SEE YOU SOON

DANGEROUS BLOOMS

KATE BREITFELLER

Ebook ISBN:978-1-7353048-6-1

ISBN:978-1-7353048-7-8

❦ Created with Vellum

A girl should be two things:
who and what she wants.
Coco Chanel

PROLOGUE

New York City
   August

Cara Bloom would have given just about anything to avoid this argument with Declan. She tore her eyes from the East River glittering forty floors below her half-brother's office, and brought them back to his face.

"I'm not *ruining* my life. I'm starting a new one."

Cara jumped as Declan surged to his feet and stalked to the small bar against the wall. The knot in her stomach drew sickeningly tight.

She wished she could tell him why she was so desperate to relocate, but it would only make everything worse.

"A little early for a drink don't you think?" she joked warily, watching him splash a liberal amount of amber liquid into his glass.

The veins in Declan's neck bulged, and his nostrils flared. He tipped the glass up, draining it in one swallow. After a dramatic exhale, he turned his head and pinned her with another of his enigmatic stares.

Cara struggled to hold onto her temper. She adored her half-brothers, all three of them, but they could be obnoxiously over-protective. She might be their baby sister, but she wasn't a child anymore—despite the words Declan had flung at her moments ago!

He means well, she reminded herself… but still!

Declan paced the length of his large office and then back again. Finally, he came to a stop, and swiveled to face her.

"Let me see if I understand what you are saying." His violet eyes, so like her own, were clouded with frustration. "You've suddenly decided that your life's ambition is to be a makeup artist, and you're moving to Atlanta to go to beauty school? Is that correct?"

"It's a cosmetology school. And it's not *my life's ambition*." She mimicked his sarcastic tone. "You know I want—"

"So, you're not going to finish your degree? You're just going to quit?" he interrupted. "You only have one more year! Once you have your MBA, I can set you up here at Bloom Capital with a real job."

"You aren't listening! I don't want to work for your company." She threw her hands in the air. "Let's be honest! I didn't even earn the undergraduate degree I got! The university only gave it to me so Dad wouldn't pull back all the funds he'd promised. I *want* to go to cosmetology school."

Cosmetology school was the first step in her grand plan to build something for herself—away from her family's famous last name and everything that went with it.

But her plan for the future wasn't the only reason she was leaving. If she shared with *any* of her brothers why she was suddenly desperate to start a new life almost a thousand miles away, or why she planned on using her mother's last name instead of Bloom— they'd definitely try to force some sort of security detail on her!

She had to hide the truth about why she was desperate to

escape from her life. To start over. Someplace where whoever was sending the increasingly frightening messages couldn't find her.

Even after she changed her phone number and email address, the unnerving notes still found her. Cara rarely left Declan's house in Connecticut anymore, and she was tired of feeling trapped. The stalker's last note proved, that even with all the precautions she'd taken, he was still watching her.

Her brothers falsely believed that her self-imposed isolation was because she was still dealing with their father's death and her *very* public scandal. It had been a terrible year for *all* of the Bloom siblings, and she didn't want to be the one to make it worse... again.

"*Atlanta?* But not with Luke? How are you going to pay for that?" Declan challenged.

"I'm not asking you to pay for it, if that's what you mean. I only want you to promise that you won't try to keep me from accessing what's left in my trust account."

Declan's lips parted slightly, and his eyes flickered with what looked suspiciously like hurt. "I would never do that."

She shouldn't have said that. Her brother was insanely generous with his siblings. In the aftermath of her father's death and the shocking discovery that Cara and her brothers had been practically disinherited—in favor of their father's new wife, Courtney—her brothers made sure she was shielded from most of the ugly fallout.

In the chaos that followed, each of her brothers thought they had the single right answer for what Cara should do next. Declan wanted Cara to finish her graduate degree so she could get a corporate job. Luke offered her a place to live, with him in Atlanta. His twin brother, James, suggested she spend some time with friends—regroup and plan for the future.

James's option sounded like the most fun. So, after a quick text, Cara's best friend, Amara sent her a plane ticket to join a group of their friends in Ibiza, including Cara's on-again, off-again boyfriend, Erik.

And then her scandal—or *the incident* as her brothers referred to it—erupted across the tabloids.

"I'm sorry, Declan. That was mean. I'm not planning on using it. Well, not a lot anyway. I may need some for deposits and stuff, but everything else will be paid for by however much I make. I'll get a job."

"*However much you make?*" Declan repeated her words softly. "And how much do you think that will be?"

Cara fidgeted, her hands damp despite the air conditioning.

She wasn't a complete idiot. Cara had researched her plan and knew roughly how much money she could expect to earn as a makeup artist starting out in Atlanta. If it took longer than she thought, there was always her trust fund. But she didn't want to use any more of it.

She had wasted too much in the months following her father's death. She was counting on what remained to act as the seed money for her dream. Cara wanted her own beauty line.

"I don't need all this stuff, Dec!" She waved her hand at his modern glass and steel office, high above Water Street in the Financial District.

"Your Amex bill says differently," he said with a small smirk.

Cara resisted the urge to smack him.

"If I'm no longer living in this environment, I won't need all these things. I won't be going to parties and charity galas—I can't do this anymore!"

After someone she trusted sold nude photos of her to the tabloids, it felt like her life was over. Then the messages began, and she found out just how much worse it could get! After the latest email, when she had been *so* careful, she knew the stalker was too close. She had to go!

See you soon.

Three terrifyingly simple words.

Declan's lips lifted in a sad smile. "I understand, Cara. I do. Dad's death and then a couple of weeks later those pictures—" He roughly cleared his throat and averted his eyes.

She pressed her tongue to the roof of her mouth grateful he didn't spell it out. Declan strode over to his desk and lowered himself into the leather chair. His voice was gentler when he continued. "I heard your mom is getting married again. I know you had planned to do this makeup thing with Corinne—"

Cara bit the tip of her tongue, the sharp pain reminding her not to yell at her brother. "I wasn't thrilled when she ran off with Alessandro, but it wasn't shocking. She's done this six times before!"

Corinne Blease was a hopeless romantic who loved weddings. And cocaine… and men… and parties… and freedom…

"I know you're disappointed, but that doesn't mean—"

Cara cut him off. "Yes, my mother backing out of plans to start a makeup line with me influenced this decision. But not in the way you think." And it had nothing to do with why she really needed to move. "It made me face all the concerns you and the twins brought up when I first told you about my idea. *Just because you like to play with makeup doesn't make you qualified to run a business.*"

Declan blanched as she parroted his words back at him. "But I *do* love makeup and skin care—If necessary, I'll finish my MBA. You were right. I need to know more than YouTube tutorials can teach me. That's why I enrolled in a school."

Declan waved a hand dismissively. "I'm happy to see you excited about something, but I don't understand why your hobby needs to take the place of your future."

"It *is* my future!" Cara gritted out. "I'm twenty-six years old. It's past time for me to take control of my life! I need to do it by myself!"

As independent as she hoped it sounded, Cara didn't really

have a choice anymore now that Corinne had pulled out of their plans. Without her mother's famous face, Cara would never find investors.

Declan opened his mouth to interrupt, but Cara held her hand up to stop him. "I know you would take care of me, but that's exactly my point. I've been taken care of my entire life. If we learned nothing else from Dad's death, it's that nothing is certain. I need to be able to fend for myself."

Her brother leaned his massive frame back, his shoulders filling the leather desk chair, and steepled his fingers in front of his mouth. Just when she thought Declan would continue the argument, he suddenly placed his hands palm down on the glass desk and winked.

"So be it. I'm sure you'll be grand."

Cara watched suspiciously as his lips curled up into a smile. Declan's Irish accent was thicker than usual, and that only happened when he was drunk… or putting on a show.

She pursed her lips. "I will be."

Cara had just reached the double doors leading back to the marble reception area when her brother's voice sounded again, more natural than it had before.

"If it doesn't work out though—" Cara looked over her shoulder at him and softened at his worried look. "You know you always have a home here. With me."

"I know." Cara grinned. "And I love you, too."

CHAPTER ONE

ATLANTA

January

ANOTHER WEEKEND, another bridal show.

It wasn't that Cara minded the wedding shows so much. She was just exhausted. In addition to school, she was working a variety of freelance jobs for photographers and hair salons—this bridal show for example.

Luckily, because Georgia licensing laws weren't as strict as some states, she was allowed to do basic makeup applications even though she hadn't finished her courses. But she was tired of applying lashes and the same dewy, ultra-natural, no makeup-makeup look to one pretty face after another.

"Be sure you use the setting spray." Stephanie, the owner of the salon, reminded everyone as she spritzed hairspray onto one of the models' ringlets. She stepped back, eyeing the woman's hair before quickly assessing the hair styles on the other models seated in a row in front of her. Stephanie frowned.

"Has anyone seen Melody?" The woman consulted a clipboard

where she had a list of all the models her salon was responsible for. The other stylists shook their heads, and Stephanie muttered something about it not being her problem.

The model she was working on got up from the tall chair, and Cara set her brushes to the side, scanning the crowd. Not seeing anyone headed her way, she put her arms over her head and stretched. She'd been doing makeup for over two hours and was dying for a break.

Cara picked up one of the society magazines that had been left and flipped through the glossy pages, stopping on a collage of pictures from a black-tie event. Laughing up at her in full color was her ex-boyfriend, Erik, and his parents.

Rage burned hot in her stomach as she stared at his happy smile, before fear gripped her. What was Erik doing in Atlanta? Only after she flipped the magazine over to check the date did she exhale. The issue was from last month, but it made her skin crawl to think he'd been in the same city.

"Hey! Are you free? I'm sooo late!" Cara snapped the magazine closed as a beautiful but harried woman hopped up on her chair.

Cara blinked hard, banishing the memory. The woman in front of her was stunning. Thick, black hair had been pulled up into a soft chignon, with several curled tendrils framing her dark eyes.

She dropped the magazine in a nearby trash can. "Sure, I'm Cara. Are you already prepped?" Technically, Cara wasn't supposed to apply moisturizer, but makeup on dry skin was a nightmare.

"Melody. Yeah, though feel free to hit me with a spritz. I was up a little late last night." She peered closely at Cara. "Do I know you?"

Cara's stomach sank, but she was saved when Stephanie spotted the new arrival.

"We aren't going to have time to do your hair, Melody," Stephanie snapped.

Melody flashed the woman a saccharine smile. "Already done."

It was plain that Stephanie wanted to say something about the fact Melody had clearly done her own hair but was distracted by one of the bridal shop employees calling her over to repair someone's hair.

Cara squeezed a small amount of primer onto her sponge and began dabbing it on the model's face while assessing the woman's skin. The dark circles shouldn't be a challenge to cover up, and her skin was smooth with an even tone. Easy! Up close, Cara detected a few more fine lines around Melody's eyes than the other models.

The majority of the women in the show were in their late teens and early twenties. At first glance, Cara had put this woman in the same category, but now with her face only inches away, Cara suspected she was closer to her twin brothers' age—early thirties.

"You're a little dehydrated, but I don't think it will be a problem."

"Cool. I just don't want to look cakey in the pictures."

Obviously a pro, the woman sat still as Cara went to work applying the different layers the designer had asked for. She'd done it so many times that morning, her mind began to wander. She slammed the door shut when it tried to veer to Erik and forced her brain to work on her more immediate problem.

She'd never admit it to her brothers, but her plan hadn't worked out quite as well as she'd hoped. Cara liked what she was doing, but after the first month, it was clear that her budget was going to be tighter than she'd anticipated. She'd made it work these last six months, but now she had a whole new problem to deal with.

"What?"

Cara paused blending the cream blush onto the woman's high cheekbones.

"You're frowning. Is something wrong with my look?" Melody asked.

"Oh no! Sorry, I was just thinking about my roommate."

Melody wrinkled her nose. "Ugh. Roommates are the worst! If they aren't late with the rent, then they're taking your Adderall or accusing you of taking their Chanel knockoff."

Cara kept her face neutral.

"My roommate's moving her boyfriend in, and in her words, they need *privacy*." Like that had ever stopped them before! "I'm going to be homeless at the end of the month."

"That sucks. Have you lived with her long?"

"Look up for me," Cara instructed, using a thin brush to touchup where tiny flecks of eyeshadow had fallen. "No, I only met her six months ago through school. I recently moved to Atlanta and don't really know anyone. Makes it hard to find someone to live with."

"Where are you from?"

The tip of Cara's tongue peeked out from between her lips as she peered closely at her work. Behind her, she heard the show coordinator calling for last touches.

"All over," she muttered vaguely, as she pulled the tissue paper away from Melody's shirt. "Close your eyes." Cara patted a final layer of setting powder over the model's décolletage and applied the setting spray.

Melody opened her eyes and peered at herself in the hand mirror Cara offered. "See you around."

Cara cleaned her brushes slowly, listening to the familiar frenzy before the first look went out. It was a safe bet to pack up most of her stuff. She might be called on to do touchups, but most of her tools could be put away. Melody almost recognizing her had been unsettling, particularly on the heels of learning Erik had been in town.

So far, no one in Atlanta had put together Cara Blease with Cara Bloom. Everyone seemed to accept she was who she said she was—a young woman studying to become a makeup artist—and not the socialite heiress she used to be. At least the move to Georgia had been successful in one regard. Her admirer had disappeared.

"You did a great job," Stephanie said, appearing at her shoulder. "You can go if you want. Renee and Dharma are going to stay for the touch ups."

Cara swallowed a sigh. As tired as she was, she needed the extra money she would have made staying for the whole show. Stephanie handed her an envelope of cash.

"You do really good work. I appreciate that you don't get flustered and actually show up when you're supposed to. Call me later this week, I have some appointments you could cover in the salon."

"That would be great!"

Cara finished cleaning her things and packed them neatly into her rolling makeup case. Her brother James had sent her a bunch of confused-face emojis when she sent him the link to what she wanted for Christmas. However, he still had the exact makeup case she'd asked for delivered to his mother Anne's house where Cara spent the holiday with the twins.

She frowned thinking of Declan. He had declined Anne's invitation as well as the one from his own mother, Siobhan, to spend Christmas with her and his older half-brother Seamus in Dublin. Instead of spending the holiday with family, for the first time, Declan went skiing with friends.

Cara chewed her lip as she closed the clasps. She worried about her brother. Declan was pulling further and further away from his siblings, and she didn't know why. Cara, Declan and the twins shared a father, but had different mothers. Despite the potential for disaster, the women had chosen to raise David Bloom's children as a family—long-distance but still family. The boys and their respective mothers were the only true family she had left.

She loved her mother, but Corinne had her own issues. Growing up, Corinne had been far from maternal and even now only spoke to Cara when she needed something—usually attention.

Cara edged around the perimeter of the room, stopping at the doors when classical music filled the air. She glanced over her shoulder as the first of the brides made their way down the runway. Her mind immediately relived all the shows spent backstage as a young child, following her mother around the globe. The smells of champagne, cigarettes, and makeup mixed with sweat and too much perfume.

Once surrounded by sycophants and hangers-on, her mother typically forgot Cara was even there. She would trail behind, trying to stay out of the way, as her beautiful, magnetic mother was transformed into whatever fantastic creature the designer had envisioned for the show. It fascinated Cara—like grown-ups playing dress up.

Corinne's hair was twisted up in horns or covered by bubblegum pink wigs—bold colors, feather eyelashes, icy palettes with iridescent crystals glued to her mother's flawless face—Cara couldn't get enough. She loved those moments before the signal to walk was given, the final minutes with seamstresses adjusting fits and everyone scurrying into place.

When the show was over, Corinne would rush backstage with the other models and designers, gushing over each other, unless of course she was in conflict with someone, which was frequent. Next, the celebrities and various VIPs would arrive. When Cara was little, she tried to stay out of the way, but as she got older, it was inconvenient for Corinne to have her child standing next to her, reminding everyone of her age. That was when Siobhan and Anne had stepped in, convincing Corinne that Cara needed more structure in her life.

Making her way to the parking deck, Cara tried not to be discouraged. She was learning a lot about makeup, and getting to practice on so many different skin types was great, but the free-lance jobs didn't pay enough. She needed to find steadier income. One of the many production companies in Atlanta would be ideal, but she didn't have the experience or the connections necessary to get a job like that. Not as Cara Blease, anyway.

Cara stowed her rolling case in the backseat of her car and drove back to the small condo she shared with her soon-to-be ex-roommate. She looked longingly at the cute restaurants lining the streets but forced herself to keep driving. As much as she would love to pick up a specialty salad for lunch, her budget told her to eat the groceries at home.

Thankfully, the condo was empty when she arrived. Zoe and her ever-present boyfriend, Jeremy, were out. After fixing herself a salad, she opened her computer and pulled up the spreadsheet where she tracked her expenses.

Cara had hated business school! She spent more time with her friends and worrying about when her next vacation was than actually preparing for the courses. But she wasn't completely devoid of how to function in the real world. Taking in the numbers on the screen, she flopped back on her bed with a frustrated breath.

Her savings from selling her BMW had gone fast! And now she needed to find a new place to live which meant solo rent and all new deposits. She chewed her lip. Almost as if she'd conjured him, her brother James's handsome face flashed on the phone screen lying next to her on the bed.

"Hey, Car-Bear," his deep voice said when she answered.

"Don't call me that!" Her response was automatic. "Shouldn't you be at work or something?"

"It's the weekend. Federal courts are closed."

"That's not what I asked." She grinned smugly even though she knew her brother couldn't see it.

"Just doing some reading." James never wanted to discuss cases with his family. "I'm actually heading to the gym in a bit, but I wanted to check in. How's it going?"

"Everything's fine," she lied. "I had another bridal show today."

"That's good. How much longer do you have left in that school before you're licensed?"

"Just a few more weeks."

"Do you have a plan for after that?" Cara loved James, but she didn't know if it was his military background, or the fact he worked for a federal prosecutor, that he couldn't conceive how people went through life without a step-by-step plan. Maybe it was time to share hers.

"Short term or long term?"

"Wow! Who is this girl?" Her brother teased, but the approval in his voice made her chest swell, and banished, at least temporarily, her money problems. "Tell me all of them."

"Short term, I'd like to get a job with a production studio in order to get more experience and have a steady paycheck. Long term..." Cara took a deep breath. "I still want to have my own business." She hesitated. "Originally, I wanted to do a makeup line with my mom. It seemed like an easy thing to do with her connections... But now that I've learned more, I'm more excited to do a skin care line. Something affordable with mostly natural ingredients."

Cara had quickly discovered that the luxury products she normally used were now out of her price range, and using what she had learned at the school, she began experimenting with making her own. Cara found it to be fairly simple, and she could scent everything with her favorite essential oil.

"Really?" James sounded surprised.

The last time she mentioned what she wanted to do to her brothers, they had laid out a litany of reasons why her ideas were impractical and wouldn't work. At least on that subject, the three of them could agree. Looking back, she realized she *had* been naïve. These last months, supporting herself and living without the benefit of her father's last name, had opened her eyes to how difficult it would be to break into the competitive beauty industry—but that didn't mean she had completely changed her mind.

"I think that's great. You seemed different when I saw you at Christmas. You've really turned your life around. I'm proud of you."

Cara's jaw fell open. James was the most taciturn of all her brothers, so for him to say anything of the sort was… weird.

"Thanks, James."

He grunted. "Don't get carried away."

She bit her lip to keep from laughing.

"All I'm saying is that your life now, compared to six months ago… You've come a long way. I thought you were nuts when you said you were going to go to beauty school."

"Cosmetology," she corrected.

"Whatever. That you were going to do this and live off what you earned… I wouldn't have said it then, but I didn't think you could do it. So, yeah," his voice was gruff again. "I'm proud of you."

Cara grew a little queasy as he continued to talk. It hurt to hear him say he hadn't believed in her, even though she knew that was how all of her brothers felt. Hearing it out loud was different.

There was no way she could mention that her savings were almost gone now. Or that the money she made at her jobs barely covered her bills. Oh yeah, and she *definitely* couldn't say she was about to be homeless!

"Glad I could live up to your low expectations."

"I didn't mean it like that, it's just… You never had to work for anything before—"

"I get it, James. Did it ever occur to you that was because I was never given the chance? It's impossible to work toward some-thing when it's handed to you automatically."

It was a lame excuse, and she knew it.

"I'm sorry, Car-Bear. That came out wrong. I was trying to say I think you are doing amazing and to keep it up."

Cara sighed. For someone who made their living convincing juries, he was remarkably bad at communicating his own feelings.

"I'm not mad, James. Thank you. Seriously."

CARA FIDGETED, watching the weather through the tall windows. The storm was not improving and neither was her life, she reflected miserably. No sign of a new job and now nasty weather. An unseasonal thunderstorm had killed the power in the space, and everyone was forced to wait for either someone to restore the electricity or to tell them all to go home. A crash of thunder shook the windows, and a couple of people let out squeals. The angry weather suited Cara perfectly.

This was it. She was going to have to admit defeat.

She was out of time. Apparently, a new place to live that fit her budget didn't exist. So, unless she was going to embrace the prospect of sleeping in her car, Cara knew she was going to have to ask her brother Luke if she could stay with him for a while.

I won't have to give up on my plan entirely, she consoled herself. Cara would save money staying with her brother. There was no doubt he would say yes, and she could even use her trust fund until something came up. However, it would also mean lecture after lecture from her brothers.

She blinked back angry tears, her conversation with James ringing in her ears.

None of them thought she could do it.

Turned out, they were right.

She sniffed, fully prepared to wallow in self-pity. Almost to make a mockery of her bad luck, the lights flickered on, and the room erupted in automatic cheers.

"What's wrong with you?" The model in her chair asked, looking up from her phone.

Cara plastered a fake smile on her face. "Nothing." She scanned the woman's face and reached for the eyeshadow brush she had been using before the lights went out.

"We lost a lot of time, people!" the events coordinator called out. "Do what you can and wrap it up! We have less than ten minutes."

"Great," Cara muttered, going to work.

"We've met before. You did me two weeks ago. At the Georgian Terrace show?"

Cara leaned back and looked at her again. "Melody?"

"You looked all pinchy that day, too. Something about roommates, right?"

Cara's surprise must have shown in her expression because Melody continued. "It's important to remember people's names. You never know when one might be able to hook you up."

Cara was cynical enough that she knew the model was right. Melody's eyes closed as Cara blended the trio of colors on her lids.

"I use clues. Something about the person when I first meet them, to remember their name. In your case, it was the hair."

Cara lifted her brush. "My hair?"

Melody's dark eyes flashed open. "Don't be offended. It's nothing bad. Your hair is fine and blond—like air. Air. Care. Cara."

"Um, okay." It seemed like a reach, but Melody *had* remembered her name so it must work for her. Cara reached for the blush, hurrying now as several models around her got up from their chairs.

"Did you find a place to live?"

She remembered that?

Melody shrugged at Cara's skeptical expression. "Originally, I used 'concerned Cara,' but I actually already have one of those, and she has red hair. So, I needed something different for you."

Cara dusted powder on the woman's nose, choosing to ignore Melody's convoluted thought process.

"So, did you? Find a new place?"

"No," Cara said, taking a final look. "You're done."

Melody lifted herself from the seat in no apparent hurry to join the scramble of women and girls being put into gowns.

"I've got a room in a little house. My roommate totally flaked on me, and even though my landlord would let a couple months' rent slide, I don't want to have to deal with him." She rolled her eyes.

Cara's brows scrunched together.

"It's tiny, but it's nice enough. I pay next to nothing cause he has a little crush on me." She winked. "Come by tomorrow, and we can talk about it. Are you free?"

"Melody!" The coordinator bellowed. Melody gave him the finger.

"Here." She grabbed one of Cara's lipsticks and scrawled a number across the top of a stack of blotting papers. "Call me tomorrow. We'll set it up!"

Is she for real? Crazy?

Cara picked up the blotting pad and entered the number into her phone.

At this point, did she have a choice?

THE NEXT DAY, she arranged to meet Melody at a little house near the Chamblee area. It wasn't the greatest neighborhood, but the houses appeared well-tended and in decent shape. Melody showed her around the small two-bedroom home that came fully furnished—another plus because Cara didn't have any furniture.

It was tempting, but she didn't know this woman! At least she'd had classes with Zoe before the room in her condo became available. However, after Melody told her what her rent would be, it was a no brainer.

When Melody told Cara that she didn't need to sign a lease, Cara felt a moment of pause. But it was too good a deal to pass up. Without a lease, she could leave if it didn't work out.

"You don't smoke do you? Pets?" Cara shook her head. "Good, I can't stand little furry things running around making a mess, and smoke wrecks my clothes. If you're going to smoke, go on the deck." She pointed at the small wooden deck visible through the sliding doors in the center of the main room.

Cara nodded. This was moving fast, but since she didn't have time to waste…

"When can I move in?"

CHAPTER TWO

"YOU CAN'T BE SERIOUS! YOU'RE LEAVING? TODAY!" WES EVANS folded his arms tightly across his chest.

Melody barely glanced up from where she shoveled the million-and-one products that normally littered her bathroom counter into her toiletry bag. "I just got the call. This could finally be it! Fabrizio D'Gallentine is like *the* biggest photographer. My agent thinks this could be my big break."

She zipped the bag closed and then pivoted back to where Wes's broad shoulders leaned against the bathroom door, blocking her exit.

He was very experienced with what he called a 'Melody tornado', and he knew the second she got through the bathroom door she would continue whirling through the apartment and disappear before Wes could get any more info out of her.

"Wes!" Melody let out a dramatic sigh. "Move! My flight leaves tonight, and I still need to get my clothes from the cleaners!"

"Give me two minutes! I only got here three days ago, and now you're leaving?" Wes knew he'd failed to keep the frustration out of his voice when Melody's face folded into the sad, puppy-dog expression that always made him give in. It had worked for her since he was fourteen, so why stop now?

"Wes, the shoot is just for a few days. Then, I'll be back. A week tops." Melody put both hands on his chest and shoved gently. He stepped back, and she brushed past him into the bedroom, pressing a kiss to his cheek. "I know we had plans, but I'll be back soon. We'll hang out then."

Wes planted his hands on his hips, his shoulders bunched. This was supposed to have been his chance. For the first time in years, he and Melody were living in the same city. Wes had moved to Atlanta, and using the excuse of house-hunting, had been crashing in Melody's extra room. Now, less than a week later, she was jetting off to Europe for a photo shoot and had apparently offered his room to someone else.

Wes was happy for her. He truly was. He knew better than anyone how much she had struggled, and she deserved this break —it was just—this was supposed to be his shot at showing Melody they could be something more than childhood friends. He wasn't the same scrawny teenager who had a crush on her at fourteen.

Melody stopped her manic packing for a second. Her bright smile flashed, and she flipped her glossy black hair out of her eyes. His heart caught. It was one of her rare, genuine smiles. Normally Melody wore a mask, rarely letting her guard down. Life had taught them both that it was best to never be vulnerable, to always be aware of who or what might hurt them.

He sighed. "Do you need a ride?"

"That would be great! You're the best! Wes, you're the only one who's never let me down." She surveyed the room, taking in her scattered clothes. "It's a mess! Would you mind?" She gestured at the room, and Wes squashed the flare of irritation. Melody was in a rush, and it wouldn't take him long.

"I'll clean it up."

Melody grabbed her keys from the hook by the front door.

"My flight's at ten so, leave by… eight?" she tossed casually over her shoulder.

Wes frowned. "Seven at the latest."

Melody flashed another smile, and with a wiggle of her fingers, she was out the door dreaming of catwalks in Milan.

CHAPTER THREE

"Ow!" Cara grunted, her elbow banging the corner of the door. She wedged the door with her hip, while simultaneously wrestling a box through the narrow opening. "Stupid door!" she cursed, catching her elbow again.

"Um, do you need some help?" The deep voice laced with amusement made her jump. It wasn't so much that the person behind the voice was laughing at her, but that it was distinctly male.

"I've got it, thanks."

Great, another roommate with a boyfriend. Melody was gorgeous so the situation wasn't wholly unexpected. Please don't be another Jeremy situation, she begged the universe. She didn't need any more roommate drama.

"I'm good." She lifted her eyes, a polite smile ready to soften her snappish tone, and froze.

Two things hit her at once.

One… he was hot, really hot. Two… he wasn't wearing a shirt, which meant, because of her short stature, she was eyeball level with a very sexy, sculpted pectoral muscle.

Her heart skipped a beat. When was the last time she was this close to a half-naked man? *Too long,* she thought, quickly followed by, *why isn't he wearing a shirt? It's winter!*

"I can do it myself," she snapped, irritated by her reaction to him.

His caramel eyes widened slightly, and for the briefest of seconds, she felt bad. "It's not heavy, just awkward."

"I could hold the door." He held his palms up. "Just to make it easier."

His lips spread in a disarming smile, and Cara sighed. "Thanks."

An arm extended over her head to hold the door open, and Cara blinked at the bicep flexing in front of her. A jolt of attraction shot through her when the narrow space made her slide across his bare chest.

Good grief! He's your roommate's boyfriend! Get a hold of yourself!

Cara carried her box into the main living area and set it on the small accent chair facing the sliding glass doors. The house was noticeably cleaner than the week before when she visited. Her spirits lifted. The fact that Melody had made an effort was a good sign. The granite countertop, separating the small kitchen on her left from the main living room, was spotless. Her eyes ran over the tan sofa facing the large TV on the wall and the remote controls neatly lined up on the coffee table in front of it.

Huh! Melody hadn't struck her as the tidy type. Cara's eyes strayed to a small kitchen table that took up the remaining space between the kitchen counter and the sofa. It might be a little snug with three people, but she could make it work.

"You're in there." The man gestured to a door situated next to the television on the wall to her right. Cara nodded. She already knew that, and her unease returned. Melody hadn't mentioned her boyfriend stayed there, and he had a distinctly proprietary air about him.

When she turned back, the stranger stood by the kitchen

counter. "I'm Wes Evans." He gave her a broad smile that lit up his eyes.

Cara stared at him blankly. Was that all he was going to say? "Cara Blease." She looked toward the bedroom door past the kitchen. "Is Melody around?"

Wes's brow wrinkled for a moment, and then his lips pressed into a flat line. "Melody is in Milan."

"What?" The already unsettled feeling in her stomach turned into a rock. Melody wasn't here, but this guy was? Cara sent a quick glance to the front door. This was starting to feel like a massive mistake!

Wes straightened, and Cara tensed ready to take flight. "Don't touch me! My brothers will kill you!"

The man's face slacked in shock. "I wasn't going to! I was—"

"I don't know what kind of messed up thing you and Melody have going on, but people know I'm here!"

Wes shook his head vigorously, his wavy, chestnut hair flopping widely. He looked almost as horrified as she felt.

"No! I'm just staying here temporarily while I house hunt. I had no idea Melody hadn't told you she wouldn't be here! She'll be back in a few days!" Cara watched him closely. He *seemed* sincere.

"Prove it."

For a second, he looked confused. "Prove what?"

"That you aren't a human trafficker."

His mouth formed an O, and for a split second, her traitorous brain thought he looked adorable.

"How do I do that?"

Good question. If she were being honest with herself, her unease had already begun to slip away. For a human trafficker, he was an awfully good actor. His shock seemed real. Plus, greeting the victim at the door shirtless didn't seem like the best plan.

His tongue crept to the corner of his mouth, and his eyes

sought the ceiling, clearly thinking—which was in itself reassuring. If he were a criminal, he wouldn't bother with the act. *Right?*

"What if you take a picture of my driver's license and send it to a friend? Like insurance?"

That actually wasn't a bad idea even if she didn't currently have any friends she could send it to. But he didn't need to know that. She nodded, and by the time he returned with his wallet, she was pretty convinced he wasn't going to sell her—but she still made him toss her the card.

Keeping her eyes on him, she pulled the phone from the back pocket of her jeans and snapped a picture. She sent it to her brother Luke. She would think of a story later but just in case….

"Are we good?" he asked, interrupting her thoughts.

"Did you just move here? Your license is from Virginia."

"I said that. Can I have it back?"

She scowled at him. "I don't know why you're giving me attitude. I'm not the one who greeted a strange woman half-naked. You do know it's the middle of winter, right?"

He looked down at his half-dressed body with surprise, then narrowed his eyes at her. "I don't think I gave you *attitude*. I was working out, and you were struggling with the door. I was trying to be nice."

Technically, he hadn't done anything wrong. It was just that she hated feeling uncomfortable. And unfortunately, every time it happened, her automatic reaction was always her mouth. If she hadn't lost her temper in Ibiza, Erik wouldn't have wanted revenge.

"Let's start over," she said. "I'm Cara, Melody's new roommate."

His shoulders relaxed. "Wes Evans, temporary roommate."

"And Melody's not here? She's in Italy?"

"It was a last-minute photo shoot. I thought she'd let you know. She'll be back in a couple days."

Cara nodded slowly, her mind assessing her options. She

could stay with this strange guy, sleep in her car, or she could stay with her brother until Melody returned. None of them sounded especially appealing.

Her phone buzzed, and when she looked down, she saw a text from Luke.

LUKE: WHY ARE YOU SENDING ME A DRIVER'S LICENSE?

She chewed her lip for a second.

CARA: SORRY, JUST A GUY I MET. DIDN'T MEAN TO SEND IT TO YOU.

"Needless to say, this isn't the living situation I thought I was walking into," she said aloud, meeting Wes's gaze.

"I can imagine. But I'm not a psycho. Promise."

Cara was more cautious than she would have been the year before, and this might be a terrible mistake but... "I kinda feel like that's what all psychos say, but..." She lifted a shoulder. It wasn't his fault his girlfriend put them in this position.

Picking up the box, she placed it on the floor by her bed. She would just ignore him. When she returned from her car with the next box, Wes had put on a pair of black athletic pants and matching hoodie.

"Do you need help?"

She shook her head.

"I'm going to the grocery store. Need anything?"

She tried not to let her relief show. It would be a lot less awkward to get settled without an audience.

"I have some food, but thanks."

Once he was gone, Cara finished unloading her car and put the few groceries she had brought with her in the kitchen. She didn't want to take the time to make a meal, so with a bag of carrots and a tub of hummus, Cara retreated to her room. She called the number Melody had given her but was forced to leave a voicemail. For good measure, she also sent her new roommate a terse text asking for an explanation.

Times like this, she wished she hadn't isolated herself from everyone. *You could call Amara,* a voice in her head whispered. She ignored it. After her father's death and Erik's betrayal, she had learned quickly how shallow most of her relationships were.

Once she could no longer afford their lifestyle, many of the people in her life were no longer interested in knowing her. The pictures in the tabloid had been the final straw. In her old social circle, it was one thing to do something risqué, provided you didn't embarrass your family. It was another to have nude pictures on the front page of a tabloid.

Only Amara had remained loyal, and Cara had rewarded her best friend by shutting her out. After the pictures had been published, all Cara had wanted to do was crawl in a hole and be left alone.

The closest people in her life now were her brothers, but she wasn't about to tell them about the predicament she found herself in. Not until it was settled anyway. They would most likely find a way to use her situation to blame each other. All they seemed to do lately was disagree.

The tension and emotion around their father's will and her own scandal had exacerbated the fissures already existing among the men. Instead of bringing them closer, their different points of view of what should be done to fix things pushed them apart. As the baby sister, she had been exempt from the finger pointing, but watching her formerly close family change and knowing it was partially her fault had been intolerable. She wouldn't do anything to worsen the family tension.

An hour later, Cara heard the TV come on at low volume and realized Wes was back. She gnawed on a carrot stick. Between asking if she needed something at the store, and not blasting the television, he was already a more considerate roommate than Zoe had ever been. Still, she wasn't quite ready to make small talk with a stranger alone in a new house. She'd listened to her fair share of true crime podcasts!

Cara crept to the door, and silently turned the lock. She positioned her suitcase in front of the door and stood back looking at her makeshift security alarm. It was pretty pathetic, but it was all she had. Propping her phone on a pillow, Cara scrolled through the internet finally settling on one of her favorite makeup vloggers, one ear out for her new roommate.

The next morning, the main area of the house was empty, the door at the end of the short hallway on the far side of the kitchen closed. Cara chugged a glass of water before putting in her earbuds and heading out for a run.

She hadn't slept well, waking at the slightest noise. Periodically in the night, she heard what she thought was typing on a keyboard but hadn't been brave enough to look. When the sun peaked through the blinds, she finally gave up trying to sleep and got out of bed.

Wes hadn't attempted to come into her room during the night, which was reassuring. And if it was some sort of set-up, it seemed unlikely he would have waited for her to settle in her room. The more likely scenario was he was just another person that Melody had forgotten about when she made her plans. Cara was an adult. She'd make the best of it.

Normally, Cara ran for half an hour. But this morning, her normal distance took longer than usual because she was unfamiliar with the neighborhood. Her running app set for her preferred distance, she jogged slowly, overly conscious of her surroundings. She wasn't in the mood for any more surprises.

The rhythm of her legs and breath took over her anxieties, each stride further easing her. She welcomed the endorphins that coursed through her body. Growing up, Cara had never enjoyed exercise, but she had taken up running at her mother's urging.

"Darling, unfortunately, you are built like your father. You can either starve, or exercise. There's no way around it."

Her mother had imparted this nugget of wisdom during one of the rare school holidays Corinne chose to spend with her daughter. Even at thirteen, Cara understood her mother didn't mean to be unkind. She was stymied by Cara's appearance. Cara knew she'd gained weight that year, and standing next to her willowy, supermodel mother, she had felt like a hippopotamus.

Cara picked up her pace, pumping her arms faster to banish the memory. She liked the long, low hills of the neighborhood and how the post-war homes mixed with new construction. The mature trees filling the lots were winter-gray and bare, but it would be a great route in the summer when the thick leaves would provide shade.

CHAPTER FOUR

WES DIDN'T LOOK UP AT THE SOUND OF THE FRONT DOOR OPENING. A dull headache throbbed behind his eyes, the result of waking at four a.m. from a nightmare and being unable to get back to sleep. He hadn't had the dream in a long time. *Why now?* Wes suspected it had to do with the petite, curvy blonde who had first looked terrified and then unhappily resigned to her new living situation. Like a woman who had run out of options.

MAMA SQUATTED LOW, hugging him tight into her neck. Her shirt was drenched in her favorite perfume. It would make him stuffy later, but he didn't care. Something was wrong; he could feel it. His tummy churned like the time he ate the whole sleeve of cherry Lifesavers.

"Don't go. Stay here with Gram and Poppy," he pleaded. Something hot and wet hit his cheek, and when she pushed away from him, he saw she was crying. "Don't cry, Mama. Don't be sad."

The sick feeling in his belly grew, and it was hard to breathe.

"It's okay, buddy. You're going to stay with them for a little bit. You'll love it," she insisted with a smile. Even though tears no longer fell,

her eyes were wet and shiny. "You are going to have so much fun with Gram and Poppy. Be a good boy, and I'll call you soon." She smoothed a hand over his hair, pushing it back from his face. "My beautiful boy."

"Tiffany." Gram's voice sounded the same way it did when she told him not to chase the dog. His grandmother stepped closer, and Wes felt her hands gently rest on his shoulders. "Don't drag it out. It's not fair to him."

Mama jumped to her feet. Wes craned his neck back, watching the splotchy red patches spread up her neck. Her eyes weren't sad anymore; they were mad.

"Fair?" She looked down at Wes and took a deep breath. She squatted again, pulling him away from Gram's hands. Her hands were rough and pinched a little.

"Ow, Mama!"

He squirmed and then instantly regretted it because she dropped his arms, and Gram hissed.

"See. You don't—"

Mama ignored her, leaning forward to press a kiss on his lips.

"I love you, little man. More than anything! I'll be back as soon as I can. Promise." She came to her full height and stared angrily at Gram and Poppy. "I will! Then Wes and I will be the kind of family I always wanted."

Then she was gone, down the steps, and running to the white Ford Probe where the angry man who thought Wes was too loud waited.

Wes lifted a finger to where his mother had left her sticky strawberry gloss on his lips. Gram grabbed his finger and wiped the sweet shimmer away with her fingers before rubbing them roughly across his lips to remove the last of Mama's kiss. Wes heard a weird, gasping sound.

"Are you sure we are doing the right thing?" Gram asked Poppy nervously.

"Take him inside and clean him up. He's got snot running down his face."

Only then did he realize the scary sound was coming from him.

~

Wes finished pouring coffee into his favorite mug to give her a chance to realize he was in the house. He still couldn't believe Melody hadn't let her new roommate know he was going to be there! He realized the second she registered his presence because she froze in the middle of pulling her earbuds out.

"Cold outside?" It was a dumb question. Her cheeks were pink with the cold, and she wore a headband that doubled as earmuffs —but other than dumb small talk, he wasn't sure how to put her at ease. People were not his strong suit.

"Yeah." She unzipped her jacket to reveal a bright pink shirt. His eyes fell to his coffee in order to avoid watching the material stretch tight across her chest as she shrugged out of the jacket. She already thought he might be a creep—the last thing he needed was for her to think he was staring.

"I run, too."

Wow! Good one, Wes.

He picked up the coffee pot to cover his embarrassment only to find his cup was still full. Cara's lips twitched when he set the carafe back in the machine. Apparently, his awkwardness had done what his lack of conversational skill could not.

"Do you want some coffee? I made a whole pot."

"Thanks, that sounds great." Cara threw her jacket on the back of the couch and joined him in the small kitchen. Reaching into the cabinet, he pulled out one of Melody's white coffee mugs.

"Sugar? I'm pretty sure she has that, but if you want cream, you're out of luck."

"Black is fine." She smiled but took the cup to the other side of the kitchen counter, putting a physical barrier between them. Wrapping both hands around the mug, she took a sip, and moaned. "This is perfect!"

"I know this whole thing is awkward and—"

"What's that?" Cara interrupted, squinting at the mug in his hand. He turned it to face him.

"Captain Picard." His voice was neutral. However, instead of the snarky comment he usually got about being a nerd, she stayed quiet, her brow furrowed. "From Star Trek."

"Oh," Cara said, as if she understood, but it was obvious from her expression she didn't have a clue what he was talking about.

"The TV show?" Still, no sign of recognition. "You've never seen Star Trek?"

"I've heard of it... sci-fi, right? About aliens... the guy with the pointy ears?"

Wes gaped at her. How was it possible that someone had never heard of Star Trek? Had she grown up in a cult somewhere that didn't believe in television?

Wes took a sip of coffee to prevent himself from saying something that would wreck whatever tentative truce was happening. But... seriously? Star Trek! "Yeah, but Captain Picard is from a newer version."

She shrugged. "How long have you and Melody been together?"

"I've known her pretty much my whole life—since I was fourteen. We grew up together in Athens."

"Wow! So, when did the two of you become a couple?"

"We aren't exactly dating," he said carefully. This is where it got tricky, and he wasn't sure he wanted to explain his and Melody's complicated relationship to a stranger.

"There's no shame in friends with benefits. I think everyone's done it at some point."

Wes didn't miss the way her eyes briefly scanned his body. "Um, not exactly that either."

Wes had this same conversation with his friend and business partner, Jin, only a couple weeks ago when Wes decided to move back to Atlanta. It sounded insane when it was put into words. That was only because it was impossible for an outsider, who hadn't been through what he and Melody had, to understand their connection.

Cara's expression turned wary, and he knew her mind was back to wondering what he was doing staying in the house.

"I'm in love with her. I always have been."

Her mouth fell open at his outburst, and Wes felt his cheeks heat. He sighed, setting down the coffee cup. She already thought he was a weirdo, might as well spell it out so she stopped looking at him like he was going to bury her body in the backyard.

"Melody and I have always been close, but I was living out of state, and she was trying to get her career going... The timing was never right. Now we're in the same city for the first time in more than a decade, and we are going to see how things go."

"Hmm, okay."

Wes watched a progression of emotions flash across her violet eyes.

"So, you're not *together*, together?"

"Not officially." *Not at all.* "I only got to town a few days ago. Then she got the call for the shoot, so we haven't had a chance to talk about it yet."

Cara's nose scrunched. "Does she know how you feel?"

"I think so."

"Ah."

"What does that mean?" Wes knew he sounded defensive, but who was she to question it? He should have kept his mouth shut. "I know it sounds crazy, but Melody and I are different than other people."

Wes bristled when she smiled sympathetically. She thought he was deluded. *Fine.* He didn't care what Cara thought. When Melody got back, Wes was confident—well, semi-confident—she would agree it was time to really give them a chance. They'd both grown up in messed up families. If anyone understood his dream of a home and family, it was Melody.

"I'm sure it will all work out for you," she said, putting her mug in the sink. "I'm going to take a shower. Thanks again for the coffee."

After she was gone, Wes took his mug to the kitchen table, where he had set up his computer. He sorted through his inbox, filtering through emails. Nothing from Melody, but there were several from potential new clients. His chest swelled with satisfaction. His new company's reputation was growing.

This was the other piece that had held Melody back from dating him—not that Melody had ever said it out loud–but he knew the type of man she pursued, and what they had been able to give her. He didn't blame Melody for making money a romantic requirement, but he knew others did.

Wes made the mistake of mentioning it once to Nina, Jin's wife, and she didn't even try to hide her disapproval. She and Jin had both grown up in solid, middle-class families. They couldn't understand what the lack of security meant to kids like Wes and Melody.

Until the last couple of years, he didn't have enough to offer Melody. She dreamed of a big life, and while he had made a comfortable living, it wasn't enough to support the lifestyle she craved. That she deserved, he amended. Now everything was different.

Wes answered the emails he could and then sent Jin and Nina messages asking their availability to meet with some of the prospective clients. Wes's technical skills might be better than his business partners, but the couple was better with the clients. He tended to talk too much about the intricacies of the code and how his patented method and algorithm would protect their intellectual property. Nina had told him more than once that he had a unique gift for putting people to sleep.

Wes was just pulling up the project he was working on for his biggest client, an independent movie studio in Atlanta, when Cara emerged from her room. She hesitated as if she wasn't sure what the protocol was with a roommate-but-not-a-roommate situation.

"I'm heading to school and then I have a job after." Her eyes fell to his laptop. "Do you work from home?"

"Mostly. Where are you in school?"

"Atlanta Cosmetology. I'm getting my license." She chewed the corner of her lip. "I probably won't be back until late afternoon."

"Great! Have a good day!" She didn't move. Was he supposed to say something else? If this was a test, he was totally failing. "Hope you have a good show." Her brows came together. "Shoot? Sorry, I never know what to call it."

She shook her head slowly. "I have a makeup application for a local photographer."

"Oh, I assumed you were a model. Melody said she met you at work…"

A shadow crossed her face, and her eyes narrowed as she snatched her car keys off the hooks by the door. "You shouldn't make assumptions."

Evidently, he'd hit a nerve. "I didn't mean to upset you—"

"You didn't," she snapped, but the way she slammed the door said something different.

Wes didn't understand her reaction. Wasn't it a compliment to be confused for a model? It was an easy mistake for him to have made. She was objectively beautiful… long, fair hair and huge, violet eyes, but… She *was* pretty short. Maybe Cara had wanted to be a model but was too short? Hadn't he heard Melody constantly blame her own height for why she never achieved the success she deserved?

With the puzzle solved in his mind, Wes returned to the program he was running. He would always prefer computers to people. Create an input, receive the expected output. No tears, no confusion, no misunderstandings. Reliable, predictable technology would always be preferable to people.

CHAPTER FIVE

It was an offhand comment. Why had it bothered her so much? Because it felt false, patronizing. Cara wasn't blind. She knew she was attractive, but she had long accepted that she wasn't beautiful like her mother, and she had zero ambition to be a model.

It needled at her, popping up inconveniently when she should be paying attention to things that actually mattered. Who cared if he felt he had to give her an empty compliment? She didn't want attention from someone clearly hung up on someone else no matter how attractive he was. Cara loaded her groceries on the belt and crossed her fingers when she handed the clerk her card. The first time she had a purchase declined, she had wanted to fall through the floor in humiliation. Since then, she kept close track of her balances, but she hadn't forgotten the feeling.

Cara hoped Wes wouldn't be at the house when she was done shopping, but the same green truck was parked in the driveway. She had been less than thrilled to learn he worked from home and that he appeared to view this house as his home. *Is he going to be here all the time?*

Sitting in the driveway, she pulled out her phone to send another text to Melody.

> CARA: YOU NEVER MENTIONED THERE WAS A GUY
> LIVING HERE!

Melody hadn't responded to her text from the evening before, and with the time difference she wasn't expecting a reply. So, Cara was shocked when the bubble appeared indicating Melody was typing.

> MELODY: SRY. JOB CAME UP COULDN'T SAY NO. B
> BACK IN COUPLE WEEKS. DON'T WORRY ABOUT
> WES. HE'S THE BEST… LIKE MY BROTHER… HE'S
> HOUSE HUNTING.

A couple of weeks? What the hell!

Wes was in the same spot at the table when she unlocked the door, a pair of expensive-looking, noise-canceling headphones covering his ears. By the way his head bobbed to the beat of whatever he was listening to and the rate his fingers flew over the keyboard, she realized he hadn't noticed her return.

She walked past him to put the plastic bags full of chicken and veggies on the counter. He jumped, ripping off his headphones.

"I didn't mean to startle you," Cara said. "You looked like you were in the zone."

Wes draped the headphones around the back of his neck and rubbed his hand along the scruff on his jaw, glancing out the sliding doors to his left at the dark landscape. "What time is it?"

Cara's eyebrows rose. "A little after six."

"Shit, really?" Wes pushed back from the table, closing his laptop and placing the headphones on top. He rolled his shoulders and stretched his arms over his head, exposing a band of muscled skin where his shirt lifted.

Longing hit Cara with surprising force, and she averted her eyes, unloading the groceries. He certainly didn't have the body of a computer nerd!

Wes took in her haul where she spread it on the counter. "Big chicken eater?"

Cara caught the teasing tone but kept her reply short. "Yup."

Grabbing his glass from the table and putting it in the sink, he headed toward the back bedroom, stripping his shirt off as he went. His back was all lean muscle and broad shoulders that tapered to—she jerked her eyes back to her food, as heat crept up her face.

"I'm heading to the gym for a bit," he called from his room.

That explained why he didn't look like he spent all day at a desk.

Get it together, Cara! You live with him now!

Lusting after a roommate would only complicate things. She hadn't been around men, attractive or otherwise, in far too long. That's all it is, she told herself. She was lonely. Cara retrieved a cutting board from where she had stored it the day before. She sliced the chicken and veggies, until two cookie sheets were full with her dinners for the week.

"That's a lot of food." Cara spun, knife in hand, at the sound of Wes's voice. "Hey! I was just joking! Eat what you want."

Cara lowered the knife. "It's for the whole week. It's healthy and makes it easier when I have a long day."

"Smart," he said, filling a water bottle. "I usually forget about food until I'm starving and then end up ordering something."

Cara hesitated. If they were going to live together it would be easier if they could be friendly. "I have plenty for tonight. I could save you some."

Wes studied her for a second, a slow smile spreading across his face. "That would be awesome. Thanks!"

Cara knew she hadn't been the best roommate to Zoe when she had first moved in. Cara never had a roommate before, except for Amara, and that had been at school. She was suddenly flooded with homesickness and regret. She had handled everything so badly, and now so much time had passed….

Cara slid the pans into the oven and set the timer. She wiped the counters and did the dishes, her thoughts returning again and again to the same thing.

Why not call Amara? What's the worst that happens? She doesn't answer?

No, the worst would be if Amara yelled at her, telling Cara how selfish she had been. And she would deserve it.

Blowing out a hard breath, Cara typed Amara's number into her phone and added a simple "Hey, it's Cara" text. The fact that she had to identify herself perfectly illustrated the status of their friendship.

The constant hang-ups Cara received after the photos were published forced her to change her phone number. It had been her choice at the time to only share it with her family. She didn't want to talk to anyone from her old life, and that had included her best friend.

Cara hit send before she changed her mind and set the phone on the counter. It was a start. It gave Amara time to decide whether or not she wanted to respond. Cara didn't even know where on the planet her friend was or what time zone she was in. She might not even...

She froze when her phone began to ring, Amara's number dominant on the screen. Cara *had* to answer. She'd sent the text less than a minute ago. If she didn't answer, then it would... Cara grabbed the phone.

"Hey, back!" Amara laughed, and a wave of relief washed over Cara.

"I was taking the coward's way out," Cara admitted.

"No kidding! I'm not letting you get away with it! How are you?"

On the surface, it was a normal question. The standard conversational opener when you hadn't spoken to someone in almost a year. But Cara sensed the layer underneath it—the one that seriously wanted to know how she was after the scandal.

Understandable since Cara had cut off contact with everyone, but she wasn't ready to go there with Amara right now. Maybe she never would be.

"I'm good. I just moved actually. I have a new roommate, and it made me think of you."

Amara was silent. She was well within her rights to lay into Cara, but after a beat, it appeared she was going to let it go in her typical carefree style.

"No one could possibly replace me. What's her name? Where are you living?" The silent question was there. What have you been doing? As someone who had lived her life so openly on social media, Cara had essentially fallen off the edge of the world when she deleted all her accounts and holed up at Declan's.

"I'm in Atlanta."

"Are you living with your sexy ass brother? Tell him I said hi."

Cara laughed. Amara never failed to flirt with Luke when she saw him, but it was harmless. It was more of a game at this point. "No, but I'll tell him you were asking. Her name's Melody."

"Hmm. I refuse to be jealous of a newbie. What's she like? Is she nice?"

Cara thought about it for a second. "I don't really know. I only met her a couple times, and the day I moved in, I found out she left the country for a photo shoot." Telling Amara the story made Cara realize how crazy it was.

"You're living with a stranger?" Amara sounded concerned. "You couldn't get a place of your own?"

"No." Cara's tone was sharp, and Amara got the message to back off. Amara still lived in the privileged world they had grown up in, where money was never an issue.

While she hadn't gotten what she had expected in the will, her father had left her some money—a fortune by some standards. However, Cara had been oblivious to how much her lifestyle cost. She had run through almost a quarter of her inheritance in a month before she'd even realized it. She needed to save the rest to start her own business.

"It's not all bad. She's not here."

"I guess that's good."

Cara hated the pity she heard in her friend's voice and searched for something to change the subject. "I'm not alone, though. A friend of hers is staying here while he house hunts."

"He?" Amara teased. "Is he cute?"

An image of Wes shirtless flashed in front of her. "Yeah, he's hot. A little dorky, but seems nice enough."

"Nice! Worse things in the world than having someone to make out with when you're bored."

Cara laughed. "I don't think that's in the cards. Even if it weren't for the fact that I'd still have to live with him after, he has a thing for Melody. He told me straight away."

Amara booed. "He's not with her though, so fair game."

The timer sounded, and Cara tucked the phone under her chin and pulled out the pans.

"Actually, I feel kind of bad for him. When Melody finally texted me today saying she wouldn't be back for a few weeks, she said he was *like her brother.*"

"*Brother?* Ouch. Well, that settles it then."

"I'm not going to make out with my roommate. That has disaster written all over it."

"Lame. What about other guys? Are you dating?" The cautiousness was back in Amara's voice.

"As a matter of fact, I was thinking about that tonight." Cara put a chicken breast and a cup of roasted veggies into each heavy plastic container. "I haven't since… But, I have to eventually, right?"

Amara was quiet, and Cara squirmed. She shouldn't have brought it up.

"What Erik did, sending those pictures to the tabloids, was

horrible. But you can't let him win. He's a spoiled piece of shit. If you hide away, not living, you are doing exactly what he wants."

Cara closed her eyes. Amara was right, but it wasn't that easy. She still didn't know *how* Erik had gotten the old photos of her. She had certainly never sent him any. Declan had threatened the tabloid with legal action because they could prove she was underage when the pictures were taken, but the editor refused to tell him who had sent them the photos.

The magazine took the images down from their digital site, but the damage was done. Everyone she knew had seen them. It wasn't that she was ashamed of taking the pictures—it was the violation of knowing the decision to share them was taken out of her hands.

It had been humiliating to face her family after the story broke. As if they hadn't had enough to deal with in regard to their father dying only a few weeks before, she'd dumped this mess in her brothers' laps. It had been too much for Cara to deal with and she had retreated from the world.

Unfortunately, the world wouldn't stay away from her. When the phone calls began, she thought it was Erik finding new ways to torture her. But soon after came the emails and messages on her social media account, detailing what she had done on certain days, making it clear that whoever was sending them was close by. It hadn't been difficult to find out that Erik was still in Europe. Which meant it was someone else.

"The pictures are gone," Amara said quietly.

Cara heard a burst of laughter in the background.

"Are you at a party?" Cara asked, nerves prickling under her skin.

"My parents are having a thing. I'm outside. No one knows I'm talking to you."

"I'm sorry. I want to let it go. I really do..."

"What about a dating app? You could use whatever name it is you're using now."

"What do you mean?" Cara hedged.

"Duh! I googled Cara Bloom, trying to find out where my best friend had disappeared to, but all that's out there is old stuff. Don't be so paranoid. Not everyone is out to get you, you know. Even Colin was asking about you the last time I saw him. People care about you and think what Erik did was really shitty."

Cara rubbed her forehead. "I don't want to talk about this anymore."

"Okay, let's talk about dating apps then. Which ones do you have?"

Cara wrinkled her nose. "Dating apps? I don't know—"

"I'm on one."

"You are not!"

"I am. Unless I'm going to keep dating in the weird, incestuous circle that is our friend group, I need to meet some new people. It's designed for high net worth or high-profile people. I can refer you—" Amara stopped suddenly.

"Pretty sure I wouldn't meet their requirements anymore," Cara said dryly.

"Whatever. So far, they're mostly snobs. You're better off without it. You should sign up for Mingle or something though! Even if it's just to meet new people."

Cara grinned. "I'll think about it."

"I've got to catch a flight tomorrow. My mom wants me to put in an appearance for the start of polo season in South Africa, some retailer they want me to schmooze. I'm going to call you in a few days, and you better have at least one account set up."

"Yes, ma'am," Cara laughed.

"Ugh! My mother is giving me death eyes through the glass, so I better go. I wonder if she realizes she could make much scarier faces if she didn't have so much stuff injected?"

Why had she waited so long? It was nice to hear Amara's voice, but she didn't miss the fake social whirl and all that came with it. Maybe she *should* start opening herself up again. *It can't get any worse...*

CHAPTER SIX

New York
Ten Months Earlier

"Damn it!" Declan's fist slammed against his desk, toppling the Guinness pint glass, and scattering the pens he kept inside across the slick surface. Cara trembled and bit her tongue trying not to cry. She wanted to throw up. Declan had seen the pictures.

His back was to her, muscles heaving under his dress shirt as he bent forward slightly. He braced his palms on the desk, his arms fully extended, as he struggled to control himself. She'd never seen him this angry. Not even a few weeks before when they found out their father had essentially cut them all out of his will, and Courtney forced him out of Bloom Communications.

She had done this. Her brothers were already arguing about Courtney, and Cara added this to the pile of shit they dealt with.

"I'm sorry. I'm so sorry, Dec—"

She heard him drag in a ragged breath, and then he pivoted to face her. His eyes shone with unshed tears.

"Don't you **dare** say that." His eyes burned, and one tear slipped free *sliding silently down his cheek, which only made her feel worse. Her brothers never cried, and the thought that she was the one who caused Declan to, destroyed her.*

In two strides, he reached her, enveloping her in his arms. "You have nothing to be sorry for, mo chroi." He kissed the side of her head the way he had when she was little. Declan hugged her hard and then let go, clearing his throat.

Steely-faced, unemotional Declan, she knew. It was reassuring. Declan crying? That must be a harbinger of the apocalypse.

"Your hair was pink?" He framed it as a question, but it was clear he knew the answer and was only verifying.

"Yeah." Cara's cheeks felt like they were on fire.

Declan's throat worked as he swallowed. "So, you were what? Fifteen?" His voice was controlled, but his violet eyes were almost black with fury.

"I don't know. Something like that. I did a lot of dumb stuff back then. I mean we all did. But, I'm not stupid. I didn't send them to anyone... It was just a silly night with my floormates. When you're snowed in at boarding school, there's only so many ways to entertain yourself."

Cara was babbling. She remembered the night the photos were taken —sort of. Someone had a bottle of peach schnapps, and they had all played strip poker. There was a vague memory of dancing—it was just one night of many that she had long forgotten. Until she had gotten a phone call from Amara, letting her know that the nude pictures they had taken that night were suddenly everywhere.

It was devastating. The comments on some of the sites had been brutal, stabbing at every insecurity she'd ever had about her body. She didn't even know it was possible to have ugly ears! Everyone she knew had seen them—her brothers, strangers. It was almost unbearable.

"Who was there that night?"

"I don't remember exactly. Amara—she reminded me where they were from. So probably Lisel, Tamar, maybe Kerstin?" She shook her head. "I'm sorry. I just don't remember. It was over ten years ago. It was

supposed to be something silly, for just us girls. I thought we all agreed to delete them."

"Whoever sent them has been holding onto them." The muscle in Declan's jaw ticked. "They waited until our father was gone before they leaked them. The fucker wouldn't have dared while Dad was alive! They must think that our father's will neutered me, and the bastards thought they could get away with it. I'm the one who should be sorry. It's my fault."

"Declan!" Cara gasped, but he ignored her, pacing behind his desk and keying his computer to life. He seemed to have forgotten she was there. "Declan!" Her sharp tone got his attention, but she was taken aback by the light in his dark eyes.

"I failed you, mo chroi. It won't happen again. Our father may not be here anymore, but that doesn't mean people should forget how dangerous the Blooms can be!

CARA FIXED herself a plate of the food and then put an identical plate in the oven to keep it warm for Wes.

"Your food is in the oven," she called out when the door opened, not looking up from her phone.

"Thanks."

She heard his keys clatter on the counter and then the bedroom door shut. Cara frowned. She'd been expecting a little bit more of a response. She took another bite of broccoli and made a face at her phone.

Wes emerged from his room and brought the plate to the chair across from where she was sitting. "Thanks again for the food."

She nodded, still glaring at the phone. "Is something wrong?" he asked between bites.

"No, just stuck on what to write." She looked up and for a second was caught by his warm eyes. His driver's license said brown, but now up close, with only a few feet separating them, she could see the light caramel only had tiny flecks of brown sprinkled with gold across the iris. His hair was wet, hanging in waves over his forehead, and his clean scent reached across the table. Tingles started low in her stomach, and she dropped her eyes back to the phone. *This is Amara's fault.*

"What are you writing?"

When she didn't answer right away, he lifted up to peek over the top of her phone. The dating app's logo was prominently displayed at the top.

"Mingle?" He shook his head disapprovingly.

Cara gritted her teeth and closed her phone. She picked up her plate to return it to the kitchen.

"You need to be careful with those apps."

She met his gaze. "Thousands of people use them."

"And they get hacked all the time because of it."

Cara blinked. That wasn't what she expected him to say. "Hacked?" Of all the problems associated with meeting people on the apps, hacking wasn't one she'd thought about.

His shoulders lifted. "You could be hacked any time. Why make it easy for them? Hackers set up a fake profile with a phishing virus attached, and the second you click on 'Jake' your phone is infected."

"You seem to know a suspicious amount about it."

"It's what I do?"

"Hack people's phones through Mingle?"

"No." He smiled. "Cybersecurity. I help people *not* get hacked. Businesses primarily—movie studios, record labels."

"How?" Cara didn't have much experience with computers, but after her pictures were leaked, she was *very* interested in how someone could invade her privacy again.

"By hacking *them.*"

"Excuse me?" Cara coughed a laugh, and he grinned.

"Best way to find out if a system is vulnerable is to hack it.

Then I identify the vulnerabilities and build something better to protect them."

"You're a hacker?" Something she couldn't identify flashed in his eyes, and he pushed to his feet with his plate. "I'm sorry. I didn't mean to insult you. It's just you said…"

"I'm not offended." He set his plate down on the kitchen counter. "I *am* a hacker. A very good one, but I don't break in anywhere I haven't been invited."

"A white hat."

His eyes widened at her use of terminology.

"I read an article," she lied. Cara wasn't about to explain that she knew what a white-hat hacker was because Declan hired one to scrub the images of her off the internet. Even though the tabloid had taken down the photos of her, others had snagged screen shots and shared them to other sites.

Her stomach turned over at the memory. She had no idea how many people had seen the pictures, and she dreaded the day she met someone new, and they recognized her.

"People pay me to do it. I'm helping them." His voice was defensive.

Cara realized he had misinterpreted her silence. "I agree. It's actually kind of noble."

He pushed his wet hair back off his forehead. "I wouldn't go that far. My clients are mainly corporations trying to protect their profits. Pirating is a huge problem in the entertainment industries. Streaming services, movie and music executives are all desperate to protect their products from being leaked early. And I'm making money from it."

Wes looked uncomfortable, and since she didn't want to reveal her own interest in the topic, her eyes roamed the room looking for some way to change the subject. It was still early, and she didn't want to spend another evening by herself trapped in her bedroom.

"Do you mind if I turn on the TV?"

"Of course not. It's your house, too."

She gestured at his computer. "I didn't know if you still had work to do."

"It's a laptop. If the noise bothers me, I can go in the other room."

Cara relocated to the couch and heard Wes making microwave popcorn as she scrolled through the menus of the different streaming services that were loaded on the TV. Nothing looked particularly interesting.

"What was the name of that show you mentioned? The one on your mug."

"Star Trek. Do you want to watch it?" His tone was so hopeful, she had to roll her lips in to smother a laugh.

"Why not." Cara shrugged and typed the show into the search bar. "There's more than one?" she asked over her shoulder, and then had to stifle another giggle when his face morphed into outrage. Messing with him was just too easy!

"More than one?" He shook his head, grabbed the bowl of popcorn, and collapsed on the sofa next to her. He took the remote from her hand. "There are five! But we'll start with the best. Unless you think chronological order is better?"

Cara felt her whole body relax. He looked so intensely frustrated, as if the choice of which old sci-fi show they watched was the most important thing in the world. Not for the first time, she wondered how someone who looked like him could be such a dork. She pulled the fuzzy blanket, folded under the coffee table, over her legs and snuggled back into the cushions. Something bubbled in her chest—something that felt distinctly like happiness.

"Let's start with the best," Cara said, taking the bowl from him and putting it on the arm of the sofa.

"Nice try." Wes leaned across her to take the bowl back. He set the dish between them, pointed the remote at the screen, and flipped through the menu until he got to the selection he was looking for. The intro music began, but Cara couldn't look up because she was too busy trying to keep the full bowl of popcorn from spilling all over the cushions as Wes tried to get comfortable. The small couch was not designed for someone his size, and the constant crossing and recrossing of his legs was bouncing the bowl dangerously.

Cara rolled her eyes and then leaned forward to pull the coffee table closer.

"Just put your feet up. I won't tell. It's the only way you'll be comfortable."

"I'm fine. Really."

"Don't be stubborn. I have three overgrown brothers. There is no reason for you to be uncomfortable." She waved her hand. "Brothers, roommates, it's all the same." Or at least that's what she kept telling herself.

Wes paused and looked at her with a funny expression. "Don't tell Mel. She'd kill me."

"Your secret's safe with me."

"I think I might like this little sister thing," he said, tossing a popped kernel in the air and catching it with his mouth.

Cara's eyes lingered on his profile as he chewed and felt a stab of disappointment. She'd started it, and she knew it was necessary to keep a mental barrier up—but she was also acutely aware of how the muscles in his forearm flexed each time he reached for the popcorn. The *feelings* she was experiencing were anything but *sisterly*.

CHAPTER SEVEN

THE EPISODE HAD BEEN ON FOR FIFTEEN MINUTES WHEN CARA turned to him, eyes brimming with delight, and pointed at the screen trying not to laugh.

"What?" Wes squelched the disappointment he felt. Why did it matter if she liked his favorite show? He braced himself for the ridicule he knew was coming. Even Melody hated Star Trek.

"Is this a space soap opera?"

Wes scowled. "No, what are you talking about?"

Cara snatched the remote from him and backed the program up several frames until the characters of Commander Riker and Counselor Troi were centered on the screen, staring at each other.

"That!" She jabbed her finger at the image. "Super dramatic, longing looks! Unrequited love if I've ever seen it. And why is she wearing a miniskirt?"

"What? No!" Wes looked at the screen fully prepared to defend his favorite show. "They're not..." he stopped. "Okay, I can see how you could think that, but the series isn't like that."

"Mmkay, if you say so." She grabbed at the last handful of

popcorn. "I'm cool with it. I love a good romantic subplot; I just hadn't pegged you as the type."

Wes shifted forward. This had been a mistake. What had he been thinking? "I'm not. Never mind. I should probably get to bed." He braced his hands to push himself up, angry at himself.

"Don't be a baby." Cara pushed the play button and the show resumed. "You're as bad as my brothers! Now shh, I want to see what happens."

Wes sat rigidly next to her, counting the minutes until he could make his escape. But as the episode continued, he found his eyes returning to her face over and over. Her full lips curled up in delight several times, and Wes finally settled back against the cushions, his breath coming easier.

The thought of Cara making fun of him shouldn't bother him so much. He didn't even know her. And she certainly wouldn't be the first girl to find Wes's obsession with Star Trek nerdy, but... He snuck a glance again. She seemed to like it.

He took the opportunity her interest in the show gave him to study her. Her pale blond hair was caught up in a clip of some sort at the back of her head, wispy bits sticking out everywhere in a messy halo. Her lips parted in laughter again at the action on the screen, and he found himself smiling along with her. It was rare that he was comfortable with other people, and he could count on one hand people he trusted. But there was something about her that was... easy.

"Are you going to make some more?"

Cara's voice broke through his thoughts, and he realized she was asking about the empty popcorn bowl. He glanced at the TV and saw the show was over. Had she caught him ogling her?

"Sure. Do you want to watch something else?" he asked, taking the few steps into the kitchen to stick another bag in the microwave.

"No way! It says it was part one of two. So, we have to watch the next one. I know that Q is supposed to be the bad guy, but he's my favorite so far." She pressed the buttons on the remote to advance the episode.

Punching in the time for the popcorn, Wes turned and leaned a hip against the kitchen counter. "Should I be concerned that you like the manipulative, all-powerful character?"

"Maybe." She winked, and his gut clenched in response.

He shook himself mentally. Calm down, he ordered his body. It didn't mean anything—just a normal healthy response to an attractive woman.

That's all it could be.

He pulled the steaming bag from the microwave and poured it into the bowl, adding salt. Oblivious to his reaction, Cara pushed play and turned up the volume.

Wes did his best to ignore his new roommate and concentrate on the television, but now that his body had given him an unmistakable reaction, he was uncomfortably aware of her next to him. His brain was suddenly fixated on identifying the faint floral scent that drifted his way every time she shifted. Warmth radiated off her soft curves, and for a second, he wondered what would happen if he slid his hand under the blanket, up her leg...

Don't be that guy, Wes. Melody. Think about Melody and the future you have planned out.

It was only when Cara pushed to her feet that Wes realized the episode was over.

"Obtuse piece of flotsam." She chuckled, quoting a character. "I'm going to have to use that. Night, Wes. Thanks for introducing me to the show. I really liked it!"

"You're welcome," he said, as Cara gave him a small smile before shutting her door.

He rubbed his palms down the tops of his thighs. Shit! There was no point in denying he was attracted to her, but that didn't mean anything. Attraction is just a chemical reaction. That's all it was.

He'd never lived with a woman as a roommate before. His

body was clearly just confused by the false intimacy. Once he got to know her better, it would resolve itself. That's it. They'd be friends–buddies–and you don't lust after your buddies. Not that he was lusting after her, he assured himself.

Wes ran a hand back through his hair with a groan. He was overcomplicating things. She hadn't seemed to notice so there was nothing to worry about. He set the alarm on his phone and placed it on his bedside table, unable to escape the unwelcome thought that this attraction could hamper his plan with Melody.

He couldn't let that happen.

THE NEXT MORNING when Wes emerged from his room, he was greeted by the rich aroma of coffee and the sight of Cara pushing egg whites around in a frying pan.

"Good morning!" She sent him a sunny smile. "Did I wake you?"

He shook his head and poured himself a mug of coffee. Wes watched her cook for a few minutes, and then she slid the egg whites on to a plate. She took her plate to the table but snuck repeated glances at him. Something was bothering her. Wes grabbed a granola bar from the pantry and chewed it slowly, waiting for her to decide if she was going to say something.

"Have you talked to Melody lately?"

Was she still worried about living with him? Had he made her uncomfortable last night?

"She texted me yesterday," Cara said into the silence, interrupting his thoughts. "I'd asked her about you."

"Seems fair."

Cara nodded, and Wes caught himself staring again when she chewed her lip. "You haven't talked to her though?"

Wes frowned. What was she getting at? "No."

"Maybe I misunderstood what she meant… She said she

would be back in *a few weeks*. Not at the end of the week, like you said."

He shook his head. "She said the shoot was no more than a week." But in the back of his mind, Wes wasn't surprised. It wouldn't be out of character for Melody to suddenly change plans but— "What exactly did she say?"

Cara got up to retrieve her phone and tapped on the screen before handing him the phone. He felt his cheeks heat as he read Melody's words.

"Huh, I guess I should give her a call." He tried to be nonchalant, but he was pissed. Had she taken another job, and not bothered to tell him… again?

"It's just…" Worry was plain in Cara's eyes. "I don't even know where to send the rent? I never signed anything and…"

"Don't worry about that." He waved his hand. "It's already taken care of."

"But—" Cara's brow wrinkled.

Wes wasn't interested in reassuring her at the moment. "I need to make a phone call."

Taking his phone onto the deck, he dialed Melody's number, tucking his hands under his arms to stay warm in the cold morning air.

"I was just about to call you!" Melody said, in lieu of a greeting.

"Right."

"Yeah, plans changed. Things are going really well here. Fabrizio and the representatives from the line I was shooting for love my look! They want me to stick around to work with them in their studio. Isn't that amazing!"

"That does sound great. But, Melody, what the hell? How long are you going to be there?"

"I don't know," she said breezily. "As long as they want me, I guess."

"And what? I'm supposed to stay in the house with this girl you moved in?" A muscle ticked in his jaw.

"You're only there temporarily. Aren't you looking for a house?"

"Yes, but that's not the point. We had plans—"

"Don't nag," Melody whined. "It's easy for you to judge. You're successful, and I'm still trying to make a name for myself. It's like you don't even want me to succeed!"

"It's not that at all." Wes pinched the bridge of his nose. Conversations with Melody could be exhausting. "We haven't seen each other in a really long time. I was looking forward to spending time with you."

"And we still will! We have all the time in the world!"

"What about Cara?"

"What about her? Is she messing up my place or something?"

"No." He loved Melody, but she could be remarkably self-absorbed. "What do I tell her? She wasn't expecting to live with a strange guy. You didn't even tell her where to send the rent?"

Melody blew out an exasperated breath. "Just tell her to hand it to you. You are being so over dramatic, and it's boring me. Find a house, and then you can move out."

"I was kind of hoping you would want to help me pick one out." He had hoped it would be a house they could live in together and start a family.

"Aww, you're such a sweetie. I'm sure anything you pick will be great! I gotta go, but it was great to hear from you. Ciao."

Melody ended the call before he had a chance to reply. Her behavior wasn't that unusual. She'd always been careless of other people. Wes scowled. That's not what he meant. His frown deepened. Right now, he had the more pressing problem of what to tell Cara.

However, when he slid the glass doors shut, Cara was nowhere in sight. Her door was open, so he assumed she had left. Sure enough, thirty minutes later she returned from a run, but

Wes was on the phone with Nina and only gave her a half-hearted wave.

He was running the initial threat detector on a local private school's website when Cara appeared again, her wet hair pulled into a sloppy knot on top of her head. When she walked past him to the kitchen, he got a strong whiff of the same floral scent he noticed the night before. It was familiar, but he couldn't put his finger on it.

Wes listened while she filled a glass of water behind him. He needed to address the Melody situation, but he wasn't sure how she would take it. Glancing at the software, he saw that it still had several minutes left to run. Wes half-turned in his chair to face her.

"You were right. Melody took another job so she's going to be there longer."

"A couple more weeks?"

He grimaced. "She didn't say. But you don't need to worry about the rent. I actually own this house. I've been renting it to Melody for a couple of years now."

Cara's eyes became saucers as they bounced around the house. "This is *your* house? You said you were house hunting."

"I am. It's an investment property. I really was just crashing here until Melody left. I'm looking to buy a house to live in, but I was taking my time. I hope my owning the house doesn't make this weird."

He could practically see the thoughts racing around her head. Finally, she shrugged. "I guess it doesn't really change anything, and if something breaks, my landlord is right here for me to complain to."

Wes's shoulders sagged with relief. He appreciated that she seemed to roll with the information. He'd half expected her to immediately move out. Between him and Melody, they had thrown one surprise after another at her over the last few days.

Her smile was bittersweet when she said, "I don't have a lot of options."

His stomach sank. Wes felt like an ass to have put her in this position, but he didn't know what to say, so he only nodded before turning back to his monitor.

Cara took her water to the sofa and picked up the television remote. Wes tried to concentrate on what he was doing, but his thoughts kept returning to how annoyed he was with Melody for putting them in this situation.

"Are you watching Star Trek again?" he asked, surprised when the familiar music played.

She didn't turn around because the answer was obvious. He stared at the back of her long neck for a minute before dropping his eyes to the project he was working on.

I'll just take a little break, he promised himself as he joined her on the sofa. If she gave the slightest indication he wasn't welcome, he'd get up, but she only glanced in his direction before tucking her feet up and leaning against the arm of the sofa.

After the third episode, he finally asked, "No school today?"

"Nope, I have the day off." She looked over her shoulder to where his computer sat unused. "Aren't you supposed to be working?"

"Probably." He gave her a lopsided grin, and she shook her head with a laugh as the next episode began.

CHAPTER EIGHT

Cara was just getting home from school the next day when her phone buzzed with a text from Amara.

AMARA: HOW DID THE DATING APPS GO?

All of her free time over the last few days had been spent watching Star Trek with Wes. She'd forgotten all about the apps and that she was supposed to be out meeting new people. It was weird how quickly she had become comfortable in Wes's company. She'd only known him for a couple of days, but there was something about him that made her comfortable and secure.

He was confident, quietly sure of himself without the bravado or arrogance most of the guys she grew up with had. They had never questioned that their pedigrees and money would pave their way in life. Wes was making his own way, and she admired that.

It *had* been a weird moment when he told her he was actually the owner of the house. She had been concerned that it would change the dynamic between them. But he seemed more nervous about telling her than she was about receiving the news. She remembered Melody's comment about the landlord having a crush on her and giving her a deal on rent. Cara was starting to wonder how well Wes actually knew Melody.

CARA: NOT YET BEEN GETTING TO KNOW MY 'ROOMMATE.'

Cara unlocked the door and hung her keys on the hooks by the door. Wes was seated as usual at the kitchen table with his headphones on, completely lost in his world of numbers and code. Today, however, he'd added a pair of black square-framed glasses. He rested his jaw on his fist for a second, causing the muscles in his forearms to flex. A flash of heat spread low in her belly, and her pulse picked up pace. *Since when are forearms hot?*

He needed a haircut, but she liked how his hair curled and waved, the overhead lights picking out little bits of gold in the thick chestnut. She could cut it for him—practice for school, of course. Her mind drifted, imagining her fingers combing through the waves, holding his head still... Her phone buzzed with Amara's response.

AMARA: BORING. YOU'VE GOT TO START GOING OUT!

Cara shook her head at Amara's enthusiastic use of eggplant emojis. She smirked, and raised her phone to take a quick picture of Wes.

This time she couldn't hold in the laugh when Amara's reply came through.

AMARA: HOLY SHIT THAT'S YOUR ROOMMATE????

Wes looked up and gave her a warm smile of greeting, and then pointed at his computer to let her know he was still working. She gave him a little wave on her way to her room. She didn't want to run today, but the thought of the giant bowls of popcorn she'd consumed had her reaching for a sports bra. Then again, she reasoned, I've been on my feet all day doing practicals.

Graduation was coming up fast, and she still had hours she needed to complete. Only a few more weeks to go and then she could look for a steady job. She didn't have any work booked for this week, and she was worried about some of her bills.

Her phone continued to light up on the bed signaling she had multiple texts and notifications from her new social media account. Cara quickly pulled on a pair of sweatpants and a loose top and scrounged for slippers. She scrolled through Amara's rapid-fire texts.

> AMARA: ARE YOU SERIOUS? HE LOOKS LIKE SUPERMAN WHEN HE'S NOT BEING SUPERMAN.

> AMARA: SEXY CLARK KENT...

> CARA: DIDN'T CLARK KENT HAVE DARK HAIR?

> AMARA: SHUT UP YOU KNOW WHAT I MEAN. WHAT HAVE YOU BEEN DOING? (FOLLOWED BY ANOTHER EGGPLANT EMOJI)

> CARA: WATCHING TV PERV. HAVE YOU EVER SEEN STAR TREK?

The dots appeared, then disappeared before appearing again.

> AMARA: ARE YOU BEING SERIOUS?

> CARA: IT'S ACTUALLY PRETTY GOOD. CHEESY BUT GOOD.

> AMARA: THAT'S IT I'M COMING TO ATLANTA. WHO ARE YOU AND WHERE IS MY BEST FRIEND?

> AMARA: CUDDLING ON THE COUCH? ALL IT TAKES IS A HAND SLIP...

> CARA: NOPE IT'S A NO GO. HE'S IN LOVE WITH MY REAL ROOMMATE REMEMBER.

> AMARA: BUT THEY AREN'T DATING.

> CARA: NO.

> AMARA: THEN... WHAT ARE YOU WAITING FOR.

> CARA: I DON'T NEED THAT KIND OF DRAMA IN MY LIFE.

> AMARA: PFFT.

CARA: THANKS FOR LIKING ALL MY POSTS BTW.

AMARA: OF COURSE! I'M GLAD YOU'RE BACK ON.

CARA: IT'S FOR WORK. THE INSTRUCTORS AT OUR SCHOOL SAID WE NEEDED TO HAVE ACCOUNTS TO SHOW WHAT WE CAN DO. A VISUAL RESUME.

AMARA: MAKES SENSE. YOU CAN DO MY MAKEUP ANYTIME. GOTTA GO TALK SOON.

PREHEATING THE OVEN, Cara pulled one of her containers from the refrigerator and put it on the counter. She glanced at the empty bag of Fritos and the half-eaten package of Oreos on the table next to Wes. Stretching across the counter, she tapped him on the shoulder.

"Are you hungry?"

His gaze fell on her container resting on the counter. "Are you sure?"

"Don't get excited. It's chicken and broccoli again."

"That sounds perfect." His lips curved, and Cara found herself staring at his lips. She spun to the refrigerator and jerked it open. "No problem."

Wes closed down his program, and after filling a glass with water, lounged casually on the opposite counter of the kitchen. "Those are pretty handy." He angled his head at the two containers she was putting in the oven.

"One of the ladies I go to school with told me about them. Fewer dishes, and when you're tired after a long day, you don't have to think about what's for dinner."

"My grandmother used to do that with the crockpot."

"I don't think I've ever used a crockpot," Cara said diplomatically, not completely sure what one was. "If it's low maintenance like this, I'm open to anything. Ask her what would be good for beginners."

"Can't. She's dead." His voice was flat.

"I'm so—"

"It was a long time ago. I was a kid."

Cara shifted, wishing she had something to do with her hands. She shouldn't ask. She barely knew him, and it was completely inappropriate! But now the question that had instantly formed at his comment was burning its way through her brain.

"Does it get easier?"

He frowned, his eyes holding hers in a level stare. "Grief?"

Cara wanted to tear her eyes away. She felt trapped and vulnerable. The black of his pupils seemed to bleed into the caramel as they bored into her.

"My father died last year." Why did she tell him that? "I miss him." She bit her lip, emotions she had pushed down over the last year threatening to surge up and choke her.

"It changes." His voice was quiet. "But you never forget what you've lost. The hole is always there."

"My brothers won't talk about it. Everything changed when he died, and now they barely speak to each other. I don't even know what they are so angry about. It feels like I lost my whole family that day!" She covered her mouth in horror. The words spilled out of her before she had registered them.

A dark cloud hovered over his face, and regret knotted in her stomach. "I'm sorry I shouldn't have said…"

His throat bobbed. "Unfortunately, I know exactly what you mean. One minute everything is fine. The next your world is spinning, and you don't know which way is up. People respond to grief differently. Sometimes anger is all they can manage."

Cara thought about that. Was that why her brothers fought so much lately? As they grew to adulthood, they'd all chosen different paths, but each seemed to pick a path guaranteed to irritate one of the others. Luke was a criminal defense attorney, his twin, James, worked with a federal prosecutor, and Declan seemed to have followed in their father's footsteps. Cut-throat and ruthless–anything to win.

"How did your parents—"

Wes cut her off. "My mother is gone, too, but my grandparents raised me."

Her mouth fell open with a tiny gasp of dismay. "You were alone? How old were you?" Cara felt sick. She was a grown woman and still had her mother. He said he'd been a child….

His jaw sawed back and forth, but he didn't walk away like she expected—that must mean something.

Maybe he needed to talk about it as much as she did.

"I had just turned fourteen." He inhaled sharply through his nose. "There was no other family that would take me, so I ended up at the Children's Home in Athens."

"Oh, Wes!"

"One star—do *not* recommend." His lips twisted in a grotesque attempt at a smile, and he pushed away from the counter, carrying his glass to the table.

Cara was saved from responding by the oven timer—because what do you say to that? She had no experience with this at all. Her parents hadn't been nurturing, but they'd been there—in their own ways—and she'd had Anne and Siobhan, her surrogate mothers. She carried the two containers to the table and took her seat.

Wes took a bite while Cara searched her brain for a way to gracefully break the tense silence that enveloped them.

"It wasn't all bad," Wes surprised her by saying, pushing a piece of broccoli around with his knife. "It's where I met Melody. She was a year older, but she'd been in care most of her life." He stabbed a piece of chicken.

"That's awful."

Wes chewed the bite slowly. Was he also wondering why he was sharing all of this? "It was. If it hadn't been for her showing me the ropes—how to get extra food, how to fight dirty—I don't know that I would have survived. It was so different from where I'd come from—I owe her everything."

"I'm glad you had her," Cara murmured, pieces of their relationship finally starting to make sense.

Wes speared another piece of the meal. "What about you? You've mentioned your brothers several times."

"I have three half-brothers—Declan, Luke, and James." She smiled.

"Did you all grow up in Georgia?"

Cara hesitated, taking a bite for cover. How much did she want to reveal? Where she came from everyone already knew about her father and his romantic exploits. How would it look to someone new? But... Wes had been open with her, and it only seemed fair.

"No, we all had different mothers, so we grew up in different places."

Wes's fork paused on the way to his mouth. "Ah."

"We're a family, though. Siobhan, that's Declan's mom, and Anne, the twins' mom, always treated me like one of their own. They even made sure we spent most holidays together. Until Declan graduated from college, the four of us spent summers with my dad. We're unconventional but it works. My dad stayed friendly with all of our moms."

Wes looked skeptical, and she laughed. "I'm serious! I think in part it was because they were all brutally honest about what they expected from each other. My dad loved women. *Loved* women. He was a confirmed bachelor for most of his life, and I know it makes him sound like a cliché, but he didn't do long term relationships. He made that clear from the start. He loved each of them in his own way." Cara smiled. "First of the baby mamas was Siobhan. She was married before and had a young son, Seamus. They met while Dad was working in Dublin. Her family owns several bars and restaurants there, and they met at a party. Then, there was Anne. She was a professor at Brown University. They met when my father was invited to give a talk at the business school. They were together the longest, even after the twins were born. And then there's me. I was the result of a short fling."

"That's… unusual."

"It is. What about you? Have you always been into computers?" She winced, but Wes appeared to accept the abrupt topic change.

"No." He sat up straighter in his chair. "I took a computer lab as a freshman in high school and was fortunate to have a teacher, Mr. Phelps, recognize I had an aptitude for them. He encouraged me to sign up for more challenging classes and join the computer club that met after school." His smile was wry when he continued. "I would have done anything to get out of the Children's Home for a few extra hours. It gave me something to focus on…"

"And the hacking?"

"There was a contest in Atlanta, though they advertised it as a cybersecurity demonstration, and I won." His eyes brightened. "I loved it. Mr. Phelps was a great guy. He never brought it up, but he seemed to understand how much I was struggling. He's the one who introduced me to lifting weights, too. The stronger I became the less of a target I was."

His tone was dispassionate, but Cara looked down at her hands, her throat thick.

Cara pushed her chicken back and forth, and Wes lifted his chin at her conspicuous fidgeting. "Just say it."

She sensed, rather than saw, his body tense up. She should keep her mouth shut, but she was dying to know. His eyebrows rose impatiently.

"What happened with you and Melody? Why didn't you stay together?"

Wes's body deflated with relief, and Cara wondered what he thought she was going to say.

"We weren't together in high school. More like best friends. She's older and always dreamed of going to New York and becoming a famous model." His lips twitched. "My dreams were a lot less lofty. I wanted to go to college, get a steady job, and start a family of my own. Right before she turned eighteen, she ran away from the home to get started, and I still needed to finish high school. It's not that exciting." He chuckled. "I got a scholarship to Georgia Tech, and now I'm doing what I love."

"Melody?" It didn't appear as though the model's dreams of fame and fortune had panned out.

"Mel tried really hard. She had a few big jobs, but it just didn't work out. It's a tough industry. She worked part-time jobs to survive, but never got her big break. I helped her when I could. Eventually she moved back to Georgia. She hoped she would have an opportunity with all the TV and movie production that's moved here from California in the last ten years."

It didn't sound like a love story, Cara thought. There had to be more! "You stayed in touch though?"

Wes finished his meal and picked up his container to carry into the kitchen. "Yeah, sometimes months would go by. At one point, it was a year. But Melody always knew she could count on me if she needed to."

Cara bit the inside of her cheek. She wanted to point out that, from what he described, the friendship was one-sided. But if he was convinced it was love, then it was none of her business.

"This was great! Much better than the mushy veggies that I usually have delivered."

Cara put her container in the dishwasher, and when she straightened, she saw he was watching her thoughtfully.

"You do this every week?"

"I try to do some sort of meal prep every weekend."

"I have a proposition for you. If I pay for the groceries, would you make enough for me?"

Cara considered the idea. It wouldn't be much extra work, and she could save a lot of money if he were paying for the food.

"Deal!"

"Just one thing? Any chance we could have a little more variety sometimes. I love chicken and broccoli, but..."

Cara laughed. "That's just what I was making this week. Make me a list of foods you like, and I can work around it. Particularly if you're paying."

Wes grinned, his eyes lighting up. Cara's heart flip flopped in her chest.

She needed a date... soon!

CHAPTER NINE

OVER THE NEXT COUPLE OF WEEKS, THEY FELL INTO A PATTERN. Most days, Cara was out of the house finishing her program at school and working at the hair salon. Wedding show season had morphed into fundraising season in Atlanta, and she was grateful for the work because, even though she had sent out what felt like a million resumes, she hadn't had a single phone call showing interest. But, as worried as she was about finding a job, she was happier than she had been in what felt like a very long time.

Every night she came home and reheated what she had made for herself and Wes, and they ate dinner together before inevitably ending up on the couch watching Star Trek. If anyone from her former life could see her now, they wouldn't recognize this new domesticated Cara. She preferred these quiet nights with Wes to the overly loud club scene she had previously inhabited. She felt like a different person, and she liked it!

The only sticking point was her extremely inconvenient and persistent attraction to Wes. She'd hoped being around each other every day would lessen his effect on her ovaries—that she would become immune. But every time he wandered out of his room without a shirt on, her stomach flipped. And it was getting worse. She found herself staring at the back of his neck, where his hair curled too long, wondering if it would feel as soft between her fingers as it looked.

Each night she fought the urge to lean against him when they were on the sofa together, warm under the fuzzy blanket they now shared. The worst part was she *liked* him. If it were just physical, she could scratch that itch herself—and she had tried—but she suspected her feelings were starting to shift. And that was a problem.

He had been more than clear. Wes wanted Melody. He had a plan for his life—wife, kids, white picket fence—and she understood a hot fling with a woman he just met didn't fit. Still... He hadn't mentioned Melody since the night he revealed their history together, and to Cara's knowledge, he hadn't spoken with Melody either. The weeks slipped by, and no one mentioned when she might return.

When Cara had first started seeing Erik—scum of the earth—she talked about him to Amara incessantly—and that had *never* been love. If he were truly *in love* with Melody, wouldn't he want to talk about her? Or maybe it was just Cara's out of control hormones feeding into her wishful thinking.

HER COMPLACENT LITTLE bubble popped on a Saturday afternoon in late February. She'd been watching the notifications on her phone, and the second she saw her package had been delivered, she rushed to the mailbox. One of the instructors at the school had noticed the scent from her skin cream and asked her where she had gotten it. After Cara explained she made her own, the instructor had her give a short presentation to the class.

At first, she was uncomfortable standing at the front of the room, but her classmates seemed genuinely interested. Cara explained that while she used a honeysuckle essential oil for her personal products, almost any scent would work. She'd even started playing around with body oils. Cara pulled the small box from the mailbox containing her order of essential oils and instantly spotted the oversized cream envelope nestled next to a large red one.

She stared at the two cards, making her way up the driveway. One covered in hearts was clearly a late Valentine's card, but her attention was on the heavier stock envelope. Usually, when one of her mother's wedding invitations arrived, Cara had a mix of emotions. Most common ones being exasperation and amusement. This time when she stared at the Italian return address, all she felt was annoyance.

She would have to attend. Corinne was still her mother, but Cara couldn't help but begin to mentally calculate how much time she would lose from work and the cost of a plane ticket. Her mouth flattened. Just so her mother could realize *He's not the man I thought he was* in less than a year.

A few minutes later when her phone rang, she answered with a terse, "Yes, I got the invitation."

"What invitation?" Declan's voice rumbled.

"My mother's latest wedding invitation—Italy. At least it will be warmer than last time. Remember her Winter Wonderland wedding in Prague. Freezing!" Cara tore open the red envelope and tossed the other mail on the counter. As she suspected, it was a Valentine's card, with a gift card to a makeup chain tucked inside. She smiled. Even unsigned, she knew it had to be from Anne, the twin's mother. She was always sending thoughtful gifts like that.

"That's not why I'm calling." He sounded distracted, his voice strained. The Valentine was instantly forgotten.

"Everything okay, Dec?"

"Have you had any contact with Courtney?"

His question about their stepmother startled her. "No, why?"

"I heard she was planning a trip to Atlanta. I was worried it had to do with you."

Cara's brow creased. "Why would Courtney come to see me? She hates me."

It was strange. When David Bloom first started seeing Courtney, Cara had liked her. Courtney had recently sold her executive gift business, a company she had built as a single mom of two boys, and Cara was impressed by her independence.

But after David and Courtney married, her mask had fallen away, and she was a completely different person. Every time Cara was around the couple, Courtney made biting, pointed jabs at Cara whenever her father was out of earshot. Cara was spoiled, Cara was stupid, Cara was rude. Amara thought the woman was jealous of David's obvious affection for his only daughter, but it didn't make any sense to Cara. She wanted her father to be happy.

"Trey graduated from college. I think she's shopping for a job for him," Declan said, mentioning Courtney's youngest son.

"Am I supposed to know what that means?"

"It means, she's trying to buy his way into a company. It looks like Atlanta is where she's looking."

Cara was stunned. "Why Atlanta? How do you know about it? Are you spying on her?"

"I keep myself informed. I know the three of you think I'm being paranoid. I have more information now. I'm going to prove she killed our father."

"Declan," she breathed; chill bumps rose on her arms. "Dad was sick—"

"Don't worry about it. I'll handle it. You don't need to be involved."

"He was my father, too! If you've found something, you have to tell me. I have a right to know!"

Declan's frustration was palpable over the phone, and a knot formed in her stomach. Luke and James thought Declan was obsessed with their stepmother and refused to discuss the possibility that their father died of anything other than natural causes. But Cara had always thought Declan might be right. The way Courtney had behaved during his illness and the extreme conditions of the will *were* suspicious.

"I had lunch with Mrs. Woodson."

"Our Mrs. Woodson?"

"Yes.

"You had lunch with Mrs. Woodson? Dad's housekeeper?"

"Are you going to repeat everything I say?" Declan snapped.

"Sorry."

"I've been meeting her for lunch every few months."

Cara's eyebrows flew to her hairline. She knew Declan was fond of the woman. She had worked at the Rhode Island estate for as long as Cara could remember, but the idea that Declan and the elderly woman went out to lunch somehow surprised her.

"That's nice of you."

"We owe her."

Cara and her siblings weren't the only ones who had suffered under the new will. All of her father's long-term employees, with the exception of Vince Menardi, head of security, had been excluded. Declan had personally given settlements to each of the staff that had been promised a bequest in the previous will.

"You offered her a job, Dec."

"She's worked enough. Taking her out to lunch is the least I can do." His voice was gruff, and she could tell he was embarrassed.

"What happened at lunch with Mrs. Woodson?"

"She told me that, in the last months of his life, our father suspected he was being poisoned."

Cara's heart fell into her stomach, and a chill swept over her. "What are you talking about?"

"I tried to talk to her about Dad's death before, but she always became so upset. I didn't press. Yesterday, it was all she wanted to talk about. We compared notes, and I'm now more convinced than ever. I think, given time, she'll remember more about what was happening in the house."

"Compared notes?"

"I've gone over his medical records, but there's nothing there. I can't find any neglect, and Dr. Keller seems to have ordered the tests one would expect."

"How in the world did you get his medical records?" Cara frowned. "And why does she think that's what he believed? Did he tell her? If Dad thought someone was poisoning him, he would have done something about it. He wouldn't have just let himself be murdered!"

"I don't think Mrs. Woodson took him seriously at the time. He didn't tell her explicitly, but now that we've been talking, she's remembering certain things. Like how fast he declined. Almost from one day to the next."

"We talked to Dr. Keller. He said it was old age—the natural progression of whatever illness he had."

"Idiopathic," Declan sneered. "The catch-all for, 'We've run out of ideas.' What if it was poison? She said he refused to eat anything that wasn't prepared by her in the house."

"You're getting ahead of yourself. He didn't die suddenly. He was sick for months! Wouldn't they have looked for toxins or something?"

"They did," Declan conceded. "However, certain poisons require special tests or are only detectible in an autopsy—which Courtney refused and then promptly destroyed any evidence by cremating his body.

"You don't trust Dr. Keller? He was Dad's closest friend." She rubbed at the headache building between her brows.

"I'm not saying that. From what my experts say, he followed every logical step and referred Dad to specialists when he couldn't diagnose him." Cara heard a car door slam, and the car's Bluetooth took over. "There's something else Mrs. Woodson said.

Just before his death, Dad took a trip. He didn't say where he was going, only that he had business that had to be done in person. She tried to talk him out of it because he was so ill, but he insisted. The only other person who knew was Vincent. He handled the travel. But he seems to have disappeared."

Pieces of a memory fell into place. "He went to Ireland." Cara stared blankly at the wall.

"How the fuck do you know that?"

"Don't yell at me," Cara snapped. "I just put it together. When I told Corinne Dad was dead, she was shocked. She said she had just seen him. She ran into him in Dublin." Her mind raced. "The last time I saw Dad—a week or so before—it ended in an argument. But before we argued—when I saw how sick he was–I asked what the doctors were doing to help him. I didn't think much of what he said at the time but now…"

Was Declan's paranoia contagious? Was she seeing something where there was nothing?

"What! What did he say?"

"Something like, don't worry, I'm taking all the precautions I need."

Declan inhaled sharply. *"Precautions?* That's the word he used?"

The scene flashed in front of her. The violet eyes she and Declan had inherited dulled to gray, his skin pasty—nothing like the virile man he'd been. "One last puzzle, little star," she murmured.

"What was?"

Cara swallowed, her throat thick with regret. "The last thing he ever said to me. We argued; it was stupid. I wanted a job with more impact in Bloom Communications. He told me that what I was doing was important and not to worry." Her voice caught. "That one day I'd figure out where I needed to be, but for now, I served him best by being his 'perfect little star.' I was so angry, but he was tired, and I dropped it. He told me we would talk again. He needed to solve 'one last puzzle.' I was hurt. I was talking about my life, and he was talking about one of his stupid riddles. If I'd known…" Cara's eyes welled up.

"I'm sorry, Car-Bear."

"That's why I remember it so clearly. I was never able to get him on the phone again. Courtney always said he was too sick. I should have forced her. If we hadn't argued, maybe he would have found a way—"

"You can't think like that!" Declan's voice was sharp. "*He* is the one who shut *us* out."

A horrible thought began picking at her. "Declan, if he thought he was being poisoned, and then he changed his will… Doesn't that mean he thought one of us had something to do with it?"

"I don't know how Courtney did it, if she coerced him or threatened him. But I don't believe our father would betray us like that. Take away *everything* we'd been promised."

Cara's heart clenched. Declan and their father had been inseparable at one point, and she knew Declan had done everything humanly possible to earn their father's approval—until David Bloom must have gone too far, and Declan said no. The two men were broken after that, too stubborn to make peace.

"Not everything, Dec. We still have each other."

After a moment of silence, he answered, "You're right. I'm sorry. I still have my family. I have to go, Cara. Be careful."

"Okay." Cara wished she knew what to say to make it better for her brother, but she was worried that the wounds he'd accumulated before and after their father's death would never be fully healed.

"I love you, Dec." *I'm worried about you.*

"Love you, too."

CHAPTER TEN

"Hey!" Wes speared a zucchini noodle and stopped halfway to his mouth. He glanced up at her and then down again at his food. "I have tickets for a thing this weekend. I bought them a long time ago... I thought Melody and I..." He paused again. "I wondered if maybe you would want to go?"

"I don't have anything going on this weekend. What is it?"

Wes's eyes shifted. "Trek Atlanta. It's a convention—for Star Trek fans."

Cara's lips parted slightly, but the laugh he half expected didn't come. Instead, she smiled.

"Yes! Is it like Comic Con?"

His shoulders dropped with relief. "Basically. They have panels with actors from all the different franchises, and people get together—clubs, online forums—we don't have to do all that, if you don't want to."

"Sounds like fun! I've never been to anything like that."

"Cool." Wes sipped his water, fighting the urge to grin. "They're actually VIP tickets. I got them from Peachtree Pictures —that movie I'm working on. A woman I knew in high school works there. She introduced me to a couple of people last time I was at the studio. They all seemed nice."

Wes wasn't particularly interested in socializing, but Cara had mentioned more than once that she hadn't met a lot of people in the city.

Her eyes lit up. "Who are we going to go as?"

"Um, what?"

"Which characters are we going to be? The easy answer is I could be Counselor Troi, but I don't want to. She's kind of a know it all, and she irritates me. But then again, I could wear a wig, and that's always fun."

"I wasn't going to dress up." Wes shook his head to emphasize his point.

"Of *course*, we are going to dress up. Are you kidding me? This will be the first time I've had a chance to practice some of the tricks I've learned on YouTube!" She made an exaggerated pout. "Pretty please, Wes."

His brain froze like the dreaded wheel of death on a computer monitor right before it crashed. His gaze fell to her plump lips, and a sudden intense need to lean across the table and claim them consumed him.

"You can be Data. It won't require too much latex."

Cara gnawed on her lip the way she always did when she was thinking, and his body seized, watching her teeth work at her plump lower lip. Heat raced through him, and Wes was grateful he was sitting, the table keeping him from embarrassing himself. What was wrong with him? He was acting like a teenager!

"Can you order the costumes?"

Her question broke through the haze, and he dragged his eyes from her mouth.

"Wes?"

"Yeah, sure. Whatever you want." He couldn't imagine saying no to her when she looked at him like that.

"Great!" Cara chattered on about what she could do to transform them, but Wes barely heard a word.

Fuck.

This was getting out of hand if he couldn't even share a meal with her without getting an erection!

He stood abruptly and hurried into the kitchen with his dish. "I'm going to the gym."

"I thought you went earlier?"

Wes didn't answer, only grabbed his keys and ran.

CHAPTER ELEVEN

"Stop fidgeting." Cara swatted at Wes's hand, when he attempted to scratch the latex pad she had attached to his chin that morning. "You won't be able to get through." Cara placed the backs of her fingers under his jaw and rubbed.

Wes groaned, "That's not helping."

"This isn't supposed to be uncomfortable!" She put her hands on her hips. "Let's go back to the room, and I'll take off the chin piece. I brought the white crème foundation. I should be able to blend it."

Wes rolled his shoulders in his polyester costume. "But we have fast passes for Brent Spiner."

"I don't think Commander Data will mind if you don't look exactly like him."

Wes huffed, but Cara could see he'd reached his limit with the heavy makeup. Flashing their badges at the security guard, she steered him to a chair inside.

Peachtree Pictures had provided a hospitality room for those with VIP passes, and it had filled up since they left hours before. Most were standing in small groups talking, but there were a few seated with their feet up. She and Wes were among only a handful in costume, and she could practically feel his embarrassment.

"Hang on." Cara grabbed the bag she'd stuffed under a table that morning and began to loosen the glue with her latex adhesive remover.

"That shit sticks, huh?" Cara lifted her eyes to see a woman (at least she thought it was a woman) dressed as a Ferengi, arms crossed watching her work. "You need to use a lot more."

"Ahhh! I'm already making a huge mess!" Cara exclaimed, as the liquid dripped onto the leg of Wes's Starfleet uniform.

"Here." The Ferengi shoved a handful of napkins at her.

"I've got it." Wes snatched the napkins out of her hands, when she began wiping up the spill on his lap.

The woman looked around the room, and the part of her mouth not covered in a molded latex piece curled. "Brian can afford VIP tickets and a room here, but I can't get funding for a real team." She waved at someone across the room, before her attention returned to where Cara was crouched in front of Wes, trying to prevent the dark curls of her wig from sticking to his thick, white makeup as she worked on his face.

"I can't believe you dressed up, Wes!" the woman said, as Cara carefully inched the latex chin pad from Wes's skin.

"Me, either."

"Is this your handiwork?"

Cara nodded. "It's my first time using the latex, but I was happy with how it came out. Who did yours?"

The woman was completely transformed with what must be several sculpted latex pieces and a wig."

"I did. I'm the lead makeup artist on *Love in Arms*," she said, referring to the Peachtree Pictures movie Wes was working on.

Cara opened the jar of white makeup and began sponging it gingerly onto Wes's reddened chin.

"You should clean and moisturize that first." The woman pointed out.

"I know. I didn't bring everything I needed and," she gestured to where Wes's eyes were screwed tightly shut as if he were being tortured, "my client's patience is limited."

The woman laughed loudly. "I'm Skye by the way. He must really like you to let you do this. Never in a million years did I think I would see Wes Evans in a costume."

Cara felt her cheeks heat.

"Leave my roommate alone, Skye," Wes said.

Skye's eyes widened slightly behind the makeup.

"I thought you bought a house when you moved back?"

"Still looking."

Cara kept her mouth shut as she finished blending the edges of the old makeup with the new. Wes hadn't looked at houses in weeks. She sat back on her heels. The chin didn't look great, but it would do for the next few hours.

"You're free. Don't touch it for ten minutes. Give it time to dry."

Wes got to his feet and immediately stretched his mouth, cracking the thick makeup. Cara sighed.

"Cara's really talented. It would be awesome if she started having models other than me," he said, giving Skye a meaningful look.

She looked at Cara consideringly. "Are you licensed, or is this something you do for fun?"

"I have my license, but I'm just getting started."

"Don't listen to her," Wes interrupted. "She spends all of her time on YouTube learning. She's got these creepy heads all over her room that she's always playing with. She's really, really good. You should hire her."

Cara blinked at his blunt statement, not sure which part stunned her more, his compliments or the fact that he had just told the woman to give her a job.

"I don't *play* with the mannequin heads."

Skye ignored the comment. "Are you interested in working

on a production? I wouldn't normally do this, but the other makeup artist just flaked off with all of his assistants, so I'm kind of screwed. The film is mostly done, but I can't do it by myself. It's a tiny cast with only a few extras, but the budget is extremely tight which is why we were using so many assistants under Tomas's supervision, instead of MUAs, make-up artists," she clarified for Wes. "When he went, his minions went with him, and now I have no one. It doesn't pay much."

"I'd love to work on a movie!" Cara sounded too eager, but she didn't care.

Skye stared hard at her. "I can't believe I'm doing this—I'm desperate. I can see you're competent, and we don't do anything particularly complicated. Would you be interested? You'd be supervised and doing the absolute basics."

Cara didn't hesitate. "Yes!"

"It's not glamorous," Skye warned. "It will mostly be cleaning brushes, making sure the rollers are plugged in, prepping extras, that kind of thing."

Now that Skye had made a decision, she wasn't wasting any time. "Wes has my email. Send me a resume and a portfolio of your work as soon as you can, just in case someone checks up on me—which is unlikely because Brian is barely keeping it together," she muttered. "I'll send you all the forms you need to fill out, and I'll need you by Wednesday. Can you get all that back to me by then?"

"Absolutely!"

"I'll message you on social media. I don't always look like this." She indicated her face.

"I'll give her your number, and she can send you her username. It's a flower, right?" Wes asked.

Cara nodded. "I don't have a lot of followers." *Don't say that.* "I do have a few loyal bots that like everything I post and leave the classic 'you're so beautiful' and 'let's talk' comments." She joked to cover her anxiety and was gratified when Skye groaned.

"I hate those! They are always some account with four or five fake pictures claiming to be either military or a doctor. I guess that's what the Russian bot farms think American women like."

Both women laughed but Wes scowled. "You should delete them. Those bots are usually farming for your personal info."

Skye and Cara looked at each other and rolled their eyes, but Wes didn't seem to mind.

"Whatever. I'm getting a cookie." He ambled off towards the hospitality table.

"Thank you so much for this opportunity," Cara said. Did she really just get offered a job?

Instead of responding, Skye's eyes followed Wes and then brought them back to Cara, cocking her head.

"It's nice to see Wes finally found someone who loves Star Trek as much as him. How did y'all meet?"

"I don't think *anyone* loves Star Trek as much as Wes. I'd never even seen it until I moved in with him." Cara didn't know why she felt the need to explain, but she found herself babbling. "I only met him a few weeks ago. I thought I was moving in with Melody, but then she suddenly had a job overseas… So, now it's just us until she gets back."

"Melody Spires?" Something about the way Skye said her name grabbed Cara's attention.

"That's right! You went to high school with Wes! You must have known Melody, too."

Skye's lips flattened, and her gaze went to where Wes was loading up a plate of the catered food. "Yeah, I know Melody. I didn't realize they were living together."

"They aren't—as a couple." *Again, with the overshare!* "He's crashing at her place while he finds someplace to live."

"Then I hope he finds someplace fast. Anyway, it was great to meet you, and I'll see you Wednesday." Skye gave her a little salute and went to join a group of fellow Ferengi just entering the room.

After the group left, Cara forced herself not to skip over to where Wes was scarfing down potato salad.

"Oh my god! I can't believe it. My first real job!" Cara squealed. "This wouldn't have happened if you hadn't brought me here! Thank you so much for introducing me to her."

Wes grinned back, his caramel eyes sparkling. "You're welcome. But if you hadn't done such a good job, Skye would have ignored anything I said. This is the best I've ever looked at one of these things." Taking one last bite, he dumped his plate in the trash can and caught her hand in his. "Come on, Counselor Troi! The real Commander Data is waiting for us."

CHAPTER TWELVE

After glancing at her ID and checking her name against his list, the security guard waved her onto the studio lot. Cara's pulse raced. It was actually happening! She had spent the last three days reading everything she could online about what to expect on a movie lot, and studying the film synopsis sheets Skye sent over.

Cara followed the road around the facility's perimeter, past the sound stages and what she assumed were warehouses and office space. She found a large parking lot at the back of the property, bordered by a heavily wooded area. Following Skye's instructions, Cara strode up the slight hill toward the sound stages, pulling her rolling case behind her. Skye had let her know that morning over text that she would be working in the vanities trailer on the far side of the four large soundstages.

She made her way between the buildings, glancing through the folding barn doors on the ends at the film sets inside. Excitement bubbled through her, and Cara knew she was grinning like an idiot. Her brothers had all been appropriately happy for her, but only Amara had shrieked with excitement.

Cara found Skye sorting through brushes in the small trailer.

Three makeup stations, divided by large, round vanity lights over one long counter, faced tall makeup chairs. An assortment of containers held everything from cotton balls to sponge wedges, and drawers beneath were labelled with the type of product to be found inside.

"Thanks for being on time," Skye said, not looking up. "We don't have a lot of time before the first principal arrives. She'll be here in ten minutes." Skye moved to the next station, looking it over and rearranging a few items on the counter. "Did you read the synopsis of the movie and look at what we are shooting today?"

Cara swallowed and tried to appear confident. "A diner scene between the love interests first, and then the fight in the apartment later this afternoon."

Skye nodded approvingly. "It's set in post-war 1945. The director loves a bright-red, matte lip and lots of eyelashes." Skye rolled her eyes. "I tried to explain to him that it wasn't completely accurate for the time, but he's seen one too many film noirs. Everything super matte, so be sure you use plenty of powder. Zero glisten under the lights."

She began pulling items out of drawers, holding them up one by one to show Cara. "I'll be doing most of the applications, but I need you to be sure both principals are moisturized to the gods! I swear, if Chandler comes in hungover again, I'm going to murder him." She cut her eyes at Cara. "You didn't hear that."

Cara pretended to zip her lips closed and throw away a key. Skye looked at her watch and leaned back against the long vanity counter running the length of the trailer. "Makeup on set isn't like what you learned in school. It's not that it's more difficult. It's just different. As long as you do what I tell you, and pay attention to the details, you'll be fine. But," she held up a finger, "the number one cardinal rule of the vanities trailer is nothing is ever repeated. The actors have to trust us. If they think we are going to repeat what we've talked about, or gossip about them, it can make things really difficult. On this shoot, no one is in the chair long, but if you make this your career, you might be spending hours only inches from someone's face."

She swirled her finger around in the air. "Circle of trust, got it?"

Satisfied by Cara's nod, Skye resumed educating Cara about each of the products, and in what order she wanted them to be used.

She hadn't finished when the door opened, and a stunning auburn-haired woman stepped hesitantly into the trailer. She smiled shyly at Cara and took the seat on the far end. Skye introduced her as Lia Everton, playing the lead female character Helen.

"Please call me Lia," the woman said quietly. Skye supervised Cara's preparation of Lia's skin for the long day of shooting, while she put rollers in Lia's thick hair.

"On this shoot, we double as hair," she explained to Cara. "Good ol' budget cuts."

Lia made a face in the mirror but didn't say anything.

"Lia, today is Cara's first day, so I'm going to be explaining what I'm doing as I go. Okay?"

"Of course." Lia smiled and sat almost preternaturally still, her moss green eyes staring straight ahead. It was a little unnerving, like she had retreated into her own world, but Skye didn't seem to find anything out of the ordinary. Cara turned her attention to the techniques Skye employed and her explanation behind them.

"Today they're shooting indoors, a diner scene, which is going to require Lia to drink?" She looked to the actor for confirmation. "We need to use a different lipstick than normal. I'll still do several layers with powder in between for staying power, but this baby," Skye held up a purple tube of lipstick, "is the gold standard. Won't budge."

"How's it going this week?" She directed her question at Lia while applying her foundation.

Only Lia's lips moved when she answered in her melodic voice. "I think Brian and Stephen are fighting. Stephen wants more location shoots, but Brian said it's impossible." Her green eyes sparkled. "My money is on Stephen."

"The director," Skye explained, when Cara looked quizzical.

Lia and Skye chatted about the set and the latest gossip. The main topic being whether or not the lighting director was sleeping with the line producer and was the head of cinematography jealous.

Skye was almost done, having just begun to layer Lia's lipstick, when the door to the trailer flew open and an exquisitely handsome man bounded up the stairs and into the small space.

"You're early, Chandler," Skye said pointing at the empty seat next to Lia. "This is Cara; she'll get you started for me."

"I bet she will." He smirked at Cara, sipping coffee out of a travel mug.

"Behave. It's her first day. Let's let her hold onto any delusions she might have about the glamor of movie making for at least a few hours," Skye said, patting Lia's lips with powder. "Cara, can you make sure he has plenty of moisturizer and primer, and then I'll have you finish up Lia."

Cara nodded, moving to get the products Skye mentioned. Cara had done makeup on men before, but her hand shook as she began applying the product. She didn't know if Chandler was any good, but he certainly looked like the quintessential leading man.

"Am I making you nervous?" He ducked his head trying to meet her eyes.

"First day jitters," she said repressively. He flashed a bright white smile, which he obviously thought was charming. Chandler was handsome, but his cocky attitude made her hackles rise. She bit the inside of her cheek to keep herself from saying something she'd regret.

"According to the costume sheet, he's wearing a shallow V-neck sweater, so be sure you cover his neck and the first couple inches of his chest, too," Skye instructed.

Cara had turned to retrieve sheets of tissue paper to protect his clothing when Chandler surprised her by pulling his shirt over his head revealing, what she had to admit, was an impressively muscled torso. "Don't worry about the tissue paper." He winked.

Even though Cara was new to the job, she was fairly certain it wasn't normal for an actor to disrobe in the makeup chair. Cara looked to Skye for guidance. She only glared at Chandler, but Lia's thin shoulders had curved inward and she'd closed her eyes.

"I'm just trying to make it easy on you girls." Chandler smirked, his eyes sliding to his co-star. "Lighten up, Lia! It's not like you haven't seen it before."

Cara thought Lia flinched, but she wasn't sure. Ignoring his antics, Cara concentrated on doing a good job, and thankfully, Skye took over a minute later telling Cara to finish Lia's lipstick.

Cara painted another layer of the crimson color on Lia's full lips, and then covered it with powder again for good measure, while Skye began creating a long scar that ran down the length of Chandler's face and the side of his neck.

"Poor Bob took some shrapnel in the war," Chandler said, when he caught her looking. He reached out to pat Lia's hand where it rested on the arm of the chair, chortling when she jerked it away. "His faithful Helen waited for him. Such a good girl."

Cara wasn't the only one who caught the slight sneer in his voice. Skye looked troubled and turned her attention to Lia, her eyes running critically over her face.

"Looks good. Keep the rollers in. Jerrod will finish your hair once you're in costume."

Skye had barely finished speaking before Lia bolted from the trailer with a muttered, "Thanks."

"I don't know why you bully her," Skye snapped, dabbing a taupe color to the wound.

"It's not bullying. She's wound way too tight. Lia is talented," he said grudgingly. "But if she doesn't develop a thicker skin, she's never going to survive in the industry."

Skye didn't disagree with him. However, Cara's questions about the interaction would have to wait. The door to the trailer opened again, and the first of the extras entered.

Skye continued to work on the fake war wound, while keeping an eye on what Cara was doing. Fortunately, not much was needed for the extras who would make up the other customers in the diner. Skye explained, "Just enough foundation and color so they don't look out of place on camera with the principals."

Cara finished with the extras and was cleaning her station when the walkie-talkie Skye placed on the counter crackled. A voice announced that everyone had five minutes to get to set.

"You better hurry."

Chandler didn't seem concerned and blew Cara a kiss before leaving. "See you around."

"You did good," Skye said, once they were alone. "Nice job not reacting to Chandler. He's basically harmless, but he'll push as far as he thinks he can get away with."

"What's the deal with him and Lia?"

Skye's eyes became cautious. "They were dating a while back, but it didn't work out. I'm sure the studio will have them get back together any day now, for publicity." She looked at her watch and then her clipboard. "We've got about an hour before we need to be available for touchups. I'll give you a quick tour."

They claimed a golf cart nearby and Skye began pointing at various buildings they passed. "That's mainly production offices and HR," she said, pointing at a large, mirrored building with a low pull-thru portico and then to a large warehouse next to it. "That behemoth is wardrobe and storage. I'll introduce you to Jerrod in a bit. You'll love him—or not—it's a toss-up. I have to love him though because he's my brother-in-law. In fact," she mused, "now that I think about it, I like him more than my brother, Todd."

Cara laughed as Skye wheeled them through the open spaces between large soundstages arranged in a square. "Normally we use this area as base camp, but Brian, he owns Peachtree Pictures, only has two films in production. Our film, *Love in Arms*, and a romcom—but they aren't shooting yet."

The lot wasn't large, and soon they had circled back to the trailer adjacent to soundstages three and four. Pulling to a stop, Skye asked, "So what do you think?"

"It's great." Cara smiled, but her doubt must have shown through.

Skye grimaced. "Peachtree used to be bigger, but the last couple of big-budget films were a bust, and then the superhero movie that was supposed to save the studio got leaked before it was ready. That ruined everything. Social media destroyed the film before it was even released. Which wasn't fair because everyone knew it hadn't cleared postproduction. When it was officially released, it bombed. That's why Brian hired Wes's company. Brian's super paranoid about the dailies being leaked."

Before Cara could respond, Skye's walkie-talkie crackled again.

"Skye to channel four. Skye to channel four." Instead of changing the frequency, she set the device down, and grinned at Cara.

"That's Jerrod. It's our code for *come here I have gossip.*"

A short, bald man, dressed in herringbone tweed pants and matching vest, greeted them when they cleared the massive warehouse door. Jerrod didn't hide his perusal of Cara, going over her from head to toe and back again. Cara didn't mind. She was too busy taking in the massive rows of clothing hung from racks layered almost to the ceiling.

"Chanel?" Jerrod quirked a brow at her.

It took Cara a second to realize he was looking at her sneakers. He pursed his lips taking in her black pants. "And Prada Gaberdine." She couldn't tell if he was impressed or not.

"They were gifts," Cara said quickly. Which was technically true. Everything Cara owned before a year ago, her father had paid for.

"Don't explain yourself!" Skye said, with a hand on her hip. "If you work hard and want to buy yourself nice things then that's your business!"

Cara squirmed inside. She hadn't bought them, but that independence was what she craved.

"What's the deal? I don't have a ton of time," Skye asked.

"Brian is looking to sell!" Jerrod pressed his palms together and raised them in front of his lips, his eyes alight with glee.

Skye gasped. "How do you know that? Why do you look so happy? We could all be out of a job!"

"Valentina heard him on the phone when she went to argue about her budget being cut again. He has a prospective buyer coming in a couple of days. Originally, they were going to invest, but now he thinks they might buy the studio outright."

"Great," Skye said unhappily. "I was counting on that romcom movie. I guess I could reach out to Tina, see if they need anyone over at Magnolia."

Cara was equally dismayed. She'd finally gotten a steady job, and now it looked like it might disappear before it started.

"Don't be such a sourpuss. I didn't say Peachtree was *closing*. If he gets a new buyer, things might get better. Besides, dear sister," Jerrod said, when she gave him the finger, "maybe you'll be able to hire a team again. No offense." His last comment was directed at Cara.

"None taken."

Skye frowned and looked at her watch. "We better get going—unless you have more unhappy news? I need to pack my bag and get to set in case they need touchups."

"Nice to meet you," Cara said with a wave, following Skye as she stalked away.

"It's easy for Jerrod," Skye groused, as she pushed the pedal on the golf cart. "My brother makes tons of money and would love for Jerrod to stay home with their baby. He doesn't know what it's like for the rest of us."

Cara wisely kept her mouth shut.

On their way to the trailer, and as they gathered the tools they would need, Skye went over what Cara should keep in a touch-up kit and what they could expect for the rest of the day. Cara typed notes into her phone as Skye outlined what looks they'd be doing for the scene later in the day. She may not have the job for long, but she planned on making the most of the opportunity.

Between the two main scenes being shot, they were dismissed for lunch. Cara accompanied Skye to craft services, joining Jerrod already seated at one of the tables set to the side.

"How long have you been in the business?" Jerrod asked her, plucking a chip from the bag in his hand.

"Not long." Cara hedged, poking at her salad. "This is my first job on a movie."

Jerrod turned raised eyebrows to Skye.

"She's a friend of Wes's."

"Am I supposed to know who that is?"

"Wes Evans. He went to high school in Athens with me and Todd. The cybersecurity guy. You met him." Skye was clearly exasperated by Jerrod's blank look.

"Cyber—oh, you mean Hacker Hunk!"

Cara snorted with laughter. "That's pretty accurate."

Jerrod's dark eyes glinted. "Are you dating him? Please tell me you're dating him. I have so many questions!"

"Not dating, just friends."

"They live together." Skye and Jerrod exchanged a look.

"Interesting." Jerrod drew the word out.

"It's not. I only met him a few weeks ago, I was supposed to live with his friend but—"

"Melody." Skye interrupted Cara, the look she gave Jerrod speaking volumes. They didn't like her.

"Ah." Jerrod's eyes were less friendly when he asked, "You're friends?"

"I only met her a couple of times. I was in a jam, and she needed a roommate."

The other two exchanged a look again.

"Okay, what? What is it about Melody? You guys are starting to make me feel like I've moved in with a demon!"

Jerrod curled his lip. "Not far off."

"She's not that bad," Skye reproved. "She's just… What's the word…"

"Opportunistic? Selfish? Greedy?" Jerrod sneered.

Skye hummed a sound of agreement.

Cara was curious. "In what way?"

Jerrod looked at Skye and when she shrugged, he said. "One example—she was hired for a small role on a production here last year. No experience, but she was hooking up with the director—the very married director. She flaunted it!" He said the last bit to Skye when she made a slashing motion across her neck. "She was always late, never knew her lines, and eventually most of her performance was cut, but…" Jerrod smirked. "She got a lovely vacation to St. Barts out of it and a new line on IMDb. She tried latching on to Brian, but he wasn't interested. Melody is the type that is always on to bigger and better and only has time for you if there is something in it for her."

"She had a tough start, Jerrod," Skye said quietly, sliding her eyes to Cara. "She and Wes both did. It wasn't easy for them in school."

"Hmm, but one owns a cybersecurity firm, and the other is still taking freebies for doing nothing."

Cara was uncomfortable with how the conversation was

going. She didn't know Melody, but she knew how Wes felt about her. This felt disloyal. "I have some phone calls to make. Meet you back at the trailer?" she asked, gathering her trash.

"Don't mind us," Skye said, waving her hand. "I've never liked Melody. Even when we were young, she took advantage of people. The only one who never saw it was Wes."

For Wes's sake, Cara hoped that wasn't true. Wes was smart and sweet—why would he care so much about someone who everyone else thought was awful?

CHAPTER THIRTEEN

Cara spotted Luke stretching at the end of the parking lot and couldn't help smiling. It didn't matter that they were just going for a walk in the woods. Luke, like his twin James, approached everything with a completely unnecessary level of competition. Cara had hoped for a pace that would let them to have a conversation. But, if some good old heart-pumping exercise put Luke in a good mood, then it would only help.

She hadn't anticipated how long her days on set would be. It wasn't unusual for her to work twelve or more hours. Cara wanted to talk to Luke and James about what Declan thought he'd discovered, but she wanted to do it in person—and this was the first day off she'd had since being hired.

Cara didn't begin to understand her brothers' brains or why they seemed to get on each other's nerves so much. But the not talking had to stop. There was no way she was going to allow her brothers to continue to fracture their family.

Luke gave her a friendly wave as she approached, and she noticed a couple of moms with jogging strollers surreptitiously checking out her older brother, who in turn gave them one of his blinding smiles.

"Really? Even the ones with babies?" She punched him in the arm.

"What? I'm just being friendly."

"Uh-huh, I don't think the wink was necessary."

Luke draped one of his giant arms around her shoulders. "Maybe not to you, but the redhead seemed to like it."

Cara glanced back over her shoulder, and sure enough, the woman was now openly trying to catch Luke's eye.

"One of these days your flirting is going to get you in trouble."

Luke shrugged and, using his arm around her shoulders, tugged her toward the trail disappearing into the woods.

"I'm single and being friendly. I can't help it if women like to flirt with me."

"She had a baby." Cara tried to sound exasperated, but it was almost impossible to stay annoyed in the face of Luke's good humor.

"What's your point? Come on. We need to walk a little faster for a warmup."

Cara picked up the pace. "My point is that with a kid that young, she's most likely in a relationship."

"How's that my problem? You're overthinking it. All I did was smile at her. You sound like James."

"Slow down a little!" she said, panting.

"Oh my god! Why are you so short?" But he immediately adjusted his pace to match hers.

Cara decided to let the matter drop. She rarely got to see her brother even though they lived in the same city. She didn't want to waste time arguing about his conquests.

After a minute, Luke broke into a slow jog. Without a word, they loped along for almost a mile. They passed the mile marker sign, and the trail sloped downward toward the river. Within minutes, she could hear the Chattahoochee flowing over the rocks.

Cara was tiring, but she'd rather die than admit defeat to

Luke. She watched the trail carefully, but when she tripped over a root for the second time, Luke tugged her elbow.

"Let's walk."

"Sure, if you need a rest," Cara said, between giant gulping gasps of air.

Luke ignored the jibe. "I'm glad you insisted we get together. It's been a crazy year now that I've gone out on my own."

"Do you have a trial coming up?"

As a defense attorney, her brother was always cagey about who or what he was working on. He didn't deal with the nicest people in the world, and he had told her once that he wanted to keep that part of his life as far away from his family as he could. She understood his need to protect all of them, but sometimes she worried about who was protecting him?

"Always. Fraud case. Nothing particularly complicated."

Cara took advantage of a bench overlooking the river and collapsed onto it, unhooking her water bottle.

She offered it to him, but Luke shook his head. Cara might be a little out of shape from the long hours of work, but Luke looked like he'd barely broken a sweat. *Jerk*.

"I saw Mom the other day." Luke stared thoughtfully out at the green water rushing over the rocks. "She asked about you."

Cara felt a twinge.

"I need to call her. I keep meaning to, but…"

"I get it. She's not mad or anything. You know how Mom is. She loves you, same as us. She worries." He hesitated. "She hasn't been feeling well lately."

Anne had been diagnosed with multiple sclerosis several years ago, but it was only in the last few that the disease had taken over her life, forcing her to retire from the work she loved.

"I'll call her this afternoon. Shooting is supposed to be lighter this week. Maybe I could drive out and see her."

"She'd like that." He took the water bottle from her hand and finished it with a giant gulp.

"Hey!"

Luke grinned again. "Big brother rights." He wiped his mouth with the back of his hand. "So, what's new with you? Loving the movie life? Meet any celebrities?"

"Not yet."

"How's your roommate, the model? Do her model friends come over a lot? Maybe you should invite me over," Luke teased, nudging her with his elbow.

Cara managed a weak smile. She still hadn't told her brothers about her living arrangement.

"What's that smile?"

Cara schooled her face into a more neutral expression. "I talked to Declan last week."

Luke nodded, but his eyes became guarded. "How is he?"

"Focused."

Luke chuckled. "When's he not?"

"You know he's been looking into Dad's death and the will."

"Cara," Luke groaned, rubbing his hands over his face, and then clasped them loosely on top of his head. "I don't want to talk about that. I don't want to fight with Declan, and the last thing I want is for you to get pulled into it. Leave it alone. Dec and I will get our shit sorted out eventually. We just need a good fight and a couple drinks. No need to worry, Car-Bear."

He reached out and ruffled her hair pulling several chunks out of her ponytail.

"Quit it!" She smacked his hand away. "I'm not trying to get between you and Declan. You're both so pigheaded it's not worth the trouble."

Luke grunted.

"I've stayed out of it for the most part. I don't know what I thought immediately after Dad died. Then right after was the tabloid disaster, and I felt..."

Luke shifted uncomfortably on the bench next to her. Her brothers and feelings were like oil and water.

She tried again. "I agree with you and James that Declan is fixated on breaking the will and proving Courtney is to blame. I thought it was his grief... But he said something that made me think."

Luke sighed, his eyes on the river.

"Did you know that Declan takes Mrs. Woodson out to lunch once a month?"

A smile played around the corners of Luke's mouth, lightening his expression a fraction. "Does he really?"

"I think he feels responsible for her."

Luke scowled again. "Of course, he does. Who doesn't Declan think he's responsible for?"

"She told him, that in the weeks before he died, our father refused to eat or drink anything that wasn't brought to him by her."

Luke sat up straighter on the bench, his brows dipping, before he relaxed again. "He wasn't well, Cara. You know that."

"I'm well aware of that, Luke!" she snapped. "I'm the only one who actually went to see him."

Luke's lips thinned and his gray eyes turned flinty. She thought he would snap back, but instead he pulled in a slow breath through his nose and rose to his feet, extending his hand to her.

"I regret that. I do. But you and I don't see the old man the same way. Never have. You're my baby sister, and I love you. I'm not going to fight about this."

"I didn't mean it the way it came out."

"I know." He stretched his arms over his head and took another deep breath, letting it out in a loud exhale. "It's gorgeous out here, but we should start back."

Cara didn't want to fight either, but she needed him to hear what Declan had learned. Taking his elbow, she pulled him to a stop. The resigned expression that stared down at her told her that, even though he thought she and Declan were wrong, he would listen just to humor her.

"Dad might have been paranoid; he might even have had the beginnings of dementia. But what if there is something to it? Declan's gone over the medical records. Dr. Keller did order tests for toxins. They didn't find any, but Declan thinks it might have been something that would only show up in an autopsy."

"How did Dec—never mind, I don't want to know. If they tested for poison and didn't find any, that's proof there wasn't any. Dad was paranoid. It's not unusual for the elderly to become confused."

"Why do you think Courtney had him cremated so fast?"

Luke's expression darkened at the memory, and then he echoed her own thoughts. "Could just be she's a heartless bitch. If that's true, and the will is real—Cara, don't forget there were witnesses to it—that means Dad thought one of us was behind it."

He pulled her into a sudden, fierce hug so that she had to turn her face against his chest to breathe. His breath was uneven, too. No matter how much he wanted to deny it, Luke was just as affected by their father's death as she was.

"David Bloom put on a good show to the world of loving us. But it wasn't real. We were just one more asset he could show the world. If he knew us, he would know none of us would ever hurt him."

"Mrs. Woodson's settlement was changed, too," she insisted.

Luke's eyes looked sightlessly past her shoulder.

"Why would he do that?" Cara asked. "According to Declan, he trusted her most of all because he only wanted her to handle his food."

Luke shook his head. "Unless she's lying. People lie for all kinds of reasons. Mrs. Woodson always adored Declan. Maybe she's telling him what she thinks he wants to hear."

Cara arched an eyebrow, and he chuckled before his brow furrowed again.

"Courtney wasn't the only one who benefitted from the new will. Matt would never have become CEO if Courtney hadn't inherited the shares necessary to push Declan out, and I'm sure she'll be just as generous with Trey," Luke pointed out. "Keep in mind, she didn't have to kill him to get what she wanted. She might have simply poisoned his mind against us and had him rewrite the will in her favor. That's far more plausible than that she's a murderer." He shook his head. "She is significantly younger; she wouldn't have had to wait long."

Cara opened her mouth to object, but Luke held up his hand.

"I can see why what Mrs. Woodson said made you take another look, but it just doesn't make sense. Declan is angry. *So* angry. He can't accept what Dad did. He's destroying himself going down this path. Don't let him take you with him."

They finished the last hundred yards in silence, as Luke walked her to her car.

"I love you," he repeated, pressing a kiss to the top of her head. "And call Mom?"

Cara promised and with a quick squeeze she slid into her seat. Was Luke right? Was Declan projecting his anger at their father onto Courtney?

LATER THAT AFTERNOON, Cara stared at her hands covered in aloe vera as she attempted to answer her phone with her elbow.

"Hey, babes!" She heard Amara's faint voice through the phone. "I have the best news!"

"Hang on. I'm covered in goop!" Cara quickly washed her hands and pushed the button to put her friend on speaker.

"Okay, what's the news?" Cara asked, picking up a jar of honey and pouring it into the bowl with the aloe vera gel.

"I'm coming to Atlanta for a week!"

"When?" Cara was excited about the prospect of seeing her

friend, but there were also nerves. What would Amara make of her new life? She looked down at her pajama shorts and T-shirt that she'd put on after her shower, both now spotted with the concoctions she was working on.

"Next week! There's a birthday party for some business associate of my parents at an art museum, and since they can't be there, I have to put in an appearance for the family. A couple other meetings, but nothing major."

Cara wrinkled her nose. "That doesn't sound fun."

"No, it won't be." Her voice was matter of fact. "Buuut, it means I get to see you and meet the ridiculously hot roommate. How come you never put him on your Insta? You'd get more likes."

"I'm sure my loyal Russian bot friend would like him. It seems to be reaching the limits of its English vocabulary." She laughed. "Every picture, it writes 'so talented' or 'great job.' It's ridiculous."

"How do you know it's a bot? Maybe it's someone who just likes what you do. The pictures you've put up recently from the set are gorge! You should be proud of yourself."

"I am," Cara said, but Amara's comment bothered her. Of course, it was a bot. The responses were too quick, too automatic. The 'like' and comment always appeared within minutes of her posting. No one was sitting around with her account as part of their notifications, unless… Her heart started to race, and she felt lightheaded.

"Hello? Cara?"

Cara licked her lips. "Sorry. What did you say?"

"I asked if you'd banged your roommate yet?"

Cara quickly took her friend off speaker and cast a nervous glance at Wes's shut door. She had met Luke early so that she still had time to play what Wes had begun calling 'kitchen chemist' before it was time for dinner.

"Stop! We're friends. That's all it's ever going to be. Remember? Melody?"

"Pfft. He's just confused. After what you told me those movie people said, I don't think he even knows her."

Cara had started to think the same thing. She didn't ask any more if Melody was returning. It had been six weeks, and Cara loved her new living arrangement.

Except for the rampant sexual frustration.

"I still think you should make a move. Keep it physical. Get it out of your systems. Maybe reenact that dream."

"I never should have told you about that!" Cara hissed.

"Whatever," Amara hummed. "So, there's one little teensy tiny thing I need to tell you." Cara froze, her entire body tensing. "It's not just me that is coming."

All the air in her body left in a whoosh, and her knees felt weak. She didn't want to hear what she knew Amara would say next.

"I didn't know you were still close." Cara's voice was wooden.

"Aw, don't be like that. I don't have a choice. You know how these things are."

Tears pricked at the back of Cara's eyes. They had never been able to prove that it was Erik who sent the nude pictures of her to the tabloids, but everyone in their circle knew it had to be him. He was the only one with a motive. Cara understood the pressure Amara was under from her parents, but the betrayal still stung.

"It's fine." Cara's movements became jerky, and the wooden spoon clattered on the tile floor. "Did you tell him that I live here now?" Her chest rose and fell quickly, and there was a faint buzz in her ears.

"No! Of course not! I haven't even told anyone we're back in touch. Look, my parents are trying to get an exclusive contract with Erik's family's new hotels. It's just business."

Cara lost her grip on the bowl as she moved it from one area of the counter to the other, for no reason other than she needed to do *something*! It thudded loudly on the counter, thankfully staying upright. Cara wiped her damp hands on a dishcloth, vaguely aware of movement at the end of the hall.

"Who else?"

Amara sighed. "It's Erik, Colin, Heather, and Liesel. The usual crowd—I promise I haven't told—"

"It's fine. You guys will love it. Atlanta is a beautiful city, lots to do." Her words sounded strangled. "I'm not sure I'll have a lot of free time. The shooting schedule has been crazy, and it's a lot of long hours."

"Not a chance." Amara's voice was firm. "I know you are upset, but you aren't going to run away and hide again."

"Amara, I can't see them." Her shoulders crept toward her ears.

"Duh, I'm not suggesting that. You and I *are* getting together. I'll call you when I'm done."

Wes appeared beside her, his warm hand on her shoulder, offering his wordless support. She looked up at him. His eyes were concerned behind the lenses of his glasses, but they settled her racing heart.

Everything was fine.

Cara exhaled a long breath.

"I'll see you soon."

CHAPTER FOURTEEN

"Everything okay?" Wes asked when Cara hung up the phone. She reached forward to place it on the kitchen counter but didn't step away from his hand. He should move it, but the warmth of her skin through the thin, cotton shirt seemed to have forged them together. He forced himself to lift it away.

"Everything's fine. Amara's coming to visit."

"The bestie?" he asked in a teasing voice. "That's good, right? She's…"

He stopped. He didn't know anything about Cara's friend other than they went to school together and had some kind of falling out a year ago. Cara had made it clear whatever had happened was a red-light, full-stop, conversation ender whenever he probed.

"Where's she from?" Wes suspected that if Cara weren't so rattled, she wouldn't have answered so quickly. The words fell from her lips automatically.

"South Africa, mostly."

He hadn't expected that. "I thought you lived in Connecticut?"

Cara's eyes flashed up, and he was shocked by the alarm he saw in them. And how protective it made him feel.

"I didn't tell you that."

She was afraid of something. It almost killed him, but Wes took a step backward. Every instinct made him want to wrap his arms around her and tell her that she was safe from whatever it was that scared her.

"You did," he said slowly. "A couple of weeks ago, when it was so cold. You made fun of me for wearing long johns and earmuffs when I went running. You said, 'This isn't cold. You'd never survive a Connecticut winter,' and I said I survived DC…"

The clouds in her eyes lightened, and her cheeks bloomed red. Cara turned away and fidgeted with the bowl.

"I'm sorry," she exhaled. "I've had a rough day."

Wes stared at her back, wishing he could think of something clever to say that would make her smile.

He looked skeptically at the mixture in the bowl.

"Uh, what is that? It's disgusting."

Cara cleared her throat. "It's not disgusting. It's aloe. It's really good for your skin. It's good for eczema, burns, irritations, cuts…" She didn't turn around, but the more she spoke, the more even her voice became.

He wanted to press her on why the phone call had upset her so much. But in the brief time they had lived together, he'd learned the instant he pushed too far she would shut down.

"I get it!" He joked, gratified when the tense lines of her body slowly softened. "You'd think by now I would have learned not to ask."

"Can you open the freezer for me?"

"I don't think you have enough room in there." He watched her dubiously try to fit her concoction into the packed freezer. Wes reached over her shoulder and grabbed the two pints of ice cream from where they blocked the bowl from sliding in.

"Are you planning on eating both of those?" Cara lifted her chin and glanced over her shoulder before he straightened. Her nose brushed his neck and all the blood in Wes's body went south. His breath caught. He needed to step back, but neither of them moved.

Slowly, Cara faced forward and carefully set the bowl down as if it might explode. Wes stepped away, retrieving two spoons from the drawer, while she arranged the freezer so the door would shut.

"I think we should finish these. You know, so they don't go to waste."

"We should have dinner." She eyed the ice cream.

He could tell she was weakening. "We will. Later." Wes didn't wait for her to reply. The skin near her eyes still looked pinched, and her mouth was turned down in the slightest of frowns.

He didn't like it.

Wes settled on the sofa and wiggled one of the spoons in the air at her.

Cara laughed softly. "You are nuts."

Wes pulled up the next episode on their Star Trek list, and Cara took her usual spot, tucking her legs under her. He noticed that when she took the ice cream, she was careful not to brush his fingers.

By unspoken agreement, they let the moment between them pass. It was for the best. Besides, something else was bothering her, and he wanted to know what it was.

Wes waited until the episode was over and Cara set her now-empty ice cream tub on the coffee table. She leaned back into the corner of the sofa, looking exhausted.

"Do you want to talk about it?"

"Talk about what?"

"Whatever it was about the phone call that upset you so much you inhaled a pint of ice cream."

"You made me eat it!"

"Did I though?" He smiled to soften his words. "Something must have bothered you enough that you bent your rules. I've never seen you eat ice cream. Ever."

"That's not true."

"It is one thousand percent true."

Cara pushed to her feet, grabbed the ice cream container, and threw it angrily in the trash, turning to glare at him. Wes's eyebrows met in the middle. "It wasn't a criticism. I'm happy that you arcn't only eating lean protein and vegetables."

Cara crossed her arms across her chest. "I eat other stuff. There's nothing wrong with eating healthy."

"I don't care about the ice cream. I care why you were so upset."

Her expression stayed mulish. "It's none of your business."

Wes reared back. "You're right." He slowly got to his feet, an ache spreading through his chest and huffed an angry laugh. "It's not. I thought we were friends, but when I think about it, I know next to nothing about you."

"That's not true." But she didn't meet his eyes.

"Right," he said with a nod.

She stepped into his path and tilted her chin up.

"I told you about my brothers, our family… how worried I've been. I've never told anyone that. We've been living together, eating together." She waved her hand at the paused image on the television. "What more do you want to know?"

Everything.

The word flashed in his brain.

He folded his arms across his chest, mirroring her. "I want to know why you are unhappy your best friend is coming to visit. And why you looked at me like I had suddenly become a serial killer when I said you were from Connecticut?"

Her entire body appeared to deflate in front of him, and his frustration was replaced with concern. Her face tipped to the floor, and the knot she had tied her hair up in slid to the side, giving her a lopsided appearance when she finally looked back at him.

"Fine." She brushed past him and retook her seat.

A wave of relief washed over him—until he saw the look in her eyes. She looked defeated, and a stab of guilt hit him square in the chest.

"What do you want to know?" she asked when he was seated. She picked at her nails, not looking at him.

"An easy one—where are you from?" He'd meant it to be funny, but her lips twisted.

"Not as easy as you'd think."

"Okay, where did you go to school?"

She let out a resigned sigh. "I didn't go to a real school until I was nine. My mother… traveled a lot for work, so I was homeschooled. Except my mom usually forgot to hire someone, or they quit because they couldn't deal with her moods. Eventually, Siobhan and Anne confronted her about it. They saw I wasn't getting the education I needed and made my dad step in."

Wes's mouth fell open. "Did you go live with your dad?"

Cara chuckled. "My dad loved me, but he wasn't interested in being a full-time parent. My mother knew people who had children around the same age. They sent their children—Amara and Colin—to a boarding school in Switzerland. She decided that was the best place for me." She glanced at him for the first time. "It wasn't bad. In a lot of ways, it was better than being with my mother. I spent most school holidays at Siobhan's or Anne's, and like I told you before, I was with my dad for the summer. Amara and I roomed together almost the whole time. We're more like sisters than friends."

A spasm crossed her face. "Or at least that's how we used to be."

"What changed?"

She leveled a flat stare at him.

Right. Red light.

"Why did you have a rough day?" He tried again.

Her brow wrinkled. "What do you mean?"

"Earlier, you said you had a rough day? Was it just the phone call? I thought you were meeting your brother."

The corners of her mouth turned down. "I want him to call Declan to talk about something, but he's refusing to. I'm sick of them being so stubborn; it's stupid!"

"Why aren't they talking?"

Cara's face shuttered, and Wes didn't think she would answer. She looked down at her hands in her lap. "Do you remember when I said things changed when my dad died?" He nodded. "That wasn't strictly true. Everything changed when my dad got married."

"I thought you said he was a 'confirmed bachelor'?"

"You remember that?" Her eyebrows lifted in surprise, her eyes on his.

"Of course." Wes held her gaze.

Cara exhaled a sad breath. "He was. Then he met Courtney. At first, it was the same as it had always been when he had a girl-friend. I don't want you to get the wrong idea about him. He was kind and generous, and he was always upfront with the women in his life about how he lived. I actually thought from things he had said that he was close to ending things with Courtney, but then suddenly he announced they were getting married. We were shocked, but my dad refused to discuss it. Declan was furious—he never liked Courtney, and it only got worse when Dad gave her oldest son, Matt, a job in the company. That company was Dec's life, and Matt was in no way qualified. I think Luke and James were more hurt than angry. There was already tension between them and our father, but this was the final straw. After that, they were done with him. Their mom Anne married someone else eventually, but she always loved our dad. I think the twins were upset for *her*."

Cara was quiet for a minute. "It did hurt if I'm honest with myself. My mom never had a real relationship with him, but it was kind of like why was Courtney worth marrying if our mothers weren't? I'm never getting married. It doesn't mean anything. It's just a status thing."

"What?" Wes was stunned. "Of course, marriage means something! It's a promise that you will always be there for each other. Someone to lean on when you need them!" He took a breath trying to slow his pulse.

It didn't matter to him that Cara didn't believe in marriage, he told himself. What she does with her life is her business. Wes's heart pounded painfully in his chest.

Cara lifted one shoulder. "I've seen a lot of relationships, my dad, my mom, my friends' parents. Romantic love that lasts a lifetime isn't real. It's just lust mixed with familiarity. My dad understood that. He enjoyed his relationships, and when they weren't fun anymore, both parties moved on." Her lips firmed. "Look at what happened when he finally got married. My mother's been married six times, and I just got the invitation for her seventh! Each time she insists that 'this is the one' and 'I've never been so in love.' She believes it. I'm not saying I don't believe in love. Of course, I do. I just don't believe love lasts."

"Maybe you've just never been in love?" Wes had to stop grinding his teeth to answer.

"Maybe." Her violet eyes held his. "Is that enough of a deep dive into my life for today? I want to heat up dinner and then go to bed."

Wes was too caught up in his thoughts to reply. For the first time since they met, they ate their meal in silence.

CHAPTER FIFTEEN

THE PASTE GLOOPED OFF THE WOODEN SPOON INTO THE BOWL. Cara gave the concoction one more stir before peering at the mixture and making a note in her binder on the counter. She wanted to make this unexpected day off count! Just before dawn she'd gotten a text.

> SKYE: LIA HAS THE FLU. PRODUCTION IS SHUT
> DOWN FOR THE DAY.

Cara felt bad for Lia, but she was thrilled to have the day off in the house by herself. For once, Wes was actually out of the house, meeting clients with his partners, Jin and Nina. Cara planned on taking full advantage.

Cara carried the bowl and spoon to where she had spread a towel over the sofa. She pressed the button on the remote with only the tiniest twinge of guilt. It's not like Wes hadn't seen them all before, she reasoned.

She pushed a terry cloth headband back over her forehead to protect her hair and used the wooden spoon to scoop a large amount of the homemade mask into her hands, before smearing it liberally over her face. Wiping her hands on the towel, she set the timer on her phone and leaned back ready to see what wisdom Captain Picard would dole out today.

The mask had just begun to sting, indicating the enzymes were working, when she heard Wes's key in the door. Cara grimaced. She didn't need a mirror to know how absurd she looked.

It doesn't matter. He's just my roommate.

Looking gross and foolish in front of your hot roommate was totally acceptable.

Wes set his computer bag on their kitchen counter and circled around the furniture to gape at her. "What the hell is all over your face?"

Cara's tongue snuck out to catch a piece of pineapple that had migrated to the corner of her mouth, not missing how Wes's eyes followed the action.

"Honey, oatmeal, and pineapple mask."

"Are you watching without me?" he accused, when she pushed pause.

"Please, you could probably recite all the lines." Her words caused more of the mask to slide onto her mouth. Her tongue flicked out again to catch it.

"Should you be eating that?" His voice was slightly breathless, and Cara made a point of taking another taste.

"It's perfectly safe. Not to mention, a little tasty."

Wes squinted, bending close to her face, his clean scent reaching through the citrus. He gingerly reached out a finger, stopping just before it touched her cheek. Her stomach swooped. What was wrong with her? *This is not a sexy moment!*

"What's that yellow stuff?"

Cara batted his finger away. "I told you. It's pineapple."

"And why did you make a fruit snack on your face?"

"Because it's good for my skin. I'm trying out a new ratio." She tilted her head pretending to inspect his skin. "Wouldn't hurt you to try it. It would take care of those dry spots where you use that terrible shaving gel."

Wes rubbed a hand over his jaw. "I don't have dry spots."

Cara arched a brow. "If you say so. You know, just because you like to hibernate like a computer bear, only taking breaks to run—in the sun without sunscreen." She gave an exaggerated shudder. "Doesn't mean your skin isn't taking a beating. You won't always be this attractive. Particularly when you're covered in brown spots and wrinkles."

"But you think I'm attractive now?"

His eyes suddenly dipped to her breasts, his pupils flaring. Expecting to be alone, Cara hadn't bothered with a bra, and by the flush on Wes's face, he'd noticed. Cara felt the energy pulse between them and was grateful the thick mixture hid the heat she felt rising on her cheeks.

"Don't get too excited," she managed to say. "I'm in the beauty business. I can objectively recognize symmetrical features and appreciate how yours are put together."

"How they are put together?" he echoed, lips twitching, but his eyes came up to meet hers.

Cara knew he was laughing at her, but it didn't bother her. He knew he was handsome, and they'd both know she was lying if she denied it.

"They are put together nicely, but..." She pursed her lips pretending to concentrate. "If you don't start taking care of those problem spots. There, and there." Cara waved her hand at Wes's smooth skin.

She grinned when he tentatively touched where she had pointed.

"I don't have problem spots!"

Cara reached for the spoon.

"What are you doing?"

"Nothing." She widened her eyes innocently.

Wes leaned back. "Don't even... Oh my god!" He exclaimed as

the cold mixture hit his cheek. His nose wrinkled. "I can't believe you just did that."

Cara grinned. "Don't pout. Let me practice."

Wes grimaced. "Do I have to wear one of those?" He gestured at the terry cloth headband.

Cara screwed her mouth to the side and nodded with mock seriousness. "I think it's best."

Wes's eyes were full of laughter when they met hers. "I can't believe…"

Cara bounded up and raced to her room for supplies. Before Wes knew what was happening, she had him seated on a towel, a pink headband pushing his hair back.

The phone's alarm went off. "Don't move," she commanded, before racing away again. She quickly rinsed off her mask, worried Wes would leave before she came back. She eyed her bra lying on the bed.

She should put it on.

No reason for temptation.

She kept walking.

Cara was still blotting her face with a washcloth, when she saw he hadn't moved. A happy warmth spread through her.

She sat on the coffee table between his knees and dipped her fingers into the bowl. Technically, Cara should use a brush, but she wasn't going to give up the chance to touch him.

"This won't hurt a bit," she said solemnly, as she leaned forward. His eyes fell to her chest again, and Cara's pulse beat frantically through her veins. Desire, hot and fierce, flowed through her.

Wes shifted his seat a little. "You've got… there's a little…" He cleared his throat and gestured at her chest. "Something."

Cara looked down and saw that she had gotten some of the mask on the loose neck of her tank top. A flush spread its way down her chest. She wasn't the only one breathing a little harder.

With her clean hand, Cara wiped at the mask mixture that

had landed on her top. "Occupational hazard," she murmured, her nipples tightening at his strained expression.

This is a bad idea. I need to stop.

What had begun as a silly game was now escalating to dangerous levels.

We're roommates. Friends. Buddies.

She repeated the mantra to herself even as she smoothed her fingers over his face, smearing the mixture. She made quick work of covering his forehead, but her fingers slowed as they traced his cheekbones and then trailed lower to his jaw.

His pulse was visible at the base of his throat, and she knew that he was just as affected as she was. It fluttered against her fingertips as she stroked a thin layer over it. Heat pooled low in her belly, and her own heart threatened to burst from her chest. Cara squeezed her thighs together as the sensations grew stronger.

He was so close. She could smell the spearmint of his breath and see the light gold band around his irises. His pupils darkened, and she couldn't look away.

Cara's breath hitched and her gaze fell to his mouth. Slowly she dragged her thumb against his lower lip, fascinated by the movement. Wes was so still she thought he might be holding his breath. Her gaze fell to his lap, his arousal clearly evident.

Slowly she leaned back, breaking the connection. She was flushed, feverish, every nerve ending on fire.

Too far. She'd gone too far.

"I—I got some on your…" She held up her thumb to show a tiny fleck of pineapple. "It's not good for your lips."

Cara rose under the guise of putting the mask away, but in reality, they both needed the distance. She turned her back and tried to get her body under control again. She washed her hands for too long under the cool water of the faucet, but it did little to help.

She felt like she was on fire.

"Is it supposed to sting like this?"

Cara closed her eyes and braced her hands against the counter. He sounded normal, whereas basic lust still throbbed in her veins.

"Um, yeah. It's the enzyme in the pineapple."

"What's that do?"

She appreciated his attempt to inject a sense of normalcy. One of them had to be the adult, and it clearly wasn't going to be her sex-starved self. They lived together. If they gave in to their attraction, it would ruin everything. Cara knew she was developing feelings for him, but Wes would end up resenting her… She wasn't the one he wanted.

Cara rinsed the bowl and the other utensils, consciously relaxing the muscles in her body and focusing on her breath until it was slow and even.

"It eats your dead skin cells." When she turned back around, her smile was easy again. Nothing like dead skin cells to kill the mood.

"Uh. Ow." His face contorted in discomfort.

"It's not that bad. If it's stinging, it's working. On a scale of one to ten, what would you say?"

"Like a nine?"

Cara grabbed a dishcloth and put it under the faucet. "That's not good. You might be having a reaction. Let me get it off."

"I'm just kidding. It's maybe a two." He grinned at her, bits of the mask dropping into his lap.

"You are the worst," she said throwing the cloth at him, but there was no anger behind the words. "You have about ten more minutes if you can bear it."

The doorbell rang, startling them both.

"Are you expecting someone?" she asked with a frown.

Wes shook his head and bolted for the bedroom. Cara almost fell over when the door opened, revealing her brother taking up most of the doorway.

"Luke?"

"Surprise!" He looked over her head into the house. "You mentioned you weren't working today, and I had a meeting with a client nearby, so I thought I'd stop in and see where you live. Since you've never invited me before," he added archly.

For good reason she thought. She never told her family that she was living with Wes. Not that they *should* object. She was a grown woman after all, but... She knew her brothers, and they were frequently unreasonable. Sometimes being the little sister sucked.

"Cara?" His brows came down in a frown when she put her hands wide to block the doorway. "Move."

She sighed, stepping back. Maybe Wes would stay in his room. Luke paced into the single common room glancing at the kitchen, his expression lightening.

"It's cute. Where's your room?"

Cara pointed to her doorway, but Luke's attention was caught by the frozen image of the television. "I didn't know you liked Star Trek."

"You've seen it?"

Luke looked at her like she was insane. "Of course! Everyone has seen it."

"That's what I said." Wes's deep voice sounded behind them, and Luke's head swiveled from her to Wes and back again before a slick smile appeared. Cara groaned inwardly. She recognized his cross-examination face.

He stepped forward extending his hand to Wes. "I'm Luke, Cara's brother."

"Wes Evans. Cara's told me a lot about you."

"Really?" Luke dramatically lifted his eyebrows. "She hasn't mentioned you—at all."

"He's Melody's friend," Cara blurted out. "He's staying here while he house hunts."

"And where's Melody?" Luke looked pointedly around the room. "I was looking forward to meeting her."

"She's out," Cara said, sending a silent message to Wes. "Did you want to see my room?"

Luke looked back suspiciously at Wes, but Cara grabbed his hand and towed him to her bedroom. The room was small, and the tour consisted of Luke standing in the doorway and looking around. Thankfully, when they were done, Wes had disappeared back into his bedroom, the door closed.

Luke stared at the door for a moment but didn't make any further comment. Cara exhaled. "Don't you think you should invite me to dinner?"

Luke grimaced. "Sorry, Car-Bear, I have an event tonight. I just wanted to check in on you." He jerked a thumb at the door. "What do you know about him."

"Wes?" She kept her tone breezy. "He's really nice."

"What does he do? Where does he work?"

"Luke," Cara groused.

"Should I ask him?" He took a step in the direction of the kitchen, and Cara caught his arm.

"He owns a cybersecurity company. He's harmless. Honestly, just a nice guy. He's interested in Melody."

She didn't think her brother would appreciate the fact that, just before he arrived, she had been thinking about getting Wes naked and enacting some of the fantasies she'd been indulging in lately.

Luke pulled her into a hug and kissed the top of her head. "Don't be mad, Car-Bear. I'm allowed to worry."

Cara hugged him back. "I know and I'm being careful. Promise."

She waved until he was out of sight, wondering how long it would be before she got phone calls from Declan and James. However, if it got the three of them talking again, it wouldn't be all bad.

CHAPTER SIXTEEN

FUCK!

Wes gripped his hair and stared blankly at his reflection in the mirror over Melody's dresser. Thank God, Cara had the sense to pull back because he had been seconds away from giving in to the impulse to yank her into his lap and test whether or not her lips tasted as good as he'd imagined—pineapple masks and all. He groaned.

The second she'd stopped, he had instantly missed her featherlight touch on his face. His brain automatically wanting to know how it would feel on the rest of his body.

He exhaled hard.

It was just physical attraction. A beautiful woman in close proximity. The fact that his body responded was just nature, he assured himself. There wasn't a man on the planet that wouldn't have reacted to Cara in that top, without….

He paced across the tiny room.

If it had been one sided, it wouldn't have been so bad, but he'd seen the flush on her skin and the matching arousal in her eyes. It had taken all of his self-control not to palm her full breasts as they hovered at his eye level. His body hardened at the memory. Wes balled his fists, banishing the image.

He couldn't mess around with his roommate.

Even if he *weren't* planning a future with Melody—which of course he was—he cared too much about Cara to risk their friendship.

He had never made friends easily, but when he was with her, he could be himself without worrying what she thought of him. She was sweet and funny....

Wes caught himself smiling in the mirror and froze.

He shook his head at the reflection. "No!"

He had a plan and needed to stick to it. He'd only known Cara for a short time. He'd known Melody forever. And, if his heart whispered that he'd never felt this way about Melody, he chose to ignore it. Cara said herself she didn't believe in a love that lasted. That was all he had ever wanted in life. A love to build a family on.

The family he'd always wanted.

He needed to put some distance between them, physical and mental. In the house where her different concoctions scented the rooms, he couldn't think clearly. All it did was remind him of her warm skin.

Argh!

Wes picked up the phone and texted Jin, inviting him for an early dinner. And so what if he peeked out his bedroom door like a coward to see if Cara was still in the main room. Phone in hand, he called out to Cara that he was meeting a friend for dinner and escaped through the front door.

They were spending too much time together.

That's all it was, he told himself, as he backed out of the driveway.

CHAPTER SEVENTEEN

Even with the barn doors open at the end of the sound
stage, Cara could feel sweat dripping down her back. She rolled
her shoulders forward a bit and flapped the top of her long-
sleeved shirt. It had been chilly when she left home that morning,
but she was quickly learning that March in Atlanta was a little
bipolar. Enclosed in the soundstage with all the lights, the
temperature had climbed quickly.

"There's no avoiding it," Skye said, casting her a sidelong look.
"It's inevitable. We all have gross sweat marks by the end of a
long shoot. Boob sweat is just another one. Just wait until your
first summer."

"Easy for you to say. You probably aren't even wearing a bra!"
Cara squinted suspiciously at her friend dressed in overalls and a
white tank top. "You aren't, are you?"

Skye shimmied her shoulders. "Having small tits has its
advantages. It's all about the layers."

Before Cara could think of a good comeback, radios crackled
around them, and then Brian's voice could be heard. "We are
code green, folks."

Skye sighed.

"What's a code green?"

"It means Brian has invited some investor or potential buyer to come play movie star for a day in the hope they will bail him out."

"Okaaay." Cara waited, but no further explanation seemed to be coming. In fact, with how irritated Skye looked, Cara was almost afraid to ask.

"Do we need to do anything or just carry on?" Cara looked around the set, noticing that her coworkers all wore sour expressions.

"If they come on to our set, try to look busy and stay out of their way." Her mouth flattened into a thin line. "The last two he brought through were tech bros, and all they cared about was finding out who had the best blow and if casting couches were still a thing."

Cara stared at Skye trying to decide if she was being serious. From the irritated energy radiating off her, Cara suspected she was.

"Great."

The shoot continued, and by the time the clapper board went down the final time, Cara was more than ready to go home. Possibly attracted by the warm lights, a long, black rat snake had found its way onto the set, and while Cara totally sympathized with the actors who jumped on set pieces to get away from it, it caused a major delay. First, the snake had to be caught, then there was a spirited debate as to whether or not it should be killed.

After one of the supporting actors sobbed that she was a member of PETA and wailed about them even considering killing an innocent animal, the director ordered it relocated. Cara suspected however, by the look on the face of the unlucky grip chosen to transport the snake in a trash bag, the director had told him to kill it.

The histrionics had required the props and furniture to be reset, and several members of the cast needed their hair and makeup fixed.

Cara was dirty, and sweaty, but also somehow inexplicably cold. She was helping Skye pack up their bags in preparation to take them back to the trailer when Skye's eyes narrowed.

"Do you know him?"

"Who?" Cara straightened abruptly from her bent over position, and her stomach fell to her feet.

Shit!

Declan's words about Courtney shopping for a job for her son, Trey, rang in her ears. *Why here?*

"Are you okay? You're as white as a sheet!" Skye put her hand on Cara's arm.

"Just stood up too quick," Cara mumbled, her eyes still fixed on where her stepbrother—was he even technically still a stepbrother?—had come to a dead stop, blocking the people behind him. Trey's behavior quickly drew the notice of his mother and brother, Matt.

Matt's eyes went wide when he spotted her and then laughed, pointing in her direction. Trey stood uncomfortably next to his mother and shuffled his feet.

For a split second, she thought Courtney would pretend she didn't know Cara. She saw the hesitation on Courtney's face, but their reaction to Cara had been noticed by others nearby. Everyone looked back and forth between them, muttering behind hands.

Cara brushed the loosened hairs from her braid out of her face. There was no avoiding it. She could only hope that Courtney was in a good mood. With one last regretful scan of her dirty, disheveled clothes, Cara pasted a smile on her face and answered Skye's question.

"It's my stepmother and her sons."

Skye's eyes were saucers.

With an elegance that belied the monster beneath Courtney's beautifully put together façade, the woman approached Cara and Skye with an exaggerated, sympathetic moue.

"Oh, darling! What's happened to you!" Courtney cried out, pitching her voice so that even those on the far side of the set could hear.

"Damn!" Skye muttered.

Cara noticed Jerrod and a few others angle closer to better hear whatever drama was about to go down. It was abundantly clear that Brian's guests were not happy to see the makeup assistant.

"I'm not sure what you mean, Courtney." Cara kept her tone saccharine sweet, inclining her head to Trey when he and Matt stopped just behind their mother.

Matt was an ass, but Trey looked like he was embarrassed by the whole thing. He sent her a sympathetic smile and then resumed his study of the floor. He knew, as well as Cara, that Courtney wouldn't let the opportunity to embarrass her husband's daughter slip by. The only question was how vicious would she be?

Courtney glanced around in disbelief. "Do you…" She waved her hand limply at the set. "Work here?" Her voice dropped to a horrified whisper.

Skye took a few steps back. Cara didn't really blame her. If Courtney ended up being the new owner of the studio, then it was in Skye's best interest to distance herself from Cara. It hurt even if she recognized that the woman didn't owe her any loyalty. They were new friends, and this was Skye's career.

Anger bubbled inside her. Cara loved this job and was starting to make real friends. Courtney had already taken so much from her and her family. There was no way Cara was going to let her waltz in and take this away, too! At least not without fighting back.

"I do. I love it!" Cara knew she had put a little too much enthusiasm in her tone when Matt smirked, and Trey risked a glance.

"That's…" Courtney's eyes drifted insultingly down Cara's body, "different." Her lip curled and her nose scrunched. "So, you're… an actor?"

It was obvious that Cara wasn't.

"I work in hair and makeup."

"Hmmm." Courtney pressed her red lips together. "I'd heard you ran away to Georgia, but I didn't realize you blew through your inheritance so fast."

Courtney made a tsking sound, and Cara stiffened feeling the curious looks of her coworkers fall on her.

And there it was.

She hadn't hidden the fact she grew up with money and had a trust fund tucked away, but she hadn't volunteered it either. For the first time in her life, she wasn't being judged by her last name, but by who she was and how hard she worked. She loved it.

Cara bit the inside of her cheek to keep herself silent. Defending herself would only play into Courtney's game, and who knew what other bombs she would reveal. Cara couldn't take that risk.

She met Courtney's smug expression with a neutral smile. Courtney's smirk slipped, and she took a breath prepared to let loose a verbal barrage.

"If you need money, we could always find you something more—" Matt visibly flinched under Courtney's fiery glare.

Courtney reassumed the pitying look and shifted her Balenciaga bag higher up her arm.

Cara narrowed her eyes. *Is that mine?*

It wasn't a particularly special bag, but it had been one of the things she still kept at her father's house—her belongings that Courtney claimed she couldn't find. After the reading of the will, she had barred the Bloom siblings from the property. Courtney followed Cara's gaze and moved her other hand protectively over the bag. Then realizing how she had given herself away, she dropped her hand to her side.

Hot pressure built behind Cara's eyes. She was *not* going to cry over a handbag! Cara sniffed as tears clogged her throat. In her periphery, she saw matching expressions of fascinated horror on Jerrod's and Skye's faces.

"Matt wants to play producer, so Mom's going to buy him a studio," Trey burst out, buying her a moment away from everyone's intense scrutiny. Had Trey done that to help her? "I'm going to work in postproduction on the graphics."

Cara vaguely remembered Trey had studied graphic arts in college. Frankly, he lived so completely in Matt's shadow, sometimes Cara forgot he was there. Why was he risking his brother's ire by speaking to her?

Matt's face flushed dull red, and he took a step toward his brother as some of the crew tittered quietly. White-faced, Courtney stepped between her sons and placed a hand on Trey's face, her painted nails stark against his pale cheeks. Identical, pale blue eyes looked down into his mother's face. With her next breath, Courtney's anger dissolved, and she patted Trey's cheek fondly.

Veins bulged in Matt's neck, the red in his face rapidly becoming a deep purple, and Cara had the stray thought that he might actually stroke out in front of them. Trey had always been the baby. But even Cara was surprised by Courtney's preferential treatment.

"Shh, darling. You both will have the company."

"I thought Bloom Communications was the company you gave Matt?"

The words were out before Cara realized it, but she didn't regret it. Rage rolled through her, obliterating all previous plans to be the bigger person and get through this encounter. "That was the big move, right?" She cocked her head, her voice dripping with sarcasm. "To install Matt with his vast business experience as CEO? That's why you pushed my brother out of our father's company? Because Matt was going to play businessman."

Did you kill my father for it?

Skye's hand came up too late to hold in her burble of laughter.

Courtney's eyes narrowed to slits. "You spoiled little—"

"Oh great! You found the set." Brian practically jogged through the barn door to where they stood.

His radio crackled, and Brian twisted the knob to silence it. He turned a pained expression to Courtney while Cara scanned the people still watching the tableau play out. Someone must have radioed Brian that there was a problem with his potential buyers.

"So, did you see everything you were hoping for? Any questions?" Brian tried to slip an arm around Courtney's waist to steer her away. "Let's go back to my office and I can show you—"

Courtney planted her feet and swiveled back to face Cara. "No need for that."

"But—"

The smile she gave Brian didn't reach her eyes.

"Send the paperwork to our lawyers. I can't *wait* to buy your little business." Her eyes gleamed when they met Cara's. "It's going to be life changing."

Cara's chest constricted. That was it then. She'd be fired; her shoulders slumped.

Confusion warred with relief on Brian's face. Relief won.

"Fantastic! This calls for a celebration. I have champagne in my office!"

Without another word, Courtney allowed Brian to escort her away, Trey slouching along behind them. Cara was rooted in place. Her limbs felt heavy, and her throat ached.

A gentle touch on her shoulder brought back the realization that she had an audience.

"You all good?" Skye's eyes were full of concern.

"Yeah, I'll be fine." Cara took a deep breath through her nose. "I just need to have a word with my *brother*."

Matt still stood nearby, staring at her angrily. It was clear he had more to say, and she would rather not have everyone hear it. Skye gave her a meaningful look.

"Let's meet for drinks, and you can give me all the details."

"Sure," Cara lied.

"My, my, my! How the princess has fallen." Matt sneered then chuckled. "It's like you're the anti-Cinderella. You're supposed to end up as the princess, not the maid."

Here we go, Cara thought. If Matt thought he could hurt her with his pathetic insults, he would need to think again. After everything she'd been through, his words couldn't hurt her.

"A movie studio, huh? I guess if you get tired of playing movies, you can just tell Mommy, and she'll let you go back to pretending to be Declan." Cara pushed her bottom lip out making an exaggerated pout. "Was pretending to be the CEO of a global media empire too difficult? Needed something with training wheels?"

Matt slowly clapped his hands. "I'm glad to see that your natural bitchiness survived the sudden descent into poverty. Or do you think it made you bitchier? I can't tell." He shook his head in disgust. "You are filthy!"

"It's called actually working for a living, Matt. Not just playing a role that Mommy picked out for you."

Matt's eyes narrowed, and then as if a switch flipped, all traces of the hatred that had been written so clearly across his face, disappeared. Instead, he frowned and shook his head in fake sorrow.

"Your father was always so proud of you. Always telling my mother how beautiful you looked, how poised, how classy... He liked women who looked, dressed and..." he paused with a slight sniff, his face wrinkling, "smelled like a woman. I can't imagine how humiliated, how *disappointed* he would be—his only daughter out in public like this. Ruining his reputation by looking like the trash you always were."

It felt like something had sucked all the oxygen out of her body.

She'd been wrong.

Words could still hurt her.

CHAPTER EIGHTEEN

Wes raised his arms high above his head and angled his head from side to side stretching his neck. He'd been working on security protocols all afternoon. It wasn't his favorite thing, but it was the engine behind their business. He preferred coding, but Nina had caught the flu going around. He had to pick up her most urgent client deadlines.

Lately, they had several businesses add e-commerce, and they were *all* asking about leaks. Everyone wanted a shopping app on their webpage but worried about their customers blaming them in the event of a data breach. No one wanted their brand attached to a hack.

Checking the time on his screen, Wes logged it on the digital time sheet Nina insisted they use. She wanted him to log every hour and code it to the correct project. Wes might complain, but the business would have crumbled without Nina and Jin's business acumen.

Pushing back his chair, Wes wandered into the kitchen and grabbed a beer, collapsing on the couch in front of the TV.

Did Cara have a late shoot tonight?

Wes checked his phone, but there were no missed messages or

texts from her. He didn't remember her mentioning it either, he mused. He sent her a quick text and when she didn't respond, he called her. Straight to voicemail. Wes frowned. She's probably just busy, he told himself.

He scrolled through several shows feeling increasingly restless. Wes checked the call sheet Cara had hung on the refrigerator.

She should have been done by now. It's always possible they ran long, he told himself. There was no reason to worry.

Wes turned on a basketball game but couldn't concentrate. He couldn't shake his unease.

There were plenty of reasons why Cara might not text him back. They might still be shooting, or she went out with Skye after work—or she'd been in a car accident.

He took several long, deep breaths but couldn't completely shed his tension.

As the evening wore on, his eyes rose to the dark front windows each time a set of headlights approached. But none turned into their driveway.

Where the hell is she?

When his phone rang, Wes snatched it from the table, but instead of Cara's smiling contact pic, it was Jin's avatar displayed across the illuminated screen, and his heart sank.

"What's up?"

"Sorry, did I wake you up?" Jin asked.

"It's only eleven," Wes said, mostly to reassure himself.

"Normal adults are asleep at this hour. *You're* usually asleep now," Jin pointed out.

"If it's so late, why are you calling?"

"Okay, cranky," he drawled. "I didn't know if Cara mentioned it, or if she even knew we had an appointment at the studio tomorrow, but they've cancelled it. Apparently, Brian sold the company today." He snorted. "He said he'd give our information to the new owners, but that they've shut down production for a few days."

Wes frowned. "Are they going to finish the movie? It's so close to being done."

"No idea, but if I had to guess, I'd say yes. Why buy a movie studio and then scrap an almost finished movie?"

"I'm sure Cara will appreciate the days off." Wes said. "They've been working a lot of long days trying to make up the schedule from when Lia was out."

That was one bright spot, he thought. Lately, Wes had noticed the dark circles under Cara's eyes were more prominent than usual against her pale skin. She always looked worn out when she got home from the late shoots. Wes frowned as he registered what Jin said. "She's still not home."

There was a pause. "They wrapped a couple hours ago."

"How do you know that?"

"Because I talked to Brian—that's how I knew he had sold the studio."

"Then why isn't she here?"

"She probably went out with friends after work to celebrate the unexpected days off. Why do you care?"

"Well, she could have at least let me know."

There was another long pause from Jin's side before he quietly laughed. "You want your roommate to let you know when she's going to be late?"

Wes scowled. "It's just manners. Keep the people you live with informed."

"I don't remember you ever worrying about where I was when we were roommates."

"She's a girl."

Jin snorted with laughter. "I wouldn't say that to her if you want to live."

"Good point." But Wes wasn't ready to let it go. It suddenly became imperative that his best friend agree with him. Agree that he had the right to worry, that it was totally normal and not because he had anything other than totally boring, platonic feelings for his roommate.

"But it's rude, right? She normally texts when she's going to be late from work. She even sticks up her call sheet so I can put whatever weird, new healthy dish she has for us in the oven. What if I'd put her food in the oven already? Her dinner would be ruined!"

"Her dinner would be ruined? Can you repeat that?"

The words had an odd echoey sound. "Did you just put me on speaker?"

"So, to be clear, you're upset because it's late and Cara didn't tell you she'd be late today, and you don't know where she is or when she will be home, and that's a problem because dinner was ruined?"

Wes ground his teeth when Nina's laughter rang out.

"But you're not into her. Got it." Nina howled. "Thank you so much for this. I've felt crummy all day, and this is the funniest—"

"Never mind." He cut her off. "You're both idiots, high on cold medicine."

They were still cackling when he ended the call.

They were wrong. It was an absolutely ordinary and common thing for him to want to know where Cara was, he thought.

But Nina's words had sent his brain into a tailspin. He didn't have feelings for Cara.

Okay, he was attracted to her—very attracted—but he couldn't help his body's physical reaction. It's a physiological response.

That's not the same as *feelings*. Well of course I have feelings, he thought pacing the room. We're friends. I have friend feelings.

Friends worry about each other.

Everything was totally fine.

Wes pushed his glasses up onto his forehead and pressed the

heel of his palms into his eyes. He was exhausted. He should go to bed. There was another project due to a client tomorrow.

He stopped in the middle of the room, staring at Cara's dark doorway. Jin was right. Cara was an adult, and she could take care of herself. Besides, most likely she went out with Jerrod and Skye. The three had become friends.

He lay back on the sofa, staring blankly at the television. He could text Skye something like, "Hope you're out having a good time since you got a surprise day off."

Most likely she'd text back what they were doing, and then he'd know—or he could check Instagram. Cara didn't use it for personal things, but Skye did, and she always posted where she was.

Wes was reaching for his phone when it hit him.

What am I doing? This is crazy. It's not like she's my girlfriend!

He was only having these weird reactions because Melody had been gone for so much longer than she'd originally thought. He ignored the voice in his head that said, "You haven't seen Melody for much longer periods. It had never made him feel like this about someone before."

No! Melody was his future. That was the plan.

Picking up his phone again, his thumb tapped rapidly across the keyboard, and before second guessing himself, he hit send.

> WES: WHERE ARE YOU THIS WEEK? I THOUGHT I'D
> FLY OVER FOR A COUPLE DAYS. VACATION
> DESPERATELY NEEDED.

He instantly felt better. There, course correction. He would go to Melody if she weren't ready to come back. And when he got back, everything would be normal with Cara again.

Wes was just shutting his bedroom door when he heard the front door softly closing. His door ajar, he watched as she tiptoed in, and annoyed as he'd been, he couldn't help smiling at her elaborate efforts not to wake him.

She was home. She was safe.

His hand was on the door to push it all the way closed when he saw her swipe at her cheeks and let out a little sniff.

Was she... *crying?*

Fury filled Wes's body as he swung the door open. He reached her side in three long steps, causing her to yelp in surprise.

"Wes? What the—?"

Wes gripped her chin with his forefinger and thumb and turned her head to each side as his eyes feverishly checked her face. He didn't see any bruises, only the plain evidence that she'd been crying.

Cara twisted her head away, and he instantly dropped his hand.

"Are you okay—"

"Wes, what's—"

They spoke simultaneously.

"Why are you crying? Did someone hurt you? Who was it? I'll..."

CHAPTER NINETEEN

Wes's chest heaved as if he struggled to draw a full breath. Cara gaped back at him in silence. His eyes scanned down her body but not with heat as they had in the past. His pupils were wide, and his lips trembled a little.

Whatever he saw—or didn't see—seemed to calm him, and his shoulders slumped. Then just as suddenly, the skin across his cheekbones tightened, and the lines by his eyes twitched as he tried to smile. His voice was gentle when he asked, "Is it something I can't see? You can tell me."

Cara's entire face scrunched in confusion. What was he talking about? What did he think—terrible understanding hit her.

"I'm okay. Why would you think—"

Wes took her hands brushing his thumb across the tops of her knuckles. His gaze was slightly unfocused, and she wasn't sure that she was the woman he was seeing in front of him.

"It's nothing to be ashamed of. Do you know who it was?" His face darkened again, and Cara met his eyes. The pain she saw there caused her heart to squeeze painfully in her chest.

"I promise nothing happened," she said carefully. "Promise," she repeated when his eyes were still uncertain. She squeezed his hands before letting go. "But I love you for caring." The words had slipped out and she was immediately embarrassed.

However, her comment seemed to release something in Wes, and his mood morphed from concern to anger.

"Where the hell have you been?"

"Excuse me?"

"It's..." He raised his elbow and made a show of looking at his watch. "Almost midnight!"

Cara narrowed her eyes, but he missed the warning.

"Were you out with Skye?"

"No."

Wes frowned, and she glared back. Anger was better than the miserable rabbit hole she'd sent herself down for the last several hours. If he wanted a fight, she was more than happy to give him one.

"Jin said you weren't at work..."

"Are you spying on me?

"No, Jin happened to mention it." He planted his hands on his hips.

"Why are you even still up?"

An expression crossed his face that she would think about later.

"I was worried about you."

Cara's lips parted, his words immediately dissolving her anger.

They stared at each other in awkward silence.

"That's it. I'm having wine," Cara announced, before opening the refrigerator and pulling out a bottle. "Should I get you a glass."

Wes stared at her blankly. "Nothing's wrong, but you're drinking?"

"Just because I don't drink a lot, doesn't mean I don't drink at all." She opened the cabinet door where the wine glasses were stored. "So, yes or no? Do you want one?"

There was just enough left in the bottle to fill each glass which was probably a good thing, she thought. She would love to numb herself to everything that had happened that day.

She handed him his glass, but he blocked her path, his face set along determined lines.

"You're physically okay, but something is obviously very wrong."

"Why were you so worried?" she countered. "I'm not that late."

His eyes were soft when they met hers, and the first pricks of guilt hit her. His concern was genuine. Wes had been worried about her. Cara's heart turned over with a heavy flop.

"It's midnight. I texted you. Even called. You didn't pick up, and you're never late." His hands were back on his hips. "I'm your roommate. Who else is going to notice if you don't come home someday?"

"I'm sorry. After I left work, I just needed to drive around for a while."

"Why?"

Cara's eyes searched his face, fighting the urge to hurl herself against his chest. She wanted him to hold her and tell her everything was going to be all right.

But she couldn't. He wasn't hers.

"It's a long story," she warned.

Wes took her hand and led her so that they were seated side by side on the sofa. She folded both legs on the cushion, and Wes sat facing her.

Was she really going to do this? What if it changed things? But as she watched Wes's familiar face, patient and kind, her chest eased. She wanted to tell him. Wanted him to understand. Wanted him to know her.

"I told you about my brothers and their moms," she trailed off.

"Three years ago, my dad started dating my stepmother, Courtney."

Wes nodded. She had told him some of this before. "Everything was great at first. Courtney was nice, fun even. She made my dad laugh. I spent part of that first summer with them. Her oldest son Matt was around some, but her younger son, Trey was away at college. I didn't get too attached though. I knew it wouldn't last."

"Why?"

"It never did." Cara toyed with the stem of her glass. "There was nothing wrong with Courtney. Well, at least at the time, I didn't think there was. My dad's relationships always had expiration dates. After about a year or so, things inevitably cooled between them. He didn't mention her as much. He gave Matt a job at his company, and when Trey was struggling, my dad helped him get into a college closer to home. We all thought he was putting a red ribbon on her life as a going away present. It happened every few years." She smiled wistfully. "My dad was extremely successful at business and very generous with the people he cared about. But, even though all the signs of an imminent break-up were there, out of the blue, he announced they were getting married."

She took a large sip of her wine. "Declan is the one who told us. My dad didn't even call us himself. Declan only found out because of a corporate memo. Luke and James pretended they didn't care, but I know it hurt them as much as it did me and Declan."

Wes's brows knitted together.

"It hurt," she explained, "because it was so fast, and it was clear we were unwanted. Courtney and my dad planned the ceremony and sent each of us invitations without ever speaking. My father wasn't answering the phone… It was like we were distant cousins they were obligated to invite. Not his children."

Wes reached out and caught her hand, giving it a sympathetic squeeze. She inhaled a shaky breath and studied Wes's face in the dim light. Wes met her gaze, and she felt something settle inside of her.

She'd never talked about this, how the wedding had affected her—not even to Amara. Cara should wonder why she was so comfortable opening herself up to someone she'd only known for a couple of months, but she didn't. It was Wes.

Now for the part that could make it weird.

Her father's money always did.

"What happened today? Why were you so late?"

"Are you sure you want to hear this?" she paused. "You might feel differently about me. About how I grew up."

"Now you *have* to tell me." He stroked his thumb over her fingers with a lopsided grin.

She took a deep breath. *Just get it over with.* "Like I said, my dad and Courtney got married. I was the only one of my siblings to attend. I think Dad knew Declan wouldn't come—they'd been estranged for a while. But he really believed the twins would come. I'm not sure Luke and James ever had a conversation with him again." Cara felt the dull pain in her chest twist into a sharp ache. So much pain and regret for all of them.

"What did he do to them?"

"What do you mean?"

"Three of his four kids didn't come to his wedding. That sounds like something happened."

"Courtney happened," Cara snapped.

"I'm not buying it." Wes shook his head. "Every time you talk about your brothers, it's always how smart they are, how successful they are. That description doesn't match a group of grown men not speaking to their father because he finally got married to someone who wasn't their mother."

Cara's mouth opened and shut a few times. He wasn't wrong. Put like that, her brothers sounded like petulant children, but it was hard to explain. Even she didn't completely understand where things went so wrong between Declan and their father—he wouldn't talk about it.

The only time she tried to discuss it, her father told it to drop it. She knew it had something to do with Declan's brother Seamus and the family business, but that was it.

One thing she did know, however, was that everything was worse after he met Courtney.

"It's really complicated," she finally said. "Declan and my dad had some huge disagreement. I'm not exactly sure what the deal is with Luke and James, either." Cara frowned. Now that she thought about it, her family had a lot of secrets from one another.

"Luke is the brother who lives here?"

Cara brought her attention back to the conversation. "Yeah, his twin, James, lives in Miami. They were never close to Dad like Declan and I were. The twins hated being associated with our family name. The press and stories about our Dad… At one point they even thought about legally changing it to Anne's maiden name, but they never did. I think they both worried how it could impact them professionally. Not only because they didn't want people to think their achievements were based on their last name, but my father had a reputation for being a bit… aggressive. All of my brothers are proud to the point of stupidity."

She stared out the dark doors behind Wes. "Part of me thinks the fact that Anne was with Dad longer than anyone else influenced them. No one ever talks about it, but I suspect of all of them Anne may have been the most hurt by our father. My mom, Corinne, was a fling. There were never any true feelings between them even though they got along, and my dad looked out for her. He was with Siobhan throughout her pregnancy, but she was never going to leave Ireland or her family. She already had Seamus, from a previous marriage and wasn't looking to get married again. They also remained good friends."

"That's…" Cara could see Wes was looking for the right word. "Unusual."

It was. She had heard plenty of jokes over the years about the Bloom Harem, but she was grateful that all of their parents had stayed friendly. It allowed Declan, Luke, James, and herself to be a family. Nontraditional to say the least, but still a family.

"Once when I was about thirteen, we had Easter in Dublin, and I overheard Siobhan and Anne talking. From what Siobhan said, I got the distinct impression that Anne was still in love with my father. The twins are smart. They had to have picked up on it if it were true. Maybe that's why they wouldn't let him in their lives. They adore their mom."

"It's very possible. It's the worst feeling in the world when your mother is sad." He turned his head slightly, the shadows cast by the kitchen light lengthening on his face. "Particularly when there is nothing you can do to help."

There was no doubt from the pain in his voice, that he was speaking from experience. Is that why he was raised by his grandparents, she wondered?

Cara pressed two fingers against her temples and rubbed as pressure built behind her eyes. It had been a long, emotional day, and the last thing she wanted to do was make Wes relive a sad memory.

"It's late. We should probably get to bed," she murmured.

"I want to hear what happened." His thumb stroked over her knuckles again, soothing her. "Please."

Cara gnawed her lower lip. He had been in foster care, had literally lost his whole family. There was no way she could tell this story and he not think less of her.

She would sound like the entitled, spoiled brat she had been. But part of her was relieved to have it out in the open. For him to know where she came from.

"After the wedding, my dad changed. He was angry. I didn't see him a lot. I was… working." She wasn't quite ready to tell Wes she'd been a club rat. "And that kept me away from my dad. When I tried to see him, there was always an excuse. Courtney started answering his phone, claiming he wasn't feeling well enough to talk, always promising to give him the messages. He almost never called back, and when he did, he only wanted to talk about what I was doing, who I'd seen. Superficial things.

"He used to call me his little star." Cara smiled remembering the endearment. "He got sicker and sicker and the doctors couldn't figure out what was wrong. A couple weeks before he died, we had a… disagreement."

"About what?"

"Technically, I worked for the family company, too, but I wanted to change what I was doing." She glossed over the fierce argument with her father. She couldn't face those emotions tonight, on the heels of everything else. "He said no, and I was hurt. Anyway," she rushed on, "he died before the doctors could find a treatment. We weren't even told he was gone until after Courtney had him cremated the next day."

Cara swallowed past the lump in her throat. The pain of missing that time with her father still tormented her. Too wrapped up living her own life, she hadn't even noticed how much Courtney had isolated their father. She would be ashamed of that until the day she died.

If she hadn't been so self-absorbed, would he still be alive today?

Wes moved closer, tugging gently on her hand. She allowed herself to sag against him, relishing the comfort of his warm body. She tucked her head against his chest, listening to his heart beat, strong and steady.

"I'm so sorry," he said against her hair. "That's a horrible way to find out."

Cara cleared her throat roughly to cover the thick tears clogging it. "She's awful. Every time I thought things couldn't get worse, they did."

"What did she do?"

Cara started to pull back, but Wes brought his arm around her shoulder, holding her in place. "That's the billion-dollar question. What *did* she do? Did she do anything at all, or was it what my father wanted?"

"I'm not following." His chest rumbled under her cheek.

Cara sighed. She wanted to burrow in, his strong arms around her, and forget the ugly scene a year ago.

"We were all there for the reading of my dad's will. I knew something was off the second we got to the house. Courtney had security there, and Andrew looked like he wanted to throw up."

"Who's Andrew?"

"Andrew Reinhart. Dad's personal lawyer. Originally it was Andrew's father, but when he retired, Andrew took over the practice. At first, I thought it was just because Dad had died, and he was upset. Andrew had known him all his life, but unfortunately for me and my brothers, it wasn't that simple." Cara's hand came up to rest next to her cheek, smoothing his shirt in restless tiny movements. "Apparently, days before my dad died, he had redone his will. In the new will, Courtney got just about everything."

"You thought he would leave you something?"

Cara's lips twisted bitterly. "I knew he would. He wrote a new will when he and Courtney got married, and he told me not to worry. He was going to leave Courtney a small amount so she couldn't contest the will, but our, his children's, portions wouldn't be affected. Instead, this new will completely reversed that. It also left out the bequests to staff and friends that were in the previous will."

"Ouch." Wes winced. "That must have hurt if you thought it was coming to you."

Understatement of the year.

In regard to my known natural born children, Declan Bloom, Luke Bloom, James Bloom, and Cara Bloom, I bequeath to each the sum of $200,000.

To just about anyone else, it was a huge sum, but her father had owned a billion-dollar media empire and raised his children in that lifestyle. It was a slap in the face, and by the smirk on Matt's face, everyone knew it.

She had a vague memory of Declan roaring at Andrew, and James letting out a full, deep belly laugh. Then, James clapped his twin, stunned by the news, on the shoulder and walked to his car in the front drive. Cara was told that Luke led her outside and drove her to a hotel, but her memory was hazy. Looking back, Cara thought she might have been in shock.

It wasn't the loss of the money—though later when she realized what it meant for her life, it had been a blow. The pain that wracked her body, the rushing of blood in her ears that day sitting in her father's study with Courtney beaming at them, came from the realization that her brothers had been right all along. Their father never truly loved them; they were accessories. As James used to joke, "The Bloom giveth and taketh away," but he had been referencing his own struggles with his father's approval. In the end, David Bloom had chosen Courtney and her sons over his own children.

Pulling herself back from the memory, Cara licked her dry lips. "The next day, Declan explained to me what was happening. Courtney had barred us access to our father's house which wasn't a big deal for the boys, but I still had stuff I kept there. Worse, we weren't allowed any mementos of our childhood to take with us. A few days later, Courtney revealed what must have been her plan all along." Agitated, Cara used her hand on Wes's ribcage to push away. This time he let her, but his concerned eyes watched as she finished the last swallow in her glass.

"After the reading when Declan was ranting that he'd given her *everything*, I thought he meant the house, the money, the plane... It never occurred to me he meant the majority shares in the company."

An odd look crossed Wes's face. She brought her feet down flat on the floor and placed the glass on the coffee table.

"I feel so stupid that I didn't think to question him at the time! Because Declan knew! He must have known the second Andrew read the words. When he said *everything,* he meant it. Declan dedicated his entire life to Bloom Communications, and she kicked him out, like it meant nothing. There was nothing Declan could do about it though. He ended up starting his own company, Bloom Capital using his connections." She sighed, staring morosely at the empty glass. "Declan claims he prefers private equity, but he'd been essentially running Bloom Communications for the last seven years. He's brilliant, so it didn't take him long to build up his new business, but I know he was heartbroken to lose the family company."

She was afraid to look at Wes and see what he thought of her family's dirty laundry. Her frown deepened. "After Dad died, Courtney didn't even bother to pretend she was a decent human anymore.

"I thought for sure she would see sense about Declan. How was she going to run the company without him? I thought if she knew how much it meant to Declan—" Cara huffed a bitter laugh. "But when I cornered her at an event, she laughed in my face. Courtney said it was time we all learned to stand on our own two feet instead of hanging on Daddy's wallet. So now Bloom Communications is under the control of a non-Bloom, and the four of us had to move on.

"To make things worse, Declan told me recently that he thinks he has proof that our father suspected he was being poisoned. Our old housekeeper told him that our Dad would only eat food and drink prepared by her... But it's all hearsay and theory. I can't decide if it's true or just Declan's paranoia!"

Cara sighed. "Today, Courtney showed up on set and bought Peachtree Pictures. She was thrilled to see me, so my guess is I'm fired. Seeing her made me so angry I just needed to drive around and listen to music for a while! That's why I was late." Cara glanced down at her shirt. "I should get in the shower. I'm gross." After a moment, she realized Wes was staring at her with giant eyes. He'd recognized the company name—her family's name— she knew it would happen.

Which of the many stories written about my family has he read? Or is it the fact I just told him my step-mother might have murdered my father...

Her stomach knotted, and every muscle in her body drew taut. "I never lied to you. I told you I was starting over. Just because I grew up wealthy doesn't make me a bad person. Not everything they say about us is true."

Wes's face had undergone a rapid color change, and now he was white and pasty.

"Are you going to be sick?"

CHAPTER TWENTY

"BLOOM CAPITAL," HE REPEATED DUMBLY, HIS TONGUE HUGE IN HIS mouth.

It was impossible!

Bits of information pulled from all over his brain cascaded together and brought him the unavoidable truth. Bloom Capital had hired his company a year ago to scrub pictures of the CEO's sister off the internet. Which made Cara…

"You're Cara Bloom! That's not the name you're using." His chest closed like a vise on his lungs.

She wrapped her arms around herself. "I'm using my mother's name. Something… something happened last year, and I wanted to start over without that last name. That's why I'm using Blease."

Wes did his best to recover, to not let her see how thrown off he was. But the truth was he was reeling. Cara's expression shuttered. She pushed to her feet, and he said nothing to stop her.

He *should* say something! Before she had retreated behind that blank expression, protecting herself, he'd seen the vulnerability on her face. But Wes was having trouble forming a coherent thought and could only stare at her speechless.

It couldn't be her! Could it?

Cara was the girl in the pictures? His stomach rolled, disgust and anger at what had been done to her fighting for space with... pity.

It wasn't the first time his company had been hired to remove a socialite's indiscretion off the internet. This one had been memorable not because it had been difficult. It had actually been laughably easy. The sites that had been sharing the photos weren't run by geniuses. The job had stuck with him because of how much they'd been paid to make it happen!

They hadn't been given much information. Photos had been stolen and sold to a tabloid. The only daughter of a supermodel and a billionaire meant price was no object. The tabloid had removed the photos, but not before screenshots had been taken and disseminated across the web. His job had been to find the photos and erase them. He rubbed a hand across his mouth.

The client wanted the sites, most using revenge porn content, punished. Wes had attached viruses to his phishing attempts in order to corrupt their users. Jin and Nina had worried it would get him in trouble again, but he was careful. No one would trace it back to him.

"Wes?"

He jerked his eyes up to meet hers then slid to a spot by her ear.

"I told you it would change how you saw me?" Her voice was cold. "Who I was doesn't change the person you know now. I knew I shouldn't have told you."

Cara's words finally penetrated his brain, and he saw the rigidity of her body, her hands fisted at her sides, as she began to walk away.

Wes swiftly came to his feet, catching one of her fists. Their gaze locked for a timeless second, before he wrapped his arms around her and pulled her tightly against him. One hand rubbed between her shoulder blades until he felt the rigid muscles start to ease.

"I'm sorry," he said against her hair, the familiar scent of honeysuckle tickling his nose. "I'm so sorry all that happened to you."

Cara slowly brought her arms up and wrapped them around his waist, leaning into him.

"I'm sorry I worried you tonight," she said, her voice muffled by his chest.

"My mother left me when I was six."

Cara startled against him, and Wes clasped his arms tighter, feeling her heart gallop against his chest. He wasn't sure why he told her—the shameful kernel at the center of his life.

Wes needed to tell her he knew about the pictures. That he knew what had happened to her–but he couldn't.

He knew her secret, even if she didn't know he knew.

Wes's heart pounded, and he rested his chin on the top of her head. "You shared your secret with me. I want to tell you mine."

She stilled. Wes didn't know what to say to make her feel better about what had happened with her father, her brothers or even the stepmother still causing havoc in her life. He *never* knew the right words. But in this moment, with the darkness outside and Cara in his arms, he wanted her to know everything.

"She was fifteen when she had me. My grandparents were evangelical Christians in a small Georgia town. They were devastated that their teenage daughter had sinned, and now everyone would know. They wanted her to give me up, and she refused. At least that's what she said. She couldn't stay in their house though, and she moved in with the first of a series of boyfriends."

Wes exhaled a slow breath. It was an old story, most of which he only remembered through fragments of memory mixed with what his grandparents had told him later. "None of them were good guys. She was an addict."

Cara didn't need to hear about the bruises on his mother's tiny body—the tears and hiding under a bed in a stranger's trailer.

Cara stiffened and started to pull back. He knew she would say something sweet to try to make him feel better, but he needed to get the words out. Holding her, he wasn't afraid. Wes resumed the slow rub, up and down her back, as much to comfort him as her.

"Sometimes my grandparents would let her stay when it got really bad. They wanted to see me, so I was her leverage. She loved me, but she couldn't even take care of herself. I don't have a lot of clear memories of her, but I do remember her watching Star Trek. My grandparents later told me it was her favorite show—that she'd named me Wesley after one of the characters. I started watching it as a way to feel close to her." Wes heard Cara's slight, dismayed gasp. Even Melody didn't know that.

He swallowed against the thickness in his throat. "One day when I was six, she took me to stay with my grandparents. She would leave me with them sometimes for a few weeks at a time. But she always came back for me. Until she didn't." Wes's throat closed making his voice hoarse.

"My grandparents raised me after that. Then they didn't come back either. They were killed one night in a car accident."

"They didn't come home either." Cara's breath caught. "Is that why you were so worried tonight?"

Had it been?

Not consciously.

Jin's words prickled under his skin. He hadn't worried when Jin didn't come back at night when they lived together, and he didn't worry when he hadn't heard from Melody for days.

Only Cara.

Wes had sat up in the dark waiting for her because he needed to know she was okay.

This is not good!

Wes set her back from him, hands gently clasped around her arms. "Yeah. Maybe."

"Thank you for sharing that with me." She gave him a tremulous smile, and guilt stabbed him in his gut. Tell her about your role in her past, his brain screamed at him.

Cara lifted up on her toes and pressed a kiss to his cheek. Did he imagine that she lingered, or did he only wish she did. "Good night."

Wes was left staring at her closed door, thinking of all of the things he should have said.

CHAPTER TWENTY-ONE

WES'S DOOR WAS OPEN, THE HOUSE SILENT WHEN CARA FINALLY crawled out of bed the next morning. The late night, combined with an emotional hangover, made Cara sleep in. Despite the hours she had spent in bed, she still felt bruised and exhausted. Her heart ached for the fifteen-year-old girl innocently naming her baby after her favorite TV character.

Her mind drifted to Wes's face last night when she had crept in, the worry and concern that quickly changed to anger. She grew up with three protective brothers, so she understood that his anger was rooted in his anxiety. At first, she had been secretly thrilled that he cared about where she was, but then when she found out it stemmed from his childhood, she felt like a jerk.

Cara pulled a pillow over her head. She was losing it! Wes was her friend. She just needed to keep reminding herself of that fact and she'd be fine. Maybe she should put a rubber band around her wrist and snap it every time she thought about ripping his clothes off.

And then there was the Courtney situation.

Cara was almost definitely fired which was bad enough, but Declan was going to have a fit when she told him about her run in with Courtney. He loved Bloom Communications, and when he found out Courtney was cavalierly spending company assets to give her sons a project….

Did she have to tell him? Cara was weighing the pros and cons of calling her brother when she caught the rich, warm smell of coffee.

The mug she used every day sat on the kitchen counter. On it was a yellow sticky note with Wes's precise handwriting.

Had an early meeting but will be home early afternoon.
Wes
Ps. See it goes both ways!

Warmth spread through Cara's chest at the smiley face he'd drawn. But her smile dimmed as she filled the mug.

She knew he had grown up in foster care, but hearing the details of how he ended up there made it more real. She shivered. If her father hadn't been who he was, what could have happened to her? Corinne wasn't fifteen, but she had been very young when Cara was born.

Even with the money she made as an international super-model, Corinne had never been interested in taking care of a child. Cara hadn't said it last night, but she fully understood the sick uncertainty of a parent who was an addict.

The stomach-churning anxiety of not knowing who your parent would be from one hour to the next. She may not have lived in a trailer, but there were plenty of times that her mother had forgotten that, as a small child, Cara needed to eat.

Corinne's diet mostly consisted of a handful of calories, ciga-rettes, and cocaine. If it hadn't been for Siobhan and Anne... And then Wes had lost his grandparents, too! Grief for that young boy, alone in the world thrust into the harsh reality of a children's home, made her chest ache. As much as her brothers made her insane, she couldn't imagine life without them.

She would call Declan.

Her brother would be hurt if he thought she had information and hadn't shared it with him. Still, Cara thought sipping the rich liquid, there was no reason it had to be right this second. She didn't want to start the day with an unpleasant conversation with her eldest brother.

Settling on the sofa with her coffee, Cara opened her phone and began absently scrolling through social media. If a job hunt was in her future again, she needed to update it. Her bot-boyfriend had liked more pictures on her account. However, the latest comments were slightly different, more specific to the movie she was working on—*I'm looking forward to seeing your talent on film*—which was a little weird, but not overtly creepy. Was she being paranoid?

Amara's voice in her head, Cara clicked on the account name. Ice washed over her. The only account it followed was hers. That doesn't mean anything, she assured herself. There is no way whoever sent her the messages last year could have found this account. Different name, different city... But her family followed her, and now so did Amara.

Is that why this had started up again? Had he found her?

Cara had accounts on each of the main platforms. They were strictly limited to following other professional accounts and a few celebrities. After *the incident,* she deleted all of her personal social media accounts. It wasn't only the constant stream of images of her friends having a good time—a life she was no longer a part of—that bothered her. The main reason had been that she couldn't bear for her face to be on the internet anymore.

After Cara was bombarded with messages from people who had seen her photos, she wanted to crawl into a cave until everyone forgot what she looked like. Most of the messages were lewd. There were even some from adult magazines offering her a feature. Of course, they wanted full nude this time and were willing to pay her. By this time, everyone knew that of all the Bloom siblings, Cara was the one who was broke.

The worst of the comments by far had come from one account. It referenced things no one should know about and always ended with the phrase 'See You Soon.'

Cara had begun to feel watched but kept her fears to herself. She already felt so guilty about adding to her brothers' stress with her tabloid scandal; she didn't want to worry them further.

Cara intentionally used a sprig of honeysuckle as her contact picture and never included anything personal, only pictures of work she'd done. It was unlikely someone had gone to such great lengths to track her down, but she blocked the new account for good measure.

In the message portion of the app was an invitation from Skye, begging Cara and Wes to join her that night at one of the luxury hotel bars in Buckhead. It was Skye's extra line about a *friend* she wanted Cara to meet that made her wary.

Cara didn't feel like socializing. Last night had been intense, but as her fingers hovered over the keypad, ready to type out a thanks-but-no-thanks, she found herself instead telling Skye to send her the details.

Why shouldn't she have some fun? They'd been working almost nonstop. Message sent, Cara washed her coffee mug, dressed, and brushed her teeth. Finally, unable to justify putting it off, she clicked on Declan's number.

She glanced at the clock. He was probably at work. Cara crossed her fingers for voicemail, worried how Declan was going to react to the news of her confrontation with their stepmother.

The phone clicked, and Cara opened her mouth to leave her prepared, upbeat message when she heard her brother's voice, "Morning, Car-Bear."

Cara froze.

Crap.

She must have been silent too long because her brother

sounded amused when he said, "Hello? Cara?" Then louder, "Did you pocket dial me? Cara?"

"Oops, sorry, Declan! I dropped my phone." Cara winced at the ridiculous lie.

"No problem," he laughed. "What's up? You don't normally call me on a weekday."

"We got some unexpected days off, so thought I'd call and see how everything is going." That much was true.

She heard a splash of water and then the sound of wood scraping. Cara couldn't imagine what in his glass, minimalist office could have caused that sound. "What are you doing?"

"I'm on the river." Declan said it in an offhand tone, as if it weren't groundbreaking news that her brother wasn't at work on a weekday morning.

"Do you see any pigs flying near you?"

"What?" Declan sounded bewildered, but Cara couldn't help chortling when he finally got the joke and groaned. "Ha ha. Very funny."

"So, that's a no?" She couldn't resist. "What about locusts?"

"I took the morning off. You act like it's the most unheard-of thing and yet *you* called *me*."

Cara went silent, humor forgotten.

"Is everything okay?" The wood scraped again, and she knew he was pulling the oars up.

Shit. She should have gotten it out while he was distracted.

"Yeah, everything's fine. I shouldn't bother you while you're on the river. You'll need both hands."

"I have ear buds in, and I'm just pulling into the boat house now, so chat away."

"I saw Courtney yesterday," she blurted out.

Real smooth, Cara!

"Where?" Declan's barked.

Cara sighed. "She came on to the set yesterday. The owner needs money, and from what I heard her say, it sounds like this is the company she's buying for Trey. He's going to work in post-production. It's not a big deal though! Nothing happened!"

That wasn't true, but it didn't feel especially necessary to share what Matt had said. Declan already wanted to rip their stepbrother's head off. Cara wasn't going to be the one to give him another reason.

"You spoke to them? What did she say—exactly?" At Declan's dark tone, Cara had the first stirring of uneasiness.

"Not much. It lasted less than five minutes."

"They didn't ask about Luke and James? My business?"

"No."

Frustration warred with sadness. Declan was so paranoid when it came to Courtney. The woman was a bitch and wouldn't miss an opportunity to needle them, but it was a bit far-fetched to believe she had an active vendetta against David Bloom's children.

Why should she? Courtney had everything she wanted, and they had no proof she was involved in their father's death.

"They came in, said hi, and that was it."

"Bullshit!" Cara jumped. She'd heard her brother use that biting tone before, but never with her. "They said, 'Hi, Cara. So good to see you. See you around?' Don't lie to me!"

"Fine. She made some shitty comments about how I was a lowly working person now, and Matt made a comment about me being dirty."

There was a beat of silence before Declan spoke again, murder in his voice. "He said something about—"

Cara instantly realized her error and cut him off. "No! Not like that! It had nothing to do with... before." A wave of embarrassment flooded her chest. "I was filthy from the set, and he made a comment about my appearance. It wasn't a big deal."

Heaviness weighed down on her, and her throat thickened. She hated to think about what had just popped into her brother's mind.

"What's the name of the studio you work for again? Something flower?"

"Peachtree Pictures. Why? Declan, don't do anything. I like my job, and if I haven't already lost it, I'd like to keep it. Don't interfere. It doesn't matter anyway. She bought it yesterday."

"How much was that?" It sounded like he was talking through his teeth.

"I have no idea, Declan. Does it really matter anymore?"

He ignored her question. "You should stay far away from them. I'm serious. Don't talk to them. Not a word, not even the littlest one about me or the boys. You never know what she'll use."

"Declan, don't you think—"

"Just promise me."

"I promise."

"By the way, Chris is in Atlanta for work. He'll probably want to take you to dinner."

Cara's eyes narrowed at the phone. Chris Keller was one of Declan's oldest friends, and the son of their father's doctor.

"I don't need a babysitter."

"It's not babysitting. He's known you since you were a little girl. Just go to dinner with him—don't make this a big deal."

"Whatever."

"I have to go, Cara. Be careful."

This is exactly why she didn't tell her brother about the odd messages she'd received. They were most likely harmless, but Declan would put her on lockdown.

She'd handled it before, and if it became a problem, she would handle it again.

CHAPTER TWENTY-TWO

"Did Skye text you about going out tonight?"

Wes was seated as usual in front of his computer, working. Cara set the water glass she'd filled next to him on the table. He looked up with his sweet smile and tucked one side of his noise-canceling headphones behind his ear. Her heart turned over in her chest at the memory of how warm and solid he had felt, when he'd held her the night before.

"What did you say?" he asked, taking a sip of the water.

"A group is going to the St. Regis tonight for drinks. I know it's not your scene. You know," she chuckled, "people. But it could be fun."

Butterflies took flight in her belly as she watched his face. Why was she nervous? She was being dumb.

A cloud passed over Wes's face. "I don't think so. I still have a lot to get done tonight, and Nina gets mean when I miss deadlines."

Cara had yet to meet Wes's friends and business partners, but she knew an excuse when she heard it. She matched his bland smile.

"No problem. It was just an idea." She walked to her door before tossing over her shoulder, "I'll be late though."

Cara didn't wait to see Wes's reaction before closing the door. Why was she so irritable? *It's not like he rejected me*, she thought. *It's a group outing, and he has work.*

She flopped back on her bed. So, what if he was super-hot with his stupid wavy hair and nerdy glasses? It's not the first time she'd lusted after someone. Cara threw an arm over her eyes.

She was beyond absurd. In a short time, he had become one of the most important people in her life. Did she really want to give in to her hormones and risk ruining it?

Wes had a plan for his life. He wanted a happily-ever-after with Melody; if that stung a little, so be it. Cara wasn't her mother. She wouldn't rush blindly into one love affair after another, convinced she'd found *the one* just because a guy set her panties on fire. Cara didn't even believe in the kind of happily-ever-after Wes wanted. There couldn't be a future for them.

A moment of sexual release wasn't worth the awkwardness that would come after. And that's all it was, Cara assured herself. Anything that happened between them would be purely physical, and even if she could live with that, she knew Wes couldn't.

A little while later, Cara heated their dinner, and when she handed him his plate, Wes looked up looking slightly sheepish. "You aren't mad, right? Fancy bars and groups of people..."

"Not at all. Skye is trying to set me up with a guy, and I thought a wingman would come in handy in case he's a complete dud."

Why had she said that? But Cara knew. Her pride wanted Wes to want her as much as she wanted him. Even if neither of them ever acted on it. She cringed, but before she could speak, he pulled his headphones back on, pushing the plate away.

"I'm sure you can handle yourself."

Cara stared at the top of his head for a second.

What the hell! Last night, he was beside himself because she was late, but tonight Cara could be drugged and dragged off from a bar and he didn't care?

Ass.

NORMALLY, it took Cara twenty minutes to get ready. Leggings and a T-shirt, along with a warmer layer, had become her uniform. She spent so much time putting makeup on other people, she rarely liked taking the time to put it on herself. But tonight felt different—and Cara chose not to examine why. She hadn't dressed up and gone out in over a year. Tonight she took her time.

Maybe this guy Skye had told Cara about would be the perfect way to break the weird obsession she had with her roommate? If she made out with someone else, maybe she wouldn't feel like climbing Wes like a tree every time he touched her!

Cara rolled her long hair until it fell in thick waves down her back. She kept her makeup deceptively simple. It might look natural but had taken Cara almost an hour to create the look.

She chose a soft, yellow dress with a deceptively modest V-cut in the front and back that tied with ribbons over each of her shoulders. It wasn't cut deep, just enough to expose her full cleavage. Being cold for the few minutes in and out of the car was worth it.

She had picked the dress up in Milan, at one of the ateliers her mother loved. It was one of the few designer pieces she brought with her to Atlanta. The fabric felt like butter as it skimmed just above her knee. Slipping a handful of delicate bangles over her wrist, she stepped into a pair of nude heels.

When she opened the door, Wes had disappeared from the table. Her shoulders dropped. So much for her entrance! Cara checked the app and saw her car was four minutes away. She was transferring her keys and wallet into a tiny purse when she heard

Wes's bedroom door open. Cara glanced up, and her mouth went dry. Freshly showered, Wes had swapped his normal athletic attire for a pair of dark jeans topped by a fitted T-shirt and sport coat.

Holy Shit!

Need swirled low and hot. Their eyes met across the small kitchen.

Wes's eyes were riveted on her face. They slowly traveled down her body and back up again. His Adam's apple bobbed as he swallowed. "You look… incredible."

A shock of desire hit her, her nipples tightening under his blatant perusal. Wes's gaze fell to where the thin fabric did little to hide her reaction. His tongue swept against his lower lip, and Cara's knees went weak. She wanted to launch herself at him.

No! Roommate! Bad!

"You changed your mind." Her voice was breathy, and she coughed to clear it. "I'm glad."

Wes grunted, his eyes still staring. Normally, she'd be thrilled by his stunned response, but when his eyes had pinned hers, and she felt flames lick up her thighs, she realized that teasing Wes could burn her, too.

He held her coat while she slipped her arms in the sleeves with only a muttered, "You're going to freeze."

Goosebumps rose on her nape when he lifted her hair free from the collar. Wes helped steady her as she gingerly navigated the steps down to their sidewalk. The feel of his warm fingers gripping her elbow started a slow throb between her legs.

She needed to get it together.

Or get laid.

One of the two was definitely a priority.

CHAPTER TWENTY-THREE

THE FORD FOCUS THAT PICKED THEM UP HAD VERY LITTLE LEG room, and for the twenty-minute ride, Cara could feel the heat of Wes's leg through the material of her dress. He fidgeted for a minute as their arms crowded each other. Finally, he lifted his, and with a strained expression, placed it along the seat behind her.

"Do you mind?"

"No, it's fine." Cara's breath caught as the car hit a pothole, and Wes's arm slid, his fingertips grazing the top of her shoulder. When he began sliding his fingers through the long strands of her hair, Cara held still, afraid that if she moved, he would stop the delicious movement.

She would ignore it. The same way they both ignored the fiery tension that pulsed between them... They were playing a risky game. Both pushing the limits just far enough.

By the time the car dropped them under the large stone portico in front of the hotel, Cara was more determined than ever to meet someone new. The sexual stalemate she and Wes were in was killing her!

Cara's nerves were taut, her body vibrating with awareness of

Wes's large frame beside her. She strode a few steps briskly away from the car in an effort to put a little physical space between them. She had never been as aware of another human the way she was of Wes.

But he was in love with someone else.

Cara scanned the lobby looking for the bar entrance. Even though she had never been to this hotel before, the expansive marble floor and sweeping grand staircase in the center of the lobby, combined with the delicate perfume piped through the air conditioning system, made her feel simultaneously at home and anxious.

Most of her life had been spent in and out of hotels and homes that resembled this lobby. Comfortable, neutral sofas and wingback chairs were grouped in front of the large, white stone fireplace, and she could see several tables on the floor above through the wrought iron railings. Money oozed from everyone, whether they wore a three-piece Brooks Brothers ensemble or a Louis Vuitton track suit.

These had been her people.

Now she felt out of place.

"I think it's this way." Cara pointed up the stairs.

They climbed the carpeted steps, and stepped into a bar that could have easily doubled as a private British club. Chesterfield sofas and small occasional tables were clustered along the walls with smaller groupings of chairs and tables situated closer to the wooden bar. Skye waved at her from across the room.

Cara recognized several people from the studio. They had pulled three of the small tables together in front of an upholstered banquette to make room for everyone. It was Friday night, and the bar was packed. It was an eclectic mix and impossible to tell who was who—influencers, business people, the idle rich, sports figures, as well as one or two familiar faces from the entertainment industry.

Skye caught her hands and made a show of ogling her. "Holy

shit! Have you been hiding this body the whole time? Look at your tits!"

Cara felt her cheeks heat. "Nope, I bought them today at Phipps Plaza," she joked, catching Wes's frown out of the corner of her eye.

"I'm going to get a drink at the bar. What do you want?" His eyes dipped to the generous amount of cleavage on display, before he jerked them away. His lips compressed into a thin, angry line.

"Surprise me. I'll get our next round," she said, as he stalked away.

Skye angled her head to where Wes was now waiting at the end of the bar. "I can't believe you got him to come! He never agrees to come out." Skye's eyes ran down Cara's dress, and then slapped her friend on the ass. "But I think I see what might have enticed him."

"Where's this friend of yours?" Cara asked. She didn't want to talk about what she couldn't have. She glanced around the group, but none of the faces were strangers.

"He's not here yet." She cast a speculative look back toward Wes. "Are you sure this is going to be okay?"

Cara was saved from answering when Wes reappeared and handed her a cut-crystal tumbler with a lime. "I got you a gin and tonic."

Cara smiled. "Perfect."

Wes took a sip of his whiskey. "So, where's the guy?"

"That's just what I was asking!" Cara plucked the lime from the rim of the glass and sucked at the sour juice. Wes leaned into her space, to avoid a group passing behind them, throwing her off.

Skye checked her phone. "He hasn't texted, so he should still be coming. He may have gotten stuck on location."

"Location? What does he do?"

"He's in production."

"Is that all you're going to tell me? 'He's in production.' That's so specific." Cara rolled her eyes.

"If I tell you any more, you'll google him. That would defeat the whole purpose of a blind date. I didn't give him your name either, not that he'd find much about you." Skye made a face. "You're the only person I know without real social media. You're like a ghost."

Cara shivered as a finger of unease ran down her spine. A warm palm slipped under her hair and cradled her neck, settling her nerves. Her eyes darted to Skye, but in the low light and bodies packed together she didn't think her friend had noticed Wes's movement.

"I don't have any." Wes's voice was even; whereas, Cara found herself barely able to follow the conversation. All of her attention was on the tender skin of her neck where his strong fingers lightly massaged.

"Yeah, but you're a super-paranoid computer geek," Skye said, oblivious to the fact that Cara was about to dissolve in a puddle at her feet. "Besides there *is* stuff about you, where you went to school, your business, etc."

"Trust me, if I could run my business and scrub the internet of my information, I would. It's insane the amount of private data people have floating around."

Was his voice raspier than before? Cara fought the urge to lean back into him.

Jerrod suddenly appeared before them, and grasping Cara's hands, he pulled her forward. She instantly missed Wes's touch.

"You came! Yes! I needed a night out!" Jerrod's dark eyes were happily unfocused as he swung Cara's arms side to side, almost spilling her drink. "You are too cute!" He reached forward tipping her glass to her lips. "You've got to catch up."

Cara arched a brow but finished the drink.

Satisfied, Jerrod grinned blearily and wagged a finger. "No baby talk tonight."

"No," Cara agreed with a laugh.

"Hey!" Skye objected. "Don't talk shit about my niece!"

Jerrod's eyes rounded. "Never. But this is daddies' night out!" He swung his arm around a heavy-set man watching indulgently.

"Don't worry, Sis. I'll get him out of here before it's a problem," Todd said to Skye, and she snorted.

"Are you being stood up?" Wes's leaned close to her ear, to be heard over the bar noise. His warm breath on the sensitive skin reignited the heat between her legs.

If Cara closed her eyes for a moment to savor the feeling, who was to know?

She rattled the ice cube in her glass, desperate for a distraction before she did something to embarrass them both. "I don't know. I'm going to get another. Want one?"

Wes lifted his still-full glass. "Don't worry about it. I'll get it for you."

"But…" Wes was already walking away when Skye laughed.

"Let the guy buy your drinks! That shit's expensive!"

Cara scowled. "Just because he makes more money than I do doesn't mean he should always pay."

Skye patted her on the shoulder. "You are adorable! But if he doesn't mind let him."

"He's saving for a house. He shouldn't be buying me sixteen-dollar cocktails. He's only here to be my wingman—what?" Cara asked, when Jerrod and Skye gave her a funny look.

"You know he's loaded, right?"

"Wes? No, he's not. Why in the world would you think that? His company is just getting started."

Her friends laughed again, but sobered when they saw she was serious.

"Do you really not know?" Jerrod was definitely leaning to his left now, his husband catching his elbow.

Skye peered at her as if she weren't sure if Cara was making a joke. "The fancy encryption device that he sold? Before he came to Atlanta?"

Cara shook her head, the gin she had downed so quickly making her a little fuzzy. Her gaze bounced between her friends, apprehension tickling under her skin.

What weren't they saying?

"Oh, baby," Jerrod said. "You don't know anything."

That got Cara's hackles up. "What don't I know?" She glared, but it didn't have the desired effect.

Instead, Jerrod laughed. "You know about how he got out of jail, right?"

Cara's jaw dropped and for a minute she forgot to breathe.

Skye elbowed Jerrod hard. "Shut up."

Todd kissed his husband on the side of his head, and Jerrod frowned. "You two are the ones who told me! That he was arrested, and then suddenly he was living in DC and not in jail. Don't act like it was just me! You two were obsessed with finding out what happened! Melody told you he worked for the government—"

Skye poked him again, her drink sloshing. "Damn it! I borrowed this top from wardrobe."

Cara's eyes went to where Wes leaned on the bar waiting for her drink.

Jail? Government?

Doubt consumed her, and her heart rate picked up its pace. What did Cara really know about him?

He must have felt her eyes on him because Wes looked back and flashed her a smile. Cara tried to make her lips move, but they wouldn't obey.

"Don't worry about it," Todd said, taking the drink from Jerrod's hand. "It was a really long time ago."

"Why—"

Skye gave a smile that didn't reach her eyes. "You should ask him. It's not our story to tell. But it's nothing bad, I promise."

Nothing bad? He was in jail!

Skye's phone pinged, and she groaned. "Sorry, babe, but he just cancelled."

"Who?" Cara couldn't look away from Wes's profile. His familiar, she'd seen it a hundred times next to her on the sofa watching Star Trek, profile.

"Martin. My friend?"

Cara stared at her blankly. "Oh, right."

"Are you going to freak out?" Skye asked, following her attention to the bar. "Wes is a nice guy. He made a mistake. Just ask him about it. He probably thinks you already know."

Cara shot Skye a 'yeah, right' look.

Wes turned to come back to their group, her drink in his hand. Acid rose in Cara's throat. "I've got to go to the restroom."

CHAPTER TWENTY-FOUR

Wes watched puzzled as Cara bolted from the bar.

"Everything okay?" he asked when he rejoined the group. No one would meet his eyes. "Is Cara okay?"

Skye heaved a heavy sigh and pointed at Jerrod. "This idiot just told Cara about…" Her face contorted, her gaze sliding away.

Foreboding settled over him. "About?"

"About what happened at Tech," Todd said quietly.

Wes took a step back, his brain scrambling. "What about Tech?"

Skye rubbed her nose. "About your arrest for breaking into the university's system, and then your work for the government…"

Wes swallowed convulsively, his chin tucked to his chest.

How the hell did they know about that?

He certainly didn't broadcast it. Wes's eyes flew to the door, his mouth going dry.

Fuck.

He needed to explain it to her. What if she'd left? Panic twisted around his heart. Cara appeared in the doorway, and Wes sucked in a breath.

"Man, I'm sorry," Todd said, but Wes only cared about the stone-like mask Cara was wearing.

Her eyes faced stubbornly forward when she reached his side, taking the drink from him. Wes wanted to beg her to look at him. He needed her to listen.

Wes could only imagine what was going through her head. He frowned when her hand trembled as she lifted the glass to her lips.

"Cara," he started to say, but she turned her back and looked over to the bar, only to whirl back to their group, her face a frightening blend of whitish green.

Her hand gripped his forearm, and she lifted her eyes to his. Fear, stark and vivid, shone in her violet eyes.

"What is it?" Wes looked over his shoulder to see what had scared her. He heard Skye ask Cara what was wrong, but his attention had been caught by a group of men sitting at a low table near the bar.

One of them stared fixedly at their group. His expression looked confused or maybe disbelieving. With the dim lighting, it was impossible to make out which. As Wes watched, the man nudged his friend and gestured toward their group. Cara's death grip on his arm loosened, and she tipped her glass up, downing the entire contents. Wes's eyebrows lowered.

"I'm going to the bathroom."

Cara pressed the glass into his hand and slipped away, walking briskly out of the bar. Skye, Todd, and Jerrod looked bewildered.

"Again? Is she sick?" Jerrod slurred. "Maybe you should check on her, Skye. I thought she was going to hurl. I'm not sure I've actually seen anyone that color. Well, without theatrical makeup anyway."

Their words came to Wes from a distance. He was torn between wanting to go after Cara and approaching the group of men who were now in an argument with a woman.

She was tall and striking, with near perfect features. She leaned over the three men with a finger in one of their faces. The gold jewelry in her waist-length braids glinted in the candlelight of the bar, as her hair swished with her angry motions. Two of the men looked amused by her fury, but one, with ginger curls, looked nervous, his eyes flicking to his friends.

Abruptly, the woman whirled away and stalked across the bar in stilettos and fitted leather pants traveling in the same direction Cara had gone.

"I'm in love!" Skye breathed, her eyes glued to the woman striding out of sight. "That is a work of art!"

Jerrod and Todd nodded, but Wes's body was on alert. He wanted to charge after Cara, but he wasn't sure she wanted to see him right now.

"Could you check on Cara?"

Skye took one look at his expression and handed her glass to Jerrod. She had just reached the entrance when the extraordinary woman was back hesitating at the doorway. She looked upset. Skye, distracted from her mission, stopped next to her and appeared to be trying to strike up a conversation.

Wes's confusion grew as Cara appeared and gave the strange woman a hug. She looked in the bar and then tugged the two women out of sight. Cara knew her. The pieces clicked into place. *Amara.* Cara said she was coming to town.

He tried to ignore the little curls of anxiety that grew in his stomach. Amara was her friend, but he couldn't forget how upset Cara had been when she first heard Amara was coming to visit.

"I'm sorry what did you say? It's loud in here." Wes said, once he realized Jerrod had been speaking to him.

It wasn't that loud, and by their looks, the two men weren't buying it.

"I asked how Melody was doing? Is she coming back?"

"Of course, she is." Wes's response was defensive, and worse, automatic. He frowned.

"So, you've talked to her?"

"Yes." When *was* the last time he'd spoken to Melody? Weeks? More than a month? He knew she was doing well because she posted photos of Italy on her social media every day. But when was the last time they actually had a conversation?

What was taking Cara so long? He took a step toward the door.

"Interesting."

"What?"

"Nothing," Jerrod took a sip of his drink, not hiding his smirk. "It's only—"

"Uh-oh," Todd interrupted his husband. Wes swung his head to see where Todd was looking and saw Skye frantically gesturing for them to come.

Instinctively, Wes looked to where the men had been sitting.

They were gone.

His shoulders tightened, his pulse picking up speed, as he hurried across the room.

As soon as she saw him approach, Skye disappeared again. Angry voices echoed in the two-story marble lobby. He followed the noise to the small alcove between the bar and the bathrooms.

When Wes turned the corner, his body went rigid.

Cara wore an angry expression on her face, but what had him seething was her arms wrapped protectively around her stomach. Skye stood off to the side, clearly at a loss for what to do.

The ginger and one of the other men leaned against the wall, their ankles crossed, enjoying the show.

Amara stood next to Cara, her eyes flashing. The man who had stared so intently at them in the bar had his back to Wes, but he could clearly hear the patronizing voice.

"Chill, Amara. No one is *doing* anything to Cara. I just wanted to say hello. I haven't seen her for a long time. I mean in person." One of the men snickered, and Wes saw bright red spots appear on Cara's pale cheeks.

Her chin jutted forward, and despite her distress, her voice was steady. "And I would prefer if I never saw you again, Erik. Amara and I were having a conversation, and you interrupted. You can go away."

"You aren't still mad that I fucked that girl in Ibiza, are you? You were a super bitch when you saw us. Made quite the scene, but I'm prepared to forgive you—if you ask nicely." Erik sent his friends a leer over his shoulder.

Wes clenched his fist, every cell in his body wanted to pound the guy's face in.

Cara's mouth had dropped open, but when she caught a glimpse of Wes stalking forward, her eyes widened in horror. Her expression made the others turn. Amara's eyes flashed recognition and gave him an assessing look. The two men against the wall straightened, and Erik shifted his weight as if he were expecting an attack.

Wes moved slowly and deliberately, his gaze fixed on Erik. He didn't know all that had happened between them, but he *never* wanted to see that look on Cara's face.

Erik's sneer slipped when Wes walked straight at him. At the last second, Erik shifted to the side to avoid Wes plowing into him.

Taking Amara's place at Cara's side, he wrapped his arm completely around her.

Amara grinned.

"You were taking so long, I had to come find you." Wes brushed a kiss against the top of Cara's head. He met each of the men's gazes. "Is there a problem here?"

"Who are you?" Erik's voice was dismissive, but he wasn't skilled at hiding the anger in his eyes. They darted repeatedly to where Wes's palm lay possessively on Cara's stomach, betraying how much it bothered him.

Cara didn't wait for him to answer. "He's none of your business. Go away, Erik!"

She took a step forward, forcing Wes to drop his arm from her waist.

"Clark Kent," Amara muttered, still smiling.

Cara shot her a look, but Amara only lifted her eyebrows back at her.

"Is this your boyfriend or something?" Erik scoffed.

"Or something…" Wes said silkily.

"Are you surprised?" Cara's voice lashed out. "That someone on the planet wanted my—how did you put it—homely, fat ass? And now that I was broke, you couldn't pretend you wanted to be with me anymore, and no one else would either? Something about if I needed cash, I could join you and the bartender, and you'd pay me as much as her even though I wasn't worth it."

Blood whooshed through Wes's ears, and he growled, stepping toward the man.

He was going to murder him.

A surprisingly strong hand caught him, and he looked down to see Amara give a quick shake of her head, before stepping to Cara's other side.

"And what was it you said, Cara?" Amara tapped her lips like she was thinking, and then her lips curled in an evil smile. "Oh, yeah! She was happy that you were finally able to get it up, Erik. Because she thought you must secretly be in love with Colin, since you could never keep it up long enough to get her off." Amara tossed a look at her friend. "Cara was worried it was a family problem, and that was why your mom had so many—"

"Enough, Amara. I shouldn't have said that. It makes me as ugly as him."

Erik's face twisted. "Fucking bitch! Don't be sorry now. I already *made* you sorry."

Wes didn't recognize the sound that came out of his mouth as he charged forward. Cara stepped in his path blocking him while Erik's friends grabbed him and pulled him into the bathroom.

"Stop!" Cara pushed against his chest.

Wes's pulse beat behind his eyes, his breath coming hard and fast.

He was going to rip the prick apart.

"Wes!" Cara's voice was sharp. He dropped his gaze to her. She was hanging on by a thread. Adrenaline dilated her pupils and her face was flushed. She swayed slightly.

He needed to get her out of there.

Home.

He'd take her home and wrap her in the fuzzy blanket she loved....

Wes didn't clearly remember the walk down the stairs to the front of the hotel or what—if anything—he said. Later, he had a vague recollection of Skye saying she'd called for a car. Cara pulled her phone out of the tiny purse and bent her head close to the screen.

Wes's body still thrummed with anger, but he knew he needed to check on her. See if she was all right after the nasty scene. He put his hand on her back and his heart contracted when she flinched away. He felt helpless while they stood on the curb in silence waiting for their ride.

Cara's knuckles were white where she gripped the phone, her other hand stabbing at the screen. Her coat forgotten on a chair in the bar, Wes wasn't sure if her trembling was from cold or the shock of the adrenaline leaving her body.

"What he said—" Wes's blood coursed hotly. "He was the one—"

"Not now." Cara sounded like she'd been chewing glass. Wes slipped his sport coat off and laid it over her shoulders, but her trembling only increased. His molars ground together.

She must have found what she was looking for because he heard her exhale a shaky breath, and for a split second, she looked up as if she might say something.

A car pulled to a stop in front of them, and Cara opened the back door. Before she climbed in, she wordlessly extended her arm behind her, offering him the phone.

Wes didn't want to look. He suspected he already knew what she wanted to show him. In the back seat, Cara turned her whole body to look out the window, and he could only stare at her back as the car pulled away from the hotel, wishing he had the right words.

Wes looked down once to confirm she had in fact pulled up a news story detailing the tabloid photo scandal. He pressed the button to power the phone off and set it in his lap.

Cara's shoulders rose and fell in ragged little breaths, making Wes feel like someone had hollowed out his chest. She had recoiled from his touch before, but it was all Wes had to offer her.

He took one of her hands, gripped stiffly in her lap, and pried her fingers apart, pulling her to face forward. The driver looked curiously at them in his mirror, but Wes ignored him.

Wes applied very little pressure to her hand before Cara was turning and burying her face against his side. He shifted so that he could bring his arm around her back and bent his head to place his cheek against the top of her head, the honeysuckle scent of her blonde hair filling his nose.

CHAPTER TWENTY-FIVE

Wes unlocked the front door and stepped back so she could go in first. She paced several steps then turned to face him, looking tiny and vulnerable in his coat. His heart broke. Her eyes were puffy but dry, as if she refused to cry.

Cara folded her arms across her chest and raised her chin. "Did you read it?"

He shook his head, and little furrows appeared between her eyes.

"Why? I want you to." She shoved her phone at him again. "I want you to read it!" Her voice pitched higher, and it occurred to Wes this might be her way of controlling what had happened.

"I already knew." He kept his eyes on hers.

"What? How?" Cara's lips quivered, and her eyes took on a hunted look.

He hated it.

She licked her lips. "This whole time?"

"No! I didn't put it together until the other night." Wes shoved a hand back through his hair. How was he going to explain this?

Cara slowly took his coat off and draped it over the back of the sofa, pivoting to retreat into her room.

"Wait!" His voice broke. "I swear to you. I didn't know until you told me your real name."

Cara turned slowly, her expression wooden. "You saw the pictures."

"I did. It's not what you're thinking… You know what I do…" His voice was anguished. How could he make her understand? "I only look at photos long enough to identify them. I never *looked* at them—I knew from the client request that age was an issue…"

He trailed off as all color rushed from her face and then flooded back, an angry red.

"It was you! You were the white-hat hacker Declan hired." She laughed bitterly. "Wow. The two of you must have…" She stopped, shaking her head. "I really am as naïve as my brothers accuse me of being."

"Unless you told him, as far as I know, your brother has no idea we even know each other." Wes held her gaze, hoping she would see he was being sincere. "I should have told you the second I knew, but I didn't know how. You were already so upset that night. I didn't want to make it worse."

Her lip curled.

"Cara, what can I do to make you believe me? I would never hurt you. Tell me what I can do!" He knew he sounded desperate, but he didn't care.

Her beautiful eyes held his in an inscrutable stare.

He shifted on his feet.

"Why were you in jail?"

"I… I," Wes fumbled his words.

"Everyone seems to know about it except me. You've seen me naked." She waved a hand down her body. "Or close enough. Let's put it all out there. Get naked, Wes."

Wes felt like he couldn't breathe.

"You asked what you could do. This is it. Let's lay it all out on the table. No more secrets." Her tone was defiant, but he could still hear the hurt underneath.

The room wasn't large, but it felt like a gulf had opened between them.

"I hacked into my college's computer system."

"That can't be all," she challenged, and Wes sighed.

"I had a scholarship that covered all the basics. But there was no extra living stipend. At first, I tried to work to cover the other costs, but Tech is hard, and my grades were slipping. Which meant I was at risk of losing my scholarship. On top of that, my computer broke, and it didn't matter what I did. I couldn't pay my mounting credit card debt."

Her eyes flickered.

"I needed a way to make money, and honestly, my skill was hacking. It started with our study group, getting early copies of tests. Then, it just kind of spread through word of mouth."

Wes hated sharing how he had struggled. How sometimes he went without eating because the dining hall hours didn't always line up with his classes. He stopped running for a while because he had worn holes in his shoes and couldn't afford to buy new ones. At eighteen, you are aged out of the foster care system. Wes was one of the lucky ones. He had skills that gave him opportunities, but it wasn't a comfortable life.

"I sold tests." He shrugged. "Then I realized I could make more money changing grades. I got greedy and changed too many, too fast. It alerted the university that something was wrong. They hired their own specialist to trace the breach." Wes huffed a laugh. "I was young and arrogant. I used my computer in my dorm room. It was easy for them to trace the IP."

Cara chewed her lip. "You were arrested? Were the charges serious?"

Wes walked into the kitchen and opened a beer, as memories flooded in.

It had been awful. The police came into the lecture hall, and he was handcuffed in front of the entire class. He'd never forget the terrified look on Jin's face—the fear his was the next name they would call. Because, of course, his roommate knew what he was doing. Jin helped Wes do it.

"The university wanted to make an example of me. After all, it was a school full of computer and math geniuses. They wanted to make sure it didn't happen again. Ten felonies. Nineteen years old and my life was over."

He gulped the beer, but it tasted sour.

"Oh my god," Cara breathed.

"So, you see, I know all about making a catastrophic mistake when you're young."

"You must have been terrified. I had a family..." her voice cracked.

"Yeah, it was bad." Wes made sure he kept his voice neutral. "I pleaded guilty. There was no way I was getting out of the charges. I wasn't exactly a criminal genius covering my tracks. My public defender said I might get a more lenient sentence if I saved the state a trial."

"It must have worked. You're here. Now."

He shook his head. "I was facing twenty years."

Wrinkles creased her forehead. "But?"

"I was in county, awaiting my sentencing, when I had a visit from a government agency. I was promised probation and time served if I agreed to a seven-year contract with them." His lips twisted.

"Why? What agency?"

His smile stretched. "Let's say it was a 'lettered agency' and leave it at that. I told you. I am very good at what I do. They wanted me to work for them—cyberterrorism." He held his hands out. "But that's all I can say."

"You didn't go to prison?"

"No. They gave me an advance on my salary so I could find some place to live." The government wanted to be sure he was happy in his new position. The fear of going to jail if he stepped out of line was there, but there was also the mutual understanding that once he had access to their systems, he could do great harm. They needed to be sure he wouldn't be tempted by a foreign agency's bribes.

"I wasn't the only one. There were about ten of us, all hackers, in a cube farm. None of us over twenty-five."

"Skye said you sold an encryption device. That you had a lot of money?" Cara sounded uncertain, almost like she wanted Wes to tell her it wasn't true.

"I don't know how they know about any of this to be honest. The work I did… With what we saw every day, we were *encouraged* not to discuss it."

Cara held his gaze. "Jerrod said Melody told them."

Wes shook his head. "No, she wouldn't do that. I told her—" He stopped when sympathy skated across Cara's face. The tight feeling in his chest returned.

Wes *had* told Melody a little of what he was doing. He'd bragged. Wes wanted her to see him as more than just the kid she had saved from beatings in the group home. He coughed. "She just wouldn't."

Cara's smile was sad when she said, "Someone I trusted gave Erik the pictures he sent to the tabloids. I think we've both learned that you never know who you can really trust, or even if you know them at all."

CHAPTER TWENTY-SIX

CLICKING THE BUTTON TO LOCK HIS TRUCK, WES ADJUSTED HIS grip on the messenger bag. Originally, he was supposed to have lunch with Jin and Nina, but after the meeting, he wasn't interested in being heckled anymore. Wes had been mentally off all morning. All through the meeting and demonstration with their potential client, Wes kept losing focus.

He hadn't seen Cara before he left that morning, and he couldn't help but wonder how she was feeling after last night?

At first, Jin seemed amused by Wes's distraction, but after the second time Wes missed his cue to chime in with an explanation of how the algorithm would benefit the client, his friend was just annoyed.

Nina gave him a quick kick under the table before proceeding to cover for him. Wes listened to her lay out their capabilities and explain how they would use their patented algorithm to test each point of access in the client's system.

On the way to the elevator, Nina was steaming. "What is wrong with you? This is an important get for us!"

"I know. It's totally my fault. Thanks for covering. Technically, it's not really covering though. You coded as much of the algorithm as I did. I'm just always the one who talks."

Nina glared. "We can have the 'misogynistic world of women in tech talk' another time. I *know* I'm perfectly capable of explaining what we do. I'd just like a heads up if I'm supposed to be taking lead. We looked like clowns in there. Too much dead silence while you sat there daydreaming."

"I wasn't daydreaming. I'm just tired. I had a late night. It won't happen again."

After Cara had gone to bed, Wes couldn't sleep. He did an extensive internet search on himself. The arrest was there, covered by the Atlanta papers. But there was no way anyone could have known he hadn't served his time or that he worked for a government agency, unless they were searching inmate rolls at the time he would have been incarcerated.

The only one who knew those details, and that he had sold the encryption device, was Melody. Because he'd trusted her.

Wes had tossed and turned for hours until he finally decided she must have had a weak moment. Melody liked attention. She probably didn't realize how dangerous her slip was. It was his fault for not making her understand that Wes could get in a lot of trouble for having shared the information with her. A voice in his head whispered that he was making excuses for Melody—again— but he ignored it.

"Late night, huh? Anything to do with a certain person you spend every nonworking minute with?" Jin waggled his eyebrows suggestively.

"It's not always sex, you know." Nina glared at her husband.

"Not always, but usually. Besides, you've seen how he is."

"It's true, his lack of emotional intelligence isn't usually our problem. But, if he's going to start blowing important client meetings because of it, then I guess we have to address the sexually frustrated mess in the room. Particularly, when he can't even recognize what's right in front of him."

"I'm standing right here."

Sometimes working with a married couple was a pain in the ass. It was apparent this wasn't the first time they'd discussed him and Cara—and Wes didn't like it.

"Even if I were daydreaming about sex, why would you assume it's about Cara?"

Jin and Nina looked at him and then each other.

"Just sleep with her for fuck's sake and put us all out of our misery," Nina muttered, pushing the button for the lobby.

Shocked, Wes was about to defend himself, but when Jin erupted in laughter, he decided he would be the bigger person and simply ignore their childishness.

Wes walked up their front steps, and reached out a finger to toy with the spring wreath on the door that Cara must have added while he was gone. A small smile caught his lips, and he immediately relaxed.

Jin and Nina just didn't understand. He liked living with Cara. She made things nicer. The house had taken on more homey touches since Melody had left. A new pillow on the couch, a candle arrangement on the kitchen table, this wreath.

And everywhere her scent.

Wes shook the thought away. He cared about Cara; he had no problem admitting that. He cared about Nina and Jin, too. That didn't mean Wes wanted to have sex with them. And if he'd gotten a little upset last night, when he thought she was in trouble and then told her about his past, it was just further proof. Definitely just a good friends vibe.

He heard music as soon as he opened the door—Taylor Swift blasting from a portable speaker. Wes set his bag on the table and headed for the small box to lower the volume. He smiled. Cara must have decided to put the previous ugly night behind her.

Before he reached the speaker on the kitchen counter, Cara's door was flung open. She danced out of her room, eyes closed, singing at the top of her lungs—completely offkey.

It might have been cute, her happy abandon, hair wrapped in a towel. The problem was that the only thing covering the rest of her body was another towel that hit just above the knee. Her skin was flushed rosy pink from her hairline to the luscious curves of her breasts. She danced a few more feet, parts of her that he shouldn't be staring at jiggling above the towel.

Any pretense of friendly feelings disappeared along with the oxygen in his lungs. Intense need shot straight to his groin and his entire body tightened. She was absolutely delectable, shimmying in front of her door.

Wes's mouth dried, and he couldn't help the white-hot craving that suddenly consumed him. What would she do if he stopped her dance? If he pulled her to him and held her soft body against him? If he pulled the towel away, would she be rosy everywhere? Water droplets still glistened on her pale shoulders. Would they taste like honeysuckle?

Cara opened her eyes and let out a shriek, her hand rising to her chest, blocking his view.

Wes sucked in a breath and turned away from her to hide the tent in his dress pants. He kept his back to her until he was safely in the kitchen, the cabinets hiding his reaction.

"I thought you were gone until midafternoon." She blinked at him with wide eyes.

"I skipped lunch."

"Oh." Cara still clutched the towel between her breasts. "I should get dressed."

Her eyes met his across the room, and he saw the same passion reflected back at him.

Her fingers flexed where she held the material closed. If she dropped the towel, Wes wasn't sure if he would be able to stop himself. He'd spent too many nights tossing and turning, imagining how her breasts looked, how they would feel under his palms. How they would taste.

But he couldn't. He had made a plan for his life the moment

he realized he wouldn't be going to jail. He wanted stability. Cara Bloom was not that.

"Yeah, you should." His voice came out harsher than he'd intended, and her eyes flared with hurt. Wes wanted to apologize, but he kept his lips closed. What would he say? That seeing her half-naked was torture. Or that he wanted to lay her on his bed and explore her body until she was out of his system.

He couldn't do any of those things. Mostly because he was afraid if he did give in, he'd never be able to get enough.

So instead, he walked to his bedroom and closed the door.

WES WAS deep into coding a new penetration technique when his phone lit up on the table next to him. Melody's smiling face flashed up at him, but his finger hesitated for the slightest second before swiping to answer it. He had hidden in his room until he heard Cara leave the house, and then it was another half an hour before he could focus on work. His hand constantly strayed to his phone to type out an apology text to Cara.

But what was the point? Wes told himself that he needed distance from her. It was best for both of them. "Hey, Mel."

"Wes!" Melody exclaimed.

Wes tamped down his irritation. He was still annoyed she had told people about his work in D.C.

"How's it going? Ready to come back yet?"

"You have got to come to Italy!" She gave a hum of pleasure. "It's magical."

"I texted you about coming to visit. You never answered."

"I've been so busy! This has turned out better than I could have ever dreamed. Luca's family owns this amazing fashion house. He said I'm his muse. Can you imagine? Me! A muse!"

"Luca?" Wes's skin prickled.

There was silence, and the prickle became a full-fledged

alarm in his brain. Wes propped his elbow on the table. "And what exactly does a 'muse' do?"

"What do you mean? It's a muse! I'm myself!"

"Uh-huh."

"I know this started as a job… But I love it here. And then I met Luca…"

His brain scrambled.

"He's asked me to marry him."

"You can't be serious!"

She can't do this! He had a plan. They were supposed to be the family they had both always longed for! Now she was saying she was going to be living out *his* dream with some rich Italian fuck!

"I know it seems fast, but it was love at first sight!" Melody was off and running now, enthusing over how her fiancé had shown up at the photo shoot and how amazing he was.

Wes unlocked his jaw and forced his breathing to slow.

She was engaged. It was fine. Melody was impetuous. She had gotten carried away. She'd change her mind again. She could still come back.

Oblivious to Wes's panicked thought process, Melody blithely continued. "His uncle is marrying some aging supermodel, so we have to wait until after their wedding to have an engagement party. Of course, it will be a big wedding. Luca's family is very important. You'll come, right?"

Wes's stomach turned over. She was leaving him. His plans for his life slipping away with her.

"I have to go."

"Aren't you going to congratulate me?"

A plan. He just needed a new plan.

"Congratulations," he said dully.

CHAPTER TWENTY-SEVEN

"DON'T YOU DARE HANG UP!"

"Amara, I really don't want to talk right now."

That look on Wes's face. He wanted her. Cara knew he did. But he had made it clear it wouldn't happen. On the heels of seeing Erik last night, Wes's rejection cut deep.

"Too bad!" Amara exclaimed. "I didn't have time to explain before Erik descended on us."

Cara stayed silent.

"I had no idea you'd be there, Cara! It wasn't even my idea to go last night! If I thought you were going to be out, I would have warned you."

Cara gave a bitter laugh. It might not be Amara's fault they had run into each other. That was a horrible coincidence. But the fact her best friend was hanging out with the man who ruined her life was something else.

"Are you working today?"

"No—"

"Good, then we can meet and catch up. Let's get dinner!"

Cara didn't want to meet Amara. She felt raw and exposed.

"Coffee."

"I'll take it. Where's good in Atlanta?"

Cara arrived at the café first, happy to find a parking spot in the busy area. After ordering her coffee, she sat by the front window, keeping an eye out for Amara. With her nerves stretched thin, coffee probably wasn't her best choice. She smoothed her hands across the tabletop. *It's just Amara. She's your oldest friend,* Cara reminded herself. Besides, Amara hadn't actually done anything to her.

Except stay friends with those who had destroyed her.

She was restless. Was everyone in the crowded café staring at her? Cara forced herself to take a deep breath, the rich aroma of coffee beans filling her lungs. All around her, people were busy working on their laptops or staring at their phones.

No one was looking at her. No one cared.

Cara took a sip of her coffee.

The bells above the door jingled happily as it swung open. Amara spotted her and waved exuberantly. Dressed in a blue, madras crop-top and white pants, her friend stood out amongst the casual crowd. Oblivious to the spectacle she made, Amara rushed to where Cara was seated. She stood and allowed herself to be enveloped in a familiar cloud of lemon fragrance.

"I've missed you so much!" Amara lifted Cara's coffee and took a tiny sip, followed by a 'not bad' expression. She flashed a smile, and the college-aged barista almost tripped over his feet to reach her side.

"Do you need something?"

"A coffee and something sweet, darling." The boy blushed before scurrying away.

"This isn't a table service place," Cara observed dryly.

Amara unzipped the Gucci bag strapped to her waist and pulled out her credit card. "It is now."

"I didn't realize you were already in Atlanta."

Amara evaded her gaze. "I was going to call you in a couple of days. I wanted to get the family obligation stuff over with first.

The birthday party is tonight, but I had to put in an appearance for a fundraiser the Hedin family supports."

The mention of Erik's family irritated Cara. The young man bringing Amara's items saved her from making a rude comment.

"I don't want to talk about them."

"You know I didn't set you up, right?" Amara was earnest.

"I believe you."

There was more Cara wanted to say, but she wasn't ready to hear Amara's excuses. She had some sympathy for her. Amara's parents, like David Bloom, expected loyalty, and rarely did they consider if what they asked was something their offspring wanted to do.

Cara was sure the Nkosi family would have still forced Amara to be friendly with Erik, regardless of her feelings. Last night, Amara had vocally been on her side. That was something.

"So, the roommate? He's even better looking in person." Amara put her hand to her chest and pretended to swoon. "The way he looked when he swooped in to rescue you. So hot!"

"Wes did *not* come to my rescue. I handled Erik on my own." Cara had held her ground with Erik before Wes had arrived. But she wouldn't deny she'd turned to him for comfort after. A pang stabbed her chest.

And then today he'd completely and embarrassingly rejected her.

"Wes. I like it." Amara licked icing off her lips suggestively, and Cara forced a smile.

"You are incorrigible. It's not like that." No matter how much Cara wished it were. "He thinks he's in love with Melody, the woman I originally rented from."

"*Thinks* he is?"

Cara stirred in her seat. Forty-eight hours earlier, she would have told Amara about her doubts. After last night and Wes's behavior earlier, she didn't want to share that she was developing feelings for him.

"I misspoke. He's in love with her. She will be back soon, and they are going to start their lives together."

Amara looked doubtful. "The expression on his face last night was not a 'this is my platonic roommate' look. It was a 'she's mine, back off before I disembowel you look.' Hard to believe he'd do that if he were in love with someone else."

"He's not interested," Cara said flatly. "We're roommates."

"So? Get a new place. You don't even know Melody. You don't owe her anything. This doesn't seem like a difficult problem to solve."

A tiny spurt of hope flared before reality quickly extinguished it. "I don't owe her anything. However, Wes and I have become close. I can't do that to him."

Even if Cara managed to seduce him into a one-night stand, it would ruin everything between them. She knew he believed he was in love—he'd told her his plan, what he wanted for his future. Now, knowing the truth about how chaotic his childhood had been, Cara understood his obsessive need for a secure home life. She had her doubts Melody felt the same way, but Wes knew the woman better than Cara.

His body might be willing, but she knew Wes would regret it.

Amara watched her carefully, and Cara lifted her coffee to block the perusal. They had shared a room for too many years. Amara knew her better than anyone. She knew her friend would see the truth, maybe more than Cara was willing to admit to herself.

Amara's lips parted, and her face became sympathetic. Cara blinked away the tears that suddenly sprang to her eyes and bit the inside of her cheek to stop them in their tracks.

"Plenty of hot men out there. It would be convenient to have him in the same house, but not if you'd have to move." Amara's teasing smile dissolved, her face morphing into anger.

"Hello, ladies." Erik and Colin approached their table from the doorway. Cara's stomach fell. She didn't want to do this again.

Amara glared at Erik. "What are you doing here?"

Erik held his hands up. "I wanted a coffee."

"There wasn't a single coffee place closer to the hotel? Bullshit!"

Cara pushed her chair back. She had to get out of there.

"You owe me an apology." Erik's eyes were cold. He stepped closer to Cara's chair, preventing her from getting up without bumping into him.

"You are deranged." Cara refused to let him intimidate her.

"You blamed me for leaking your disgusting pictures, and I had nothing to do with it." He sneered. "I put up with your body because it kept my parents' happy, but do you think I wanted the rest of the world to think you were all I could get?"

Fury surged through Cara, and she stood abruptly, knocking the chair backwards. Colin caught it before it hit the people behind them. Evidently, Erik wasn't done.

"Did you never wonder where they came from? How the person who gave them to the tabloid got them in the first place? Or are you so desperate and send out so many nudes you don't remember all of them?"

His voice was intentionally loud, and Cara saw that several people around them had stopped what they were doing to watch the argument. One person was even pointing a phone at them, obviously hoping for a viral video.

"You are such a piece of shit, Erik. Leave her alone." Amara had never shied away from an audience.

Cara stepped around Erik and headed for the door, leaving Erik and Amara to trade increasingly vulgar insults behind her. She was light-headed, and her fingers tingled.

The café was located on the corner of two busy streets, so Cara was forced to take several steps around the corner before she was out of sight of the café's plate-glass windows. She leaned back against the rough brick wall, trying to catch her breath.

"Sorry about that." Colin's voice made her jump. "I should

have known you'd be here. Erik insisted we come, even though it's twenty minutes away."

Cara tried to make sense of what he was saying. Not a coincidence? Only one other person knew where they were meeting. Betrayal slid over her in icy waves.

"Amara invited him?"

"What? No! Erik said he wanted local coffee and called the car."

"You just happened to end up here?"

Her sarcasm wasn't lost on Colin. He grimaced. "Erik kept checking social media. Amara always has her locations on." He shrugged. "Not difficult to guess who she is with, this far from the hotel. She doesn't have any other friends in Atlanta."

"Why can't he just leave me alone?" Cara cried. "Hasn't he done enough?" She didn't expect an answer. Colin had been Erik's sidekick for as long as she'd known him.

"You embarrassed him in front of his friends." Colin shrugged. "It's that simple. He has to win."

Their conversation was cut short as Amara chased Erik around the corner. "Erik don't!" she cried, panic in her face.

Erik stormed up to Cara. His nasty expression made her take a step back. "You were so quick to blame me for putting pictures of you on the internet! Your brother was relentless, and my family was furious with me! They took my credit cards and canceled the Bugatti I'd ordered." He leaned his face close to hers. "I didn't do it."

Cara was suddenly weary. "It doesn't matter anymore." She turned to walk to the parking lot.

"Ask yourself, Cara." He called after her. "Who took the pictures? Who else was there for your girls' strip-poker night? How would I even know about it?"

Cara froze.

She didn't have to ask. Amara looked green, guilt etched on her face.

It felt like someone had punched her in the stomach.

"Cara, I didn't. I never—"

Erik scoffed. "You had them on your phone, right? Who else had them?"

Cara felt ill. The coffee roiled in her throat and burned as it threatened to come back up.

She was vaguely aware of Amara pounding on Erik's chest while he laughed. "You took my phone! You son of a bitch!"

Cara's head whirled. The tingling that started inside the café intensified, spreading down her arms. It was too much. She needed to get home.

"Cara, let me explain! I swear I didn't give them to Erik!"

Cara barely recognized her own voice when she said, "I believe you. The question is why did you still have them? Why did you keep them all these years? I don't remember much of that night, but I remember we agreed to delete the pictures we all took. Why would you keep them unless you thought you might need them someday?"

Amara shook her head, a hand over her open mouth, tears spilling down her face.

"I don't know." Her voice shook, and the tears flowed faster. "I should have—"

"Stop." Cara put her hand up to stop her. "I can't talk to you."

Colin led her back to her car. "Are you okay to drive?"

"I'm fine."

He hesitated, looking back to the empty spot where Amara and Erik had been standing.

"I don't know this for sure." Colin fidgeted, the flush on his cheeks clashing with his ginger hair. Cara wished he would go away. She wasn't sure if she was going to cry or throw up. "I don't think Amara knew. About the pictures, I mean. I don't think she would do that to you."

Cara looked at Colin's kind eyes. She could never understand why he stuck by Erik.

"Goodbye, Colin." She pulled the door shut and merged with the heavy Atlanta traffic. Cara felt numb as she navigated her way back to the house. Putting her car in park, she stared at the front door. Wes's truck was in the driveway.

Half of her wanted to go inside and tell him what happened.

He was her best friend.

Cara didn't doubt that even after this morning, he would put his arms around her until she felt better. But she was tired of looking pathetic in front of him. She rested her folded arms on the steering wheel. "I'm not going to cry. I'm done crying over this."

Her phone had rung constantly since she got in the car. Amara's name flashing over and over across the screen. Maybe when she had time to think logically, she would realize Amara hadn't intentionally hurt her, but for now—she slid her finger across her phone, and it went silent.

CHAPTER TWENTY-EIGHT

Wes was waiting for a new infiltration device he was developing to finish when Cara called out from the door of her bedroom. He hadn't seen her except in passing since the towel run-in, though he wasn't sure which of them was better at playing the avoidance game.

"Don't worry about me for dinner. I'm going out."

He looked up. They hadn't had dinner together last night either. He frowned, disappointment spreading, before he shook himself.

That's exactly the problem. We've fallen into the habit of having dinner together every night and watching an episode of Star Trek. We aren't dating. That's why the lines have blurred.

Satisfied with his excuses, he settled his headphones on his ears and restarted the playlist he preferred when checking code. His fingers had just begun to type when an irritating thought intruded. His fingers slowed and then stopped. He pushed his headphones off.

She's going out? Like on a date? Not that I care, or have any right to—why assume it's a date? Probably a girls' night out.

None of your business, Wes, he told himself, but he couldn't stop thinking about it.

He glared at the monitor as he deleted another mistake. He looked at her door. Wes could hear faint music, but she hadn't reappeared.

The doorbell rang an hour later. Wes waited a minute or two, assuming Cara would come out to greet whomever it was she was going out with. But her door remained shut, and the bell rang again.

Shoving back his chair, he strode to the door. She knew he was working; couldn't she at least get the door for her friends?

The man in the doorway was older than Wes by several years —too old for Cara. He looked like he belonged in a 1980s country club brochure. From his brown curls cut close to the pleated khaki pants and boat shoes, he looked like a caricature.

Wes had a moment of satisfaction when it became clear he was as much of a surprise to this guy as her date was to him. By the frown gathering on the guy's face, it wasn't a happy one.

Wes took a last look at the man's fleece vest, and his mood suddenly improved. He couldn't picture Cara being with someone like that. Wes took a step back in invitation.

"Are you here for Cara?" he asked with a smile.

The man shot Wes a suspicious look before he schooled his thoughts into a bland expression. "I'm Chris Keller."

"I'll let her know you're here. Come on in." Wes walked to the table and closed his laptop before walking over and rapping on Cara's door. Chris stood awkwardly just inside, giving the room a once over.

"Cara. Your friend's here," he said through the door.

The door opened inward, creating a draft that fluttered her blonde hair back from her face, and all urge to smile evaporated. She looked beautiful.

"Wes, you're in the way."

Wes stepped back, feeling edgy. He watched as she sashayed over to the guy. Her purple top with poufy see-through sleeves, topped dark jeans tucked into high heeled boots that made her ass look...

"Chris!" Cara greeted the interloper with an air kiss on each cheek.

Wes scowled. How did she know this guy? Was she on that dating app? He told her they weren't safe!

"It's good to see you, Cara! You look gorgeous."

Cara reached for her purse sitting on the sofa, and Wes saw the jerk check her out when she bent over.

Wes clenched his jaw. She hadn't even looked back at him, just happily chirping away with Mr. no-chin. "Are you going to be late?"

Cara looked surprised by his sharp tone, but Wes's annoyance ratcheted up when she looked at Chris for an answer. "I think we are just going to dinner—"

Chris winked at her. "Unless we find something fun to do." He slid a sly smile in Wes's direction, and Wes narrowed his eyes at him. "Come on, we're going to be late for our reservation."

Wes simmered as he watched the headlights back out of the driveway.

He returned to the computer but found himself tapping on the table and not on the keyboard. He got up and paced into the kitchen, yanking open the refrigerator door. Stacked on the middle shelves were the meals Cara had made for their dinners that week. He scowled as he grabbed a beer.

Why shouldn't she date? He didn't have any claim to her. Unfortunately for him, the beer did nothing for the ache in his chest. Nor did the two that followed.

CHAPTER TWENTY-NINE

"Funny, Declan didn't mention you were living with a guy," Chris deadpanned when they were in his car. It smelled new, and Cara cuddled back into the soft leather. She could admit there were certain luxuries she *definitely* missed from her old life!

"Luke knows, but you're right. I never got a call from Dec or James, so he must be keeping my secret."

"Are you two…"

Cara burst out laughing. "No! Just friends."

"The look he gave me didn't say friends." Chris shot her a wry look as he stopped at an intersection.

"Really?" Cara hated that she sounded hopeful.

"I take it you didn't tell him who I was before I got there? When he opened the door, he looked like he wanted to punch me." Chris laughed.

Cara chewed her lip and looked out the window as Chris navigated through the congested streets of Atlanta. She wanted to believe Wes had been jealous, but he'd also made it crystal clear that he wouldn't be acting on any attraction between them. Cara mentally shook herself. She didn't want to spend the entire night brooding about Wes.

She had complained about not wanting a babysitter, but it was nice to see Chris. Cara hadn't seen him since her father's funeral. Chris pulled up to the valet stand, and after he handed off the keys, he gave her a pitying look.

Cara sighed. "You're going to tell Declan, aren't you?"

"He's been my friend for almost twenty years. I have to. It won't be as bad as you think. He knows you're an adult." Chris made a face making it clear he didn't believe his own words, and Cara huffed a laugh at his wishful thinking.

"Right, I'm sure he'll have no problem with it."

Cara tabled any conversation about Declan until their dishes arrived.

"Have you seen Declan recently?"

Chris took a bite of his swordfish and shook his head. "Not in months, now that I think about it," he said when he finished chewing. "I've been pretty busy with work myself."

"But you talk to him?"

Chris must have picked up on the worry in her voice, because he set his fork down and looked at her with a serious expression.

"Not as much as we used to. Why?"

Cara wouldn't normally share family business with someone, but as Chris said, he and Declan had been friends for what felt like forever, and his father, Dr. Keller, had been David Bloom's doctor for just as long.

"I'm worried that he's on this crusade, and he's not taking care of himself."

"What crusade?" Chris's brows drew together.

"He is still convinced that Courtney had something to do with Dad's death."

Chris shook his head. "That's crazy! I was there. He was really sick. My dad tried everything to help him…"

"I know." Cara tried to smile. "It sounds nuts, but now Declan has a new theory about what happened, and if you think about the changes to the will… maybe she forged it?" Her shoulders slumped. It sounded so melodramatic spoken out loud.

Chris's eyes widened, and he blew out a stream of air, leaning back in the chair. "I didn't realize Declan was still hung up on all that. I thought he accepted it wasn't possible."

"Why wasn't it possible?" Cara's lips turned down.

"I told your brothers—I'd assumed they'd told you. My father and I both witnessed the will signing. Your father was very weak, but adamant. We tried to talk him out of it, but he wouldn't hear it. You know how he was." Chris gave her a small smile. "I called Declan as soon as I left the house to give him a heads up. I thought he could call your dad, fix whatever the problem was, but we never connected. I honestly thought Mr. Bloom would change it back a few days later. There was no way of knowing he would die so quickly after."

"You didn't leave Declan a message?" Cara was incredulous.

He spread his hands wide. "In hindsight, I should have, but at the time, it wasn't something I wanted to leave on a voicemail. I feel terrible about what's happened to all of you. I know Declan was angry when the twins refused to contest the will with him— but they're lawyers. They knew it was a losing battle. There were no grounds to challenge it."

Cara's mouth fell open. "That's why they are all barely speaking now?"

Anger and resentment burned. They had never mentioned it to her, never asked her opinion—she was going to murder all of them!

Chris shrugged. "I don't know for sure, but Declan was furious they wouldn't side with him."

Cara forced herself to calm down and continue to make small talk. However, if the nervous looks Chris kept sending her way were any indication, she wasn't successful at hiding how furious she was.

"I'm sorry. I wouldn't have dropped a bomb like that on you if I'd known they hadn't told you."

"It's not your fault." Cara forced a smile. "I appreciate you telling me."

Cara sustained the conversation, only touching on the most trivial things for the rest of the meal, but was grateful when the check came, and she was on her way home.

CHAPTER THIRTY

"You have a package." Wes pointed behind him to the kitchen counter when Cara and her date returned. The second he heard the key in the lock, relief flooded him. The date had been a dud, and he chose to ignore why it mattered to him.

However, instead of leaving, the interloper followed Cara into the kitchen. She looked at the label on the brown box with surprise. "It's from Corinne!"

"Your mom?" Chris asked.

Wes bristled. He knew about her mom? How long had she been talking to this guy?

Cara retrieved a pair of scissors from the kitchen drawer and sliced through the tape. Despite himself, Wes turned to look. From the mass of bubble wrap and tissue paper, Cara pulled out a large snow globe with the word *Dublin,* emblazoned in red across the white base. It was the type of souvenir someone would pick up from a street kiosk.

"What in the world? Corinne bought that? Was she high?" Chris laughed.

Cara glared at him, but her face took on a worried expression.

"I don't think so. Though, I haven't talked to her in a while."

The man rested his hand on Cara's shoulder. Wes's body tensed and he got to his feet. "There's a note," he heard Chris say.

"Okay, this is weird!" Cara murmured, after her eyes had scanned down the paper.

"What does it say?" Chris leaned over her shoulder to read the message.

"She claims my father gave it to her when she saw him in Dublin." Her eyes found Wes's.

"When was he in Dublin? That had to have been years ago." Chris shook his head. "Is that it? Why is she sending it to you now?"

Cara looked at the card again and gasped. "She says there's a letter attached from him." Cara dropped the card, turned the snow globe upside down, and removed a tiny white envelope taped to the bottom.

Wes gave up pretending he wasn't interested and joined them at the counter, ignoring Chris's speculative look.

Cara pressed the envelope to her nose and inhaled deeply. When she pulled it away and offered it to Chris, her eyes were moist. "It still smells like his cologne."

Chris smiled sadly and then wrapped his arms around Cara, pulling her in for a hug. Wes's chest burned.

"What does the letter say?" Chris broke the embrace.

Wes was proud of himself when he didn't bury his fist in the smug smile Chris sent him.

Cara ran her fingers around the edge of the envelope. "I'll read it later, when I'm alone."

"Of course, it's private," Chris soothed.

Wes's jaw ached, and he worried for his teeth when the other man stroked her back. Cara pulled her lower lip between her teeth.

"Maybe I should get it over with?" Cara directed the question to Wes.

"What do you want to do?" For a moment their eyes met, and

Wes forgot Chris was in the room. Forgot they hadn't spoken in a day. Nothing mattered except an intense need to comfort her.

"If it were something bad, he wouldn't have sent a gift," he said gently.

Chris looked curiously at the two of them. "Why would it be something bad?"

Neither answered him. Cara gave a decisive nod. The paper had been folded several times to fit the envelope, but when it was finally flat, Cara read in silence. She turned the letter over to the blank side and then back again. A frown grew between her brows, and she thrust the letter at Wes, ignoring Chris's hand already extended.

"It doesn't make any sense."

Wes read the lines out loud.

My Sweet STAR. I know you're worried, and I'm sorry for the things I said the last time we spoke. I haven't been myself for quite a while, but things are clear now. You had so many questions about what was happening to me, and I had no answers. I have them now and entrust them to you. The Dublin globe has all that you need to solve my little puzzle. Bring it next time you come, but if something happens, know that I trust in you, little STAR, to discover the answer on your own.

All my love, Dad

"I don't get it," Chris said looking confused.

"It's dated last April." Wes held the paper up to show them.

Cara gave a little gasp, and Chris's mouth fell open.

"Three days before he died." Chris's frown grew deeper. "Your mom said she got this from him in *Dublin*? How is that possible? I saw him not long before that, and he was in no shape to travel."

Cara stiffened, but Chris seemed oblivious. He picked up the globe and turned it in several directions, inspecting it. "What answer was David talking about? I know my dad was worried about dementia."

If Wes hadn't been watching Cara so closely, he would have missed the angry flush start on Cara's chest.

"Your father thought Dad had dementia?"

"Hmm?" Chris had turned the globe upside down, shaking it gently.

"You said that, when you witnessed the will, he was clear-headed."

Wes's eyes widened. This man had witnessed the new will that had disinherited Cara and her brothers?

Chris's face fell, and he shot a quick look at Wes. "Maybe we should talk about this privately?"

Wes folded his arms over his chest. He had no intention of going anywhere.

"It's okay. Wes knows the whole sordid story."

Chris leveled an assessing look at him. Wes wasn't sure what the other man thought he saw, but Chris let out a heavy sigh.

"He seemed fine. My dad ordered a battery of mental faculty tests. We knew what an enormous change the new will was." He grimaced. "I hate to admit it now, but when I heard what the new terms were, part of me wished he *had* failed the mental exercises. I'm just surprised by this letter."

Cara laid her hand over his on the counter. "I'm sorry, Chris. This whole thing has me rattled, but I shouldn't take it out on you. The last time I saw my dad wasn't great, and I was worried…"

Chris's face cleared. "You had an argument with him?"

"Yeah. Not my finest hour," Cara said ruefully.

"That's why you didn't want to read the letter at first." Understanding broke across his face. "You thought because of the will change, he was still mad at you. He wasn't. That day at the house, your dad said nothing negative about any of you. We asked him over and over… We were trying to make sense of why he would change the will so drastically." Chris's smile was nostalgic. "*It's my business and mine alone*," he intoned in a gravelly voice.

Cara's expression was soft as she looked back up at Chris with warm violet eyes, and Wes had a fierce desire to shove the smaller man into the wall. Chris rubbed Cara's arms, but when he caught Wes's glare, he dropped them.

"I'm so sorry it turned out the way it did."

"I know. You've always been such a good friend to us."

Chris drummed his fingers on the counter, a worried expression taking over his face. "I don't want to worry you, Cara."

Then don't, Wes thought. But oblivious to Wes's thoughts, Chris continued. "What you told me tonight, about Declan still trying to prove it wasn't natural causes... Declan's an intelligent man. I never liked Courtney either, but I don't know that I can picture her as a killer. It's not... rational." Chris looked uncomfortable. "There have been stories recently... things he's been doing... Do you think he might need professional help?"

"No," Cara snapped. "He's suffering that's all." Chris looked like he wanted to argue the point, but Cara put a hand on his arm. "Do you mind if we call it a night? I'm exhausted."

"Of course." He gave her a smile, and when they reached the door, he leaned down and pressed a kiss against her cheek, pulling her into another hug. Wes felt his shoulders bunch again. "I'm in town another couple of weeks, so if you want to grab a bite, let me know. Also..." He glanced at Wes glowering in the kitchen. "Because I'm not interested in testing the whole 'shoot the messenger' thing, I've changed my mind. I won't mention to your brother that you're living with a guy you just met."

The door closed behind him, and Wes waited while Cara leaned her head back against the door.

"Did you tell him about your brother's latest theory? About the housekeeper and poison?"

Cara returned to the kitchen and picked up the letter again. "Chris and Declan have been friends since before college. But if Declan hasn't filled him in, it's not my place to tell him." She picked up the globe and held it close, staring into it, looking for any clue that would explain the letter.

"It's a terrible Bloom family trait. We don't trust anyone. Just family."

Cara was so fixated on the cityscape in the glass bowl, she failed to see Wes's expression. His lips parted slightly. "You told *me*."

She lifted her eyes to his, still cradling the globe in one hand. "I did."

"I'm not family," he pointed out.

What did he want her to say?

That she cared about him?

That she loved him?

Where did that thought come from?

He didn't want her to say those things.

Did he?

"No, you're not," she said, and then disappeared into her room, leaving Wes to stare after her.

What the hell did that mean?

CHAPTER THIRTY-ONE

THE NEXT MORNING, CARA TOOK HER COFFEE TO THE DECK AND watched the trees blow back and forth. Gray clouds scudded across the sky above her. The news forecast a severe thunderstorm for the day, and it suited Cara perfectly. Her robe fastened snugly around her, she stared out at the bleak landscape. She hadn't slept well.

"You told me."

"I did."

"I'm not family."

"No, you're not."

She took a sip of the scalding liquid, almost relishing the burn on her tongue, as she recalled the longing look on his face at her words. It was the closest she could come to telling him how she felt—in a way that wouldn't destroy their friendship—knowing he couldn't say it back.

She hadn't entrusted Chris, a man she'd known most of her life, with Declan's theory but hadn't hesitated to tell Wes. It simply felt right… natural. But it was also dangerous. Now, it was as if blinders had been pulled from her eyes, and she could finally be honest with herself about how she felt.

Even if there was nothing she could do about it.

She'd seen the wreckage of her parents' love affairs. They burned bright, but when they were over... Romantic love was fleeting, bolstered by hormones and endorphins that eventually faded. She valued her relationship with Wes too much to ever risk it on such a transitory thing.

She checked her phone. No text or email from Skye letting her know when production would resume. The first fat, cold raindrops hit her head, chasing her back inside. Wes hadn't come out of his room yet, and part of her worried he had seen too much in her words last night. Had it scared him off again?

Her phone buzzed in her hand, and she saw it was Declan.

Shit! Chris must have tattled after all.

"Good morning!" she said brightly.

"You lied to me." His words were clipped. "You said you were living with a model named Melody."

"I *am* living with Melody," Cara hedged. "Wes is staying here while he's looking for a house."

"His name is Wes Evans?"

Thanks, Luke. That meant a call from James was next. "Yeah."

"He works in cybersecurity?" Declan's voice was dark and low.

Cara took a sip of coffee. "He's a nice guy. I'm perfectly fine."

"Cara." Declan coughed. "Um… I need to tell you something."

She knew what he was going to say. "He told me."

"Told you what?" Declan's voice was a little too careful.

"That you hired him to erase those pictures of me last year."

There were several beats of silence. "He told you that?"

"See, nothing to worry about." Something clicked in her brain. "I take that back. You've got nothing to worry about with Wes. What you should be concerned about is I just learned you and the twins discussed legally challenging the will and said nothing to me."

"Don't change the subject. I have questions about this guy. It seems extremely coincidental that he would show up at the same house."

"The three of you didn't think I had a right to know? Patted me on the head and sent me off to Spain. Do you have any idea how hurt and pissed off I am?" She banged down her coffee mug.

"We didn't want you involved. If it had gone beyond that conversation, then of course we would have looped you in."

"*Looped me in?* I should be *part* of the loop. I'm your sister! And it *has* gone beyond that conversation. That much is clear, even though I have no idea what was said because I wasn't included," she said bitterly. "This is why you and the twins are fighting, isn't it?"

"That's oversimplifying—"

"Because you want to challenge the will, and they won't help?"

"Chris really filled you in," Declan drawled. "Fine. I was unhappy. I think they should have wanted to fight, but they thought it was a waste of time."

Cara knew her brother was trying to downplay his disappointment, but she also knew how important loyalty was to him. "You should have told me."

Declan grunted, but Cara left it, knowing arguing was a waste of energy. Declan rarely apologized.

"I might have some news on that front. Corinne is closing up her apartment, to prepare for her wedding in a couple of weeks, and she came across a gift Dad bought for me right before he died."

"How did she get it?" Declan asked.

"She ran into him in Dublin, and they spent the afternoon together."

"You never said they spent the afternoon together!"

"Declan, be quiet for a minute and let me finish my story!"

Declan grumbled but stayed quiet as she told him all she knew about the snow globe.

He was quiet for a moment and then said, "I think I might know what the Dublin connection is."

"What?"

"He kept a vault there at a private security company. Dublin has a few sites that offer these services. I'm not sure which one was his… Let me look into it. Andrew told me that Courtney has been after him about an alternative way to get into a secure vault. That must be the one. She has the paperwork that proves she inherited it, but she doesn't have the four-digit code necessary to access it. I'll call Mam and ask her if she knows about the visit. Hopefully, I'll turn up something that will help unravel his message. Why couldn't he spell things out?"

They spoke for a few more minutes, and Cara was glad that by the time they hung up Declan sounded hopeful.

Not long after that, Wes emerged from his room and poured the rest of the coffee into his Picard mug, taking it to the table. He glanced through the deck door at the trees twisting in the wind.

"We might lose power." He pulled his headphones on. "A lot of old trees in this area, and that wind is supposed to get worse. I need to get as much done as I can. Might want to charge your phone."

Cara got the message that he didn't want to talk and went to her room to get dressed for the day. When she returned to the main room, Wes was standing at the front door holding an enormous bouquet of red roses in a crystal vase, his face as stormy as the sky outside.

"Those are pretty," she said.

"They must be for you," He placed them on the table harder than necessary. Cara winced at the jolt to the delicate crystal. Despite his sour expression, Cara couldn't help the smile that spread across her face. She couldn't think of the last time she received flowers.

"Really? Who are they from?"

Wes plopped back in his kitchen chair, snatching up his head-phones. "How should I know?"

Cara picked up the flowers and carried them to the kitchen counter. The smile didn't budge. If she didn't know better, she would think he was jealous. "They're probably from Chris. He's sweet like that." Cara hid her smile when she caught his profile scowl. Why should she be the only one to suffer?

She said it to get under Wes's skin, but it was likely that the sender was Chris. It was possible it could be from her brothers, but that would make it a first. Particularly because it wasn't a holiday or her birthday. Cara pulled the rose stems apart, looking for an envelope. She frowned.

"That's weird."

"What?" Wes twisted in his chair to look at her.

"There's no card. You didn't see it, did you? Maybe it fell out?" But her quick survey of the floor revealed no envelope.

"Of course not. Why would I care who sends you flowers?" he grouched.

Cara rolled her lips in. She was enjoying this. "They must have forgotten it. I'll just call the florist. Who was it?" Wes looked at her blankly. "The uniform?" Wes shook his head again. "The logo on the van? The car?"

"They were on the front step. I opened the door to look at the weather, and they were sitting there."

"I'm surprised they'd leave them in this weather. They must not have been there long, or they'd have been shredded in this wind." Cara shrugged. "Well, whomever they're from, they're gorgeous."

And expensive, she thought. Other than her brothers and Chris, she couldn't think of anyone in her life that would send her flowers, particularly in a crystal vase. With that thought in mind, Cara sent off a rapid thank you text to each.

She was combining the ingredients for an egg white scramble when the response texts came.

CHRIS: I SHOULD HAVE THOUGHT OF THAT! HOW
DID YOUR ROOMMATE TAKE IT?

Cara didn't bother to answer.

JAMES: NOT ME. WHY IS LUKE SAYING YOU'RE
LIVING WITH A STRANGE MAN YOU FOUND ON THE
INTERNET?

Cara rolled her eyes.

LUKE: YOU'RE WELCOME. JK CAN'T TAKE THE
CREDIT.

"Huh," Cara said, as she divided the eggs between two plates. She set a plate and fork next to Wes's elbow, before picking up her plate and carrying it to the sofa. "None of them sent the bouquet."

Wes forked a bite into his mouth. "So, who is it? Did you match with someone on that dating app?"

Cara thought Wes sounded like he was trying to not choke on the breakfast. She considered teasing him, but said, "Nope. I haven't even talked to anyone on it. I honestly have no idea who could have sent them." A new thought popped into her head. "You didn't—"

A weird, pinched look passed over his face and was just as quickly gone. "No."

Cara narrowed her eyes at his bowed head. She picked up her fork and stabbed a clump of egg. Her pleasure at receiving the flowers had dimmed. It could be a mistake, she supposed, but she had been home all morning and should have heard the door. It's possible the delivery person knocked when she was on the deck, but that would have been extremely early.

"I talked to Declan earlier. Hang on." She retrieved the snow globe from her room and set it on the kitchen table between them. "I told him about getting this in the mail and the note attached. He thinks there might be some connection to a vault Dad had in Dublin. It's near where my mom said she ran into him." Cara explained about Courtney trying to access a vault.

"You think the four-digit code is hidden somewhere in the snow globe?" Wes mused.

"It's possible. We need a magnifying glass." Cara chewed her lip. She slowly rotated the snow globe, tipping it in different angles. "I don't see anything! I thought maybe there would be a number on the building or something," Cara said, frustrated.

"What about the letters in the word Dublin?"

"There's more than four." Cara picked up the globe and wound the mechanism until the song played.

"Twinkle Twinkle Little Star." Her face wrinkled. "What the hell does that have to do with Dublin? Watch while I wind it! Maybe something happens when the music plays."

"What did the note say again?" Wes asked, dutifully peering through the glass.

Cara frowned. "I'll get it." She walked from her room reading the message out loud, "*know that I trust in you, little STAR, to discover the answer on your own.* It would have been a tad more helpful if he'd given me a hint."

"A security device usually uses a numeric pad," Wes explained. "Could there be a correlation between the lyrics and numbers?"

"My dad didn't know anything about that kind of stuff."

"But, if it was a key to a vault, he might have tried or asked someone who knew."

"That's a good point. The answer has to be there. Why else would he have my mom send it to me?" She trailed her hands through her long hair, fidgeting with the ends.

A loud crash sounded somewhere in the distance. Seconds later, there was a loud click and the kitchen lights blinked out, followed by the beeping of Wes's battery backup in the other room. Even though it was morning, the house was dimly lit, darkened by the trees behind the house and heavily overcast sky.

"Great!" Wes groaned. "There goes the Wi-Fi."

"I'm sure the power will be back on in a few minutes."

Wes arched a brow at her. "All these trees and aboveground utilities in the middle of a storm? We'll be lucky if we get it back by tonight."

"Oh." She frowned.

"I need to wrap some things up before my battery dies." Wes turned back to his computer.

Cara finished breakfast and retreated to her bedroom. She tried to stream some shows on her phone, but the poor connection made her nuts, and she eventually gave up. After cleaning her room and reorganizing her makeup, she plopped on the bed desperate for some other way to keep busy.

Her phone pinged with an email notification. Skye had emailed the call sheet for the next few days with the message, "Looks like we are back in business." Cara wasn't sure if she should be relieved or worried that Courtney hadn't fired her yet.

She wandered back into the main room that had grown much darker as the storm intensified. Thunder crashed around the house. Cara carried the candles from the kitchen table to the coffee table and lit them.

"Want to play a game?" she asked hopefully, when he looked up. He shook his head, continuing to tap away at his keyboard. Cara made a face at the top of his head. She was bored!

Checking her watch, she saw it was close to lunchtime. Not particularly hungry, she pulled open the refrigerator door, and… storm days were like holidays, right? She pulled an unopened bottle of Chardonnay from the fridge. When she walked past with her full glass, Wes's hands lifted from the keyboard.

She held up a finger on one hand and took a large sip from the glass in the other. "Not a word. I just got an email from Skye. We are back to work tomorrow, so this could be my last day off for a while."

Wes set his headphones to the side. "So, the evil stepmother didn't fire you?"

Cara took another swig. "Not yet. My guess is she either wants to do it in person or find ways to torment me a little while longer. So, today… I day drink."

Wes looked from his computer to her and back again. He clicked a few keys, closed his laptop, and grabbed a few beers from the kitchen.

"I think I'll join you."

"Really? Wanna play cards?"

"Not really."

Cara ignored him and retrieved the pack from her room.

"Has anyone ever told you that you're bossy?" he asked dryly, when she returned and sat cross-legged facing him on the sofa.

"Yes." She shuffled the cards on the cushion between them. "What do you want to play?"

"Gin rummy?" Wes suggested.

"Okay, grandpa."

"I used to play it with my grandparents all the time. They weren't fans of popular television, and I found it preferable to Bible study."

Cara scrunched her face. "Sorry, that was an asshole thing to say."

He gave her a soft smile, and part of her melted. "It's okay. I'll even keep score."

"That's good," she sipped her wine. "Because I don't know how."

He laughed, and she grinned back at him. They played several hands, teasing each other whenever they won a hand. When Wes got up to grab a few more beers, he brought the bottle of wine, filling her glass.

"Such a gentleman," she joked, as he pretended to give a half-bow. Warmth spread through her body. She knew in part it was the wine, but it was also simply sitting there with Wes. There were so many complicated things going on in her life right now. It was nice to be somewhere where she felt so comfortable. Safe.

"What's that smile for?" Wes's voice caught her off guard, but instead of hiding it, her smile widened as she met his eyes.

"I'm happy."

He appeared to consider it, his smile growing until it reached his eyes. "Me, too."

Wes dealt the cards, and as casually as he might ask if she wanted more wine, he said, "Melody's getting married."

An emotion she couldn't identify flowed through her. She searched her mind for the right words, her mouth opening and closing, making her resemble a goldfish.

"That was pretty much my reaction." His lips twisted.

"I'm sorry, Wes. I know you'd hoped you could have a future with her."

He drew another card. "I'm not giving up. She's not married yet."

Cara bit the tip of her tongue. They were having a nice time, and she didn't want to have an argument—but he had to hear how insane he sounded.

"What are you expecting tomorrow?" Wes asked, changing the subject.

"Make you a deal? Let's have fun today. No Melody, work, or family drama talk." She stuck her hand out, and Wes clasped it in his warm palm, giving it a firm shake.

Thirty minutes later, Cara was slowly going out of her mind. She was tipsy, alcohol happily humming along her bloodstream, and thinking this was the best day she'd had in years. Who would have thought playing cards on a rainy afternoon in a tiny house could be this perfect? She smiled goofily. Her brain drifted. The only thing that would make it better would be if… her eyes roved over Wes.

He'd shrugged out of his hoodie earlier, and now only a thin white undershirt covered his chest, doing little to hide the muscles beneath. He sat with one leg bent in front of him and the other dangling off the end next to her thigh.

Cara had a sudden vision of crawling toward him. Pushing Wes back against the cushions... Her breath hitched, her pulse doubling its speed. Her gaze fell to his hands, where his long fingers deftly shuffled the cards. She suddenly, desperately, wanted to know what else he could do with those hands.

"Are you okay?" Wes asked when she failed to pick up her hand. "You're flushed."

"Must be the wine." She snatched up her cards and began arranging the matches, trying to hide the fact that her entire body throbbed with need.

When Cara finally lifted her eyes, Wes was staring intently at her. Her arousal must have been written across her face because his golden eyes darkened. Wes's gaze fell to her breasts, the skin around his mouth tightening. His chest rose and fell rapidly as his eyes returned to hers.

The air between them grew heavy and thick. The current of attraction pulsed along with the electrical storm still visible through the glass doors.

Later, she would take her pick of what to blame: the wine, the candlelight, or the intimacy of sitting in the near dark as a thunderstorm crashed around them. Cara set her cards down, rose to her knees, and settled back on her heels, watching him. The slight movement caused the candles to flicker, illuminating the ripple of his jaw where the muscles tensed, his eyes boring into hers.

Moving slowly, anticipation fizzing low in her belly, Cara rose on her knees and inched toward him, giving him more than enough time to stop her. The cards crinkled under her knees, and Wes shifted forward to meet her. She would have smiled, but it was taking all of her concentration not to throw herself against him.

Every fantasy she'd had, since moving in, streamed in front of her.

The urge to feel his skin under her hands, to finally taste him, was almost unbearable. Cara placed a hand on his firm shoulder, his skin scorching her through the thin material. She met his eyes.

Is he going to back away again?

Cara would have collapsed with relief when his large hands settled on her hips to pull her closer if the movement hadn't set her body humming. He tugged her against him, her knees on either side of his hips. Cara ran the back of her fingers from his temple, down over the scruff of his jaw and swiped slowly across his soft lips.

Wes growled, surging forward, and pulled her flush to him. His rigid length pressed hard against her, and she moaned. Wes lowered his head. From the tremors she felt rippling through his body, she expected the kiss to be fierce... wild. Instead, he stopped a breath away and licked his lips. Cara caught a slight whiff of beer, and what would normally be a turn-off was suddenly sexy as hell.

Agonizingly slow, Wes slicked his lips back and forth across hers, until he pulled her lower lip into his mouth sucking it between his teeth, before releasing it with a groan. He angled his head, deepening the kiss, his hand tangled in the back of her hair holding her still as his tongue stroked inside to find hers.

Cara thought she might be having a heart attack.

Her pulse thundered in her ears running straight through her body until it was centered between her legs. Her breasts tingled as she tried to get even closer, rubbing against the sculpted planes of his chest. Cara scratched her nails at the nape of Wes's neck, slipping her fingers through the waves of silky hair and pressing her full weight against his erection, desperately seeking the pressure she craved.

Wes trailed kisses from her mouth to the shell of her ear, sending shivers down her spine. His nose nuzzled under her jaw, inhaling deeply.

"I'm never going to smell honeysuckle the same again," he

muttered, sounding so aggrieved Cara chuckled. "It's not funny." He pulled his head back to give her a wolfish grin. "It's one thing to get a sudden hard-on when you are a teenager, not so much for a thirty-year-old man."

"That's a shame," Cara breathed, rolling against him. Wes sucked in a harsh breath and closed his eyes as she repeated the motion.

His mouth was back on her neck, sucking at her tender skin. Wes recaptured her lips—gone were the slow, drugging kisses. In their place fierce demand, his mouth moving over hers as if he couldn't get enough of her. Hungry. Impatient. One hand slid from her hair to cup her face, the other stroked her back to the base of her spine, and then a few inches lower under the waistband of her leggings. Cara ran her fingertips down his chest and grasped the hem of his T-shirt, pulling it free to slide her hands underneath.

She splayed her hands over his ribs, Wes's heart thumped wildly under her thumbs. His hands fell, his fingers digging into her hips as she moved against him. Tearing his mouth from hers, he groaned low in his throat.

Needing to feel his skin, Cara tugged at his shirt, hauling it over his head. She leaned back admiring the ridges of his stomach. Her nails had just begun to trace the fascinating line of hair lower when Wes yanked her forward, crushing her breasts against him and trapping her hands. "Cara." The sound was more plea than a name.

Her heart stuttered.

"I want you." His eyes flared at her stark words.

Cara pulled her hands free from where they were trapped between their heated bodies. She slowed her movements on his lap, and in one fluid motion, her own shirt was gone, only her thin, cotton bra between them.

His lips parted slightly as he ran his fingertips from her collarbone to the valley between her breasts and back. He seemed mesmerized by the action, almost as though he were trying to memorize the texture of her skin.

Wes bowed his head to drag open-mouthed kisses across the top of one creamy swell.

"Wes!" Cara cried.

He lifted his heavy-lidded eyes to watch her reaction as he dipped beneath the fabric. Pinching and rolling the tight buds between his fingers. Cara's head fell back with a whimper.

Wes's mouth soon replaced his fingers, sucking hard at her nipple through the cloth, as his hands molded the muscles in her back. Cara moved urgently, her breath coming in short gasps. Rising and falling over him as she reached a fever-pitch.

Something pounded at the door, and through the haze of lust, they both froze.

Wes drew back, his eyes glazed.

The pounding came again, followed by "Atlanta Police Department! Is anyone home?"

Cara climbed off Wes's lap and grabbed for her shirt.

"Coming!" he called to the door.

"Or not," Cara muttered. She expected Wes to laugh at her joke, but he stood staring at her with his shirt in his hand. Her stomach fell to her feet.

Wes strode past her and opened the door to a uniformed police officer.

"Power lines are down at the intersection." He pointed up the road. "Georgia Power is working on getting it clear, but we're asking residents to stay in their homes until we resolve the situation."

Wes thanked the officer and then closed the door, leaving them alone. The fire that had burned between them now felt like ice. Wes avoided her eyes, and she could feel tears building, clogging her throat.

He shoved his hand through his hair. "Cara..."

"It doesn't have to be a thing, Wes." Cara gathered the cards scattered on the floor. She didn't have to ask what he was thinking. It was all over his face. "We got carried away."

"We did." His hand ruffled his hair.

She plastered a fake smile on her face. "Great, we agree."

"It can't happen again." His eyes were determined, and Cara's temper sparked. She hadn't been alone in what had happened. He had been more than a willing participant. "I have plans—"

"Oh, yes. The infamous plans," she mocked. "Plans that involve you living happily ever after with someone you've never been in a relationship with, and who is currently engaged to be married! The woman who told me you were 'like a brother.' Sex is fun, Wes! Really, really fun. You should try it sometime, instead of holding out for some fairy tale that will never happen."

Wes's face turned stony, and his hands fisted at his side. "You can't possibly understand. At least I have goals for my life, dreams of a family. Your family is a giant, dysfunctional mess, which has somehow convinced you love is a weakness, a weapon to be used. You don't even see how fucked up it is! You had the benefit of two women who worked to create a semblance of normalcy for you, despite your father—who frankly sounds like a selfish asshole—and you're convinced it was a great childhood. Instead of deciding you want something better for yourself, you've doubled down on this idea that falling in love and staying in love is a fantasy." The veins in Wes's neck bulged.

"At least I know who everyone is in my world! I don't think you know Melody at all!"

Wes stared at her and then spun on his heel, slamming his bedroom door.

Cara wrapped her arms around herself, trying not to cry. She'd been right.

Sex ruined everything.

CHAPTER THIRTY-TWO

The next day, the weather and roads were clear, and Cara left early for work. It surprised her, a short time after arriving, to hear her name called over the radio. Usually, if the director needed makeup, they called for 'Skye' or 'Makeup.'

"This is Cara, over."

"Go to channel three, please."

Cara raised her eyebrows at Skye but adjusted her radio to the requested channel.

"There's a delivery for you at production reception?" The voice was disapproving. "You need to come and get it."

"I'll be right there." The two women exchanged a confused look. "What should I do? Am I going to be in trouble? I didn't order anything."

"I'm good here if you hurry. We probably have another ten or fifteen minutes until our first application. Take the cart," Skye said, after consulting her clipboard. "But hurry."

Parking under the portico, Cara tried to look confident as she entered the building. She recognized one of the runners, Tanner, standing next to a gigantic bouquet on a low table. Her stomach knotted, a feeling of dread taking over.

"I know you're new. That's why I went to the other channel, but it's not cool to get personal deliveries. Tell whoever it is not to do it again."

"Sorry, I'll take care of it."

Cara carried the flowers, red roses again, to the cart. She sat still, staring at the crystal vase. She glimpsed a bit of white buried in the stems and let out an exhalation of relief. Thank God!

"Those are pretty."

Cara was happy her groan was silent. "They are." She didn't have a specific problem with her stepbrother, Trey, but she heard Declan's voice in her head, reminding her to stay away from the entire family.

Trey shoved his hands in his pockets and turned his head to look back at the building's front door. Cara wanted to back out, but the way he was hovering made her feel like he was waiting to say something.

"I better get back to the trailer," she said.

His eyes were on the ground, and he had such an unhappy expression on his face she felt a little sorry for him. His life with Courtney and Matt couldn't be easy. They weren't that many years apart but he seemed so much younger. How old was he? Twenty-two? Twenty-three?

"Cara," he started, and then stopped again, and Cara fought the urge to tell him to spit out whatever it was. "I'm sorry about the other day. With my mom and Matt, I mean. I know you have every reason to resent us because…" He trailed off and Cara grit her teeth. He took a deep breath. "But I'm going to be around a lot. Matt, too. And I'd like to be cordial. We were family for a while."

Cara considered him for a moment. Wouldn't it be easier if at least two of them could get along? She would still stay away from Courtney and Matt as long as she had a job, but she doubted Trey had anything to do with the displacement of her brother from Bloom Communications.

Cara's smile was guarded. "I'd like that. What do you do here?"

Trey made a face. "I'm supposed to be working in postproduction." Her confusion must have shown. "I wouldn't normally be on the lot, but my mom thinks I should be a presence on set. She thinks it will be good for me to be around people." He gave a tiny shrug. "And she said she wants me to monitor things when Matt can't be here. You know how she is."

Unfortunately, Cara did. "When Matt's not here? Shouldn't he be busy running my father's company?"

Trey flushed, and Cara instantly regretted her sharp tone.

"They've hired someone to help him out, so he'll be back and forth." Trey's eyes were on the ground again.

"Never mind," Cara said.

She shouldn't be surprised that Matt had already grown tired of playing CEO. Of all the things Matt was, stupid wasn't one of them. He had to have realized he had no idea what he was doing. All he had cared about, like his mother, was the money and prestige.

Cara's radio crackled again, and she recognized Skye's voice asking for her ETA. "I've got to go, but I guess I'll see you around."

"Enjoy your flowers."

Cara pushed the pedal down and raced to her car, sticking the flowers in the passenger seat. It was only when she screeched to a stop at the trailer that she realized she'd left the card with the flowers.

"Sorry," she muttered to Skye. But there was no time for further discussion because the principals arrived to have their makeup done.

The main scene being shot today was a fight scene between Chandler's character and some extras in a bar. Poor 'Bob' appeared to be coping with his PTSD from the war by drinking and brawling. The script wasn't bad, and the acting was good for the most part. Lia in particular shone. But Cara wasn't interested in the movie itself.

She was excited because Skye said Cara could help her feather out the edges of fake wounds. They would have a busy day adjusting the makeup as the scene progressed from pre-fight to the immediate aftermath.

Cara was grateful. If she stayed busy, she wouldn't have time to dwell on what happened the day before—like she had all night. She had alternated between her temperature skyrocketing, as she relived Wes's touch, and the cold pain in her chest, when she thought about the hateful things they had said.

It wasn't until after everyone else left the trailer, and she was cleaning their brushes that she had an opportunity to talk to Skye. If Trey and Matt were going to be on the lot, inevitably, she would run into them with her coworkers.

"Sorry it took me so long to get back. I got stopped."

Skye didn't look up from where she was putting her makeup away in the precise order she liked. "It's okay. You got back in time."

Cara wasn't sure how to start the conversation, so she blurted out, "Remember when the new buyers came on the soundstage a few days ago?"

Skye stopped what she was doing and leaned against the wall, all ears. "Of course! You said you'd explain, but then we had all those days off, and then there was the drama at the hotel."

Cara winced. This was not a good look for her.

"I swear, recent events not included, I live a really boring life."

"Uh-huh."

"I'm serious! I have a little bit of family stuff going on, but that's all it is. And the other night was just my ass of an ex-boyfriend. He doesn't even live in Atlanta."

"Hang on. Back up. That really was your family? The new buyers?"

Cara made a sour face.

"Then why the hell are you working as an assistant? With that kind of money, you could do whatever you want here! Hell, Brian would probably let you *be* in the movie. This whole industry is about who you know." Skye tried to hide the bitterness in her voice.

"That's not how I want to live my life." The anymore part, she added silently.

"You're nuts. I'd take advantage in a heartbeat."

"Even if I wanted to, it's not an option for me. The money is my stepmother's not mine, and as you saw, we're not exactly on friendly terms."

"Stepmother?" Skye's eyes widened. "She's so young! I thought you were joking the other day."

"Yeah."

"But—"

"I really don't want to get into it. Suffice to say, it's best I keep my distance. Apparently, her sons will be on the lot, though. So, in case Matt says something ugly, I just wanted you to understand where it was coming from."

"Fair enough. He won't be the only douchebag here. It's a movie studio. I'm pretty sure the electricity is run off of over-inflated egos."

After Cara finished cleaning the trailer, she and Skye collected Jerrod from wardrobe, and they walked over to craft services to grab a snack.

"So, what was your delivery?" Jerrod asked as he pulled apart the cellophane on his honeybun.

"Oh, yeah! What was it?" Skye asked.

"Flowers."

She rolled her eyes when Jerrod and Skye chorused, "OOOO!"

"Have you been holding out on us? Are you dating someone? Do tell!" Jerrod cupped his hand to his ear.

"It's Wes, right? I knew something was going on with you two! That sexual tension… chef's kiss." Skye kissed her fingertips.

"No!" Cara exclaimed, but her face heated as a vision of Wes's eyes heavy with want, just before his lips descended on her breasts, appeared in front of her.

"Says the woman, a gorgeous shade of pink," Jerrod said around a mouthful of pastry.

"Definitely not," she insisted.

"So, who were they from then?" Jerrod asked.

She shrugged, "I'm not sure. I was late getting back, and I forgot to look at the card."

Her friends exchanged a look. It was true. Trey had distracted her, and then Skye called over the radio.

"Well, where are they now?"

"In my car."

Jerrod looked scandalized. "They'll die! Go get them. I'll keep them with me until the end of the day. No one is sending me roses. I'd at least appreciate them." He sniffed.

As she took the cart to her car again, Cara told herself that she was only doing it to appease her friends—who she essentially worked for—but part of her had allowed the idea that maybe Wes *had* sent them to infiltrate her brain. It would be a joke, of course, because of the anonymous flowers yesterday. But after yesterday…

Butterflies took flight in her stomach. *No!* She mentally swatted them down.

After unlocking her car door, she pulled the flowers out and set them on the golf cart's seat. They were identical to the ones she had received the day before, down to the same style crystal vase. However, this bouquet had a simple, white envelope stuffed into it with her first name typed across the front. Maybe whoever sent it yesterday realized they'd forgotten a message, and this was a do over. The white card inside had a simple message typed across it:

My darling, I can't wait.

Wait for what? She turned the card over, looking for any sign of who had sent it. But there was nothing to identify, not even the florist it came from.

When she reached the wardrobe warehouse, she put the heavy vase on Jerrod's desk next to his scissors and pins.

"Damn!" Jerrod goggled at the large arrangement. "You must have been a *very* good girl."

He was teasing, and normally it wouldn't have bothered Cara, but something about the situation put on her on edge. The arrangement was extravagant, clearly expensive. Not the kind of thing you send someone anonymously—twice.

"So, who sent it?"

Cara handed Skye the card. She watched as her friend read the brief note and frowned. "That's it?" Cara nodded.

Jerrod read the note over Skye's shoulder, and then put his nose in the blooms, taking an appreciative inhale. "You must have some idea. These aren't grocery store roses. Smell them."

Cara kept her distance. "I'm clueless. I haven't been on a date in months and 'darling?' No one calls me that."

"Did you ask Wes?"

"It's not him," Cara said flatly.

"Still."

Cara hesitated. She didn't want to ask Wes. For some reason, it felt embarrassing to tell him she had received a second unsigned bouquet.

"Just call the guard gate. The florist had to have signed in. Then you can find out who paid for them."

Cara brightened. That was a great idea! But, after she got off the phone with the security guard, she was even more unsettled. The knot in her stomach felt like it was made of lead.

"He said it was an unmarked sedan. Nothing special about the delivery guy. The guard called a runner to take it because the driver didn't want to come on the property."

"Ah, the mystery deepens!" Jerrod looked delighted.

For the rest of the day, her friends teased her about the secret admirer. Cara smiled along, but she was frightened. It was too similar to what had happened before. Cara went through a mental catalog of all the people she had encountered recently, but no one stood out.

It was when she was sitting in traffic that the truth finally dawned on her. She had avoided Amara's phone calls. This was her friend's way of getting Cara's attention.

Cara tapped her fingers against the steering wheel. Now that she'd cooled off, she knew in her heart Amara hadn't been the one to send the pictures to the tabloids, but Cara was still pissed that she'd kept the photos.

I'll call her tonight, Cara thought, when she pulled into the driveway. There was no sign of Wes's truck, and her emotions swung between disappointment and relief.

She was glad she'd given the flowers to Jerrod. He loved them, and Cara hadn't been lying when she said she had nowhere to put them. The other bouquet, sitting on the dresser, already dominated her small bedroom. If whoever sent them didn't bother to tell her who they were, she didn't feel obligated to keep them.

A sticky note from Wes was stuck to the fridge letting her know he'd be out for dinner. She crumpled it and threw it into the trash with more force than necessary. Cara peered at her meal prep containers, closed the refrigerator, and instead stuck a bag of popcorn in the microwave. She leaned back against the kitchen counter watching it revolve, pulled her phone from her purse, and pressed the button to call Amara.

It rang several times, and just as Cara planned a voice mail message in her mind, Amara picked up but didn't say anything. Cara counted to ten and then laughed. "Our friendship would be a lot easier if we both weren't so stubborn."

"Speak for yourself." But there was no heat behind it. "I'm still really pissed at you. I can't believe you thought I had sent those pictures of you."

Cara's irritation rose. "You may not have sent them, but as far as I know, you're the only one who had the pictures on their phone. Erik said as much—I wonder if the idiot realizes it proves it was him who sent them to the tabloid. Not that I didn't already know, but it's proof."

"Asshole." Amara was quiet for a second. "Trust me, if I had any say in it, I wouldn't be within twenty feet of him. My parents have made it clear that they want pictures of us together to help their image. Positive marketing for their business deal. It's stupid. Nobody cares if Erik and I are friends, but I have to do what they ask."

Cara didn't respond. She was familiar with what it felt like to have a parent control your life because they also controlled the purse strings. But Amara chose to stay. She *could* break away. Almost as if her friend read her mind, she said. "Not all of us are cut out to work."

"I think you'd surprise yourself. I won't lie and say it's easy because it's not. Worrying about bills that are less than we used to spend on a hat... And, I have my brothers to fall back on if I get in real trouble. I've met some really talented, incredible people who only know me as Cara, the makeup girl. It's nice."

"Maybe." Amara wasn't convinced.

"The roses were a nice touch, by the way. Not to mention an effective one. Though I have to admit you were starting to freak me out a little, leaving the notes unsigned."

"What roses?"

"The flowers you sent to my house and to my work today."

"I don't even know where you live—which is insane. All I know about your job is the movie you're working on."

"You didn't send me flowers?" Cara's brows drew down.

"I just said that. Who sent you flowers? I thought you said you weren't dating."

"I'm not. That's what's so weird. They are two huge, expensive arrangements of red roses. You don't think Erik—"

Amara burst out laughing. "Erik never sent you roses when you were together. Trust me, the way he feels about you now, it's definitely not him. Why don't you call the florist?"

"I don't even know that much."

"Huh. I'm sure whoever it is will let you know. They are going to want credit."

"Good point! What are you doing tonight?"

"We're going to some club in Midtown." She hesitated. "Do you want to come?"

"No, thanks," Cara responded dryly. "Even if I wanted to spend time around Erik, I have an early call tomorrow. Call me before you leave town, okay?"

"Cara, we're all good, right?"

Things would never be exactly the same between them again. Too much had changed, but she still cared about Amara and wanted her in her life.

"All good. Have fun, be safe."

Before going to bed, Cara changed the water and allowed herself to take pleasure in the gift. Amara was right. Whoever sent her the flowers would reveal themselves. There was no logical reason for her to be so paranoid about them. Cara set the alarm clock for her early call but just as she began to drift off, she remembered the unsigned Valentine's card and the gift card inside. She typed out a rapid text to Anne, apologizing for the late thank you, and then pulled her covers up.

The first phone calls began three hours later.

Roused out of dead sleep, Cara fumbled for the phone, her "hello" groggy, but no one spoke, and she hung up. The next call came two hours later. Cara could tell someone was on the line because she heard rustling and quiet breathing.

"Stop calling me!" she hissed before ending the call. When the phone rang for a third time, Cara silenced it and powered her phone off.

Please don't let this be happening again!

CHAPTER THIRTY-THREE

Wes was trying to decide if he should go into Cara's room to wake her up. He was up earlier than usual, after a far too graphic dream about his roommate, and he heard her hit snooze three times on her 5:30 alarm.

However, Wes knew Cara slept in one of those cute, little tank top and shorts combos, and after what happened between them, he didn't trust his control if he saw her like that—warm and tousled in her bed. On the other hand, Wes could just open the door and yell something. Cara would love that. He smirked, imagining her outrage.

The decision was taken out of his hands when he heard the sound of her shower come on. She must have been quick because less than five minutes later Cara was opening her bedroom door, her wet hair up in a bun, as she rushed to the coffeepot and filled her travel mug.

"You are a lifesaver." She looked at the liquid with such longing his body twitched.

He made a humming noise. "I've heard that before. What are you looking for?"

Cara was frantically patting her pockets and scanning all the surfaces she could see. "Dang it! I have a seven o'clock call and traffic is going to be a nightmare." She began pawing through her purse. "Where is my phone?"

Wes watched her with amusement. "Do you want me to call it?"

"Yeah, thanks." Cara started to smile at him. He saw the moment she remembered, and her gaze skittered away. She planted her hands on her hips and squinted as if it would help her hear her ringtone. Wes laughed. She had no idea how ridiculously cute she looked.

"Shhhh! I'm trying to listen."

Wes pulled the phone away from his ear. "I got your voice mail. Could your battery be dead?"

Cara's face cleared. "That's right!" She disappeared into her bedroom and reemerged, wiggling her phone. "It had fallen under the bed. I forgot I shut it off after the calls."

"What calls?"

"I can't believe I overslept," she said, gathering her things again.

Wes frowned. "Who was it?"

"Hmmm?" Cara ignored him. She grabbed her purse and headed for the door, reaching for her keys where they hung on the wall. She looked at her phone and thumbed the screen. Her eyebrows drew together, her face clouding.

His instincts flared. "Is something wrong?"

Cara jumped, dropping the travel mug. The top popped off, splattering the hot liquid over her clothing.

"Damn it!" Cara tipped her head back with her eyes closed, muttering something like, "Are you freaking kidding me?"

"I'll clean it up. Go get changed."

Wes could tell her pride wanted her to argue, but she was already running late. Throwing her phone and purse on the sofa, she sprinted for her bedroom. Wasting no time, Wes grabbed her phone, thankfully still unlocked, and pulled up the call log.

Something had scared her. As quickly as he could, he took screenshots of the call logs from the night before and sent them to himself before deleting the pictures on her phone. Wes was just putting the phone back when he hesitated. He snuck a look at the still closed door and took a risk. He pulled up Amara's call information and memorized the number before returning it to the home screen and putting it back with her purse.

He should feel guilty about invading her privacy, but he hadn't liked the look on her face. It wasn't annoyance, or even anger. It was fear.

Wes grabbed the travel mug she dropped and had just begun transferring his coffee to it when she came out again. He handed it to her wordlessly and grabbed a dish towel to soak up the spilled coffee.

Her lips pressed together. "Thanks," she said, before stepping around the mess and out the door.

Wes finished mopping up the spill, tossing the rag into the laundry. He added Amara's number to his contact list. In case of emergency, he rationalized. Then, he pulled up the photos he'd taken.

He stared at them for a moment, not sure what he was seeing. She had thirty-five missed calls. Pouring what was left of the coffee, he studied the numbers. He had expected that the hang-ups would have an 888-prefix, showing they were a call center, and someone had gotten the time zones messed up, but he was wrong.

There were some repeat digits, but after the first three calls, no other phone number appeared more than once. As the hours passed, the original number had called back several times.

Wes's face darkened. It could be a prank, but someone had gone to the trouble of using a phone rotator. Why had they gone back to the number she answered?

Because Cara *had* answered?

Wes opened his computer, intending to trace the phone

numbers. He didn't bother with most of the numbers. He recognized the sequence of the numbers as the product of a robocaller. However, the first phone number that had called didn't match the sequence of the others.

Anyone can reverse search a phone number. Wes wasn't going to some extreme length, he told himself. He was just saving Cara some time because he was sure she would do it herself when she realized how many times the person had called. His excuse wouldn't hold up to any sort of scrutiny, but it was enough for him.

In less than a minute, he had it entered and the result back–"Unavailable cell user." Wes sat back, folding his arms across his chest. It would be easy to get into the carrier's server. Less than an hour. He leaned forward, his fingers hovering over the keyboard, itching to type the commands that would allow him to hack into their accounts.

Wes's jaw clenched.

He was 99% certain he could be in, get the account holder's name that matched the number, and be out before they picked up he was in their system. But, there was that 1% chance that they got his IP, and that would most definitely violate his deal with the government. Wes forced his hands to unclasp, rolled his neck, and then deliberately closed the computer.

So, someone had prank-called Cara a bunch of times? It wasn't a big deal. It's not like they had threatened her, he assured himself. It was probably some twelve-year-old at a sleepover. They kept calling her back because she'd answered. Not worth going back to prison for. Regardless of what his brain said, Wes couldn't shake the bad feeling he had about the situation.

CHAPTER THIRTY-FOUR

CARA WAS ON EDGE ALL DAY. EVEN AFTER POWERING OFF HER phone, she hadn't been able to sleep well, thinking about the hang-ups.

Anne texted her back as she was locking her car in the cast lot.

> ANNE: I'M SORRY SWEETIE, I CHECKED WITH BRUCE
> —MY MEMORY ISN'T WHAT IT WAS. WE DIDN'T SEND
> IT. ARE YOU STILL COMING TO MY BIRTHDAY
> DINNER TONIGHT? JAMES WILL BE HERE AFTER ALL.
> HIS FLIGHT GETS IN AT ELEVEN. I COULD USE A
> PEACEMAKER IN CASE THE TWINS DECIDE TO
> ARGUE ABOUT THE JUSTICE SYSTEM.

Oh no! Cara had completely forgotten. She typed back a message to assure Anne she would be there and trudged up the hill to the makeup trailer. It would be nice to see James. He rarely got time off and seldom came to Atlanta.

The skin on the back of her neck prickled. It felt like she was being watched. She cast a look over her shoulder at the densely wooded area, but her eyes couldn't penetrate the shadows.

First the card, then the social media, and now flowers and phone calls. She could no longer deny what was happening.

Somehow, her stalker had found her. She had to assume it was the same person. What was the likelihood she had two different people terrorizing her? Almost on cue, her phone buzzed. Assuming it was Anne texting again, she swiped to open her phone.

UNKNOWN: DID YOU LIKE THE FLOWERS?

Cara recognized the phone number as the one that called her the night before. She knew she shouldn't engage, maybe even tell the police, but sudden anger bubbled up inside of her. Her brothers hadn't included her in their concerns. Eric humiliated her. Wes rejected her. Now, this sicko thought he could keep intimidating her.

CARA: LEAVE ME THE FUCK ALONE OR I'M GOING TO CALL THE POLICE.

Dots appeared and then disappeared. *Take that asshole*, she fumed. She didn't need her phone on set. Anyone who needed her would use the walkie-talkies, so she powered her phone off and put it in her purse.

The rest of the day passed in a blur. Lia was off and flubbed her lines several times, resulting in Stephen, the director, shouting at her. Cara felt bad for her. Lia seemed to shut down, folding in on herself. The director called for a break, and Cara watched Lia walk over to her manager, Victor, who was always on set.

Victor gave Cara the creeps. He was always around hovering over his client. He grabbed Lia's elbow and pulled her out of sight. Cara was about to follow. She was definitely in a take-down-all-men kind of mood today, and she would be happy to let Lia's overbearing manager have it, but Skye called her over to help with some extras. When Lia returned several minutes later, she was a totally different person, and nailed the scene in the next take.

"She's a fantastic actress," Skye said, noticing Cara's interest. "She could do so much more, but that loser agent is ruining her career. Not to mention turning her into a head case."

"What do you mean?" Cara hadn't gotten that impression. Lia was reserved and didn't socialize the way Chandler did, so Cara hadn't gotten to know her as well.

"Nothing, don't worry about it." She looked over Cara's shoulder and said sotto voce, "Uh-oh, incoming."

Sure enough, Courtney had entered the soundstage with Matt.

"I'm going to the restroom. Be back in a sec." Cara walked briskly in a circuitous route to the entrance. Spying her, Courtney adjusted her trajectory to intercept her.

"Still here, I see." Courtney frowned at Matt.

Cara stayed silent, not trusting herself to speak.

"I heard your mother is getting married again next week."

Next week? That couldn't be right. Cara did some mental math. With everything going on, she had put it out of her mind. A last-minute plane ticket was going to be insanely expensive. Her shoulders drooped. How is it that a few days ago she was so happy, and now everything was falling apart again?

Did I even read the invitation? Right after I opened it, Declan called about Mrs. Woodson.

The memory centered her, and she stared hard into Courtney's blue eyes.

"Are you going?" Courtney's lips formed a thin line at Cara's continued silence. Her stepmother waved her hand dismissively at the soundstage. "I hear this will be done by then. I thought I would be nice and let you finish out your little adventure."

Cara's hands fisted at her sides. "But," Courtney continued, "I'm sure you can see why your continued employment past this film would be unacceptable. Embarrassing even."

"Embarrassing for whom?" Cara challenged.

"Oh, sweetheart." Her stepmother's expression dripped with

fake pity. "For all of us, of course. We can't have someone working like a drudge with the last name Bloom. Your father would be so disappointed. Mortified, even."

Cara snapped, lunging toward Courtney, but Matt stepped in front of her, catching her arms. He clasped her wrists hard enough to leave bruises.

"I'd be careful if I were you." Matt's eyes glittered. "Daddy's not here to protect you anymore."

"We know what you did." Cara refused to back down. "It's only a matter of time until we prove it, and then..." She shifted her eyes to Courtney, "You will get what you deserve."

"Hey!" One of the lighting gaffers approached them. "You need to get your hands off her. Right now!"

Matt dropped her wrists. Bristling with anger he turned to face the man. "You should mind your own business if you want to stay employed here."

The gaffer laughed in his face. "I'm union. Good luck with that."

Cara took the opportunity to scuttle back to the bathrooms. She huddled in the stall, her chest heaving. Her hands shook as she ripped a tissue from the roll, blotting her eyes. She couldn't do this anymore.

Cara wanted to run back to Declan's Connecticut home and hide. Let him take care of her the way he said he would.

She'd tried. She really had. But things were spinning out of control.

Her chest ached and tears welled again. Cara wanted to call Wes... to hear his voice...

She refused to play some damsel in distress. She inhaled through her nose and out through her mouth, counting the breaths until they came in an even rhythm, and she was sure she wouldn't cry.

Love in Arms would be done shooting at the end of the week. With references from Skye and Jerrod, she would find a job at one of the many other production studios in Atlanta. Courtney couldn't keep buying companies just to torment her.

Cara could find a new place to live and delete her social media—for good this time. And, if the sicko didn't leave her alone, she would call the police. This could be fixed.

Wes's image appeared in front of her, and she inhaled a shaky breath, pain slicing through her. If she had to pretend that she was okay until she found some place new to live, to protect her heart, she would. She had to.

~

THE GPS HAD the trip to Anne's suburban home taking forty minutes with traffic. As Cara battled the stoplights and stop and go movement, her sadness returned. A week ago, she had thought she might invite Wes to meet her family. Cara thought he would enjoy the relaxed atmosphere in Anne's home.

Anxiety made her want to throw up, when it came time to turn her phone back on to make the trip. To her overwhelming relief, the number hadn't contacted her again.

She pulled into the driveway and saw that Luke's Audi SUV was already parked there. She wasn't looking forward to faking it in front of both of her brothers tonight. Taking a minute to touch up the makeup she put on her wrists to cover the bruises Matt had left, she met her eyes in the rearview mirror.

"Everything is going to work out," she told herself. She was a Bloom, and she wouldn't let Courtney, or an obsessed loser, wreck her life. She was stronger than that.

"Hi, Bruce." Cara accepted the enthusiastic hug from Anne's husband. Anne and Bruce had married almost ten years ago, but Cara always felt a little awkward around him. He never made her feel anything but welcome, and she knew her brothers were happy their mom was finally settled, but she still felt like an outsider.

As Anne's sons, Luke and James belonged. She wasn't sure what Bruce made of her role in the family. Sometimes Cara worried that he saw her as a reminder of the man who had broken Anne's heart.

"Come in, come in! Anne is so happy you came!" He held the door wide, and the smell of roasted garlic hit her in a wave. It was a relief. From what Luke had said that day by the Chattahoochee, Cara assumed Anne's health had deteriorated drastically. But, if Anne had cooked her signature sauce from scratch, it couldn't be as bad as Cara had imagined.

Anne sat at the large island, sipping a glass of red wine. Her perfectly set hair was in the same shoulder-length bob it always was, though it was significantly grayer than Cara was used to. Anne always had an athletic frame, like her sons, but now her shoulders seemed narrower and her face rounder than ever. However, her bright eyes still sparkled.

"Oh, dear lord! You're supervising closely, right?" Cara lifted her chin to where the twins stood in front of the stove.

Luke tossed a dishcloth over his shoulder and shook the wooden spoon at her that he'd been using to stir the pot.

"Hey!" James cried. "You got it on my shirt."

"Luke, be careful," Anne admonished in her normal calm voice as drips of sauce hit the hardwood floor.

"Thanks for getting me in trouble, Cara! And you," Luke said, pointing at his twin with the spoon, "should thank me. That shirt is hideous."

"Yeah, well not all of us take blood money to buy new suits," James snapped.

Luke's eyes narrowed. "Everyone deserves their day in court. Maybe, if the government didn't take such liberties with the Bill of Rights."

Cara laughed as Anne threw her hands up in frustration.

"Enough! Save the problems of the justice system for another night." She leaned over and put her hand over Cara's where it rested next to hers. "I have three of my children under the same roof, and you aren't going to ruin it with squabbling." Anne smiled indulgently when Bruce came over to put an arm around her shoulders.

"Would you like a glass of wine, Cara?"

"Sure! These are for you." She handed Anne the bouquet of wildflowers she brought. Bruce beamed at the gesture. Moments like these, when Cara watched Anne and Bruce together, Cara believed that real, lasting love might be possible after all.

Luke pulled a glass down from the rack and poured from the open bottle on the counter. "Just one though, Miss Lightweight. I don't want to defend you on a DUI charge."

"Cara, can you check the oven? The sausages should be almost ready. James, slice the bread, and Luke, set the table?" The men made identical scowls but did as their mother asked. Cara's chest expanded. *This* was home. Not the house itself but having her family around her. They were only missing Declan and Siobhan.

Anne must have been on the same wavelength because she looked at James, her gaze laser focused. "When was the last time you spoke to Declan?"

James and Luke exchanged a look in that twin way they had. Entire conversations with a glance.

"I'm not sure. I should probably call," James said blandly.

"That's the same nonsense he fed me." Anne's tone was acerbic. "I don't care what the problem is. You are brothers and you need to work it out. It is unacceptable that this standoff has lasted as long as it has. He has enough to deal with between Seamus and his mother's first husband! You should try to be the calm side of his family."

Cara wanted to cheer. It was exactly what she'd been telling them!

"Don't smirk, Luke. You are just as much to blame."

Luke quickly wiped the look from his face, turning back to the stove. "Yes, Ma'am."

"Do not patronize me."

"Never." Luke cast a grin over his shoulder at his mother, and James rolled his eyes at his brother's antics.

Dinner passed uneventfully. Being around Anne's naturally maternal air always comforted Cara, and she felt more of the tension she'd been carrying fall away. At one point, as she sat next to Anne, the older woman placed her hand over Cara's and asked quietly, "Are you all right? You've barely touched your dinner."

"I've been working a lot." Cara made a show of shoving a forkful of pasta into her mouth.

"It's not something she's used to," James teased. In the past, a comment like that would have bothered Cara, but not anymore. She loved this new part of herself she'd discovered. The part that worked hard and found enjoyment in her work.

"Anne told me you work on a movie set? That's exciting!" Bruce said. "Is that what you want to do for a career?"

"It's not my long-term plan." Cara hesitated, casting a look at James, who nodded encouragingly.

Luke caught the exchange and shot his brother a dirty look. "You told this idiot and not me?"

"*This idiot* calls me," Cara pointed out, dabbing innocently at her lips with her napkin.

"You don't have a phone?" He arched a dark brow at her.

"I've called you twice. It's your turn."

Luke opened his mouth to rebut, but Anne tapped on her glass with a fork.

"You bicker like you are still children! Cara, I'd love to hear about your plans."

Cara looked around the table at the faces of her family and smiled. "Originally, when I came to Atlanta to go to cosmetology school, it was to learn the basics of makeup so that I would have the knowledge I needed to create a makeup line with my mom." Anne gave her a sympathetic smile. "But as you know, she's getting married again. So those plans are on hold—probably indefinitely—and, as Declan pointed out, I didn't actually have any experience. So, I thought I'd get the education, work in the field, and then Declan might be interested in investing."

She took a sip of ice water. "I enjoy doing makeup. I do. And I love all the special-effects training I've gotten. As much as I'm having a blast being part of a movie, and makeup is an important part, I don't think I'm passionate enough about it to keep putting in the long hours."

"It's why they call it work," Luke said dryly, and she glared at him.

"I know that. But it's on your feet work, sometimes for sixteen hours. Depending on the call time, I might need to be there before dawn, and if it's a night shoot… It doesn't really leave any time for a life outside of work."

"She makes a good point," James said, surprising her. "It's easy to get burned out."

"What is it you want to do, then? I can tell by your voice you have something in mind," Anne asked, sending a curious look at James.

Cara fidgeted with her fork. "When I was in school, I learned so much about the biology and chemistry of skin reactions. The more I work, and encounter actors with different skin types and sensitivities, I've gravitated to the skincare side of the industry. In particular, skincare using natural ingredients or products that aren't primarily artificial chemicals."

Encouraged by their attention, she continued. "I thought I might get more education about that and do a natural ingredient skincare line. I've been experimenting in my kitchen, finding ways to combine easy-to-purchase products so that, not only is it as natural as possible, it's affordable for the average person."

Anne clapped her hands together in front of her mouth, and her eyes gleamed. "I think that is a wonderful idea!"

Cara ducked her head, pleased with her response. Anne was a

no-nonsense woman, and even though she was unfailingly kind, she wouldn't say something she didn't believe.

"That's really impressive, Car-Bear." James smiled approvingly, and her chest swelled.

"Would you go back to college? Get another degree?" Luke asked. "As I recall, you weren't especially interested in school the last time you were there."

Cara smacked his arm across the table with the back of her hand. "That's because Dad told me I had to study business. And to be honest, I don't think I was mature enough at the time to take it seriously even if I had been in science classes. I needed to make the connection on my own. I'm not sure if school is the path I want to take or not. I haven't decided."

Luke tipped his head and regarded Cara like he'd never seen her before. "I like this new, motivated baby sister. Let me know if I can help you."

"Me, too. Though I'm not sure what I could do," James added, not wanting to be outdone by his twin.

"I will." Cara paused. "There is something I wanted to talk to both of you about before I leave. I need some advice for a friend."

"Legal advice? You know I charge $800 an hour, right?"

"Are you serious?" James turned wide eyes to his brother. "That's ridiculous."

"What can I say?" Luke held his palms up. "Rich people deserve fair representation, too."

"In other words, crime pays?" James shot back.

Luke's face darkened, but before they descended into a full-fledged argument, Cara said, "I'm sure you can give me a freebie."

After Cara helped the twins with the dishes, they went onto the screened porch that overlooked Anne and Bruce's wooded lot. The early spring evening was chilly, but Cara didn't want to risk Anne overhearing.

Before she had a chance, James pinned her with a stare. "Did you know this stranger you're living with is a felon?" Cara's jaw dropped. "I think you should move in with Luke until you find someplace else to live. This was really foolish of you."

Luke nodded, his face set along stern lines.

"Did you run a background check on him?" Cara asked, not sure if she should be touched or annoyed.

Luke looked at her as if she'd grown another head. "Of course, we did. You should have before moving in. We found out some interesting stuff."

Cara raised both of her eyebrows high. "You mean like how he didn't serve time because of his plea deal?" The twins exchanged a look. "Why did you assume I didn't know?" She hadn't known, but she would rather die than admit it to them.

"So, you *did* run a background check?" Luke asked. Sometimes having lawyers for brothers made it difficult to hide things.

"Wes told me himself. He told me what happened. He was a young kid who made a terrible mistake and paid his debt to society. Is there something I'm missing?"

She could tell James wanted to argue the point. "It's getting late, and I'm freezing. Can I just ask what I brought you out here for?"

Luke's lips flattened into an unhappy line. "Let's hear it."

Cara cleared her throat. "I have a friend... someone I work with who has... an admirer. Not an admirer exactly because the whole thing is very creepy. I think it might be a stalker, but she doesn't know who it is. I told her I'd ask you what she should do. If she should go to the police or just ignore it."

"You're going to have to give us a little more to go on," James said when she waited expectantly.

Cara played with the end of her ponytail. "It started with weird comments on her social media. She blocked him. Then she received flowers twice, and whoever sent them called her all night. This morning she got a text from one of the numbers that called the night before, asking how she liked the flowers. She's a little freaked out because they sent the flowers to her house and our work."

Luke frowned. "That's pretty classic stalking behavior. She has no idea who it is? She could call the florist."

Cara shook her head. "She tried that. There was no florist on the note. And when she checked with security at the lot, they didn't have a description. The delivery person had his hat pulled down over his face, so the cameras don't help either."

"And the security guard took the flowers anyway? Nothing suspicious about that kind of behavior!" James shook his head.

"That's not good." Luke's face took on a serious expression, and Cara's heart sank. Part of her was hoping they'd dismiss her concerns.

"She should file a report with the police," James said.

"Has the stalker made any threats?" Cara shook her head, and Luke sighed. "Then, it's unlikely they will do anything. Particularly, if she doesn't know who it is."

"That's not true. I'm sure APD has an excellent cybercrime division," James scowled. "They could trace the text message or the social media comment."

"You think they are going to use their resources because she has received texts, phone calls and flowers?" Luke shook his head, his face folded into an angry frown. "She should file a police report, so there is a paper trail. Unless she has some idea who they should look at, or the asshole threatens her, they can't do much."

"What is she doing to protect herself?" James asked, not disputing what Luke said.

Cara's stomach swirled. She had to wait until he threatened her? "She carries mace. Our cars are behind a gate at work, so she doesn't have to worry about that. Except, now that you've pointed out how lax our security guard is, I'm not particularly confident about that anymore. She has a roommate," Cara quickly added. "So, she has company when she's home."

Luke sighed. "She should get a good, monitored alarm system and cameras around her house. Other than that, there isn't a lot she can do. Maybe the next time he leaves flowers, it'll catch him on tape. Also, be sure one of the cameras points at the cars. Stalkers love to disable vehicles so they can establish contact by being a good Samaritan passerby. What?" Luke snapped at his brother.

"You seem to know a lot about what stalkers like. Client?"

Luke's gray eyes flashed, and a red flush crept up his throat. "I successfully defended a woman who shot her stalker, an ex-boyfriend."

"I'm sorry. I shouldn't have implied—"

"Save it." Luke glared at his twin. "I have the luxury of picking and choosing my clients now. That doesn't mean when I got started I didn't defend guilty people, but our Constitution says *everyone* deserves equal due process. My job is to make sure my clients get a fair trial."

Cara breathed deeply through her nose. She'd lost them. They could argue about this for hours. Cara rose from her seat. "I think I'm going to head back. Thanks for your help."

"Tell her to keep her head on a swivel and take a self-defense class ASAP. Also, document everything," James grimaced. "In case something happens to her, it will help law enforcement identify him later. It will help prove the case. Hey, are you okay? You're really pale."

In case something happens to her.

"I'm just afraid for her." Cara's voice was barely a whisper.

"Is there somewhere she could go? Some place she could stay away from home for a while? If he knows where she lives…"

Two words were all it would take. "It's me." If Cara admitted to her brothers that she was the one being stalked, they would have her packed and moved into Luke's high-rise apartment, complete with a doorman, before the sun rose. As a defense attorney, Luke took protection seriously.

The words were on the tip of her tongue, but she stayed silent. She was embarrassed. Embarrassed that once again, she'd gotten involved in something sordid. She knew her brothers wouldn't blame her, but Cara craved the look she'd seen on her family's faces earlier. They were proud and maybe even a little impressed that she had made such a change in her life. If she told them, it would be Cara in trouble again. And like they said, he hadn't threatened her yet. Maybe her lashing out at him this morning had put a stop to it.

There was also the piece of her that didn't want to think about moving away from Wes, which was stupid. Cara knew it was time to start looking, but she wasn't ready yet. She felt a sharp pang in her chest when she imagined not seeing him over coffee in the morning and knowing she wouldn't see him at the end of the day.

"Are you sure you are okay?" Luke peered at her. "You've got a weird look on your face."

Bruce stuck his head out the door, and said quietly, "I sent Anne up to bed, and I'm going to head up, too. Lock up when you leave, okay?"

"We'll be going. I've got an appointment early in the morning," Luke said.

"I've got an early meeting downtown, but I'll be back to see Mom tomorrow night if that's okay?" James added.

"She will love it. Don't feel you have to rush out because of us old people."

They assured him they weren't, and when they got to their cars, her brothers both gave her tight hugs.

"Thanks for coming tonight. It means a lot to Mom." Luke ruffled her hair, laughing when she scowled.

"It means a lot to me, too. It's nice to be around people who know me," Cara replied.

Luke's car beeped when he unlocked it, and James walked to the passenger-side door.

"They really love each other, don't they?" Cara stared back at the house.

James frowned. "They've been together for a long time."

"I know. I think it's really amazing how Bruce takes care of her." Cara cleared her throat to cover the tears that sprang to her eyes. "I mean, this can't be what he signed up for, but he never stopped loving her."

Luke and James exchanged a worried look.

"Car-Bear? Are you sure you're okay?"

She tried to smile. "Yeah. I don't know why I didn't see it before." The tears refused to be banished, and her voice cracked. "I think because of my mom and dad and how they lived…"

Luke stepped away from the car to wrap his arms around her. "I don't like to say things about your mom, but you know the way she lives isn't normal. It's not a coincidence your mom started getting married once every few years after she got sober. She is trying to fill something inside of her." Cara sniffled against his chest. "And our dad used women. Those weren't love stories."

"That's not fair. He was always honest with them. He didn't want long term. Our dad didn't lead them on."

Cara didn't like the pitying expression her brothers were giving her.

"He said that to absolve himself of any accountability. David Bloom was a charismatic, wealthy man. I'm not saying every woman wanted something more with him. But, I know there were times, when he turned the full force of his attention on them, that some of the women thought they were the exception. That he wouldn't be as generous and attentive as he was if he didn't genuinely care about them." James's eyes were sad.

"He hurt a lot of people, Cara. Broke women's hearts," Luke added. He looked at his twin. "Remember Tasha?"

James grimaced. "Tough to forget."

"I remember her," Cara said. "She was really sweet. She loved to play Barbies with me and braided my hair." Cara smiled at the memory.

"You know what *our* memory of Tasha is?" James's voice was flinty. "Hearing her sobs, down on her knees in the foyer, begging our father not to leave her. Dad patted her on the head, Cara. Like a pet." James shook his head in disgust. "And told her she shouldn't worry. He'd paid off her credit cards and had put a 'going away' gift in her account. A woman he had living in his home, acting like a mother to his nine-year-old daughter. He treated her like she was a commodity, and he was done with her. Our father didn't know what love was. She wasn't even the first we saw him treat that way."

Cara's eyes were wide. She'd never heard of any of this. The extent to which her brothers had shielded and protected her all those summers hit her like a bolt of lightning.

"Do you believe in love?" The words slipped out, and by the looks on their faces, Luke and James were just as shocked by her question as she was.

"Uh, I mean..." James stammered.

"I do," Luke said firmly, causing his twin to goggle at him. "I have friends who are in happy marriages." He gestured to the house. "And right there, you said it yourself, Cara." When he looked back at her, there was more understanding than she would have liked in his eyes. "I'm not saying it's easy to find the right person, but I hope maybe someday..." Luke shrugged. "Don't let your parents' failures as people be what defines love for you. You've got a good heart, Car-Bear. I know that someday when you fall in love, it will be forever."

"Gross," James groaned. "If we're done with the Oprah moment, can we go?" James winked at his sister to soften the words, and she smiled back.

Luke squeezed her hands and walked to his car.

"Which of the thousand one-night stands you've had made

you believe in love, Luke? Was it the bottle-service girl in Vegas? I get it, her tits were…"

Cara laughed, closing her car door on James's taunting.

At the stop sign at the end of the street, she was surprised when Luke pulled up alongside and James motioned for her to roll down her window.

"Do me a favor," James said across the narrow distance. "Don't be the one who volunteers to let your friend stay. I know it sounds terrible, but I'd be wrecked if something happened to you. And text us when you get home."

Luke leaned forward and called across his brother. "If something like that were ever to happen to you, tell me. I can help where the police can't. Put you in touch with one of my less white-collar clients."

"I can't believe as an officer of the court you just said that," James said, outraged.

"Oh my god, lighten up."

Cara gave a smile and a little wave as she pulled away, knowing they would bicker all the way back to Luke's condo.

Pulling into the driveway, Cara parked next to Wes's truck and did as her brothers suggested. She scanned her surroundings before almost running from the car to the front door. She practically flung it open in her haste to be safely inside. To her relief, there were no flowers or notes waiting on the porch.

Wes looked up startled, as she barreled into the house. He held his phone to his ear and his face was twisted in an irritated scowl that quickly turned to guilt.

Interesting.

He took the call to his bedroom, and Cara wandered into the kitchen to get a drink. He'd left the door partially open, making it easy for her to eavesdrop.

"Hang on, Melody, let me get a pen. Where do you want me to send it?" He was quiet for a minute, and Cara assumed he was listening. "Do you want everything?" Another pause. "How about you make me a list of the clothes you want? That'll be easier."

As annoyed as she was at Wes, she felt a twinge of sympathy for him. Was Melody *really* asking him to pack her belongings? The woman couldn't possibly be that insensitive, could she?

She heard Wes let out a breath. "Are you sure you aren't rushing into this, Mel? You've only known this guy for a few months... I'm not being negative. Of course, I want you to be happy... I don't know how far San Gimignano is from Milan... When will you be back from the wedding? I don't want to have the boxes delivered if you aren't there... okay... I'll send you a text when it's done. Wait, Mel! What about Cara?"

Cara's ears perked up.

"The woman you invited to live here. Don't you think you should let her know you aren't coming back... Wow! Fine. I'll handle it."

Wes's footsteps approached the door, and she scurried back, pretending like she had just arrived in the kitchen. Cara grabbed a glass and quickly filled it with water.

She wanted to make a snarky comment about Melody, but one look at Wes's face made her swallow the words. His eyebrows almost met over his eyes, his mouth turned down.

On the drive back from Anne's, Cara thought about what her brothers had said about Corinne and David. She wasn't ready to use the L-word about Wes, but she was past denying that her feelings ran deeper than just lusting after a friend. She wouldn't add to his hurt.

"Hey," she said.

Wes made a face. "Did you hear that?"

"Some." She shrugged, taking a sip of her water.

"She wants me to pack up her stuff and send it to her in Milan."

Cara bit her tongue. She was glad Melody wasn't coming

back. Even if Wes didn't want to be with her, he didn't deserve to be with someone as selfish as Melody.

"She's going to some fancy wedding in San Gimignano and wants me to wait until she's back." He tipped his head back, closing his eyes and breathing out through his nose. "Always on her schedule." He brought his eyes to hers. "I know what you're thinking."

Something clicked in Cara's brain. San Gimignano? Where had she seen that? She was familiar with the scenic town in Tuscany, but why did it seem like someone mentioned—oh my god!

Her lips parted in surprise before clamping shut again as a horrified giggle escaped her. Wes glared at her.

"I'm glad my life's dream falling apart is funny to you," he glowered.

Cara put a hand over her mouth. "It's not that. Maybe it's not the same but… my mom is getting married next week in a villa outside of San Gimignano. I mean, it might be a coincidence…"

Wes huffed a laugh before his face blanked. "She said it was a fashion designer and a supermodel. Your mom…"

"Corinne Blease, yeah."

Wes's eyes rounded. "Holy shit!" He studied her face. "I see the resemblance now." Cara grit her teeth, shoving down a lifetime of insecurity. "But you're prettier."

"You don't have to lie to flatter me." She curled her lip, disappointed in him. "People have done it my entire life. I know I'm not a supermodel."

"True." His tone was matter of fact, his gaze still on her face. "Maybe, it's because I see you in three dimensions and not on an ad. Your mom is stunning, but you have a warmth and glow that radiates…" His gaze fell to her lips. "And your smile." Wes's eyes met hers briefly before he looked away, red blooming high on his cheekbones.

Cara's heart hammered in her chest, and she tried to get her brain to reengage.

"Do you really think it's your mom's wedding she's going to?"

"Yes."

"How can you be sure? I don't know the names."

Cara wished he would turn back to face her so she could see his eyes. What she'd seen in them, moments before, revealed he felt the connection as much as she did.

He cared about her more than he wanted to admit.

A plan of her own formed in Cara's mind. "For one thing, my mother would rent out every villa within a hundred miles of her wedding if she thought someone else famous was also getting married nearby."

Wes stared sightlessly at the wall.

Did she dare?

This could be a disaster.

Cara swallowed over the lump in her throat, anxiety clawing at her. It would settle the issue once and for all. His entire childhood had been one of uncertainty. He had created this life plan of his in a futile attempt to control his future.

He might not admit it, but Wes feared love even more than she did. The revelation made everything clear. Wes's plan was just his way of keeping his heart from being broken. Melody was familiar, but he didn't love her, not really. Cara would bet her life on it. As it was, there was a very real chance she was betting her heart.

"Do you want to go as my plus one?" Wes whirled around his expression confused. "You could go with me. It would give you a chance to talk to Melody in person."

"Why would you do that?"

Someone should nominate me for sainthood.

She held his gaze so he would see her sincerity. "You are my friend. My best friend, really. If Melody marries this guy before you get a chance to say what you've always wanted to, you will never get over it."

His eyebrows slanted. "You want me to be with Melody?"

"*You* say you want to be with Melody." Cara set her glass down, ignoring his question. "I may not be completely convinced that love exists—though my brothers may have put a fairly big dent in my beliefs tonight. They made me realize I could do it differently than my parents did." She chuckled when his forehead wrinkled, and she gave him a soft smile. "You deserve to have your chance, if that's really what you want."

She successfully hid the pain in her chest when he said, "It is." His eyes were unfocused, lost deep in his thoughts. "Are you sure, Cara?"

Cara swallowed past the ache in her throat and forced her lips into a smile. "The wedding is a week from tomorrow, but I need to be there a day early." She pushed away from the counter and walked towards her bedroom. Tears clouded her vision, and she clamped her mouth shut to prevent her from wailing.

"Cara," he called behind her, and she paused. "Thank you."

Not looking back, she gave one nod. Just before closing her door, she called back, keeping her voice bright, "You get to buy the plane tickets, though."

CHAPTER THIRTY-FIVE

THE NEXT TWO DAYS PASSED QUICKLY AS THE PRODUCTION MOVED
at a hectic pace to meet the next day's completion deadline. Cara
had her doubts. They'd been working eighteen-hour days, and it
still seemed impossible. She hoped they would finish on time.
Cara wanted to be there when the movie wrapped. This was her
first proper job, and she was looking forward to the wrap party
the night before she and Wes left for Italy.

The night she made the offer, Cara barely slept. Was she an
idiot? Delivering Melody on a silver platter? Did she really want
to be with someone who wanted someone else?

But Wes didn't want Melody, not really. He had concocted a
fantasy based on his childhood trauma. The only way for him to
move past the issue was to confront it.

Or at least that's what her brothers had said when she was
younger. Then again, it had been their rationale for throwing her
in the pool when she was afraid to swim, so maybe not the
soundest of principles. It didn't matter. She had offered, and she
couldn't go back on it now.

As Cara finally drifted off to sleep that night, an insidious
voice in her head whispered what she secretly knew was the real

reason she had offered. She wanted Wes for herself, but she worried Melody would always be a ghost between them.

"What are your plans after this? Have you started applying for jobs?" Skye whispered next to her. They were standing at the back of the soundstage, ready and waiting for whenever Stephen yelled "cut!"

"I haven't." Cara needed to, but with everything else going on…

"You're going to Italy after we wrap, right? I'm so jealous." Skye sounded wistful.

"Mm-hmm."

Skye looked at Cara out of the corner of her eye. "Romantic. But you and Wes are just friends, right? Going to a family wedding in Tuscany. Yep, sounds totally platonic to me."

Cara's stomach rolled but some of her feelings must have shown because Skye's eyes rounded. "Are you two together?"

Cara shook her head. Skye's face fell. "I don't get you two. I have never in my life seen two people so into each other."

"We are going to the wedding because Melody will be there… long story." She held up her hand to stop questions. "She's engaged, and Wes never told her how he felt."

"So, this is what? Supposed to give him closure?"

"Something like that." The knot in Cara's stomach twisted tighter.

"Why would you do something so stupid? Oh!" Skye scrunched her nose. "Have you told him you're in love with him?" Cara opened her mouth to deny it, but a small sob escaped.

Skye glanced around, but thankfully the crew was busy and hadn't heard Cara's outburst. She patted Cara awkwardly on the back looking deeply uncomfortable.

One side of Cara's mouth lifted. "I always thought falling in love was stupid. Honestly, if this is how it feels, I think I was right." She sucked in a breath. "Can we not talk about this right now?"

"You should tell him… with actual words," Skye said. Cara shook her head, and thankfully Skye didn't argue. However, instead of making small talk as they typically would, she stood silently by Cara's side until the final clapper of the day sounded.

~

IT WAS ALMOST midnight when Cara finally made it home. As she turned into the driveway, her headlights hit a large envelope propped against the front door.

Her heart jumped into her throat, choking her. Looking over her shoulder, she grabbed the envelope, tucking it under her arm. It was heavier than she expected, and she could feel the outline of something stuffed inside.

The house was quiet, as Cara tiptoed into her room. She put the envelope on the bed and stared at it. It was a standard cardboard mailing envelope but what had her shaking, along with her real name in bold, red block letters, were the words—'**Do Not Bend: Photos.**'

She thought of waking up Wes in the other room, but the tendrils of shame were back, crawling along her nerve endings.

This is ridiculous. It's not like I haven't seen them before, she told herself. She picked up the envelope, ripped the top off, and dumped the contents on her bed. Her brow furrowed, and she blinked, trying to process what she was seeing. Photos and a small disposable phone.

They weren't the pictures of her with pink hair. She picked one up for a better look and immediately hurled it down, her hand covering her mouth. Panic sliced through Cara as she flipped through them, each showing her in various stages of undress… inside this very bedroom.

Cara heard a loud buzzing as she watched her hand reach out and unfold the paper lying on her bedspread. The message, printed in bold red ink, blurred in front of her and vomit rose in Cara's throat.

I forgive you for being rude. You should have thanked me for the beautiful flowers. You blocked me and that is unacceptable. I have chosen not to punish you yet. You Are Mine. I don't want to share these precious images of you, like I was forced to do before—but if you don't answer the phone I have left for you, I will. I love you and cannot wait for us to be together.

See you soon.

No! No! No! I can't go through this again!

Her knees turned to jelly, and she sank boneless to the floor until her forehead rested against the mattress. The burner phone rang, but Cara couldn't force her body to respond.

She needed to answer it.

The phone went silent.

Maybe he didn't know she was home yet. Or was he watching? Through the heartbeats in her ears, she heard it ring again. Slick fingers fumbled over it before she threw it against the wall.

What had she done?

CHAPTER THIRTY-SIX

WES HEARD CARA COME IN AND PUSHED HIS PILLOW MORE comfortably under his head. He was always restless until he knew she was home. Fuck, he'd been restless since she offered to take him to her mother's wedding.

He should be grateful. Happy that she wanted to help him with Melody. So why did it make him so angry?

The afternoon of the thunderstorm, Wes had been so close to throwing his dream out the window. He'd handled it badly when the police interrupted them. His heart shriveled as he remembered the hurt in her eyes. It wasn't that he regretted kissing her, touching her....

Wes rolled over and clutched his pillow to his chest. What had alarmed him was the realization that he was ready to throw away his life plan to be with her.

Cara was clear about the fact she didn't believe in marriage. Then the other night, she made the off-hand comment about her beliefs having changed... followed by an offer to help him.

Wes groaned. He shoved the sheet back and opened his bedroom door. If he wasn't going to sleep for a while, he might as well get some work done.

The sound of a telephone ringing caught his attention, and he frowned. Was someone harassing Cara again? What was that noise? He crept closer to her door, his ears straining to hear the strange mewling sound. Wes reached for the doorknob just as the phone rang again, followed by a crash against the wall.

"Cara!" The sight that greeted him broke his heart. Cara was crumpled on the ground next to her bed with her arms wrapped around her legs. Her face was pasty white, the pupils in her eyes dilated wide. She whimpered again.

Wes fell to his knees next to her. "Cara?" he whispered, placing his hand over where hers were rigidly clasped together. Her skin was damp. Was she sick? He touched her forehead. She was icy cold.

"Wes."

"I'm here, baby. What happened?" His stomach churned, trying to imagine what could have caused such an extreme reaction. She was still in her work clothes, and he saw photos and a torn envelope scattered on the bed, but before he could examine them, the phone on the floor rang again.

Cara lunged forward, scrabbling for it. Wes watched, his heart twisting in anguish in the face of her panic.

"Hello? Hello?" Her breathing was coming in quick little pants. "Who is this? Why are you doing this?" Her voice shook, and tears spilled from the corners of her eyes.

Scalding rage flooded Wes's body. Coming to his feet he ripped the phone out of her hand and snarled into the phone. "Who the fuck is this?"

"Give me the phone, Wes," Cara cried, her eyes bulging.

Wes heard the click as the caller ended the connection.

"They hung up."

Cara wrung her hands as she shook her head, looking back at the photos. "Why did you do that?" she whispered.

"What's going on, Cara?" His blood was pumping too hot through his veins for him to make his voice soothing.

Cara planted her hands on the ground one at a time and slowly came to her knees. Using the bed as leverage, as if she didn't have the strength to get to her feet without help, she rose to her full height.

Her color was slightly better, but the weary lines by her eyes seemed deeper. "That's it then." Her gaze fell to the photos on the bed. Tears streaked down her face, but Wes didn't think she was aware. "Okay, it's fine. Everything will—" Her breathing quickened.

"Hey!" Wes stepped forward, pulling her into him. He rubbed her back in soothing circles as her sobs soaked through his shirt. "You're going to hyperventilate." He pulled his head back to look down at her, brushing the tears from her cheeks. "Breathe with me. In, two-three-four. Out, two-three-four." Cara struggled to match his breaths, and after a few minutes, she calmed enough that he stopped counting out loud.

Tucking her head against his chest, he rested his cheek on top of her head, inhaling the scent that was uniquely Cara. His hand stroked down her tangle of blonde hair. "Does the caller ever say anything?"

Wes felt her shake her head.

"Okay. How often are you getting them?" he asked.

Cara's voice was low when she answered, and Wes bent his head closer. "I don't know. The first night was a lot, so I turned my phone off. I didn't get them for a couple of days. After he texted, asking if I liked the flowers, I told him I would call the police and blocked him." Her voice quavered and a wave of protectiveness washed over him. He was going to find out whoever was doing this and tear them apart.

"The flowers that were left here at the house?"

That was bad. Very bad. This guy knew where she lived.

"I got a second delivery at work, and that's when he texted me."

"Why didn't you tell me?" Fear made his tone sharp, and Cara immediately stiffened. Wes resumed his stroking, holding her snug when she moved in his arms.

"I thought I could handle it. It worked last time, but it wasn't this bad."

A chill blackness descended over him. "The last time?"

"I need to sit down, Wes." Her voice was husky, and he eased her down until she was sitting next to him on the bed. Her hands were still cold, and he rubbed them between his own.

"Will you tell me what happened before?"

Cara let out a heavy breath and then met his eyes. Wes watched as she clearly struggled with a decision. "It's all right. You can tell me anything." He lifted their clasped hands to his mouth, pressing a warm kiss to where they were joined.

"When I came to Atlanta, it wasn't just because of school. I needed to start over. After the pictures in the tabloid came out, I started getting ugly messages and emails. I ignored most, but one account started talking about things that were happening in my everyday life–nothing to do with the pictures. His messages became scarier."

"Can you give me an example?" he asked softly, trying not to spook her or let her know how his body pulsed with fury.

"It was usually along the lines of, 'hope you liked your salad,' or 'your hair looked so pretty' on days I'd been at the salon. The one that pushed me over the edge, and had me a virtual shut-in at Declan's, was the evening he said, 'I wanted to run with you today.'" Cara shuddered. "I had gone to a park to run the trails ten miles from Declan's house. I thought I was careful, but when I opened the email, I realized how isolated the spot was and that he'd been watching. He used to sign all the emails, 'See you soon.' When that wasn't on any of the messages here, I didn't realize he had found me. I thought I could start over with a different name, and he would forget. Why is he doing this?"

Wes clenched his jaw so tightly he thought he might have

cracked a molar. "Was there something more than the calls and flowers? Has he approached you?"

Cara's shoulders slumped. "No. I've run out of people I think it could be. There was a gift card around Valentine's Day. I thought it was from Anne. I thought about calling the police. Luke and James said I should file a report to get the paperwork started, but it's doubtful the police will devote a lot of time to it. Particularly because I don't know who it is."

"Your brothers know you're being stalked, and they aren't doing anything?" Wes seethed as his anger grew.

Cara stared at her hands. "They don't know it's me. I told them it was a friend of mine."

"Then your brothers are morons."

"I've never lied to them about something important before, so they trust me," she said miserably. "I never told Declan about what was happening in Connecticut. I only said I needed a fresh start. What good would it do for them to know? If there is nothing anyone can do, they will just worry—they all have extremely stressful jobs. I'm not adding to that." She cut her eyes to him. "Or, they would try to force me to move in with Luke. I don't want that." Cara finished in a whisper.

Wes's heart skipped a beat. This roommate situation was always intended to be temporary, but he didn't want to think about not being able to see Cara's smiling face every day, or not smelling the honeysuckle that trailed along with her.

She wasn't smiling now. In fact, he wasn't sure he'd ever seen someone look so hopeless.

"There's something more, isn't there?"

Cara's lip quivered, and tears filled her eyes again, spilling down her cheeks. Every cell in Wes's body compressed into a tiny knot of dread in the center of his chest. "Tell me."

He mentally braced himself for whatever it was she would say, but it didn't prepare him for what came next.

She pulled back, wiping her nose, her fair cheeks blotchy

from the tears. "I blocked him on social media and my phone, and now he's angry. He sent me a burner phone and said if I don't answer he'll release these." Cara half turned and picked up a handful of the photographs on the bed behind them.

Wes's heart jumped into his throat, and his ears pounded. A rage he didn't know he was capable of built. The bastard was watching her.

In their home.

He would kill him with his bare hands.

The photos clearly showed the bedroom they were in. Cara in a towel, Cara in lacy lingerie bent over her dresser, pulling out clothing. Living her life, where she should feel safest. She handed him a folded piece of paper and visceral anger gripped him as he read the words.

"I don't know if I can go through that again."

"Son of a bitch!" Wes surged to his feet. His eyes scanned the room, assessing which angle the stalker took the photos from. Her computer sat closed on the small end table. He picked it up and unplugged the charge cord.

"We're calling the police."

"It won't do any good. There's no way of finding who it is. Until something happens to me, I mean." Fear clouded her beautiful eyes.

Fuck that!

The police may not have the ability, but Wes sure as hell did.

"It occurred to me it might be my stepmother. This all started after she bought into Peachtree Pictures. It could just be her sadistic way of torturing me."

Whoever this person was, they were a coward and a bully. She might be right. It might be her stepmother and not some perverted psycho, but Wes didn't care. His blood flowed like lava in his veins, and all he cared about was destroying whoever was responsible.

"I'll take care of it."

She frowned. "I appreciate it, Wes. I do. But I don't know what you could do."

"I said, I'm going to take care of it. Even if the worst happens, and he puts pictures on the internet, I'll get them down." His lips lifted in a humorless smile. "But I plan on setting a trap, and in the meantime, I can find out who is behind the phone numbers."

"How?" Understanding skated across her face, and she frantically shook her head. "No! Wes, you can't! It's not worth the risk! Seriously, my being embarrassed online isn't worth you taking this risk. You would go to jail."

He stared at her for a long minute, the feelings he'd refused to accept hovering on the tip of his tongue. Without thinking, he lifted his hands to either side of her face. "You're worth it," he said and pressed a hard kiss against her lips.

"Wes!"

"Go to bed. Try to get some sleep. I promise I can fix this." He tucked her computer under his arm, his brain already ticking through a list of things he could do right away.

He needed to find the remote-access trojan, the RAT, that had been used to access her computer. That would take some time. There was no way of knowing what the virus had been originally attached to. Wes wouldn't wipe it. He would use his software to trace the asshole back to wherever he was hiding. The second he tried to spy on Cara again, Wes would have him. He bent to scoop the burner phone off the floor. "I'm going to take this."

Cara nodded. She looked so forlorn, sitting on her bed, that he paused in the doorway. She lifted her eyes to his and gave him a sad smile. "Thank you for helping me."

Apparently, five simple words were all it took to make him see the truth. There was nothing he wouldn't do for her—and that was terrifying.

Wes shook himself. There were more important things to do than make sense of his confused brain. He pulled up the pictures he'd taken of her call logs and began cataloging the steps he needed to take in order to mask his own intrusion into the telephone carrier's server.

THE SUN WAS JUST LIGHTENING the room when Wes opened his eyes. He didn't know what time it was when he finally quit, but it hadn't been light yet. He forced himself to stop when he made three careless mistakes in a row. No amount of coffee could power through that level of mental fatigue.

He swung his legs around to place his feet flat on the ground, knocking a furry white blanket to the floor. Wes didn't even remember going to the sofa to lie down. He scrubbed at his eyes. It had been years since he'd pulled an all-nighter, not since they battled with the hacker in Poland who was trying to attack a major power grid on the west coast—and Wes had been a lot younger.

Wes groaned as he stretched his stiff muscles. The house was quiet, and Cara's door stood open. Had she already left?

"Last day of shooting." Cara emerged from his bedroom, with a coffee cup in her hand and a fake smile on her face, but the dark smudges under her eyes gave away that she had had little sleep. "I hope you don't mind. I got dressed in your room…" Her eyes glanced quickly at the door of her bedroom and then away again.

"How are you feeling?"

"I'm fine." She took a sip of her coffee. "I'm going to enjoy my coffee, play make believe, and get through this day."

"I ordered a security system with lights and cameras last night. They should be here today, and I'll get Jin to help me install them while you're at work."

"Did you tell him… about?" Cara's cheeks flushed pink, and under any other circumstance, he would have thought she looked adorable. *Shit.* He still thought she looked adorable, but he hated the cause behind it.

"I only told him you have a stalker, and that they had used your computer's camera to take some pictures." He paused, waiting for her to look up. "There's nothing to be embarrassed about. You haven't done anything wrong. This parasite is…" The muscles in his neck tensed. "If he releases the pictures, I'm going to need Jin and Nina's help to get them down as quickly as possible."

Cara nodded.

"I made good progress last night. There's one thing we haven't discussed."

Cara raised both of her eyebrows.

"If it turns out to be someone you know, do you want me to hold him while you get a couple of good punches in?"

Her lips lifted at the corners as he'd intended. "I'd like to taze him right in the balls."

"Oooh, vicious. I like it."

She smiled for real then. "Oh, I can be quite vindictive when given the right motivation."

Wes pretended to shiver with fear. "Remind me not to give you a reason then."

Cara poured what was left of her coffee into her travel mug. "Skye is picking me up. She's giving me a ride. Luke said stalkers sometimes like to tamper with cars so they can rescue the person." She picked at her sweater, and then added, "I told Skye the flowers were creeping me out, but not about the calls or the pictures. I'm not ready for anyone else to know."

"I won't say anything, but I want you to do something?"

"What?"

"I want you to tell your family what's going on." Wes held her gaze.

"No."

"Cara, I know you don't want to worry them, but they're your family! That's what families are for."

"You don't know my brothers. If I tell them what's happening, they will lock me up in Fort Knox. I won't see daylight for years."

"They love you."

"I know they do, and I love them. But they'll fight over how to handle it and which one of them is to blame, which will then drive everyone further apart. Besides, you said we could handle it."

"We can." His voice was steely with his determination. "I promise I will keep you safe but... if anything were to happen, how would they feel?"

CHAPTER THIRTY-SEVEN

Wes's words stayed with her long after Skye picked her up. If something happened to her, it would destroy her brothers that she had hidden it from them.

"That's a gigantic sigh. I braked in time!"

Cara had been staring sightlessly out the side window. "It's not you. I have to have a conversation I don't want to."

"Finally going to tell Wes how you feel about him?"

"Shut up." Cara didn't have the emotional energy to defend herself. She'd tell Declan first. He'd be pissed if he weren't the first to know.

Knowing her brother was at work, she keyed a quick text asking him to call when he had a chance, fully expecting him to call her that night after work.

Two hours later, she was on her way back to the trailer with Skye when her phone buzzed in her pocket. Her brother's face flashed on her screen.

"Holy hotness! Who's that?" Skye asked.

"Gross. That's my brother. I'll call him back." This was not a conversation she wanted to have in front of anyone else.

"Fuck me sideways! That isn't someone's brother. That is sin wrapped in a skin suit!" Skye parked the cart and grabbed Cara's arm. "Seriously, why is everyone you know so hot?"

Skye's words did what Cara thought was impossible today—they made her laugh. "I thought you were in love with my friend Amara?"

"A girl can have options." Skye grinned. "Can you restock our bags? I'm heading to the bathroom. I need to cool myself off after all that." She waved a hand as she drove away.

Her humor quickly disappeared. She locked the trailer door and sat in one of the makeup chairs. Declan picked up on the second ring.

Cara stood again and fidgeted with the products on the counter. "I only have a couple minutes before I have to get back to the set. We wrap today. I didn't think I'd hear from you this early."

"I'm in the car on the way to the airport, so I thought I'd take a chance you might be free."

Cara chewed her lip. She *really* didn't want to say the words.

"Cara? Are you still there?"

"I need to tell you something, but you can't freak out and overreact in classic Declan style, okay? I wouldn't bother you, but Wes thought I should tell my family…"

She could tell Declan was trying to keep his voice calm, but he had picked up on her anxiety. "Tell your family what? Are you pregnant?"

"What? No!" She took a deep breath and then let the words out in a rush. "I have a stalker. It's the same one from last year."

There was a beat of silence. "I must have misunderstood you. Did you say, 'it's the same one from last year'?" The darkness in his voice raised goosebumps on her arms. *Oh, shit!* He was going to overreact. "Start from the beginning. And leave nothing out."

Cara was just finishing her story when someone tried the door and, finding it locked, started knocking.

"I've got to go, Dec."

"Hang on. You can't tell me all this and then go back to work!"

"Cara, are you in there?" She heard Skye call out.

"Sorry, Declan. I really have to go. I'm not in any danger. There are people around me at work, and Wes is putting in a new security system at home—"

"Not good enough," Declan barked.

"I'll call you tonight. Promise." Cara ended the call feeling horribly guilty and opened the door for Skye.

The woman cast a suspicious glance around the trailer. "What were you doing?"

"I was on the phone. I must have locked the door by mistake." Cara mentally crossed her fingers.

Skye didn't look convinced. But, after only one irritated look when she realized Cara hadn't restocked the bag, Skye chattered nonstop about the wrap party the following night.

"I'm going to get drunk and laid, and I don't care in which order. You should invite your brother and your friend."

Cara laughed. "Neither one of them is in Atlanta. Is it really that wild?"

"Not every time. Wrap parties are different. Sometimes, it's practically a bacchanalia. Other times, some pretentious ass wants to make a bunch of speeches. This one should be fun. Lia probably won't stay long. Victor always makes her leave early."

"I saw him with her yesterday. He seems a little…"

Skye's face became stony. "Victor is the worst kind of agent. He got his hands on Lia when she was young and has been running her ever since. I don't know why she doesn't leave him. She could get representation anywhere. She's really talented! Once when she was in the chair, she made a comment about signing a contract when she was young and dumb, but clammed up when I asked what she meant."

Cara frowned, but the time for conversation was over as they reached the set and were surrounded by people. She watched Lia that afternoon between scenes. Cara had noticed before that Lia had a serene, natural elegance to her, but until today, Cara hadn't been able to put her finger on what seemed off about the woman. After last night, Cara recognized the hunted expression on Lia's face.

It wasn't until they were pulling out of the parking lot that Cara realized she wouldn't be coming back to this place. She had only worked at Peachtree Pictures for a short time, but it felt a lot longer.

"What are you wearing tomorrow night? Your yellow dress is nice, but I think you need more party than pretty."

"No, thanks." Cara chuckled. "I'm not going, but I hope you have a fantastic time."

Skye turned to her, openmouthed. "I'm sorry, what? You have to go! We are going to be drunk monkeys and make fools of ourselves."

"Watch the road! I'm not in a party mood, and besides, we have a flight the next day for my mom's wedding."

"Boo! That's not a good enough excuse. At least, think about it? One last night, pretty please!"

"Are you dying? It's not one last night. We will see each other when I get back from Italy." Cara didn't want to explain that she didn't think she could fake being carefree for a party.

"But we won't work together anymore," Skye whined. "I'll come over. We can get ready together! Please, please, please. Tell Wes he has to look normal, not athletic pants and a T-shirt!"

A pinching had started between Cara's eyes at the enormity of everything going on around her. "Why would Wes go?"

"He works with the production, duh. I'll be at your place at seven? I'll bring the refreshments."

Cara tried to open the car door, but Skye pushed the button to turn on the child locks. "Are you serious?"

"Say yes, or I'm keeping you in my car forever. We'll live here.

We'll only eat at drive-throughs, and be known as the car babes…"

Cara held up her hands. "I surrender! I'll go, but I'm not staying late."

Skye unlocked the door and smiled sweetly. "I knew you wanted to go."

CHAPTER THIRTY-EIGHT

AFTER SKYE PICKED UP CARA THAT MORNING, WES TOOK A QUICK
shower and grabbed a protein bar before getting back to work.
He wished he'd had more information to give her that morning,
but so far, he'd hit mostly dead ends.

Accessing the manufacturer's database, he could see the
burner phone she received was part of a lot sent to Atlanta,
which wasn't a tremendous shock. Wes was still narrowing down
which specific store sold the phone. He brewed a fresh pot of
coffee and texted Jin to call as soon as he was up.

Jin arrived half an hour later, his computer and cables tucked
under his arm.

"You can't do this." His friend's dark eyes flashed angrily. "You
just met this girl and now you're going to break the law for her?
Risk everything you've…" Jin gestured with one finger between
Wes and then back to himself. "What *we've* built? There isn't
going to be a miracle plea offer this time, Wes. You could go to
prison!"

Wes's jaw flexed. "I'm going to do this. I'm not asking you to
do anything illegal. I just need help if Cara ends up splashed

across the internet again. She was in her own fucking bedroom!" His hand shook as anger coursed through him again.

"Damn." Jin stared at him intently. "I'd do the same for Nina. Let's get started. Have you tracked the phone yet?"

"I don't want you to be a part of that." This was his fight. Jin had a family.

"For a computer genius, you are remarkably stupid," Nina said from the door, her son bright-eyed in a front carrier. She had an alarming amount of baby equipment hooked over her arms and dangling from her hands.

"Please, make yourself at home."

Nina was unmoved by his sarcasm. "Thanks, I will. Here." She set two bags down, and with one hand released the straps and handed the baby to Wes. "Go sit over there and explain to my son that you aren't in love with your roommate, but you are willing to risk going back to jail for her—because she's your *friend*."

Shaking her head, Nina sat next to her husband. Jin set his laptop on the kitchen table opposite Wes's monitors and bent to plug in his power cord. Straightening, he pointed a finger at Wes.

"You should have let me infiltrate the carriers. I'm felony free."

Wes appreciated his friends' attempt to make him smile, but Nina's comments had hit him straight in the chest. If he was in love with Cara, what did that mean for his plans with Melody?

"Use the power strip, dummy." Nina swatted her husband's hands away from the electrical socket. "Do you think we are going to plug everything in to one?" Coming to her feet, she gave Jin a swift kiss. "I'm going to work on tracing the RAT. Is that her computer? Show me which files you've already cleared."

Wes's throat clogged with emotion. "I don't want to put you both at risk. You are a family, and this little guy needs you. This is my problem to solve. You can't get involved."

The couple ignored him, Nina offering suggestions to her husband as he keyed up a program. "I'm serious!" Wes yelled, making the baby wail. Nina gave him a dirty look before retrieving her child.

"Look what you did!" she accused.

Wes looked at his two friends. "I appreciate you want to help, but this is… You have a family to protect. I don't want to drag you into this."

Nina bounced her son, who thankfully had found his fingers, on her hip. Her look was pointed. "You're right. And that's exactly what we are doing. Protecting our *family*." Her eyes were fierce, and when Wes opened his mouth to protest, Jin interjected, never taking his eyes off the screen.

"I wouldn't. You aren't going to win this one." He looked over his shoulder and briefly eyed Wes before returning to what he was doing. "Besides, I owe you."

"You don't owe me anything. That was all my idea."

"Maybe, but I don't remember putting up a fight. And when you got caught, you could have snitched on me to get a lighter sentence and you didn't."

Nina took a step forward, laying a hand on Wes's forearm. "We will never forget. You aren't just our friend; you are our family."

Realizing the uncharacteristic emotional tone of the conversation was making them all uncomfortable, Nina shrugged and bent to put her son in a bouncy seat. "Get over it. Besides, I've never seen you as happy as you've been since you moved in with her. She's good for you. And it's really shitty this is happening. If the police can't help, we will. At some point, we'd like to meet her, just to make sure she's not some Japanese sex doll you ordered."

"Don't shame him, babe. A man likes what he likes."

"I think I'm regretting calling you," Wes groaned.

A couple of hours later, they had the name of the account holder for the number that had called Cara and texted her the message about the flowers. Unfortunately, it was a corporation,

Iveson & Co., a small subsidiary of another larger company based in New York. Nina had found the RAT, so now, the next time whoever it was tried to access Cara's computer remotely, they'd have his physical location.

Wes hadn't yet found a way to share the information with the police without revealing what they had done. However, he suspected if he gave the information to Cara's brother, Declan, the problem would disappear.

WES WATCHED Cara tip the champagne flute up again and then wave it in the air, as she shook her long blonde waves back and forth. He hadn't planned on coming to this party, but Cara had promised Skye, and he wasn't letting her out of his sight until there was an ocean between her and this perv.

She was tipsy. It wasn't something he'd seen more than once, but he was quickly becoming a fan. Cara set her glass down and pranced back to the dance floor, waving her arms over her head as her hips kept rhythm with the deep bass.

He couldn't take his eyes off her.

It had taken him fifteen minutes, including a shower, to get ready for the night, and that was with actually trying to do something with his hair. The laughter coming from Cara's room went on for over an hour, sending a warm feeling throughout his body. If she could forget what was happening for a couple of hours, he was all for it.

The voice in the back of his head reminded him he would see Melody in a few days, and after that, everything could change. The problem was, he was no longer sure what he wanted that change to be.

The bedroom door opened, and Skye and Cara spilled out, already a little wobbly. His breath caught. She wore a purple dress, simple in design, hitting her mid-thigh. Wes's eyes trailed from her nude high-heels up her toned legs, and lingered on the deep V that showcased her curves. A simple, gold disc on a chain nestled between her breasts. His mouth dried, the memory of how that soft skin had tasted on his tongue… Thankfully, the two women were so busy admiring each other and ordering a car that they didn't notice him turn away and adjust himself. This was going to be a long night.

The party had grown more raucous as time went on, and Wes looked at his watch. It was almost midnight, and Cara showed no sign of wanting to stop soon. Wes thought of their flight the following afternoon and sipped his whiskey. He didn't want to leave while she was having fun. They'd packed earlier in the day and could always sleep on the plane.

"She's a hit." Jerrod dropped into the folding chair next to Wes and lifted his forearm to wipe the sheen from his forehead. He picked up a wine glass and downed it. Smacking his lips, he looked sideways at Wes and chuckled.

Wes grunted. He was unhappily aware that he wasn't the only man in the room who thought the sight of Cara, moving to the beat in a short, tight dress, was mesmerizing. Another young man danced up close to Cara. Wes had sworn to himself that he wouldn't touch Cara again until he knew what it was he wanted. It wasn't fair to either of them.

"You need another drink."

Wes glanced at the whiskey in his hand and tipped it back with one gulp.

"Go dance with her."

Wes glared at him.

"Every time some guy tries to grind up on her, you come half out of your seat? Ah, here comes Brian with our new nepo-baby owners."

Brian, Trey, and Matt had joined the group of women on the dance floor. Wes recognized the second Cara realized it, and before he knew what he was doing, he was on his feet and striding toward her. He ignored Jerrod's laughter in the background. Matt was attempting to dance with Skye, while Trey swayed at the edge of the dance floor.

Wes was a step away when Brian put his hands on Cara's waist, and Wes didn't think. Leveling a look at the former owner, he caught Cara's hands and pulled her out of Brian's reach, until she was pressed flush against his body. He knew what it looked like. Possessive. Jealous when he had no right to be… Fuck it.

Violet eyes sparkled up at him through her lashes, and he was lost. Wes knew Cara could feel him through her dress. The second he touched her, all the blood in his body had rushed straight to his cock. His pulse thundered in his ears, but all intelligent thought fled his brain.

Wes wrapped an arm around her lower back, pulling her against him as they moved with the music. Fire raced through him, and his entire world narrowed to the feel of her in his arms and the scent of honeysuckle wafting up toward him. So sweet.

He swept her long hair to the side, his free hand finding the bare skin at the nape. Cara let out a breathy moan, and his body clenched painfully. Cara looked up, a dreamy smile on her full lips. He bent his head and whispered in her ear. "Are you ready to go?"

Cara's pupils dilated. He'd meant leave the party, but suddenly all he could see was getting her home, peeling that tight dress from her, and finding out if she tasted like honeysuckle everywhere.

Her lips curved into a wicked smile. Wes groaned. He didn't know if they would make it all the way home.

A switch had flipped inside him. Nothing else mattered but getting Cara home, spread naked on the bed, her pink mouth… Wes sucked in a breath. He needed to get himself under control, but the flush on Cara's chest, as it moved with her rapid breaths, told him she was as eager to be alone as he was.

They didn't bother to find their friends before heading for the door. The cold March breeze blew stronger than it had when they arrived. Goosebumps rose on her bare shoulders, and Wes slipped off his jacket to lay it over her shoulders.

Cara, in his jacket, felt right. A sense of wholeness hit him, and the first tendrils of hesitation began to surface. He couldn't afford to feel this way about her. Not until he spoke to Melody.

Cara must have sensed where his thoughts were going because her eyes became determined. Wes's fingers gripped the lapels where he held the jacket closed over her. She brought her hand up and slid it behind his neck, bringing his face down to hers.

"Even if it's just tonight." Emotion passed over her eyes, but before he could decipher it, her hands cupped his face. "One night," she whispered against his lips, before covering them with her own.

All doubts fled, as heat and desire consumed him once again. Cara parted her lips slightly, and she kissed him gently. When her tongue stroked over his own, his pulse skyrocketed, and he took control, slanting his mouth over hers. Using the jacket, Wes jerked Cara against him so that she couldn't help but feel his arousal pressed against her stomach. She whimpered and opened her mouth to give him further access.

"Get a room!" someone yelled, and Cara pulled away, her cheeks red, lips swollen. Wes gripped her hand, preventing her from moving farther.

They kept their hands to themselves—mostly—during the car ride home. Before the rideshare was out of the driveway, they were entwined again. Somehow, they made their way up the steps and onto the porch. Wes's hands fisted in her hair as she grabbed at the back of his shirt, wrenching it from his waistband.

"I need..." Cara gasped.

"I know." His mouth descended for another fiery kiss.

Her palms smoothed over the warm, muscular ridges of his back, followed by the bite of her nails digging into his skin. Wes stroked up under her skirt to the back of her thighs and lifted her off her feet. Cara's legs wrapped him around his waist, pushing her skirt to the top of her thighs. Wes could feel the heat of her through her thin panties, and his cock pulsed in response.

One hand gripped her ass as he turned and pushed her back against the wall next to the front door. He lifted his lips, gasping for air. "Are you sure?"

"Shhh." She yanked his hair, bringing his mouth back to hers and her tongue… He wasn't sure he was going to survive the night.

Wes pulled his head back. "Keys," he rasped, and pressed a smacking kiss on her mouth when one of Cara's hands dangled them in front of him. He didn't know where she had been hiding them, and he didn't care.

He slid Cara's body down his, one arm still holding her firmly against him, as she peppered slow kisses along his jawline. Wes groaned aloud when the key finally turned, and the door swung open.

Kicking the door shut with one foot, Wes recaptured her mouth with his, pulling hard on her bottom lip. His lips moved across her cheek, tracking down her jaw as Cara moved restlessly against him, her fingers plucking at the buttons of his dress shirt, and sighing when she found the hot skin of his chest beneath.

He walked them backward, not sure where his destination was–sofa? Kitchen table? He groaned again at a sudden vision of Cara bent over—his lips sucked feverishly at the hollow where her neck met her shoulder. She panted against his ear, writhing under his mouth. They might not make the table—

Suddenly, the world upended, and they tumbled to the ground, tripping over the items scattered across their floor.

CHAPTER THIRTY-NINE

The police arrived thirty minutes later to take their statements. Realizing what had happened, Wes had immediately sprung to his feet and checked his computer equipment, but whoever had ransacked the house hadn't damaged the electronics. Cara had nothing of great value at the house, and her computer was still on the kitchen table where Wes left it.

"Nothing was taken?" The young female patrol officer asked, eyeing Wes's misbuttoned shirt.

"Nothing valuable… it's such a mess." The contents of their kitchen cabinets were scattered across the counters, broken glass everywhere. Wes's clothes and dresser drawers had been tossed, and Cara's room had fared little better.

"But there is *something* missing?" The officer narrowed her eyes.

Cara made a face, aware of how ridiculous it was going to sound. "He took a snow globe. It wasn't valuable to anyone but me."

The officer's pen stopped writing. "A snow globe? You noticed it was missing?"

Cara shook her head. "He was carrying it when he left. Wes has the video from the security camera on his phone."

"I'll make a note of it." The officer rolled her eyes.

While Wes had been on the phone to 911 reporting the break-in, Cara called Luke. He'd beaten the police to the house by ten minutes. She needed to tell the officer about the stalker. Cara hadn't told Luke about it yet, and she didn't think Declan had either... This was not the atmosphere she wanted when she finally told him.

The officer produced a card and handed it to Cara. "If you think of anything else or discover something missing, let me know. Could be kids wanting to cause destruction..." She looked doubtful.

Cara took the card, worrying the edges. "There is one more thing." She gave her brother an 'I'm sorry' face and dove into the story. Luke paled, his jaw flexing, but thankfully he held himself in check in front of the police officer.

"Your stalker may have taken the snow globe as a personal souvenir. The crime scene team will be here soon. They'll dust for prints, and hopefully, whoever this guy is will be in the system." The woman glanced at Luke again. "Can you and your boyfriend stay with your brother?"

A muscle ticked in Luke's jaw.

"I'd like a detective here," he said, his voice steely. The officer nodded.

"My sergeant is on his way."

"Can my sister and her *friend* gather some things to take with them?"

"Not until they clear the scene." She gave Cara's party dress a sympathetic look. "It shouldn't take long, and if you tell me what you need, I'll have them bring it out."

Cara and Wes told her where to find their suitcases and which computers they needed. Thankfully, Cara had already packed her travel toiletry bag. The second the officer was out of earshot, Luke turned on her.

"Need advice for a friend, huh? Why the fuck didn't you tell me someone was threatening you?"

Cara's retort died on her lips. She knew he was worried, and she *had* lied to him.

"I wasn't being threatened at the time. It was just creepy flowers and notes. It could have been a prank… I didn't want to worry you and James."

"And you don't think your new boyfriend has anything to do with it?" Luke cast a dark look in Wes's direction, where he stood in a pool of light by the house, a resigned expression on his face.

"Wes isn't my boyfriend, and I trust him. The cameras Wes installed caught the person breaking in, but he was in a hoodie and mask. Wes has been helping me."

Luke frowned, reaching out to twitch the sleeve of Wes's jacket. Wes had insisted she put it on properly while they waited for the police because of the cool air. "Right."

A detective eventually arrived, and Cara told her story for the third time. It was another two hours before an officer brought their things out to them and they were able to leave.

"Do you think it's the same person?" Cara asked, though in her gut she knew it was.

"Could be." The detective hedged. "The scene looks staged. There are thousands of dollars' worth of computer equipment he could have walked off with, and if it was a vandal, they would have destroyed more stuff. Other than your glassware, nothing was broken. Could be he was hoping to find you here, and when you weren't, he made his presence known. You have some place to go?"

"I'm leaving the country for a few days."

The detective nodded. "That's probably a good idea. When you get back, you might consider upgrading this system to a monitored one."

"She won't be coming back here," Luke interrupted, ignoring Cara's glare.

It was almost four in the morning when they got to Luke's Buckhead condo. Cara was cold and exhausted, and she was seriously worried whether her feet would ever be the same after standing in her heels for so long.

Luke threw a pillow and blanket on his leather couch. "He sleeps here. Cara, you know where the guest bedroom is."

"Thanks." Wes's eyes looked bruised as he set their suitcases in Luke's spacious living room.

"We'll talk about this in the morning." Luke eyed her. "What time is your flight?"

"Three o'clock." Wes answered, and Luke's gaze swung to him, before falling to the luggage, as if the existence of two suitcases had just registered with him.

"You're going to Corinne's wedding?" Luke ground out.

Cara didn't like the looks that were being exchanged between the two men. "I invited him."

Luke grunted and then crossed his arms across his broad chest. "In that case, I guess you should get some sleep." He flicked his eyes down the hall to where the guest bedroom was located.

Cara widened her eyes at her brother, silently urging him to leave them alone. Luke's narrowed in response and didn't budge. If anything, his face grew stonier.

"Goodnight, Cara."

Cara scowled, but picked up her suitcase, muttering about annoying brothers.

She needed to talk to Wes. Discuss what had happened, not just at the house but between them! It was clear Luke had no intention of leaving them alone.

When they reached the airport after only a few hours of sleep, they still hadn't discussed anything.

CHAPTER FORTY

Wes and Cara boarded their flight early, and Cara let out a happy sigh when she saw he had purchased Business Class tickets.

"It was the least I could do. Besides, this is a long flight, and I wasn't going to spend it folded up like a pretzel."

"I don't care what your reasons were. I'm just glad you did!" She took the glass of prosecco the flight attendant offered.

Wes cocked his head at her. "You seem calmer than I thought you'd be today."

"I think the concept of being on the other side of the planet from this creep has put me in a better mood."

Wes was skeptical, and it must have shown because she continued, keeping her voice low so the other passengers didn't hear her. "I know we've solved nothing, and he's still out there... But after last night, I think I'm resigned to the fact that he will leak those pictures—"

"I told you we won't let that happen."

She gave him a little smile. "I know you and your friends will do your best, but odds are someone will see them. I might be numb, or maybe I'm more pissed off than I was before, but I didn't feel frightened this morning. I probably should have. He was in our house, but—" A wrinkle developed between her eyes. "I've decided to forget about it for a few days. It's going to be enough dealing with my mom. At least, I won't have to worry about the stalker while I'm there. There's nothing he can do but release the pictures."

Wes had his doubts, but if Cara wanted to live in denial for a few days, who was he to argue? "I thought you got along with your mom?"

"I do. It's just not a normal mother-daughter relationship, and she can be a bit… much."

The flight attendant came around to collect their glasses, and soon they were in the air. Cara yawned and reclined her seat. She arranged the blanket over both their legs. Wes leaned back himself, and lifted the armrest dividing their seats, pulling her closer so that she could rest her pillow against him. Cara snuggled into him, and before long, he could feel her breath even out and knew she was asleep.

Wes's throat tightened, and he briefly laid his cheek on the top of her head. Cara might feel better, but his brain wouldn't stop churning through all the scenarios that could play out over the next few days.

Everything had changed between them.

Last night, she consumed him—he'd never felt anything close to that before. He'd held off examining his feelings for so long, but the connection between them was undeniable—this level of emotion, of caring— scared him.

The life he'd imagined for him and Melody had been safe and uncomplicated—a happy family, some kids, maybe a dog. Nowhere in his mind did he envision a love that had the potential to break him. Lately, when he indulged in a daydream about his future, the woman with a toddler on her hip was Cara.

He smiled, imagining all of her potions and concoctions on the kitchen counter of the kind of house he wanted to buy. Cara told him she didn't want to be married, didn't believe in a love that would last. What would happen if he gave up his shot with Melody and told Cara how he felt? What happened if she said no?

He wasn't sure if it was a chance he could take.

~

THE CAR that picked them up in Florence finally turned off the narrow two-lane Italian highway. They came to a stop at a gate set in a limestone wall. After the driver gave the guard his identification and they underwent a quick visual inspection, the gate opened, and they were waved through. The driver pulled onto a narrow drive flanked by cypress trees and wound their way up a hill, until they reached the large courtyard of the villa Cara's mother had rented for the wedding.

Wes peered up at the two-story building. "It looks straight out of one of the Godfather movies," he said, taking in the stone walls and iron hooks that held back green shutters. Two massive wooden doors swung open at their approach, and one of the most beautiful women he'd ever seen rushed out to greet them.

The driver opened the door, and Cara muttered something that sounded like, "Here we go."

"Caralina!" Cara's mother was tall and thin, her thick blonde hair piled on top of her head. Wes had googled Cara's mother, curious about the woman Cara rarely spoke of. The flat two-dimensional nature of the pictures completely obscured the vivacity pouring off the woman who enveloped Cara in her arms.

"I'm so glad you're here! I can't wait for you to meet Alessandro! You are going to love him. So charming!" She hooked her arm through her daughter's elbow and pulled her in for a side hug. "And *so* handsome. I finally found my true love."

"Again?" Cara's tone was dry as she disengaged her arm from her mother.

A slight frown marred the otherwise smooth skin of the older woman's forehead. "He is. You'll see. It's different this time. I promise."

Cara hummed a sound of agreement, but the look on her face was pure doubt. The corners of Corinne's mouth turned down. "You are so cynical. You get that from your father." Corinne closed her eyes, raised her hands and brought her fingertips together in a prayerful gesture. "Someday you'll fall in love, and you'll understand."

"I doubt it," Cara muttered, but Corinne didn't seem to hear her.

The former model's attention shifted to Wes, her eyes twinkling. "But maybe you already have." Her smile turned coy. "Who is this delicious young man?"

Her open perusal lingered on his groin, and Wes felt his cheeks heat.

"You're scaring him." Cara laughed, but it broke the tension between the two women. By the look in Corinne's eyes before she pivoted to face her daughter, Wes was pretty sure it was exactly what she had intended. "Don't get excited. There's nothing going on with us. Wes is my roommate."

Cara's words were the truth, but they rubbed at him.

"Hmm, we'll see." Corinne threw him a wink over her shoulder as she dragged Cara up the stairs and into the villa, leaving Wes standing alone with the driver and their luggage.

The driver carried the bags up the stone stairs, leaving them in the entryway. Wes shouldered his computer bag and followed them into the house. He found Cara and her mother at the foot of the staircase talking with an older man. Wes surmised he was the groom by the way he was clutching at Corinne. Cara turned an exasperated face to him.

"Can you help me? I've explained that we aren't together, but they are insisting there is only one room assigned to me." She eyed her mother. "I find it difficult to believe that in a place this size, there isn't an extra room with a bed."

Shit! Wes struggled to keep his distance from her in the same house. He wasn't sure his self-control would survive sleeping in the same room.

"You've become so provincial, darling. You never told me you were bringing a guest. If you had, I could have reserved a room at the hotel where most of the guests are staying, but now, so close to the wedding, they are completely booked. This is a very popular event." Corinne waved a dismissive hand. "It's a large room, darling. A suite, really. And there is a chaise one of you could sleep on if you are concerned." She deliberately widened her eyes and looked between Cara and Wes. "*But* if you are just friends, I don't see why you couldn't share a bed."

Cara rubbed her temples with her fingers. Wes's brain raced, searching for a solution, but he didn't see how they could object without making a scene. It was only for a couple nights, and they'd be busy with the parties—if he really wanted to be with Melody, this shouldn't be a problem.

"I'm sure it will be fine," he heard himself say.

"Wes!"

"We'll figure it out." He forced his lips to smile.

"Wes, this is Alessandro." Corinne placed her palm against the man's chest. "My love, this is Wes, my daughter's *friend*."

Alessandro looked like he had come straight from a GQ photo spread. Between Corinne's blonde beauty and his thick, dark hair swept back from a deeply tanned face, they were almost too attractive to be real.

Corrine's hand stroked the back of Alessandro's neck, and he growled, snapping his teeth playfully at her. Cara's entire face wrinkled in disgust.

Alessandro chuckled. "Forgive us. I get carried away when I'm with *amore mio*." Corinne cooed up at him, and Cara's frown deepened.

"What time is the event tonight? We want to get cleaned up."

"Cocktails and nibbles at six, and then we have a surprise!"

"We will see you at six then." Cara moved to pick up her suitcase.

"I thought we could talk. Catch up. It feels like forever since we've had a real chat." Corinne's disappointment was palpable. But Cara only looked annoyed.

"Maybe later, if there's time."

"Of course, darling," Corinne said, but Cara had already moved away.

"Don't worry about those," Alessandro said, motioning toward their bags. "We'll have it sent up. You are the second door on the left."

Wes and Cara climbed the stone staircase to the second floor in silence. The thick wooden door swung open, and it only took one glance for Wes to realize his easy acquiescence was going to cost him.

The room was nowhere near as large as what Corinne led them to believe. Beneath two tall narrow windows was the chaise she mentioned, but it wasn't large enough for an adult to sleep comfortably on. A giant, upholstered headboard over the bed dominated the space.

Wes strolled to the open door to the left that he assumed led to the bathroom. "Not bad." Wes joked as Cara continued to gaze blankly at the huge bed. "I didn't know if we'd get our own bathroom."

Cara exhaled as she moved across the room, sinking onto the white duvet. "I'm sorry about this. In all the excitement, I forgot to tell my mom you were coming. I didn't think the room would be an issue."

"We'll make it work."

Cara worried her lip. "I didn't tell her to do this."

"I didn't think you had." Wes needed to stop staring at the bed. Imagining…

"I know you're here to talk with Melody, and I'm not going to do anything to get in the way of that."

Cara's words made him irrationally angry. Did she *want* him to be with Melody? And if she did, why did it bother him so much? A knock at the door signaled their bags had arrived, granting them a temporary reprieve.

They unpacked in an uncomfortable silence. Why were things so awkward between them here? Cara hung her dress in the armoire and laid a black silk jumpsuit on the bed. She carried her toiletry bag into the tiny bathroom, hovering in the doorway.

"I'm going to take a shower to wash off the airplane yuck."

Wes's mind immediately created a vivid image of Cara, naked, water sluicing over her…

"I'll go see if I can find us some food."

He wasted no time disappearing out the door, but once he reached the top of the stone stairwell, he realized he had no idea where to go. Cara had mentioned the villa was fully rented for the wedding, but was it okay for him to explore on his own?

The scent of roasting garlic wafted through the air, and his stomach growled, deciding for him. Wes followed the smell to the kitchen at the back of the house. It was modern for all that it tried to maintain a Tuscan quaintness. A large butcher-block topped island stood in the center of the room, but there was a huge stainless range, with a stone range hood, and a refrigerator built into the cabinets next to it. The light in the oven was on, identifying the origin of the aroma, but there was no sign of whoever had put the dish inside.

Wes grabbed an enormous bunch of grapes from the bowl on the counter and popped them into his mouth, one at a time, as he opened cabinets, looking for snacks. Neither one of them had eaten much on the plane, and he knew Cara must be hungry, too. He found a block of cheese in the refrigerator and cut off a few hunks to put onto a plate with the grapes. Something was better than nothing! Wes had just closed the refrigerator door and was trying to judge how much longer he needed to stall before Cara was safely dressed, when an elegant man about his age strolled in.

The man's dark eyebrows rose to his hairline. "Ciao! You caught me."

"Is that your garlic?"

"Si. My uncle and Corinne will murder me if they catch me cooking. I don't think either of them has ever used a kitchen. But my fiancée is hungry, and what can I say?" He gave a shrug. "Whatever my love wants, she gets." He chuckled, and Wes smiled back. The man opened the refrigerator and pulled out a ceramic bowl covered with a dishcloth. He set it on the counter and pulled a pot from the decorative collection hanging above the island, filled it with water, and set it on the range.

"Your secret is safe with me." Wes gestured at the cheese. "This was the best I could find. My..." He hesitated. The words 'my girlfriend' almost rolled off his tongue, catching him by surprise.

The man looked at him quizzically and added a hefty measure of salt to the water from a stone cannister next to the stove. "We just got in, and I wasn't sure I'd make it until the cocktail hour. Corinne said nibbles, but I hope it's going to involve some actual food."

"I heard my uncle talking earlier. They will have plenty." The man uncovered the bowl, revealing a tangle of fresh linguine. He winked at Wes. "I bribed my cook at home to send it with us. I had a feeling there wouldn't be anything besides what the caterers brought in."

"Smart man," Wes said appreciatively. "Alessandro, is your uncle?"

"Yes, more like a father really. Mine died when I was young, and Zio Alex took me in, taught me the family business." He rolled his eyes. "Delivers all the lectures you'd expect. Are you a friend of Corinne's? Your accent is American?" His eyes lit up. "Are you one of the sons?"

Sons? It took Wes a second to realize he meant Cara's half-brothers. "No, I'm here with her daughter Cara."

"Lovely!" His face took on a sheepish expression. "I'm afraid I don't know her. Corrine and Zio Alex's romance was a whirlwind, and I've been so wrapped up with my work." Wes was bewildered when the man's expression changed yet again. "I met my muse." He kissed his fingers in appreciation. "And it has changed *everything*!"

"Your muse?" Wes asked. His pulse picked up. How often did people use that word? Melody had referred to herself as a young designer's muse.

"My fiancée," the man said, oblivious to Wes's frowning dismay. Looking at the rapidly boiling water, he pushed the pasta into the pot. "I met her by chance only weeks ago, but it was love at first sight. She was on the last day of a photo shoot, and it was kismet I stopped by. There was a question about the direction it was going, and my uncle was busy." He waved his hand. "Fate."

"You're Luca?"

The man looked back over his shoulder, surprised by Wes's words, but the sound of clicking heels approaching from the stone floor of the hallway drew both of their attentions.

Melody appeared in the arched doorway, as beautiful as she had always been. In fact, if he were being honest, maybe even more beautiful because, in the moment before she noticed Wes standing there, her face looked relaxed—content. Wes wasn't sure he'd ever seen that expression on Melody's face before.

"Wes?" There was no disguising the horror on Melody's face, and Luca's previously open expression turned alert.

"What are you doing here? How did you find out where I was?"

Luca looked from her to Wes, his eyes guarded.

"Hey, Mel."

"This is *the* Wes?" Luca stepped forward, extending his hand to Wes.

Melody ignored her fiancée, her hands going to her hips. "What the hell, Wes? I didn't know you were going to be here!"

"Surprise?" Melody narrowed her eyes, and Wes relented. "I'm here as a guest, well the plus one anyway."

"Uh-huh. Because you have so many friends in the fashion industry." Wes was taken aback. He'd expected her to be surprised, but she seemed angry. Wes wasn't here to cause a problem for her, he only wanted to talk.

"He is here with Corinne's daughter," Luca said.

"Corinne's daughter? The infamous Bloom socialite?" Melody's eyes widened.

"Hey, Melody, it's been a long time," Cara said, sliding past the couple and immediately walking to Wes's side.

Melody's face creased in confusion as she stared at Cara, as if she couldn't quite place her. Cara's mouth flattened. "Cara… you rented me the room in your house, well Wes's house, but you know what I mean."

Melody's face cleared. "Oh, of course!" She had the grace to look embarrassed. "You're so out of place here, I didn't make the connection."

Cara pointed at the stove. "I think your pasta needs you."

Luca let out an exclamation and then cursed when he grabbed the hot handle.

"You've all met each other, wonderful!" Alessandro and Corinne joined them, adding to the chaos.

"Corinne, you look so beautiful, and Zio Alex, thank you so much for hosting us here at the villa," Melody simpered. "We are so happy for you, and it means so much to Luca to be included."

"Darling, you look nice." Corinne ignored Melody. Cara had put on casual loungewear after her shower. It was obvious Corinne wanted to say something more but bit her tongue. She settled on, "You'll be so comfortable tonight."

"This isn't what I'm wearing tonight," Cara said with a smile. "I just came to find where Wes had disappeared to, and to let him know the shower was free."

Melody's mouth hung open. "*You're* Caralina Bloom?"

"My whole life." Cara's voice was a shade short of rude.

"But!" Melody's forehead wrinkled. "She's the makeup girl."

"Wes, do you want to shower before the party?" Cara asked.

Wes cast a look at Melody, but she was still staring dumb-founded at Cara. "Yeah, I made you a snack." He offered the plate and was rewarded with a soft smile.

"Just friends," Corinne laughed. "Go! Get ready but come back quickly! We have some delicious drinks planned."

CHAPTER FORTY-ONE

"So, that was Luca?" Cara leaned against the door after she closed it behind them.

Wes paced the length of the room. "Did you see her?"

"Melody? She looked great."

"She didn't look like herself, she looked…" He waved his hand in exasperation. "Too slick. That's not her at all!"

"Seemed like the Melody I've heard about," Cara said under her breath, remembering the model's dismissal of her. She would bet, now that Melody knew she was a Bloom, she would suddenly want to be friends. Cara recognized the type.

Wes carried his shirt and slacks into the bathroom, lost in his own world. Cara sat at the antique vanity table and applied her makeup. Seeing Melody again had been a shock. Intellectually, she knew the model would be there. But somehow, seeing her in person, had yanked Cara out of her dream world—the one where Wes might care enough about her to forget his ridiculous *plan*.

She pictured the evening ahead and sighed. Cara didn't want to deal with her mother's attempts to pretend, for her friends' benefit, that she and Cara were close. And, she definitely wasn't interested in watching Wes chase after Melody.

Cara rifled through her bag until she found the tube of lipstick she was looking for. If ever there was a night she needed red lips, it was this one. She sat back and looked at her reflection before picking up her black liquid liner. She drew sharp cat-eyes on her lids and applied several coats of mascara to her thick lashes.

She may not be a supermodel, but she was Cara Bloom, and it was past time to rejoin the world.

~

"I NEED A DRINK."

It was the first coherent sentence Wes had made since exiting the bathroom ten minutes before. Cara had intentionally stood in the middle of the room for effect. The one-shouldered jumpsuit, with sweetheart neckline and cinched waist, showcased her full curves perfectly, and by the way Wes's jaw dropped when he saw her, he agreed.

Fairy lights strung above the large patio transformed the gardens behind the villa. The spring sun hadn't set yet, and from the patio they could see the rolling hills of Tuscany in every direction. It was still early, and only a handful of guests milled about on the patio and gravel paths that led past the pool and the stairs leading to the upper gardens.

While Wes ordered their drinks, she took a minute to look for a familiar face. Declan had texted that he would be there but wasn't sure what time.

"Damn!" Wes cursed softly as he sloshed the old-fashioned onto his wrist.

"What do you think the chances are someone twists their ankle in this stuff?" Cara asked, hoping for a smile.

He surveyed the tiny pebbles between the larger pavers surrounding them, and then glanced down at her feet. Cara had chosen flats to go with her jumpsuit. What she lost in height, she made up for in stability. "Looks like you knew what to expect."

"I'm an old pro," she joked, sipping from the coupe glass.

"Better question is," Wes tilted his head towards the water nearby, "does someone end up in the pool?"

Cara pretended to consider the narrow reflecting pool. "I've seen it happen."

"Really?"

"No," she giggled.

"To not falling in pools." Wes clinked his glass against hers.

They sipped their cocktails, watching people arrive.

"It's beautiful out here," Wes said, looking over the landscape. "I've never been to Italy. I've never really been anywhere except Mexico. I always wanted to travel."

"You should. We could take a few days after the wedding. Go to Florence or Rome." Cara bit her lip. Even if she had the budget to travel, she should remember that there was a possibility he would leave the villa with Melody and not her.

Wes cocked an eyebrow at her. "That's not a bad idea. I've got my computer with me. If something pressing comes up that Jin can't handle, all I need is a good internet connection. You're between jobs, so it might be the perfect time. I doubt you're in a rush to go back and deal with—"

"Shh. I'm on denial holiday, remember?"

He took a swig of his drink and scanned the crowd, his face folding into a scowl. "Isn't that one of those assholes we met at the hotel in Buckhead?"

Cara followed his gaze, terrified she would see Erik. The last thing she needed this week was her asshole ex-boyfriend.

"I don't see–"

A man stepped under one of the torches lining the pool, and her body relaxed. "Colin!" She lifted her hand, and he made his way toward them. "You scared me for a second. I thought you meant Erik." She said under her breath to Wes.

Wes didn't seem reassured. "What's he doing here?"

"Our mothers were friends back in the day. Well, frenemies might be a better term. When Ursula married Colin's father, they lost touch, but I guess they've reconnected. Yes, there they are." Cara pointed. "The tall brunette speaking to my mother, that's her husband standing to the side, with the red hair. He's a banker in London."

"I'm so glad I saw you," Colin exclaimed when he reached them. "Listening to my mom and Corinne try to one up each other is painful." He chuckled, then stuck his hand out to Wes. "Colin Stewart."

Wes clasped his hand—too firmly, if Colin's wince was any sign. "We've met."

"It was a terrible night. I'm sorry again." He said to Cara. "There is something about you that still gets to Erik. Can't say I blame him." He gave her a little smile and snuck a glance at her breasts before he turned to watch the crowd. "Are you staying here?"

Cara nodded. "You?"

"No, my father took a house nearby. She'd never admit it, but I think my mom couldn't stand the thought your mom was in a private home and she was in a hotel."

Cara shook her head with a laugh. "At some point, you'd think they would outgrow their competition."

"Never. I think they will compete for who has the best-attended funeral," Colin joked.

"You're probably right." She noticed that Wes's attention had strayed to the guests on the patio. Melody and Luca stood near one of the stand-up heaters with several people. Luca waved his arms, accentuating a point, while Melody stood on the outskirts of the group.

Cara's heart contracted. "You should talk to her."

"Who?" Colin looked over his shoulder to see who they were talking about.

"Are you sure?" Wes's eyes searched hers.

What did he want her to say?

Stay with me. Be with me. Love me.

Instead, Cara forced a smile and nodded. "It's why you're here." Wes needed to confront how he really felt, and get past this obstacle he'd put in his own life, even if Cara wasn't the one he wanted in the end.

Wes's eyes lingered, and then with a nod, he strolled away.

Cara followed Wes's progress to Melody's side. She must have said something to Luca because he momentarily stopped his gesticulations, and Wes and Melody strode out of sight.

Cara let out a shuddery sigh. "Can I get another one of these, please?" she asked the bartender.

"You look beautiful tonight," Colin said.

"Thanks." Cara took a fresh coupe from the bartender.

"When I met Wes in Atlanta, I thought the two of you might be together." Colin looked thoughtful, and Cara looked at him over the lip of her glass. "But I guess not if you sent him to another woman."

Colin was a nice enough guy, but he followed Erik like a puppy, and she wasn't about to discuss her feelings for Wes with him. Cara downed the rest of the drink and was slightly surprised when Colin had another ready to press in her hand. She hadn't eaten much, and the two glasses, combined with her jet lag, were already making her a little dizzy. "Do you believe in love?"

Only when Colin replied did she realize she had spoken the words out loud.

"I do. Very much so. Isn't everyone hoping to find their true love to spend their life with?"

Cara barely heard him as she searched the darkness Wes and Melody disappeared into. Had she made a terrible mistake? Despair swamped her, and a lone tear slipped down her cheek.

Cara spun on her heel and retreated further into the shadows by the tall cypress trees.

"Cara!" Colin's hand on her arm stopped her, and he tried to pull her toward him for a hug, but she stumbled in the loose gravel.

She sniffed back the rest of her tears. "I just need a minute."

"Do you want to go for a walk? Get away for a bit?"

Cara's lips trembled, and she knew there was no way she was going to make it back to the house without everyone seeing her.

"I'm sorry. I don't know what's wrong with me."

"I think you're a lot like me," Colin said, quietly. They walked farther down the path, away from the house toward the steps at the far end of the pool. The revelry from the party fell away until the only sounds that remained were faint laughter and the rustle of something small scurrying in the underbrush. They climbed the short stairs and strolled farther down the gravel lane passing the manicured hedges and flowering bushes on either side.

Cara tipped her face toward the moon and breathed deeply through her nose. She was in love with him. But it didn't matter if he never healed from the scars of his past.

"We both believe in the fairy tale," Colin continued, picking up the previous conversation. "Even when it looks like it won't work, we still believe. Once you meet the person of your dreams, you have to do whatever it takes to keep them. Be willing to risk everything."

Colin's words pierced through her. He was right. She had never told Wes how she felt. If she told him outright, would it make a difference?

Oh god! What if I've missed my chance?

Tears flooded her eyes, and Colin instantly looked alarmed. He put his arms around her and pulled her into his chest. "It's okay. You don't need–"

"Cara!" Declan's deep voice reached her through the darkness, his large, familiar outline illuminated in the moonlight. In two quick strides, he crossed the distance and glared at Colin.

"What are you doing out here in the dark?" He peered down at her face and then turned to glower ferociously at Colin, who backed up immediately, his hands held up.

"We were just walking," he stuttered. "I should get back to the party."

Her brother pulled the pocket square from his suit jacket and offered it to her. Cara dabbed at the corners of her eyes. "Am I a mess?"

"Puffy, but not terrible."

"Such a flatterer," Cara said dryly, but her brother's no-nonsense familiarity helped her regain her equilibrium.

"What's going on?" Declan cast another suspicious look after Colin.

"Nothing. Seriously. I'm just exhausted and drank too much, too fast on an empty stomach. It made me weepy."

Declan frowned. "That's not like you. You shouldn't be out here alone. It could be dangerous. Where's the hacker? Isn't he supposed to be here?"

"I wasn't alone. I was with Colin. Wes is talking to a friend, and my stalker is an ocean away."

"What friend? He knows someone here?" Declan narrowed his eyes.

Cara looked at the ground. "Melody. She's the model I rented the house from. He came with me so that he could talk to her."

"It was necessary to come to Italy to do that? Cara, what's really going on?"

"He thinks he's in love with her." Cara's voice cracked.

Declan's expression was unreadable, but he looped his arm through hers. "His loss. Let's go find some food and some of the alcohol you've been hogging. I'm not getting through this night without a barrel of whiskey." He shook his head in disgust as they reached the periphery of the party. "I don't know how I got roped into coming."

"Because your mom couldn't." Cara's lips quirked, and she cuddled into his arm. She appreciated Declan's attempt to distract her.

"Oh, yeah." He pretended to be exasperated. "Moms, they're the worst."

"Where were you?" Wes rushed toward them the second they cleared the last line of tall cypresses. "Are you okay?" He gave a quick glance at Declan looming at her side. "I looked for you and you were gone. I thought you were going to wait by the bar."

"You were so worried you left her alone at a party, knowing she has a stalker?" Declan's voice could have frozen an icicle, but Wes merely narrowed his eyes looking from Declan's violet eyes to Cara's matching pair.

"You must be Declan Bloom. We haven't met in person. Wes Evans."

"I know who you are." Declan sneered. "What I don't know is why you left her alone? Anything could have happened!"

"She was with Colin, surrounded by guests. I thought she'd be safe, but you're right."

Wes's honest answer must have surprised Declan because his tone was marginally less hostile when he said, "You and I need to have a talk."

Cara didn't want to deal with either man's testosterone. "Why were you looking for me? I thought you were with Melody."

Wes grimaced. "Some more guests arrived while you were gone." He paused, then looked over his shoulder pointedly. Declan and Cara followed his gaze. Declan cursed. "I heard them talking to Corinne, and it was obvious who they were. You never mentioned that you resembled her a little." Cara sent him a death glare.

"What the fuck is she thinking, inviting them here?" Declan stormed.

"I don't know." Cara was more baffled than upset. She didn't think her mother was friendly with Courtney Bloom, much less close enough to invite her to the wedding.

"And what is Dr. Keller doing with her?"

"Who?" Wes's forehead crinkled.

"Chris's father. He was my father's doctor and friend. But what he's doing here with Courtney?" Cara shook her head. "He's a nice man, a little soft-spoken but—"

Declan's let out a low curse, the muscle ticking in his jaw. "It never occurred to me she had her claws in him."

"What are you talking about?"

Declan's gaze met hers before flicking again to the couple. "You think it's a coincidence that Courtney is suddenly in Italy with the doctor who was supposed to be taking care of our father? He's not exactly her type, so what is she doing with him?"

"I don't trust her either, but… Dr. Keller? Chris's dad! Chris can't stand Courtney. Don't you think he'd have mentioned it if his father was involved with her?"

Wes looked thoughtful. "Whatever the truth is, they've spotted you."

"Be nice, Dec. Think of Chris. We don't know yet what their relationship is."

Declan shot her a disbelieving look.

Courtney was striking in a form-fitted, blue dress, a high slit showing off her thigh. Dr. Keller, looking more like her father than a date, fidgeted with his sport coat. He looked like he wanted to be anywhere else but at this party.

"If it isn't my precious stepchildren. How lovely to see you here!"

"Dr. Keller." Declan greeted the man through his teeth before addressing Cara. "No more wandering off. I'll see you tomorrow." Without ever acknowledging Courtney's presence, Declan walked away.

"Ass!" Courtney seethed.

"I'm surprised to see you here… together. My mother has never mentioned you." Cara didn't attempt to sound friendly, and she welcomed Wes's comforting hand on the small of her back. "I just saw Chris in Atlanta. He didn't mention you were coming to the wedding, Dr. Keller."

Elliot Keller's face drew even longer. Courtney hooked her arm through his elbow and answered for him in a silky voice. "I'm not sure he knows. Did you tell Chris about our little trip?" Her smile was cloying, and her familiarity seemed to make the older doctor uncomfortable.

"I didn't get the chance to tell him. He's been busy… I didn't plan on attending but Courtney…"

"Tuscany in the spring isn't to be missed! You don't mind that I tagged along, do you?" She pouted prettily up at the older man.

"I didn't know the two of you were such good friends." Cara didn't hide her skepticism.

Courtney's crimson lips curled up in a smile, but her eyes were glacial when they met Cara's. "I have a lot of friends."

"I find that hard to believe." The words were out before they fully formed in her head, and Wes failed to muffle a snort of laughter. However, Cara found nothing amusing about the situation. She was furious!

Cara slid her hand into Wes's and led him away, leaving Courtney fuming behind her. In front of them, the party crowd had swelled near a string quartet making Cara claustrophobic.

Instead of climbing the steps to the patio, Cara veered off the path towing Wes into the darkness at the side of the terrace, desperate to get away. Her heart pounded and her chest heaved as she tried to catch her breath. "He was my father's best friend! Dr. Keller knows what she did to Declan—how could he?"

Wes's thumb stroked over her knuckles, but anger and betrayal still rolled through her in unrelenting waves.

"He didn't look happy," Wes pointed out.

"But he *is* here! You don't understand! He and my dad were

close. Really, really close. It's how Chris and Declan met. After Chris's mom died, they were always around." Her breaths came in short, fast bursts. "He was taking care of my dad, a witness to the new will." Cara's vision sparkled, and her fingertips tingled as she fought to draw air into her lungs. "He signed the death certificate!" Her eyes were wild when they met Wes's. "Did he help her… kill my father?"

Wes framed her face with his hands and leaned close. "Slow down. Breathe." Cara's eyes squeezed shut, and she shook her head frantically, bits of hair tumbling from the pins. "You're hyperventilating. Breathe with me. In, out." Wes's voice reached her through the cloud of panic, but she couldn't match his breath. "Open your eyes, baby. Look at me."

With what felt like Herculean effort, Cara unscrewed her eyelids and met Wes's caramel eyes, only inches from her own. "Good girl. Keep breathing." He raised their joined hands and pressed them solidly against her chest. "You're okay. I'm right here with you." The panic dissipated as she clung to his words.

Cara concentrated on matching his deep breaths. Her breathing slowed, and Cara had the nonsensical thought that she could smell the orange on his breath from the old-fashioned he'd ordered. As she regained control of herself, his hands gentled on her face, but neither could look away.

The torches on the veranda above them created warm, flickering patterns across Wes's face. Cara was captivated by it. He was so handsome. Wes's eyes darkened, the black of his pupils bleeding into the gold-flecked irises. Her heart rate picked up, but this time, all thoughts of her stepmother were far away.

"Wes," she whispered. His hands fell away, and instantly she felt the loss.

"I think you're okay now," he rasped.

Wes stepped back, and Cara reacted without thinking. One step closed the distance, and she threaded her fingers through his hair, pulling his head down to hers.

He let out a guttural groan, and wrapped his arms around her waist, crushing her against his body. His lips moved over hers, sliding and sucking until her knees turned to jelly.

Cara's skin felt like it was too small for her body, and one thought hammered through her brain—*closer*—she needed to be closer. She arched her back, pressing firmly against him, seeking the friction she desperately craved.

Wes roughly nudged her thighs apart with his knee, and he making a sound low in his throat. With one leg between hers, he pressed solidly against her center, a hand at her hip holding her in place as he rocked into her. Cara gasped against his mouth.

His free hand plunged into her hair, scattering more of the pins she'd used to hold the updo in place. Using her thick hair as an anchor, his mouth claimed her lips again.

Cara whimpered when Wes's lips traveled from her mouth to feather kisses along her jaw. She sighed, angling her head to give him better access.

Her thighs tightened on his leg, and she gripped his hair, silently demanding more. Wes nipped her neck, as he curved his hands over her ass, pulling her hard against where he strained against his pants.

A bright laugh, followed by voices nearby, signaled someone was approaching.

Wes froze and then sprang backward almost shoving her away. The evening wasn't particularly cool, but Cara felt an instant chill on her fevered skin. His face was flushed, hair tousled, and she had never wanted anyone so badly in her entire life.

Cara reached for his hand, but he shifted backward, his breath still labored. Her chest constricted, and she bit her tongue to keep the tears away. He was rejecting her—again.

The group moved past, not noticing them in the shadows. Her body still quivered, but Wes's self-inflicted torment had reared its head and planted itself solidly between them.

"I'm sorry—" he began.

"Don't do that!" she choked. "This isn't some regency novel. *I* kissed *you,* and I'm *not* sorry! I may not be Melody, but don't you dare say you didn't want me!" She glanced at his pants, the rigid evidence still very much on display. "Because we both know it's a lie. You're just too big of a coward to admit what you really want!"

CHAPTER FORTY-TWO

Wes watched Cara storm off, knowing he should stop her. He needed to say something to make it better. But she was right.

He was a coward.

For more than a decade, he had convinced himself that Melody was who he should be with. Was he prepared to throw away that dream for someone he'd only known for a couple of months?

Melody knew him, understood what he'd been through, wanted the same things he did. But as Wes watched Cara walk away from him, he couldn't ignore the sick feeling in his stomach or the voice that told him he had just made the biggest mistake of his life.

Wes watched until she reached Colin's side on the veranda and while the other man filled a plate of food for her. He ground his teeth when Colin picked up her hand and pressed a kiss to the back of it, making Cara tip her head back in laughter.

He wanted to shout at Colin to take his hands off her, but he couldn't.

Wes didn't have the right. He had hurt her, and he hated himself for it. He would keep his distance, but Wes knew he still needed to keep her in sight. She may not want anything to do with him, but he would still make sure she was safe.

Luca and Melody were holding court with a group of people near where Cara sat with Colin. Wes positioned himself at the outskirts of the group, where he could still see Cara, but also observe Melody. He wasn't sure what he was looking for. A sign from the universe that Melody was the right choice? The safe choice?

Wes smiled as Melody jokingly placed her hand on a man's forearm and leaned in to laugh flirtatiously. He recognized the move. It was more polished now, but it was the same move she'd used on their foster mother, Mrs. Cobb, to get them extra food.

He snuck a glance at Cara, standing with Colin and a few people he hadn't met yet. She was smiling and seemed to be enjoying herself. Wes's attention returned to Melody, who now regaled the group with a story about a photo shoot gone wrong, repeatedly touching the man next to her. *Melody wants something from him.*

Wes quickly dismissed the thought. Just because she was flirting, it didn't mean anything.

Yet, it did.

He'd seen Melody manipulate people over the years using the same move, always for her gain—more snacks, free drinks, access to a club. If he hadn't been watching them so closely, he would have missed when Melody's eyes traveled to her fiancée, and Luca gave her a slightly approving smile.

Wes frowned, unsettled. His eyes returned to where Cara had been standing moments before, but the space was now occupied by different people. His eyes scanned through the crowd standing on the veranda and those he could see in the gardens beyond. There was no sign of her.

Wes had just taken a step to go find her when Melody's delighted voice rang out.

"Wes!"

He tamped down the irritated feeling. Had she decided it was time to include him because he had started to move away? Wes was prepared to ignore her, but he glimpsed Cara getting a glass of wine from the bar, Colin still at her side. Wes scowled.

Is he planning on following her around like a puppy dog all night?

"Wes," Melody's voice was sharper. "I want to introduce you to some people."

He wanted to go check on Cara, make sure Colin wasn't bothering her. But across the crowd, she looked up and met his gaze. She flashed a thumbs up before going back to her conversation.

He huffed an angry breath. She was having a good time without him, and he had no one to blame but himself. He rubbed the back of his neck and reluctantly joined the group, now all watching him curiously.

"Wes is my oldest friend," Melody was saying. "We've known each other since we were babies, practically." Wes let the exaggeration go. Luca smiled widely and motioned for him to come closer.

"I just met Wes yesterday and finally put a face to all the stories. You've been such a good friend to my Bella."

Wes gave a weak smile. He really wanted Luca to be a jerk.

Melody gestured to each of the others and introduced them as designers, models, and photographers. When she reached the man she had been flirting with before, she flashed him another coy smile. "And this is the great Giacomo diBenecto."

The man demurred, but he was clearly enjoying the attention. "He shoots for Vogue Italia. He's thinking about featuring some of Luca's designs in a special spread."

"Only my Bella could do justice to my work. She is my muse."

Wes struggled to keep his face blank, but if he heard the word 'muse' one more time, he was going to lose it.

Melody chuckled. "You are too sweet, my love. I'm not Vogue material." Even as she said the words, she met the photographer's eyes, daring him to agree with her. By the cynical twist of his lips,

Wes guessed this wasn't the first time someone had attempted the ploy on the Italian.

"We shall see. Now is not the time to speak of work." He raised his arms wide, encompassing all of them. "We are here to celebrate *amore*. Nothing is more important than that. Two hearts becoming one."

"Of course." Melody agreed though her smile didn't reach her eyes. "In fact, let's have a toast." Looking around, she snapped her fingers at a server carrying a tray of champagne flutes. Wes's brow wrinkled at the rudeness, but he took the proffered drink.

"To love," Luca raised his glass, "and the hope that everyone finds their perfect match, as I have with my Bella."

Melody's face softened, looking up at him with an expression that Wes had never seen on her face before.

"To love," she said softly, staring into Luca's eyes, and everyone murmured their agreement before clinking their glasses.

Wes heard Cara's laugh ring out, and his head swiveled to find where it had come from. A tall attractive man in a dark suit stood too close to Cara, whispering in her ear. The group she was with had ambled closer to where Wes stood, and under the stringed lights, he could see the blush staining her cheeks.

The man leaned down to whisper in her ear again, briefly touching her waist.

Where the hell was Colin? Wes's pulse sounded in his ears, and he didn't realize he was gripping his flute until Luca's amused voice broke into his thoughts.

"Careful, my friend, you are about to snap the stem." Luca glanced at Cara, and then gave Wes an understanding smile. Wes watched as Colin joined Cara and the stranger, positioning himself so that the lecherous jerk had to take a step back. Good man that Colin, Wes thought as he struggled to get his shoulders to relax.

"Looks like our American friend has an *amour* of his own,"

diBenecto said. "She is a beautiful woman. You are brave to let her out of your sight."

The man was joking, but he was also correct. Wes shouldn't have left Cara's side. Not because he was in love with her, he scoffed silently, but because she still had a stalker out there. They couldn't be sure he hadn't followed them.

"That's Corinne's daughter," Melody interjected. "She and Wes are friends." Her mouth turned down when he didn't answer right away. "Right, Wes?"

Melody didn't look amused. Wes should be thrilled at this sign of jealousy, but as he blankly watched Luca intertwine his fingers in Melody's and raise their joined hands to his mouth for a kiss, all he could think about was how fast he could extricate himself.

"We're roommates." His pointed comment hit the mark, and Melody made a face.

"Just temporarily, though."

Wes brought his gaze back from Cara and Colin. "Are you coming back to Atlanta, then?"

"No." There was that insincere smile again. "But you're house hunting, right? It was never supposed to be a permanent arrangement. Have you found a house yet?"

"There's one or two I saw online. I haven't really been looking."

Melody's beautiful face creased in a frown, but she quickly wiped it away.

"But you will. I wonder if Cara knows someone that can take your room. Since she doesn't have a problem living with a guy, I could give her the name of some male models I know."

Wes knew Melody was baiting him, but his gut twisted at the concept. He didn't want to think about some random guy moving in with Cara.

The thought of Cara curled up on the couch, under a blanket, watching TV with someone else was unacceptable.

"I should go check on her."

"She's not a child, Wes. These are her people. She probably knows more people here than I do," Melody said through her teeth. Luca's eyes shifted between the two of them.

"Bella, let him go." Luca brought her hand to his lips again, keeping his eyes on Wes, but all Wes felt was annoyance.

"I'm not keeping him here." Melody wrapped her arms around Luca's neck, bringing him in for a leisurely kiss. Wes mentally rolled his eyes.

"Have a good night." Wes nodded at the crowd and snaked his way through the crowd to Cara. Colin attempted to separate Cara from the man in the dark suit, but the larger man only clapped Colin on the back, knocking the shorter man off balance. Wes picked up his pace. He hated bullies.

"Cara." Was that relief in her eyes?

She cut her eyes at the man. "This is Damon. He's an associate of my mother's."

Damon's eyes narrowed slightly when Wes intentionally stepped too close, crowding his space. Damon was forced to tilt his head in order to maintain eye contact before extending his hand.

"Nice to meet you." He turned to Cara. "I think they are getting ready for whatever the surprise is."

"I'll go check with my mother and make sure she doesn't need help."

Damon's lips twitched. "I'll walk with you. I haven't seen the happy couple yet tonight, and I should thank them for inviting me." Damon put his hand on Cara's waist to pull her along with him.

For a split-second, Wes wondered how much of a scene it would be if he ripped the guy's hand off and beat him with it. Cara twisted away with a glare.

"Actually," she cast a warm look up at Wes. "I need to stop by our room first." Cara took a step closer and rested her hand on his bicep. It felt like she'd branded him, and suddenly his mind was back to the shadows, his leg between hers, and the warmth of her sex through the thin fabric of her jumpsuit.

Wes caught Cara's other hand in his.

"Meet you out front?" She said to Colin. He nodded but it was evident he was unhappy at being left behind. Wes didn't acknowledge Damon, and in fact, was proud of himself that he didn't tell the asshole what he thought of him and his pushy, handsy…

Cara tugged, trying to free her hand as they reached the crowds flowing up the steps and walking through the spacious foyer to the courtyard at the front of the property.

"Let go," she hissed, wrenching her hand away.

Wes tried to catch a glimpse of her face, but she kept her eyes straight forward, and from his height, he couldn't clearly see her expression. Her shoulders were stiff, and she was walking faster than anyone around them.

"Hey!" He reached to touch her just to slow her down, but she moved out of reach and turned a fierce look at him.

"Don't touch me."

Wes's mouth fell open. "Wait! Are you mad at me?"

"Stop talking." Her eyes blazed.

"Cara." He stopped, aware that they were drawing attention from the others standing nearby. Wes bent his head so that only she could hear, but the fresh scent of honeysuckle immediately short-circuited his brain.

Cara's gaze was on something behind him, and she stiffened before arranging her lips in a fake smile.

"Of course, I'm not mad. Why would I be?" Her lips were still smiling so anyone nearby wouldn't see how angry she was, but Wes was close enough to see the sparks flashing in her eyes.

"You came here to convince your true love to be with you. And, the fact that you and I want to fuck each other's brains out means nothing." Cara's voice had risen in volume, and she stopped to take a breath. "But the reason I'm *mad* at you, Wes, is that you made me believe love is real. That it is possible to find the one person you are meant to be with. I guess I should have learned from you and Melody. Just because you find the person you want to spend your life with, it doesn't guarantee they'll feel the same way."

Wes felt like she had punched him.

The first burst of fireworks drew the crowd's eyes upwards, but Wes couldn't take his from Cara's profile. In the subsequent bursts of light, he saw her lips tremble, the unmistakable sheen of tears in her eyes. His chest felt like his heart had been ripped out, leaving only a terrible ache behind. The last thing he wanted to do was hurt her. And that was exactly what he had done.

Wes's eyes slammed shut, emotions he couldn't identify cascading through his body. He wanted to hold her, assure her he loved her, too. Was that even what she was saying?

The entire time he'd known her, she insisted that love was a transitory, hormonal experience. How could he trust what she said now? If he risked his heart with her, and she grew tired of him, left him behind—he wasn't sure he would survive it. So, instead of comforting her, he stayed silent, hands fisted at his sides.

When the fireworks were over, and the crowd finished their applause, they turned en masse back to the villa. Some of the guests made their way to the buses and cars that would carry them back to their hotels in the region, but Wes followed miserably behind Cara into the stone foyer.

At the base of the steps, she turned. Her expression was serene—terrifying.

"Give me thirty minutes before you come up."

Wes watched her climb the stairs, and as she made the curve out of his sight, he couldn't help but feel that he had lost something. A friendly slap on the back pulled him from his thoughts, and he found Colin, a commiserating smile on his face.

"Join the club man." Colin glanced at the stairwell. "See you tomorrow."

There were still several guests milling about in the house and on the veranda. Wanting to be alone, Wes wandered aimlessly onto one of the side balconies overlooking the gardens. A laugh rang out, and he easily picked Melody out of the crowd.

He should go down and talk to her. His time was limited, his brain reminded him, but he couldn't seem to make his feet move or his heart care.

Corinne and Alessandro joined him on the balcony.

"What did you think of our little soiree?" Corinne asked.

"Very entertaining." Wes did not feel up to small talk.

"Do you know my nephew Luca?" Alessandro asked, seeing where Wes's attention lay.

"No, Melody and I are childhood friends."

Alessandro exchanged a look with Corinne. An unspoken message passed between the two, and the older man pressed a quick kiss against Corinne's lips before nodding at Wes and disappearing back into the house.

"Caralina tells me you two are roommates."

Wes was instantly alert. She was definitely sizing him up.

"We are, but we've also become very close friends."

Corinne's crystal blue eyes studied his face. "But you came to Italy with her. To her mother's wedding."

Wes hesitated. Cara would kill him if he told her mother about her stalker. "I did." His eyes strayed to Melody and Luca, and when they returned to Corinne, her eyes had darkened, and the angry light in them looked so much like her daughter's that for a moment he was speechless.

"Because of her?" Corinne's chin jutted to the group, where Melody was the center of attention.

"In part," Wes admitted. "Melody told me she was staying in Italy, and I thought I should meet the guy."

"Why?" Her genuine question caught him off guard. Corinne looked at Melody before looking back at him. "Are you gay?"

"What? No."

"I didn't think so, but I wanted to be sure."

Wes was thoroughly confused.

"I saw you tonight. I saw you with my daughter, *and* I saw you with Luca's new fiancée."

He shifted uncomfortably. Wes did not want to have this conversation.

"Melody is a lovely young woman, and I'm sure she will make Luca very happy." Was she warning him off? A small smile toyed around the corners of her lips. "They play the same game, want the same things. It's a rare thing. Anyone can fall in love," she chuckled. "I should know. I've done it enough. But there is a difference between a love affair and true love." She looked wistful as she looked out into the night. "I never understood that before Alessandro. I let the passion, the fun, the excitement, the fights..." She shook her head. "I was a fool, but worst of all, my daughter saw it all. Has she told you about her father... her half-brothers?"

Wes nodded. "My," she paused "relationship with her father was short, but it gave me Caralina and I wouldn't trade that for anything. But, between the two of us, David and I were the poster children for what not to do. Don't get me wrong, we remained friends... We knew who the other was and didn't expect something the other couldn't give." Her eyes trailed to Melody again. "I miss him." Her eyes grew misty before her lips firmed. "But just because I loved him, that didn't mean I *loved* him. Do you understand what I'm saying?" She trapped his eyes. "It worked for us... but Caralina is different. She pretends she doesn't believe in love... But, I think true unconditional love is the one thing she has always searched for, even while not believing it exists."

There was no mistaking Corinne's message, but she didn't understand. He and Melody were different. They wanted the same things, a family, children... Okay, maybe they didn't have the connection that he and Cara shared, but how much did it matter?

He shook his head. Angry at himself, and angry at her for the emotions she brought to the surface.

"If you loved David Bloom so much and care about your daughter, why did you allow her stepmother to attend the wedding? Are you aware Cara and her brother Declan suspect their father was murdered, and Courtney had something to do with it?"

Corinne blanched. "What a horrible thing to say! That's not true!"

"It *is* true, and it has been destroying Cara and her brothers."

Corinne paled, and Wes felt a tinge of regret. It wasn't his place, but his anger had now found an outlet. "Cara has been trying to hold her family together, while starting a whole new career, learning what she needs to start an organic skincare line." Corinne took a step back. "I've lived with her for months, and I don't remember her ever mentioning that she'd spoken to you. She did, however, mention how her stepmother and stepbrothers have tried to make her life miserable, and now, here Courtney is at her mother's wedding."

"I didn't invite Courtney." She defended herself weakly. "I was shocked when she showed up with Elliot."

Wes took a deep breath. Cara was already angry with him. She wouldn't thank him for fighting with her mother on the eve of her wedding.

"I'm sorry." He thrust a hand into his hair. Corinne bit her lip but said nothing, her breathing erratic. "I shouldn't have said anything. This is your wedding. I shouldn't…"

"You came here for Melody," Corinne said, her voice brittle. "You've said as much. It's interesting though, all of your anger is for my daughter." She waved her hand to where Luca and Melody were swaying together to the quartet's music. "Maybe you should ask yourself why you feel such emotion on behalf of my daughter and not for the woman in someone else's arms." With that parting shot, she whirled and stormed away.

Great! At this rate, he was going to be lucky if they didn't escort him out.

Wes leaned his forearms against the balustrade and gazed sightlessly at the dark Italian landscape. What was he doing? He thought of Cara upstairs getting ready for bed, and how he'd hurt her, but he didn't know how to fix it. Wes let out a long breath.

He wanted everything about her. Not just her lush body, but the burnt aloe, the science projects on the counters, the way she chewed her lip when she was concentrating. She was everything he'd ever wanted and more than he ever thought he deserved.

She was right… He was afraid. He was afraid of loving her and being left behind if she changed her mind. Melody didn't have the power to hurt him the way loving Cara could.

CHAPTER FORTY-THREE

THE DOOR HANDLE TURNED, AND CARA PULLED HER KNEES UP closer to her chest. Her eyes burned with the tears she refused to shed. Wes had been gone longer than she anticipated. One part of her was grateful that he had given her the space she had asked for, but the contrary part of her was angry he hadn't felt the same need to be with her that she felt to be with him.

Cara knew going into this weekend what his intentions were. He'd been clear that he was here for Melody. Wes told her what he wanted, practically the first day they met. She was the one who had chosen to forget.

It wasn't Wes's fault that now Cara wanted more.

But it *was* his fault that he was so stupid. Wes padded quietly across the wooden floor, and then she heard the quiet snick of the bathroom door closing.

Cara lifted her head to punch her pillow. He didn't love Melody, not really. How could he if he responded to her the way he did? Or was that just what she was telling herself? Had she convinced herself to believe it because she had finally risked her heart and Wes was still resisting? Scenes from the last couple of months played through her mind.

No, he cares about me. I know he does.

Just not enough to overcome his fears, she thought miserably. The bathroom door opened again, and Cara held still, barely breathing. Her pulse picked up. Would he join her in the bed? Did she want him to?

His footsteps approached the bed, and then the weight of the folded coverlet at the foot of the bed lifted off her feet, and her heart fell. She rolled her lips in, against the disappointment, simultaneously angry at herself for wanting someone who had rejected her.

The legs of the chaise scratched at the wooden floor under his weight. The antique was not designed for someone with Wes's large frame.

Wes squirmed, the rustling from his attempt to find a comfortable position growing louder, followed by silence. The walls of the villa were thick, and the silence felt oppressive, remnants of the party too far away to hear. The darkness amplified her senses, and she strained to hear his breathing.

It made no sense. They had shared a home for months now, and then in Luke's apartment the last night. How many times had she greeted him over coffee in her pajamas when he was just in athletic shorts? Why in the darkness did the thought of the sculpted planes of his chest a few feet away send fire straight to her core?

"Cara." His voice was little more than a whisper. Should she answer?

"What?" She matched his quiet tone.

"I'm sorry."

Cara bit her tongue.

The unmistakable sounds of him shifting on the chaise came again, then his feet hit the floor.

"I'm freezing," he complained, and a small smile curled her lips. She pulled the blanket higher on her shoulders. It was cool in the room, but she knew the coverlet he had taken was more than thick enough to keep him warm.

It was a mistake to offer, but she also knew this would most likely be one of their last nights together. Cara wasn't a masochist, and now that she had acknowledged to herself how she felt about him, there was no way she could go back to being just his roommate.

"Get in the bed." She tried to keep her voice light, pretending it meant nothing to her. "But keep your giant, cold feet on your side."

"Are you sure?" His deep voice in the darkness sent curls of longing through her belly.

She let out a loud beleaguered sigh. "I won't be able to sleep with you moaning all night. Hurry up! I'm tired."

The covers lifted, and Cara felt a brief draft before he slid in next to her, warmth radiating off him. She could feel his eyes, but she remained frozen, her back to him.

"Thanks." Wes lay on his back, one arm folded behind his head. Cara waited for his breathing to even out, signaling he was asleep, but it didn't come. She could practically hear the thoughts churning in his head.

Cara rolled onto her back and stared up at the ceiling, too dark now to pick out the intricate, painted patterns that decorated it.

"When you invited me to come to this wedding, you knew why I said yes."

Her heart turned over painfully. "It was always the plan."

"It was." She felt him nod. "It was always the plan. For my entire adult life, that was the plan. Make enough money so that neither Melody nor I would ever have to worry about it again. It's how I've always operated. A goal in front of me that I can work single-mindedly toward. The end game was always a family, and when I pictured it, it was always with Melody."

Cara swallowed past the lump that threatened to suffocate her. "I know all this, Wes. You've told me before."

"Then I met you, and suddenly everything was different."

Cara tried to squelch the spark of hope his words caused. He sounded so unhappy she knew there was a 'but' coming.

"We became friends and the more time we spent together, the more time I wanted to be with you. And then, when you were threatened, I…" His voice broke.

Cara fought the urge to roll toward him.

"Everything was confused. What does it mean if I let Melody go? If she marries Luca and goes on without me, where does that leave me? In reality, you and I've only known each other for a handful of months. What if it's a fling? What if I throw away what I always wanted because of how I feel right now?"

"There are no guarantees of a happily-ever-after, not outside of fantasies. Things change. I never believed it was possible to know you would love someone forever." Cara paused, her heart rising in her throat. She knew she had to take the risk. If she didn't, she would always wonder what would have happened. "Until I met you."

She felt him startle next to her. "I can't guarantee that it will work out between us. Between my father and my mother, I've seen just how wrong it can go—but I've also seen Anne and Bruce and how it can be beautiful. I've never felt the way I feel when I'm with you. You make me believe in myself. Not the name that comes attached to me. What I can build on my own. I think it's worth the risk. I *want* to take the risk."

Her heart beat in a slow, painful rhythm as she waited for him to answer. Finally, she heard him take a ragged breath. "I can't just give up without trying. I don't know how to explain it so that it will make sense to you."

Cara was grateful that the dark hid the tears that sprang to her eyes. "At some point, Wes, you are going to have to let go of your fear. You created a dream when you were a frightened child.

I understand where your need for safety and security comes from, but at some point, you are going to have to take a chance, or else you will only exist in the world, not live in it."

"I don't want to hurt you, but I don't know if I can—"

She cut him off, her throat aching in defeat. "I know you don't, Wes. Your care of those you love is one of the things I love most about you." She heard his breath hitch, but she forced herself to continue. "I know you're confused. In a way, I even feel bad for you." She let out a quiet laugh. "But I'm also furious that you are too stubborn to see that what you think is your dream never had a chance anywhere but in your imagination."

Cara rolled to her side, giving him her back. Wes let out a long slow breath, and for a brief hopeful second, she thought he would say something. Something to acknowledge that she had just told him she loved him, but he remained silent. Tears silently slid down her cheeks.

If he didn't love her, what else was there to say?

CHAPTER FORTY-FOUR

Cara filled her plate with fruit and slices of cheese from the breakfast buffet her mother and Alessandro had put out for those staying in the villa and for any early attendees. She hadn't slept well, and this morning she felt like she had an emotional hangover.

"You shouldn't frown like that. You'll get wrinkles."

Cara stifled a nasty comment. She wasn't in the mood for her stepmother. Despite the early hour, Courtney already had a full face of makeup, and wore a white suit and heels. In comparison, Cara had thrown her long hair into a ponytail and slipped into pants and a sweatshirt. She planned on dressing for the ceremony later in her mother's room.

She picked up a napkin from the end of the table and moved to walk away, intending to ignore the woman. But as she walked past, Courtney grabbed her forearm, almost causing Cara to spill her plate. Cara looked down at the scarlet nails holding her arm like a claw.

"Let go of me." Cara met her stepmother's blue eyes with resolve. "I have nothing to say to you. You are no longer relevant to my life."

The fingers on her arm spasmed, the nails digging in. Cara refused to let her see how it stung.

"You always were a brat. A selfish, spoiled brat," Courtney spit out.

"And you never belonged." The nails bit painfully deeper, "That was always what bothered you, wasn't it?"

Courtney released her arm, but pressed her face close to Cara, her thick floral perfume turning Cara's stomach.

"If we are talking about belonging, look in a mirror. You and your drug-whore mother meant nothing to David. I was the one he loved. *My* sons the ones he valued."

Cara's heart pounded with the urge to slap Courtney, but this was her chance to see how Courtney would react to being accused.

"We both know that's not true. I don't know how you did it, but I know you forced my father to change the will."

Cara saw Dr. Keller approaching. "The only question is how did you do it? We know you trapped our father into marrying you somehow and forced him to find your son a place at Bloom Communications. The way the will stood, you would have gotten very little after his death, and yet now you have everything."

Courtney leaned away with a smile. "You and your brothers only have yourselves to blame for that."

"Is everything all right?" the doctor asked, reaching their side.

Courtney's smile was insincere. "Cara is complaining about her inheritance; $200,000 is a lot of money for most people. Your father wanted you to know what it was like to earn your own way. In the end, he knew he had spoiled you too much, and you had become a useless, young woman. At least your mother had her looks to get by."

"Crystal!" Courtney whipped her eyes to Dr. Keller and shoved his arm.

"Don't call me that!" she hissed.

"You two have nicknames. How adorable." Cara sneered.

Dr. Keller looked at the ground.

"At the end of your father's life, Elliot was supportive of both of us. More than his own children ever were."

"I saw my father just before he died."

Courtney's eyes sharpened. "When? I was with him every day."

"Right before he went to Dublin." A muscle twitched under Courtney's eye, and the Doctor raised horrified eyes to Cara's stepmother.

"Dublin?" Courtney's intense gaze met the older man's.

"You weren't there, and I found my father in his bedroom." Cara left out the part about asking for a job. "He was very ill. That's why I was so surprised to learn he was planning a trip."

"Who told you that?" Courtney looked accusingly at Elliott Keller, who gave a faint shake of his head. Cara's stomach sank. She hadn't wanted to believe that the man she had always viewed as an uncle played a role in what happened.

Cara ignored the question. "Why did my father think he was being poisoned?"

Courtney's jaw fell open. "What are you talking about? Your father wasn't poisoned!" She gave a dramatic sigh, and then continued in a pitying voice. "I know it's difficult to accept when someone as powerful as David dies. It's natural, I suppose, to want to blame someone, and I guess as your father's widow, I'm the easy target." She made an exaggerated pout. "Particularly when things were so difficult between the two of you. I'm sure you hoped to show your father someone he could be proud of, and now it's too late. At least he never saw the humiliating mess you made after he died. I can't imagine how devastated he would have been if he'd known what you had done. How could he show his face knowing all of his friends had seen his daughter's tits."

"That's enough!" Dr. Keller snapped.

"My brothers and I know what you did, and we are going to prove it."

Courtney rolled her eyes, but Cara pushed on. "For a long time, I thought Declan was just bitter about Bloom Communications, but after what Mrs. Woodson revealed, I think he's right."

"The housekeeper? I can't imagine what she thinks she knows." Despite Courtney's tone, the twitching muscle was back.

"She worked for my father her entire life, and Declan has taken care of her since. Did you know they still meet for lunch?"

Courtney shrugged, but Cara didn't miss the worried glance she shot the Doctor.

"She told Declan that my father refused to eat anything that wasn't prepared by her and only drank from water bottles opened in front of him. Certainly sounds like he thought he was being poisoned. Who knows what she'll remember next?"

Courtney's skin paled. "David never mentioned that to me."

"Why would he? You were the one poisoning him!"

"Keep your voice down, you little bitch. Haven't you embarrassed your family enough?"

Dr. Keller took Courtney's arm but addressed Cara.

"This is your mother's wedding. The last thing she wants is a scene. I know you are upset, Cara, and if you or Declan have questions about David's last days, I am always available to you."

Courtney yanked her arm away and, without a word, stalked off. His eyes followed her as she made her way into the house.

"Crystal comes across as cold and uncaring, but she loved David in her way. She never left his side."

"I know. She made sure we couldn't get near him," Cara said bitterly.

Dr. Keller frowned. "I know it's hard to hear, but it was difficult for him to be around Declan. James and Luke had no interest in their father for the last decade. It's not a surprise that he didn't turn to them."

"My father and I didn't have any problems!"

"At the end, the last thing David needed was to be upset. We knew he was failing, but we were all hoping that the specialists would find a diagnosis. That trip might have been what finished him. He was supposed to go in for some more extensive tests, but he never showed up. None of us knew where he had gone."

"Exactly. He didn't tell anyone where he was going because he felt like he was in danger!"

"Then why return to the house?" His expression seemed genuine, and Cara couldn't deny that was a sticking point. If her father had believed his wife was poisoning him, why go back? Why not stay in Dublin or one of his other homes?

"I don't know why he did that, but I know someone killed my father."

The doctor's expression became serious. "Cara, your father was ill for months. David ignored the symptoms, refusing to let me do any tests. By the time he agreed it had progressed too far. He was stubborn, and because of that, there wasn't enough time." His face sagged. "David was my friend. If I thought someone was hurting him, I would have done something about it. Hell, he would have said something to the doctors at the hospital. If he believed it was Courtney, why would he protect her? She has had her struggles in life, bringing up two boys on her own, without all the privileges your siblings and their mothers enjoyed. She hasn't always made the best choices, but I've only ever known her to be fiercely protective of those that she loves."

"Courtney never loved my father, and whether or not you believe it, I know she killed him," Cara insisted.

"I know her."

"Do you?"

Dr. Keller stared at her, and then silently walked away, leaving Cara staring at the plate of food she had forgotten she was holding.

CHAPTER FORTY-FIVE

The ceremony was beautiful. The bright Italian sun shone on the couple under the arbor dripping with flowers, the rolling hills of Tuscany covered in new green vines, as their backdrop. Wes couldn't tear his eyes from where the sun glinted off of Cara's hair.

Just after dawn, he had awoken to her breath against his chest. In her sleep, Cara had curled towards him with her hands tucked under her chin. Every molecule in his body called for him to hold her close and forget about the world beyond the door, but he hadn't. A lifetime of determination warred with his heart.

At some point, he had fallen back asleep, and when he woke again, she was gone. A quick survey of the room found she had taken the dress she was supposed to wear and her makeup. Wes hadn't seen her again until she was standing with her mother. Her smile seemed happy, but he wondered what she was thinking.

Wes knew how Cara felt about her mother's marriage habit… But even someone with a heart of stone would have found themselves moved by the couple's open adoration. Wes hadn't understood a good part of the ceremony conducted in Italian, but the devotion on the faces of Corinne and Alessandro, as they faced each other, was easy to read.

His heart flipped in his chest. There was nothing safe in their expressions. Wes's eyes strayed again to Cara, where she stood with the bride and groom's close friends and family, waiting her turn for pictures.

Wes chose a seat at one of the outdoor tables with Melody and Luca. A corner of his mind realized that the clock was ticking on the time left to talk to Melody, but his thoughts returned to Cara again and again.

He had tried to catch her before the ceremony to talk about what she had said the night before. But Cara avoided him with an expertise he hadn't expected. When Wes stopped at her side while she spoke to Colin, she had refused to speak to him alone. Instead, she had laid her hand on Colin's forearm to stop him from leaving with a laugh. Her message was unmistakable. Wes had his chance, and now it was gone.

Speaking of which—she was still touching Colin. He knew they were just friends, but he didn't like how Cara was touching the man more and more. It seemed like every time Wes looked over, they were standing even closer.

"What's wrong with you?" Melody asked.

Wes rearranged his scowl into a neutral expression. "Nothing at all." He smiled and lifted his glass of wine saluting the view. "How could someone be unhappy here?"

"You seem off."

"Do I? Maybe it's just the beautiful surroundings." He winked at her. "This is my first time in Italy. Not all of us can be world-traveling models."

"Are you going to Rome while you're here?" Her words focused Wes's attention.

"I hadn't planned on it, but maybe I should take a few more days off to travel."

"Ahh, come visit us in Milan!" Luca exclaimed. "We have plenty of room. Don't we, Bella?"

A slight twitch marred Melody's perfect forehead.

"Do you remember when we dressed up as Romans for Halloween?" Wes asked Melody. "Everyone said we were too old to go out, but we didn't care, and when we came back with all that candy the other kids were jealous."

Melody's face clouded and then cleared, "Oh, yeah! I forgot about that." She laughed. "We were such dorks." She raised her hand to hide her eyes. "I can't believe I let you talk me into that. Talk about embarrassing! Then again," Melody smirked at her fiancé, "we ended up at a party with a keg of beer. That, plus the skimpy sheet that made up my toga, got that football player to ask me out. And, he paid for all new makeup at the mall, so I guess it wasn't for nothing." Luca and their friends laughed, but Wes didn't hide his dismay.

"We had fun that night," he insisted, but her mention of the party created a wrinkle in his memory. Somehow, when he replayed that night in his mind, he had blocked out the keg party.

"Oh, yeah. I'm sure we did," she agreed. "You were always a great sidekick. Without you, I never would have gotten Josh Bernard to ask me out!"

Her reaction rankled. Wes had told her, that night so many years ago, that it was his first Halloween, and later as an adult, how he looked forward to doing it with his kids someday. His grandparents had never let him trick-or-treat because they viewed Halloween as an anti-Christian holiday. Wes frowned and wracked his mind for a detailed memory of the night. The more he thought about it, he recalled Melody hadn't gone home with him.

Wes had been ready to leave. Everyone was drinking, and he had a test that week. He needed to get home, but she insisted on staying....

"We had a great time, Wes! I remember," she said, and Wes realized his thoughts must have played across his face.

"Yeah." The conversation continued around him, but he felt something massive shift inside him.

"Do you have a date for the wedding yet?" One of the group asked.

"Not yet." Luca smiled. "I'm pushing, but Bella doesn't seem to be in a hurry."

"It's not that, darling." She stroked the side of his face with a smile. "Let's just enjoy all the attention and excitement from being engaged for a while, and then we can plan a show-stopper event."

Luca pressed a kiss to her lips. "Whatever you desire, Bella."

"It takes time to plan these things you know," Melody continued telling the table. "It can't be during fashion week or while everyone is vacationing in August. I want to be sure all the important people are there." The table murmured in agreement, but Wes's brow knit again. Luca didn't seem to mind the mercenary way Melody was approaching their wedding. Wes had always known that Melody was ambitious. In fact, he had always admired that about her.

"Better enjoy the parties now before the bambinos arrive," one woman teased.

Melody laughed and then gave a mock shudder. "No bambinos in our future. If I could get myself fixed now, I would!"

"Really?" Even her fashion friends seemed surprised.

"I wouldn't mind a kid or two," Luca shrugged, "but Bella is dead set against it. Whatever she wants is fine with me."

Wes stared at her, dumbfounded. Melody wanted kids. Hadn't she always said she wanted a family, too?

"You don't want kids?" He knew his voice was too loud, and Melody avoided his eyes. "Since when?" he challenged.

Melody glared at him. "Since I realized I'm not 'mom' material."

"That's not true!"

"Really?" Melody arched a brow at him, and for a moment, it was just the two of them, as they'd always been.

"Yeah, really."

She didn't feel that way. Melody was just afraid. "I'm not saying you should have kids tomorrow, but you *never* want kids?"

"Wes…" Her voice was weary.

"Don't you want to fix all the mistakes? To prove we can do it the right way?"

Wes was vaguely aware of the others at the table following along, but this moment was too important to be embarrassed.

"Wes?" Her eyes softened, and he saw pity in them. "Don't you see? We are wired the way we are. Everything we've been through and saw—do you want to pass that genetic poison on to another generation?"

"It doesn't have to be like that." His brain flashed to Cara, saying how she would do it differently. "It could be different."

"But I don't want it to be different." She reached across the table and laid her hand across his. "I like my life the way it is." She spared a sideways glance at her fiancé, and Luca smiled in return. But the tension between Melody and Wes had set a pall over the table.

"Perhaps it's time for a refill. Come to the bar with me," Luca said.

Melody left her half-full glass on the table and followed her fiancé away.

Wes sat there awkwardly, avoiding the glances from those around him. His eyes sought Cara again where she stood laughing with her brother.

He pushed back his chair, barely catching it when it tumbled back in the grass. He stalked to the bar.

"Can I talk to you for a minute?" Wes said when he reached Melody. Over her shoulder, he saw Cara watching them, her face puckered in concern, which in turn drew Declan's attention.

"*Amico,* I know the two of you are close, but this is too much." Luca stopped when Melody placed her hand on his back.

"It's fine. Wes and I are overdue for a conversation. I haven't been the best friend lately."

Luca's shoulders tensed beneath his blue suit, but he inclined his head. Without another word, Melody caught Wes's hand and dragged him into the gardens away from the other guests.

"I didn't think you could move so fast in those shoes." Wes teased, but swallowed his words when Melody turned a fierce look on him.

"What are you doing?"

"What do you mean? I want to talk to you."

"What are you doing *here*? In Italy? At this wedding?"

Wes felt his own anger rise. This was the Melody he knew, not the polished version on display over the last two days.

"What am I doing here? What are *you* doing here?"

Melody folded her arms across her chest, making the tiny chiffon of her sleeves flutter. He waved his hand at the expensive dress. "I get it. It's what you always wanted. Fancy clothes, mansions, wine and all the cool kids wanting to be your friend, but that's not real life!"

Her finger came up, her fingernail pointing inches from his nose. "It *is* real life. It's *my* life! You're damn right this is my dream! What's wrong with that?"

"You got engaged to this guy!"

"His name is Luca, and he is amazing. He loves me and I love him. We are going to have a fabulous life!"

"Fabulous life," Wes scoffed. "Going from one event to the next, worrying about the guest list and how best you can work it to your advantage? That's not a life."

Melody's eyes narrowed. "It may not be the life you want, Wes, but it is exactly what Luca and I want."

"So, what? You were serious before? No family? Just an endless party?"

Melody reared back as if he had struck her, and Wes immediately regretted his words. "Mel, that's not what I meant…"

"Yes, it is. At least be honest, Wes. You came into foster care late. You may not have had a Betty Crocker childhood, but you were safe and fed. In their own way, your grandparents loved you. I don't even remember what my parents looked like!" Her chest heaved, but she lowered her voice. "We are *not* the same. You want the white-picket fence, two-and-a-half kids and the golden retriever…"

"Everyone does—"

"No!" She threw her hands up in the air. "No, Wes. Not everyone wants that. It's what *you* want, and that's fine, but you can't force me into it with you."

Wes felt like the world had tilted off its axis. "But you always said it was you and me. We had to take care of each other."

All the fight went out of her. Suddenly, she looked exhausted. "It will always be you and me. We have history. We always will. What we went through… But we don't want the same things. I love Luca, and someday when you fall in love, too, you'll find someone who wants the same things you do."

Melody echoed Corinne's words from the night before. As though blinders fell from his eyes, he felt like he was seeing Melody for the first time in… maybe ever.

"You really are happy? This is what you want?" Melody nodded, and he saw the truth in her eyes. To his surprise, he realized he wasn't upset. In fact, a sense of calm and rightness flooded his body. Melody was going to be okay. He felt like a weight had fallen from his shoulders.

"I love you, Wes. I always will."

Wes smiled before pulling her into a hug. "I love you, too, Mel. I'm sorry if I made things difficult for you back there."

Melody pulled back with a shrug. "Luca knows about our past. He won't mind, and as for the rest of them… Well, it's good to be a woman of mystery." She winked, and Wes let out a genuine laugh.

"Friends?" she asked.

"Friends."

"Is everything okay?" Luca asked, as he approached. Despite Melody's assertions, Luca didn't look thrilled to see them secluded. Luca loved Melody. She would be taken care of.

"Everything's great." Melody slid her arm through Luca's.

"I'm sorry if I was rude before. I'm going to blame the jet lag," Wes joked.

"It's all right." Luca's shoulders relaxed. "We always act foolish when we are in love."

Wes froze, and Melody's eyes were on the ground.

"Caralina is a dynamic young woman," Luca continued. "I can see why you are out of sorts."

He meant Cara.

"Yes, she is." Wes agreed.

In fact, in that moment, he wanted nothing more than to find her and beg for her forgiveness. Cara had seen the truth long before he had. A pit formed in his stomach. What if he was too late? Wes understood what it took last night for her to tell him how she felt, and like an absolute idiot, he had said nothing! He groaned.

"Wes is not in love with Caralina Bloom," Melody laughed.

Luca gave her a shrewd look. "Of course, he is, Bella. Everyone here can see it. The way he watches her..."

Melody scowled. "They're friends. He's just looking out for her."

Luca turned his fiancée so that she faced him. He placed his hands on her hips before pressing a kiss to her lips. "He watches her the way I watch you. When I'm with you, you are all that I see, and when we are apart, you are all that I want to see."

Wes tuned out Luca's ardent proclamation, already walking

back toward the party. Luca was right. Cara had become his entire world. How had he not understood that until right now?

"It's not the same. She's not the same," Melody insisted.

Behind him Wes heard Luca murmuring, but when he reached the area with the al fresco tables, he didn't see Cara.

Wes had to find her.

He had to tell her.

Right now!

"Where's my sister?"

The Irish lilt startled Wes as he wove his way through the crowds. The band had started, and Declan leaned close to his ear for him to hear.

"For someone who is supposed to be watching out for my sister, you are spending an awful lot of time with other women."

"She was with Colin."

"I don't like him. He's like all the rest of that group of friends. Weak and entitled."

Wes frowned. "Cara said he was a family friend."

"Not really. Ah, there she is."

Declan inclined his head toward the bar set up closest to the door to the villa. Cara sipped a glass of wine, while chatting with her mother. As if she felt him watching, she turned his way and caught him staring. Corinne turned her head to follow Cara's gaze. She turned back and said something to Cara that left her with a small frown.

"I'm leaving, but I'll be back in the morning. You and I are still due for a conver—"

He was interrupted when Corinne approached to thank Declan for coming. Slipping away, Wes approached Cara.

"You look gorgeous."

Cara averted her eyes. "I'm flying home with Declan tomorrow."

All the air in Wes's body seemed to desert him and he sputtered. "I know you are upset with me, and you have every right to be. I've been an 'obtuse piece of flotsam.'" Her lips twitched at the reference to their favorite show. "Hear me out, and I won't argue with you about leaving."

He held his breath, waiting for her response. It felt like forever before she slowly nodded. "I need to get my shawl, anyway." He followed her up the stairs to their room, but when the door closed, she walked to the middle of the room and stood with her feet apart and arms across her chest.

"This trip made me realize something I know you already figured out. I mean I already realized it… I just couldn't admit…" He groaned. "This is coming out wrong. You know I'm terrible with words!"

Cara lifted an eyebrow. "Speak or I'm leaving."

Her bottom lip trembled, giving her away. Wes's words tumbled out. "I thought I was in love with Melody. That, because I cared deeply about her, it must have meant something else. Leftover feelings of a childhood crush, gratitude for helping me when I was terrified… She's the longest relationship I've ever had in my life. I think in my messed-up brain, I was equating a sense of safety with marriage, and the only way I could make sure I wouldn't be left behind would be to make her legally obligated to stay."

"People get divorced all the time." Cara's tone was dry, but he noticed her stance had relaxed.

"That's my point. I wasn't being rational. For years, I've helped take care of Melody… in between jobs, after breakups… It felt like it was my responsibility. That's not the same as being *in* love."

Her hands fell to her sides, and he took a step closer. "Last night, when you told me how you felt, my old fears stopped me from telling you I feel the same way. The thought of losing Melody in my life never terrified me the way the thought of losing you does. I didn't want to be vulnerable. I think I believed I could stop myself from being hurt if I could control how much I cared. But with you, it's too late. I know I've hurt you and I may not deserve another chance... I'm sorry I wasn't as brave as you were."

Cara's lips parted, and Wes took a chance, taking her hands in his. "It didn't matter how much I tried not to, and believe me, I tried. It was hopeless. I love you, Cara. I've loved you for a long time, and I don't want to play safe anymore. Putting my heart in your hands is easily the biggest risk I've ever taken."

Cara's eyes softened.

"I know you aren't sure if people can love each other for a lifetime, but I know I will love you for the entirety of mine. And, if some day you decide it's not what you want anymore, it *will* destroy me." He gave her a crooked smile. "But I will always be grateful for every minute I got."

CHAPTER FORTY-SIX

"YOU DID A GOOD JOB," CARA BREATHED.

"With what?" His face filled with cautious hope.

"The words." She grinned then. "Now that I know you've been hiding this talent, I'm going to expect you to tell me you love me this beautifully at least five times a day."

A joyous laugh burst out of him. "At least!" Warm palms cradled her face, Wes's gaze falling to her mouth. "I love you." He pressed a gentle kiss against her lips. "I love you." He punctuated it with another kiss.

"I love you, too," Cara whispered against him. He drew his head back and rubbed her nose with his.

"I know I have *a lot* to make up for."

"I know exactly where you should start." Cara's arms encircled his neck, pulling his mouth back to hers. After weeks of frustrated desire, the kiss quickly became passionate. Her tongue twined with his, fueling the exquisite ache. She pressed a palm against his chest and felt Wes's heart hammering hard beneath his ribs. His touch slowly roved down the sleeves of her dress, drawing goosebumps, before sliding around her waist until his palms were on her ass securing her against him.

Scorching need raced through her body at the feel of him rigid against her belly. She moaned, her hands reaching between them to stroke him through his pants.

Wes groaned long and low, and then, it was as if even the air around them was on fire.

The slight sting as he caught her earlobe between his teeth sent a tremor of electricity straight to her core.

"Wait," he panted, trapping her hand. "If you keep that up, I'm not going to be able to go slow."

"I don't want to wait." Her entire body throbbed. "This has to be the longest foreplay in the history of the universe."

She stepped back and relished the longing in his eyes. Keeping her eyes on his, Cara brought her hands to her waist, slowly and deliberately tugging at the tie that held her velvet dress together, until the dress gaped.

Wes's mouth fell open, his eyes glazing with need. He grasped the edges of the dress, pulling it completely free of the tie and slid it down her arms until it puddled around her heels. His cheeks darkened, and he sucked in an audible breath while his gaze raked down her body, taking in the red lace bra. "Why aren't you wearing panties?" he choked.

Cara's lips curled. "Panty lines."

Wes gave a guttural groan, his fingers flexing on her waist. He ducked his head to reclaim her mouth, his tongue licking at the seam of her lips before sweeping inside. Cara plucked frantically at the buttons of his dress shirt, as his thumbs drew her bra straps down.

Wes kissed his way down her neck, and within seconds, her bra joined the dress on the floor. He cupped her full breasts, his fingers learning their shape and feel. His thumbs brushed the tight buds of her nipples slowly back and forth smiling when Cara's head fell back with a needy moan. His fingers still tormenting her sensitive flesh, Wes walked her backward until the back of her knees hit the bed. Wes stepped back, and quickly shrugged out of his shirt.

"You are the sexiest thing I have ever seen."

Cara's blood pounded as his eyes devoured her body, leaving trails of fire wherever they touched. His buckle clinked faintly as she released his belt and shoved his dress pants and black boxer briefs to the ground. His eyelids were heavy as he watched her reaction to his body.

Cara sucked in a breath, her eyes roaming from his broad shoulders to the sexy 'V' of his hips. She ran her fingertips along the length of his arousal, savoring how he hissed in a breath. "This was worth the wait."

Wes toppled them to the bed, bracing his weight on his forearms.

He arched his hips, creating a delicious friction, and Cara lifted hers to demand more. She whimpered when he repeated the mind melting motion, grinding into her.

"Wes," she tried to wrap her legs around him, but he sat back on his heels, his eyes feasting on her body. Wes trailed an open hand down her breasts, to circle her belly button, before arriving where she needed his touch the most. His fingers slicked over her, two fingers plunging inside. Cara cried out, her back arching at the delicious torment.

Wes bent to take one blush-pink peak into his mouth, sucking hard as his fingers stroked inside, his thumb pressing and circling her clit until she thought she would lose her mind.

"Wes. I can't wait! I need..." Cara's head thrashed against the pillow his fingers driving her higher and higher until her orgasm crashed over her. Wes found her mouth again silencing her keening cry. His kiss was slow and luxurious, as tremors still rippled through her, but still she ached.

Cara hooked a leg over Wes's hips, pulling him against her. He closed his eyes, a look of pain etched on his face. "We can't. I didn't bring anything," he panted.

Cara rolled her hips so that he slid against her, and licked at his lips. "Top drawer, side table."

Wes's brows slanted, making Cara giggle. "Corinne told me she stocked all the bedrooms, just in case."

His groan of relief made Cara giggle again.

"Remind me to buy her flowers," Wes grunted, as he reached for the condom and rolled it on. Cara reveled when his weight settled over her, his kiss hot and full of need. Cara wrapped her hands around him, stroking his length, and guided him to her. "Please, Wes," she begged between kisses. He buried his face in her neck, sucking and nipping.

"I'll never smell honeysuckle again and not think of this," Wes groaned. With one thrust he sank fully into her. Cara shuddered as his hand cupped her breast, rolling the nipple between his fingers.

"Oh god! Yes!"

Wes moved slowly at first, and Cara whimpered as pleasure built again. "The feel of you," Wes groaned. His hands gripped her hips hard as he worked in and out of her. Cara gasped as sensation coiled tighter and tighter inside her.

He slid one of his hands behind her knee, bending it back toward her chest as he thrust harder. Cara dug her nails into the muscles of his back, instinctively moving with him. She relished the feeling of Wes driving into her. Her orgasm caught her by surprise with its intensity as it swept over her.

Wes collapsed half-on, half-off of her and pressed a kiss to her shoulder. Cara lazily ran her fingernails up and down his biceps. Her heart swelled, and she turned her head to meet his eyes.

"That was a good start."

He arched a brow, "For?"

"Making it up to me."

Wes leaned back and grinned. "I'm just getting started."

CHAPTER FORTY-SEVEN

"Get up, sleepyhead." Cara nudged Wes with her toe. "My brother is going to be here soon."

Wes grumbled into the pillow. "You broke me. I need sleep."

Cara grinned. "I'll make you a deal. After my shower, I'll go find us some coffee."

Wes lifted his head and leered suggestively at her. "I could get up for a shower."

"I'm sure you could, but we are short on time."

Wes grumbled and closed his eyes, snuggling into his pillow again.

Cara took a quick shower, dressed, and packed her suitcase. Wes snored quietly in the tangle of sheets, and a warm glow spread through her. She pressed a kiss to his cheek, dodging his arm when he tried to pull her back to the bed with his eyes closed.

"I'll be back in five minutes. Get up."

Wes grumbled his agreement, and Cara made her way down the wide stone steps, lost in her thoughts. She couldn't remember being as happy as she was in that moment. As the foyer below came into view, she stumbled, catching herself on the railing, her happiness dissipating in the face of the reality that was her life.

Standing below, tucked into the curve of the staircase so that he wasn't immediately visible to someone coming in through the front doors, was Elliot Keller. Hearing her tread on the stairs, his head jerked up with an expression of relief on his face.

Was he waiting for her? Unease skittered up her spine. There was nothing to be afraid of. The house was full of people.

"I need to talk to you." His face was an unhealthy mix of pallor and blotchy red spots. He clutched at her hands. "Alone. Quickly, before she sees us!"

Responding to his urgency, she opened the door to one of the nearby anterooms, and seeing it was empty, gestured for him to come with her. He paced in and ran the brim of his hat over and over through his hands, eyes darting to the door.

"What did you want to talk about?"

"I called Miriam, and she confirmed what you said."

"Miriam?"

"Mrs. Woodson."

Cara was surprised. "She told you about the food."

"Yes." He shook his head, pacing back and forth. "But it doesn't make sense. The first battery of tests we ordered, after the specialists had ruled out a cancer, was to test for common toxins. They were negative."

"You had my father tested for poison?" Shock laced her words, bringing the older man to a stop, and he spun to face her.

"We'd tested for everything else. He was scheduled for more tests, but his heart gave out before. I know you don't believe me, but I would never physically hurt your father."

Something in his words sent up Cara's antennae.

"But you would hurt him in other ways? Were you sleeping with *Crystal* behind my father's back?"

He blanched at the nickname, and a sheen of moisture appeared above his lip, his face becoming waxy.

"Never while they were married—before. It was a long time ago."

Cara hadn't expected him to admit it.

"I introduced them, you know. She was Crystal back then. We lost touch for a bit. When I met her again, she had changed a lot. She created a business for herself, and after my wife died, I thought maybe we could make a go of it. She had become respectable."

"She wasn't before?"

Dr. Keller didn't seem to hear her. "But the minute I introduced her to David, it was all over." He opened his arms and gestured down his body. The doctor's body was soft, and like most men as they age, he had developed slight jowls and thickened around the middle. Cara could see why Courtney had chosen her father. David Bloom, handsome and still physically fit, would have eclipsed the doctor—and that was before you factored in her father's billion-dollar media empire.

"Did you hate him?"

His gaze met hers, and she saw the truth. "I wouldn't have killed him."

Voices sounded in the foyer, and Keller's panicked gaze flew to the doors. "I truly believed he died from whatever illness he had contracted. I never thought..."

The door handle turned, and Colin's ginger hair popped through the opening, a smile on his face. "I was looking for you!"

Go away!

"I should go." Dr. Keller scurried toward the door.

"Wait! I have more questions."

He stopped outside the door and turned his head back. "Not here. Call me when you get back to the States. I might need Luke's help."

Cara wanted to chase after him and make him answer her questions, but the hall had filled with people coming to say goodbye. There was no way he would talk now. She needed to tell

Declan what Dr. Keller had said right away. Cara was certain the doctor knew more than he had told her, or at the very least, he suspected something.

"Cara!" The way Colin said her name, she suspected it wasn't the first time.

"I'm sorry," she said absently.

"Was he threatening you?" Colin's fists clenched. "Is he after you, too?"

"If anything, I'm after him." She muttered and then his words registered. "Oh, you mean my stalker? No, I was just asking him…" She stopped. She didn't want to say anything until she talked to Declan. "Never mind. Can we talk later, Colin? It's really important that I find my brother."

Colin's face cleared. "That's why I was looking for you. He asked me to find you and tell you to meet him in the wine storage below the house."

"Where is that?" Cara threw her hands up, exasperated.

"I know exactly where you need to be."

Colin led her to the back of the house and down a set of cellar steps. Wrapped up in wondering what Dr. Keller still had to say about her father, it didn't occur to Cara, until Colin pulled the thick door shut behind them, how odd it was that Declan had asked to meet there. Colin flipped a light switch, and the narrow staircase was illuminated.

She hesitated halfway down the steps, but Colin tugged gently on her hand. "These steps are narrow, but I'll take care of you."

Once they reached the vaulted storage space, the temperature dropped by several degrees. Cara rubbed her hands across the goosebumps that rose on her arms. This didn't feel right. Why would Declan want to meet her here? Her nerves prickled.

"Are you cold?" Colin shrugged off his jacket.

"I didn't expect the temperature to drop this much. I'll just wait for Declan at the—"

Colin didn't give her a chance to finish and instead wrapped the jacket around her shoulders, holding the lapels closed with his hands. He stared into her face for several beats. An uneasy knot grew rapidly in her stomach. It's just Colin, she told herself. No reason to be afraid.

But she *was* afraid. Everything in her was telling her to get away, but when she tried to pull back, his grip on the jacket held her immobile. Colin smiled into her face.

"You're trembling."

"I'm really cold," Cara lied. She lifted her hands together quickly in front of her, forcing him to let go of the lapels. Cara blew on her hands, pretending her only intention had been to warm them. His eyes narrowed, and Cara took a couple of steps back to the stairs. Her instincts told her she needed to get out of this room.

"Don't be afraid." His tone sounded reasonable, but there was an odd light in his eyes.

"Why would I be afraid?" Her voice was weaker than she intended, and Cara took another step to the steps.

Colin wrinkled his nose. "Who convinced you that there was something wrong with me sending you gifts? I only wanted to make you smile. I've missed your smile. I wanted you to see how much I care. How far I'll go to prove I love you."

Horrified comprehension hit her. "You sent me the flowers? The gift card?" Cara licked her dry lips, and ice filled her veins.

Colin continued. "At first, I was upset you were so rude about them." His eyebrows met over his nose. "And for blocking me..." He shook his head mournfully. "I know it's difficult for you. Your family being what they are. I started to think I'd misunderstood all the signals you've given me over the years, but when you showed up and told me I was your true love, I knew I was right."

"What signals? True love? What are you talking about?" Her voice rose an octave, and she inched another foot backward.

Colin's eyes flattened. "I love you. You know that. I thought it was just a dream, but then you kept sending me your secret, little signals."

"I never sent you anything! You're Erik's best friend. Are you insane?"

Colin's face darkened. "Don't say that! Why are you being so difficult? I know Wes has been bothering you, but I'll take care of it. Nothing can keep us apart now." He lunged as Cara whirled to race up the stairs, but he was faster. Colin grabbed her arms from behind and yanked her back against his chest. His hand seized her jaw when she screamed. Pain ricocheted through her head. His hand slipped higher, pinching her nose shut while covering her mouth.

"No screaming," he whispered in her ear. "Don't make me do something we can't come back from."

Cara struggled to free herself by kicking backward and jerking her head, but Colin's hand only clamped harder, and she saw dots in front of her eyes.

No! No! Not like this.

Darkness flirted on the edges of her vision, and the pain in her head increased.

"I'm going to let you go, and you aren't going to scream. If you do, there isn't a second chance. Nod if you understand."

Somehow Cara found the strength to move her head. Just like that, the hand was gone, and she frantically sucked in oxygen.

She coughed and struggled to stay on her feet as he pulled her further into the cellar.

"I'm disappointed in you, Cara. It was one thing when you were with Erik. I know you hadn't really faced your feelings then. But you know how I feel about you now. How could you flirt with Wes?"

Cara decided silence was her friend. By this time, Wes should wonder what was taking her so long. Someone must have seen her coming to the cellar.

"Are you fucking him?" Colin's voice was harsh.

"Of course—" she struggled to speak through her dry lips, "not."

"You kissed him the other night. I saw you."

A shiver of revulsion went through Cara. He'd been the one watching the whole time. Her temper rose, but she forced herself to control it. She needed to stay calm and find a way to get away from him. "It was just kissing."

He cocked his head considering, but his hand was like a manacle on her wrist.

"Did you know I was watching? Were you trying to make me jealous?"

She shook her head vehemently, the hair that had come loose from her ponytail hitting her cheeks.

"Why did you call me a stalker?" Colin had the nerve to sound hurt "A stalker is someone who bothers someone. You liked my attention. I know you did." Cara didn't answer. "Didn't you?" he barked, bending her wrist painfully.

Cara nodded—she had to buy time. Declan should have arrived. When Wes couldn't find her, he'd tell her brother, and Declan would rip the place apart brick by brick if he had to.

"I want to hear you say it. That you liked it," he clarified.

Acid rose bitter in Cara's throat. "I liked it."

He smiled satisfied. "I could tell. The way you put on a show for the computer."

Nausea swamped Cara. It had been bad enough knowing a stranger had seen her in those intimate moments, but now that she knew it was Colin…

"Why didn't you just say something to me?"

"It's more romantic this way," Colin pouted. "Besides, I know Erik is going to be difficult when he finds out about us. That's why I stole the pictures off Amara's phone. I thought he wouldn't want you after that." His eyes darkened. "But you still didn't come to me!"

"I was frightened, Colin. I didn't know who it was…"

In one swift movement, he grabbed her ponytail at the base and twisted her head at an uncomfortable angle.

"You want a more direct approach? Would you like that better?"

She cried out when he grabbed her breast and twisted.

"No! Colin! Stop!"

"Erik always said you were boring, but I know we will be perfect together," he said, right before he smashed his mouth against hers. When she clenched her teeth to block his tongue, Colin released her breast to grip her jaw again, forcing her mouth open.

She gagged at the first touch of his tongue, then bit down as hard as she could. Colin cried out and released her. Trying not to throw up at the taste of blood in her mouth, Cara ran for the door, screaming as loud as she could.

He caught her from behind. "Why are you fighting me? I love you! Enough!" he roared, before yanking her to the floor by her hair. All traces of the friend she had known disappeared from Colin's eyes, leaving a dark void.

He was going to kill her. Through her panic, she heard thudding against the thick door, but Cara's entire existence was focused on getting Colin's slimy mouth off of hers and preventing him from pinning her to the ground. She clawed at his hands, where they fought to get around her throat.

"Stop screaming! We belong together. We've always belonged together."

She saw him pull his arm back, and then only felt fire as his fist connected with her jaw. Stunned, her hands fell momentarily away, but it was enough for Colin to wrap his hands around her throat. His thumbs pressed against her windpipe, cutting off her scream. Cara thought she heard people yelling her name, but it was too late.

"It's just you and me now. We will be together forever." The view of Colin's lips, pulled back in an obscene smile, fuzzed in front of her eyes.

Wes.

There was a crash and more yelling as she tried to stay conscious.

CHAPTER FORTY-EIGHT

"CARA." SOMEONE LIFTED HER HEAD.

She wanted to tell them to stop, to leave her alone. After the bursts of pain, the coolness of the stone felt good. Now she was being held against something as immovable as the stone floor, but it was hot. Too hot!

"Hold still, baby. You're going to be okay. I'm here. Just be still." Wes's voice sounded weird, like he was trying not to cry.

Cara wanted to ask him what was wrong, but her throat felt raw. She whimpered when the fingers on her cheek explored her injured jaw, and she heard a sharp indrawn breath.

There were other sounds, thumps and groans, but her head was too cloudy to make sense of it.

"I'm sorry, baby." Wes's voice was quiet, and then he yelled. "Where the fuck is the ambulance?"

Cara heard Declan then. His voice sounded strange, too, like he was short of breath. "She's strong. It will take more than this coward…" Declan crouched next to her. "Hang in there, Car-Bear. It's over now."

Cara struggled to keep her eyes open, but the fog was thickening again.

I'll answer them in a minute. I just need to close my eyes for a second.

"Don't let her fall asleep. She needs to stay conscious." That was definitely Declan. So bossy.

"I'm awake," Cara tried to say, but it came out as a whisper from her ravaged throat.

"Don't talk," Wes said.

"Colin?" Cara looked up into the faces of the two men leaning over her. A savage satisfied look came over Declan.

"He's not going anywhere."

Her eyes lifted to Wes's. "It was him. The whole time. The flowers, the messages, all of it." She didn't mention the computer, but she could see that Wes understood.

A flurry of movement stirred behind them, and then Wes and Declan were being moved away while two Italian EMS workers examined her.

Cara protested when another two appeared with a stretcher.

"It's not for you," Declan declared grimly. For the first time, Cara looked to where Colin lay bloody and unmoving on the floor and then at her brother's split knuckles.

"Dec?"

"Leave it." His face was implacable. "I'll talk to the police, explain the situation, and then I'll call his family. They need to understand why it won't be in their best interest to get him out of this." He turned his dark eyes to Wes. "Do not leave her side. For any reason."

Wes nodded and then gave her a faint smile. "Never."

Declan pulled one arriving officer to the side. Cara didn't know what he said, but when the officer came to her side, he assured her that the Polizia would take her statement later that day at the villa.

"Can you walk?" Wes asked, his face a mask of concern.

Cara took a ginger step. Her ribs and hip were sore from where Colin threw her to the stone floor, but she didn't think her injuries were serious. From the throbbing now making itself known in her face, Cara didn't want to think about what she looked like. She gave Wes a reassuring smile and tried not to wince when he put his arm around her waist to help her.

To Cara's dismay, upon exiting the wine cellar, there was a handful of guests lingering, drawn by the excitement. Another scandal for Caralina Bloom! At least it didn't look as if anyone had pulled their phones out to film.

Cara was suddenly exhausted and grateful for Wes's arm holding her up. Her mother ran to her, tears streaming down her cheeks.

"Your face!"

Cara reached up, feeling every eye in the place on her.

Alessandro observing her distress, loudly announced to the curious onlookers that wine was being served in the garden. He motioned for a few of his staff to help herd the guests away, as Cara, supported by Wes and followed by her mother, made her way to the stairs.

Corinne's histrionics became more exaggerated the higher they climbed. Just as Cara was about to snap at her mother, Wes asked, "Could you find several bags of ice?"

"Of course. Some arnica oil, too, for the bruising."

"Thanks," Cara muttered, as they reached the top of the steps.

Once they were in the bedroom, the door closed, Wes put his hands on her shoulders and took stock of her, his face contorting with emotion.

"God, Cara. I'm so sorry. I let my guard down. Nothing had happened since we left Atlanta, and I thought—"

"You don't need to be sorry." Her voice was scratchy.

He gently pulled her into his arms, and she buried her face in his chest, inhaling his clean scent.

"You're trembling. You should be in bed, or do you need a doctor?"

She tightened her arms around his back, ignoring how it sent twinges through her bruises.

"What I need right now is for you to hold me." Cara turned her head so that the uninjured side of her face pressed against his firm chest. His heart beat a fast staccato beneath her ear.

"You aren't going to have a heart attack, are you? Stop trying to steal my thunder."

"I thought I was going to when I heard you scream." He lay his head against the top of her hair, his breath ragged. "I was looking for you when I heard it, but I couldn't tell where it was coming from, and then I saw your brother... And then you screamed again, and we couldn't get the door open..."

"I'm sorry. I shouldn't have gone down there with him."

"This isn't your fault. You couldn't have known. He was your friend!"

"I trusted him." Cara felt stupid. How could she not have seen it? Colin was always around. "I knew he had a crush on me when we were younger." Her face wrinkled at the memory. "He was always so sweet, helpful. Constantly apologizing for when Erik was a jerk. But I never thought he was..."

Stepping back, Wes took her hand and led her to the bed, but she resisted.

"I want to take a shower."

His eyes studied hers, but then, without a word, he walked to the small bathroom and turned the water on. She pulled her top over her head.

"Wait. I'd feel safer if you stayed," she said when Wes turned to go.

Pain flashed through his eyes, but he tried to smile.

Cara dropped her filthy clothes to the floor and stepped under the stream of water, wincing when it hit an abrasion. "Are you trying to give me hypothermia? This water is cold!"

"Hot water makes the bruises feel worse."

They exchanged a look. "When you said Melody taught you how to survive, how to fight dirty… You meant things like this…"

He nodded.

She stepped from the shower and ignored the towel he offered. Reaching up on her tiptoes, she pressed a gentle kiss to his lips.

A knock at the door broke the moment.

"That's probably my mother," Cara said, as she dried herself carefully, avoiding the worst of the sore spots.

Wes retrieved the robe left for guests and extended it to her.

"In bed," he commanded, making his way to the door.

"That's really not the way I'd hoped to hear you say that." Cara slid under the sheets. She was tired and her throat throbbed.

Corinne rushed to the side of the bed, as Wes followed more slowly, holding several plastic bags of ice. Cara swallowed two of the painkillers her mother offered.

"I don't understand! Why would Colin do that? His mother is nuts but not violent crazy!"

"It's a long story."

"I heard Declan telling Colin's parents that he's been stalking you! Is that true?"

"Yes. Can we not do this now?"

Corinne looked wounded. "But if you were having problems with him, why would you go to a secluded wine cellar with him? Darling, I've taught you better than that. Men can't be trusted… And now everyone at my beautiful wedding…"

Wes growled. "It wasn't—"

Cara cut him off with a look. There was no point in trying to explain.

"He said that Declan was looking for me, and I was thinking about telling Declan what Dr. Keller said…" She trailed off. "Wes! They need to ask Colin where my snow globe is."

Corinne and Wes had identical looks of confusion. Cara

moved the ice bag off her jaw and struggled to sit up, wincing when the muscles around her ribs pulled.

"When Colin broke into our house, he took my snow globe. We need it back!"

"Cara…" Wes's face was sympathetic.

"My dad was trying to tell me something with the snow globe and I haven't discovered what it is yet. When I spoke to Dr. Keller and Courtney, I mentioned Dublin and they were both *very* concerned that Dad had been there. There has to be a connection. This morning, Dr. Keller all but admitted that he thinks Courtney might have killed Dad."

Corinne looked confused. "Do you mean that tatty snow globe David gave me in Dublin?"

Cara ignored her. "Call Declan. He said he was going to Florence where the police are going to question Colin."

"Cara, I don't think…" Wes began, but when she tossed the ice bags to the side and shifted to get out of the bed, he held up his hands in surrender. "Okay."

Corinne replaced the bags on her side and on her face, and in an uncharacteristically maternal move, brushed the hair off Cara's face.

"My poor baby." But then, in a much more Corinne-like moment, she said. "Don't worry, darling, I have the most magical creams from my plasti… facialist."

CHAPTER FORTY-NINE

Cara finally convinced her mother to leave by reminding her she had guests to say goodbye to. When the door shut behind her, Cara flipped back the blankets and patted the space next to her. "Come here."

His body still feeling the effects of adrenaline, Wes hadn't thought he would be able to relax. Although Cara insisted she was fine after her assault, she was still very pale, and her hands trembled. She chattered for several minutes about Dr. Keller and her stepmother until the shock abated.

Finally, Cara rolled to face him, and rested her palm on his chest, her bruised jaw looking accusingly up at him. Wes was nervous about hurting her, but Cara wouldn't take no for an answer, so he wrapped an arm around her shoulder, and held her snug against his side.

Eventually Cara's breath eased, and Wes realized she had fallen into a fitful sleep. His thoughts raced from one horrible scenario to the next. What would have happened if they hadn't gotten the door open? Hadn't been able to get to her in time? Wes closed his mind to the image of Colin straddling Cara, her face turning purple beneath his hands.

Fury surged through him. He still wanted to rip Colin apart. Part of Wes wished he had gotten to Colin first, but once he had pulled the bastard off Cara, she was all he could see. He thought Declan was going to kill Colin. Frankly, Wes was a little sorry that the guests, attracted by the commotion, had pulled Declan off.

Wes sighed, letting his head fall back against the pillow while he absently stroked Cara's blonde hair. At least it was over. They had captured her stalker. She was safe.

He must have dozed at some point because Wes jerked at the knock on the door. Cara blinked sleepily as he eased out of the bed, before raising her hand to her jaw with a grimace. He pressed a quick kiss to the top of her head before answering the door.

Declan gave Wes's rumpled appearance a terse once-over before pushing past him into their bedroom. He took in his sister, pulling her robe together in bed before casting a nasty glare back at him.

"You couldn't leave her alone for five minutes? After what happened!"

"Shut it, Declan. Last thing my headache needs is a lecture."

Declan immediately turned a contrite face to his sister. "Do you feel up to talking?"

"I'm fine. Probably no worse than you've had from the rugby field." Cara couldn't completely hide her discomfort when she sat up in bed and leaned back against the headboard. Her words seemed to work, though, because Declan grunted.

"But you're a puny girl, so it's not the same thing."

Wes scowled. What had happened to Cara was serious. But Cara's bright smile, followed by an "Ow" and her laugh, took away his anger. Must be a sibling thing. He'd seen firsthand Declan's murderous rage when he saw his sister injured.

"Colin's parents are being difficult." Declan held up his hand. "Don't worry. I made sure that they understand their son is seriously mentally ill. I think we'll be able to reach a compromise that keeps their son out of an Italian prison. He'll be admitted to a secure psychiatric ward under my guardianship."

Wes blinked at the cold calculation in Declan's smile, but Cara didn't seem fazed. She simply nodded, as if circumventing international courts and essentially privately imprisoning someone was normal.

He looked at Declan, considering. The Bloom family had been a media empire, and while he knew that no global business was above bending the law, her brother seemed a bit… more.

"I think we should go to Dublin." Cara drew Wes's attention back to the conversation.

"There's no reason for you to go." Declan shook his head.

"I'm going. You don't have to help me, but you know you'll feel better if you know what I'm doing. Did Colin tell you where the snow globe is? He didn't destroy it, did he?"

A muscle ticked in Declan's jaw. "He claims he doesn't have it. He wasn't the one who broke into your house."

Wes frowned. "It had to be him."

Declan spared him a glance. "I've confirmed it. He flew to London to link up with his parents before coming here for the wedding."

"He could have hired someone." Cara pointed out.

"But why take the globe?" Declan's lip curled. "I believe sickos like this are usually more interested in… personal items."

Cara's face paled. Wes suspected she was thinking of Colin accessing her computer. Declan's eyes bounced between the two of them. "Is there something you need to tell me, Caralina?"

"Nothing to do with this," Cara frowned. "If not him, then who? Did the police come up with anything? Fingerprints?"

"I checked with Luke, and he said he would go down to the police station today. He had a deposition or something this morning."

"You told Luke?" Cara groaned.

"And James. You think I shouldn't tell your brothers someone tried to murder you?"

"*Our* brothers."

"I'm trying to convince them they don't need to come. They both want to hear from you today."

"Wes, could you find my mom and ask her to come up here? I think we need to find out everything that happened the day she spent with my dad."

"No problem. I'll replace your ice, too."

"That's what you think." Cara said dryly, handing him the plastic bags now full of water. "Tearing my mother away from her grand performance won't be easy."

Cara hadn't been wrong. It took far too long for Wes to get Corinne's attention. You'd think with her daughter recently attacked, Corinne would want to know how Cara was the second she saw him. Instead, she'd held up a finger for him to wait, and as Wes moved closer, he could make out her words.

"It's just dreadful. But I guess the apple doesn't fall far from the tree. Ursula was always very jealous of me. Obviously, some of her animosity poisoned her son, and he took it out on my poor Caralina."

Wes was incredulous. "Corinne. Your daughter would like to talk with you," he said, impatience ringing in his voice.

The woman Corinne had been talking to turned sympathetic eyes to Wes. "Please give Caralina our love. Just horrible! We'd better be going…"

"Oh no! You don't need to go!" Corinne objected. The other woman cast a dubious look around the subdued crowd.

Corinne flashed her dazzling smile to Wes. "Tell my darling I'll be up after I've taken care of my guests. She'll understand."

"She probably will, but I certainly don't." Wes said through gritted teeth. "Your daughter needs you, now!"

Corinne looked surprised, but seeing he was serious, she made her apologies to the couple before swishing past Wes into the house. He stopped in the kitchen to replace the ice, and by the time he reached the bedroom, Declan was already grilling Corinne.

"I told you. It was a coincidence," Corinne was saying. "I had spent a weekend at the most delightful country house party. You remember the Zhous, don't you darling?"

"How did you run into Dad?" Cara's eyes sparked with her exasperation.

"I was going to the Sherbourne. I always stay there but decided I'd see if Siobhan was home. Why is everyone suddenly so interested in this?"

That seemed to get Declan's attention. "Who else asked you?"

"Courtney and Elliott. They said you'd told them David had gone to Dublin. They were surprised because he was so ill."

"What did you tell them?"

Corinne looked askance at her daughter. "Just that I saw him. I'm not an idiot. I don't like that woman, and if she has Elliott wrapped around her finger now then—"

"Did you see my mother? She never mentioned it." Declan interrupted.

Corinne's face blanked, and her eyes slid away. "I saw her on the street. It's quite unnerving when you make that face, you know. You look just like him." Declan stared at her, and she sighed. "Fine! David and Siobhan were in the street about a block from her place. They were arguing."

The skin tightened along Declan's cheekbones, but when he didn't ask the obvious follow up, Cara did. "About what?"

Corinne looked nervously at Declan. "I don't know."

Cara appeared as confused as Wes was. "You had to have heard them," Cara insisted.

"They were too far for me to understand what they were saying."

"What happened next?"

"I waved. I hate when people fight."

Wes thought he heard Cara snort. "We chatted for a few minutes, but David was very weak. Siobhan told him he could come in to sit for a bit, but he didn't want to. She was right. He looked terrible." Corinne's mouth turned down. "He was always such a virile man; he was a shell." To Wes's surprise, her eyes shone with tears.

Declan cleared his throat. "What did the two of you do?"

"I invited him back to my hotel for a cocktail, but he said he had an errand he needed to run. I didn't realize it, but I guess he knew the end was near, and he was putting his affairs in order. You know your father liked to keep his money in different countries for convenience." Declan and Cara nodded. "Ireland was always his favorite." She cocked her head thinking. "It's a lot of people's favorite because of the tax shelter."

"What do you mean by putting his affairs in order?" Cara asked in an attempt to keep her mother on track.

"He wanted to go to Ballbridge." Her brow furrowed. "He said he needed to update some paperwork there. You have to understand, he wasn't himself."

"Dementia?" Declan's voice was flat.

"No," she said thoughtfully. "More like exhausted, defeated… sad. I'd never seen him like that. He said he'd made a terrible mistake."

Cara sat up straighter in bed, and Declan cocked an eyebrow. "He admitted to a mistake."

Wes watched as the three of them shared a smile. "Hard to believe, I know, but yes. And it seemed to really bother him. I insisted on getting a taxi, but it could only get us a few streets away. On our way, we passed one of those tacky tourist stalls. You know the ones that sell the leprechauns and *I heart Ireland* shirts. He saw the snow globe and was suddenly determined to have it. I waited outside of the building for him. You know I hate all that boring business talk. When David came out, he seemed a little relieved, and then he gave me the package for you. He was adamant that I get it to you right away."

"But you didn't."

"Darling, I forgot! It was a silly thing. We went for a drink. He dropped me at my hotel, and that was the last time I saw dear David," she sniffed.

"If you had given me the snow globe earlier, we might have figured out what was going on sooner."

"Figured what out?" Corinne wrinkled her nose.

No one answered her, and after a few more pointed questions from Declan, it was clear Corinne had revealed everything she knew.

When it was only the three of them, Wes finally spoke. "What's the significance of the building and the snow globe?"

"It has to be connected to what was happening with his health. Remember his note to me."

"But how is a snow globe linked? And why did someone steal it? Who else knew about it?" Declan paced at the foot of the bed.

Wes looked at Cara, and her eyes fell to her lap. "Chris was there when I got it."

Declan flinched, and then his head bowed.

"He witnessed the new will along with his father," Cara's voice trembled.

When Declan raised his head, his eyes were flinty. "I'll look into the location in Dublin."

"Declan—"

"No!" Declan's words lashed out. "If Chris has the globe and is helping Courtney…" His nostrils flared.

Cara gave Wes a troubled look. "Dec, let's go to this building. Find out what Dad was doing there."

Declan hesitated, then finally agreed. "Are you sure you're up to this?"

Wes almost laughed at the insulted face Cara made. "I'd rather concentrate on this puzzle than focus on what happened today."

"I assume you want to come?" Declan came to stand by Wes.

Wes squared his jaw. Cara's brother was easily the most intimidating person he'd ever met, but there was no way Cara was going anywhere without him.

"I'm not letting her out of my sight."

Declan seemed to like whatever it was he saw in Wes's eyes because he grunted.

"I'll charter a plane. Leave in the morning." He threw the words over his shoulder, before closing the door behind him.

Cara's eyes were wide on her face. "If Chris is part of this, I'm not sure Declan will recover. They've been friends forever! And Declan doesn't have many of those."

Wes's first impression of Ireland was gray. The overcast sky and drizzle haunted them from the moment the plane touched down and they entered the private SUV waiting for them at the airfield.

This morning, Cara's bruises had blossomed into a range of purple and red. He wasn't sure what magic she did in the bathroom with her makeup, but when she emerged, the only visible evidence was a swollen jaw and slight discolorations. She tied a large scarf around her neck to hide the damage there, but he knew beneath her clothes angry bruises decorated her creamy skin.

Cara slept through the short flight, but Wes took the time to write an encrypted email to Jin, to let him know what was happening. Declan sat with his back to them in the seats across the narrow aisle.

He had spoken little since Cara revealed Chris must be the one who had stolen the snow globe, and Wes knew she was worried about her brother. Declan's head stayed buried in his phone, only once did he get up to pour a glass of whiskey.

Cara and Declan seemed uninterested in the city as the SUV

wound its way through the Dublin traffic. In contrast, Wes craned his neck, trying to get a better look at the gray stone and brick buildings, marveling at the historic architecture.

He caught Cara smiling at him, and he grinned sheepishly. "I guess you're used to all this."

"I love Dublin." Cara intertwined his fingers with hers on the seat between them. "Some of my very favorite memories are here." She reached forward and poked her brother's shoulder. Declan grunted in reply. "Hopefully, we'll have time to see some of the city after."

A shadow crossed her face, and it reminded Wes that this wasn't a vacation. They needed to find out what was so important that her father had traveled to Dublin days before his death. Wes was less convinced than Cara and her brother that this trip, and solving the mystery of the snow globe, would give them the answers they were looking for. But this was important to her, and he would help, however he could. Chris had stolen the snow globe from their home, and he hated that once again the space, where she should have felt safe, had been violated by someone she trusted.

Our home. The words felt right. They would need to find a new house—something new for both of them without all the unpleasant memories.

"What are you smiling about?"

"Just thinking about the future. When we get home."

Cara's eyes searched his face, and her expression softened as she leaned toward him. Her lips were inches from his, her signature, honeysuckle scent curling around him, when her brother barked, "Not while I'm in the car."

Cara let out a peal of laughter but settled back in her seat. Wes squeezed her fingers, and she scooted across the bench seat to press against him.

CHAPTER FIFTY

"WE'RE STAYING IN A HOTEL?" CARA ASKED, AS THE SUV PULLED up to the curb. She had assumed they'd be going to Siobhan's. She had been looking forward to one of the woman's fierce hugs. Anne was the voice of cool reason and good advice, but Siobhan was the one always ready to fight in Cara's corner. She was capable, smart, and probably even more ruthless than her son.

"I assumed the two of you wanted to stay together," Declan said, lifting his briefcase off the seat as he climbed from the car.

Cara followed him. "Look at you being all open-minded."

Declan leveled a glare at her, and she beamed back at him. The circumstances were terrible, but she was happy to be with her brother again.

"Seriously? Staying together would be an issue?" Wes whispered in her ear as they followed Declan through the glass doors. The doorman nodded a welcome and directed several uniformed porters to collect their luggage.

"Siobhan might be divorced from Seamus's dad, and then had Declan 'out of wedlock,' but she still likes to pretend she's a good Catholic girl." Cara laughed. "The whole 'Do as I say… thing."

"Ah."

377

"She's in Paris this week. I didn't think it was appropriate for us to stay there without her," Declan stated.

A man in a tailored suit came forward to greet them. "Welcome back, Mr. Bloom."

Cara and Wes hung back while Declan went over the details of their stay with the concierge. "I've reserved the floor," Declan said, when the elevator opened, and he handed them their keycards. His gaze fell to the scarf. "Still okay?"

"I'm fine, Dec, promise."

"I'm in the suite at the end."

Cara and Wes dropped their bags in their room, Wes pulling her in for a long kiss. When Cara tried to deepen the embrace, Wes pulled back.

"I'm not going to break," Cara huffed.

Wes smoothed her hair behind her ear. "You went through a traumatic event yesterday."

Cara narrowed her eyes. Wes might be worried about hurting her, but she had other plans.

They found Declan sipping a glass of whiskey, standing by the floor-to-ceiling windows in the main room of his suite. At their entrance, he poured a finger of the amber liquid into two glasses and handed them each one.

"I finally heard from my source."

Cara could feel Wes's curious eyes, but she didn't look at him or ask questions. Siobhan's family was influential in Dublin and had been for more than a hundred years. Roots in Ireland ran deep.

"Are you sure you want to be a part of this?" Declan challenged Wes. "This is our family's problem, not yours. It might be best if you didn't involve yourself, particularly with your previous record. Now that I think about it, none of this is any of your business. It might be best if you stay out of it."

Wes squared his shoulders and met Declan's implacable stare with one of his own. "Cara *is* my business."

She wasn't used to people challenging her brother head on, and she wouldn't deny it was sexy that Wes was doing it for her.

After a second, Declan nodded his approval and gave Wes a genuine smile. "In that case," he said, gesturing to the low sofas facing each other, a small table in between. "Based on where Corinne says our father went into a building, she was referring to the Waterloo Building block. There is a heavily secured, private vault business located there. That has to be where he went."

"Why would he go there?" Cara sipped her drink.

"He may have stashed gold, silver, art, documents." Declan shrugged. "No way to know until we get in there."

"How do we do that?"

"That's the tricky part. Unfortunately, even if they were susceptible to… persuasion, we wouldn't be able to get in."

"Why?" Wes asked.

"Only the account holder or the direct heir can access it. There is no override function."

"Damn!" Cara swore.

"What are the security measures? Digital or physical?" Wes leaned forward.

"Normally, it's biometrics and a 4-digit pin code."

Cara groaned.

"But when an owner dies, they can bypass the biometrics, provided the heir has the death certificate, the will, proof of ID, and the pin number. Apparently, Courtney knows where he was, too. According to my source, she tried to access it yesterday afternoon accompanied by a man but they didn't have the pin code."

"That's not great," Wes said. "If it were purely digital, I could—"

"No!" Cara smacked his arm. "I appreciate you want to help, but I'm not risking your freedom."

"No," Declan agreed. "We need to find another way."

"We don't even know if there is anything of value in there," Wes pointed out.

"It has to be something very important to my father," Cara insisted. "Why else make the trip when he was so ill? *And,* go to the lengths he did to hide where he had gone? Courtney didn't know until I told her. Which in hindsight, was a really dumb thing to do."

"Another will?" Declan guessed.

"At least, she can't get in either." Wes took a long swallow of his drink.

"What does the snow globe have to do with it?" Cara shook her head trying to make sense of what clues they had. "What did the note say? It was something like 'things are clear now, and I'm giving the answers to you.' And then he referenced the snow globe. There must be a clue to the pin number in it. It's the only piece of information none of us has. Does Courtney know what's in the vault? Maybe she's worried it will prove she poisoned our father."

"If he had proof she was poisoning him, he would have told someone," Wes reasoned.

They sat back in frustration.

"Tell me everything you remember about the snow globe," Declan demanded.

Cara shrugged. "It was a Dublin cityscape. We went over it carefully and didn't see anything."

"If we had it, we could break it apart. Chris must believe the answer is there." Declan's voice was bitter, and Cara saw the hurt he tried to hide.

"We don't know for sure he was the one."

His mouth twisted. "Don't we? He won't return my calls. He knows I know, and now he's hiding like the coward he is. They must think the clue to the pin number is in the globe, too. Why else take it? It's the only thing she's missing to access the vault." Declan drained his glass and rose to refill it.

The three of them sat lost in their own thoughts. "What about the music?" Wes asked suddenly. "Music and math are intrinsically entwined. And I'm assuming the pin number is a numeric value? What if it wasn't something visual, but a musical cryptogram?"

Declan and Cara looked at him blankly. "A musical cryptogram, it's like a secret code. You use a series of musical notes to refer to something else, like initials, or a name. People have used these types of codes for hundreds of years. It could be as simple as replacing the notes on the scale with notes on the alphabet. Even Bach had his own system."

"My father wouldn't have known about that." Cara looked dubious.

Declan rubbed a finger across his lip. "What was the song? The alphabet?"

Cara made a face at him. "Why would someone put the alphabet song in a snow globe?"

Wes stared off into space for a minute humming, and then smiled. "It's the same song."

"What?"

"The Alphabet Song," "Baa Baa Black Sheep," and "Twinkle Twinkle Little Star." Musically, they are the same notes."

"No, they're not." Cara's nose wrinkled, but Declan nodded slowly.

"He's right, they are."

"It's a four-digit code, you said. All of those words are too many letters." Cara set the empty glass down. "I don't think Dad even knew how to read music."

"A few years ago, Dad wanted to learn to play the piano. I teased him about it, but he told me he'd learned on the computer. It was learning by numbers. Could that be it?" Declan's eyes blazed with excitement, and a laugh escaped. "Could it be as simple as a learn-by-numbers song?"

"It could be," Wes acknowledged. "If he didn't have any training in cryptography."

Cara stayed quiet. The theory made sense. Their father liked puzzles, Sudoku, things like that, but he wouldn't have been able to come up with something complicated, as sick as he was, on the streets of Dublin. Her chest constricted. She had wanted to believe that he chose the snow globe and its song because of his nickname for her.

"That has to be it, then." Declan typed into his phone and then his face folded. "Damn! There are several four-note measures. How do we know which one?"

"Wouldn't he have chosen the first? Unless he practiced it so much, he memorized it."

"That's a good point. Most likely, he would have only remembered the first set, 1,1,5,5." He exhaled. "We still have a problem though. Even if we're right, the only person who can access it is Courtney. Even if we could get a fake ID for her, she was just there. They'd remember." Declan put his hands on his hips.

Cara's shoulders slumped. They were so close! If Courtney had the snow globe, it was only a matter of time before she discovered the significance of the song.

Wes was staring at her jaw, and Cara self-consciously lifted her hand to the spot. "I know you hate hearing it, but you look a bit like her."

"Hardly enough to pass for her," Declan scoffed. "Courtney has at least two inches on Cara, not to mention more than twenty years."

Wes's gaze lingered on Cara. *What was he thinking?*

"Those things can be fixed," Wes said.

Understanding dawned on her. "The hair color is a little different. I could color it, and if it's raining, wear a scarf. Some colored contacts—" She thought through what would be necessary.

"Cara, you aren't a forty-eight-year-old woman. It won't

work, and not only would it alert Courtney that we were trying to get access, you could also get arrested for using false identification. We don't even know if the code is correct!"

"Is that a crime?"

Declan paused. "Probably?"

"I think I could do it. I'd need to find a theatrical supply house, but that shouldn't be too big of an obstacle with all the theater here. As much as I hate to admit it, Courtney looks amazing for her age. It would be a simple enough aging process, similar to what we used on the set. I could use pads to make the cheekbones." She made a face. "The scarf around my neck helps. Necks are tricky to make convincing because the skin is so thin the makeup tends to crack quickly."

"What are you talking about?" Declan looked at her like she was speaking a foreign language.

Wes grinned. "Cara's great. She could do it."

"This isn't playing dress up with makeup, Cara. This is serious!" Declan's voice was irritated. "I'll think of something." He typed out something on his phone.

"Declan, I'm not playing with makeup. This is what I do for a living now."

"I thought you were an assistant." He didn't bother to look up from the device.

Frustration surged through her. What was it going to take for him to take her seriously? But before she could retort, Wes was on his feet shoving his own phone in front of Declan.

"She did these months ago. Self-taught. And since then, she has been training on the movie set. She's very good!"

Declan took the phone from him and swiped a few times, raising surprised eyes to her.

"You did this? Really?"

"From TrekCon," Wes explained, taking his phone back.

"From what?" Declan looked bewildered.

"Becoming Courtney won't be nearly as challenging. If I carry an ID with my picture on it, I won't have to be identical, only similar. They already have the paperwork, so I should be able to just go in, hand them the ID, and give the pin number."

Declan was clearly unconvinced.

"People believe what they are presented with," Cara asserted. "Why would they be looking for a problem?"

"There is a reason people use these high security vaults. Their reputation is everything. They aren't just going to take your word for it."

"But they will think I'm Courtney, coming back now that I've found the pin. Besides," Cara adopted a haughty tone. "I can play rich bitch as well as the next socialite." Declan's lips twitched. "Can you get a fake ID with my new face on it?"

"Yes." He pinched the bridge of his nose. "This is a bad idea. If you get arrested, the boys will eviscerate me."

"If I get arrested, you'll get me out."

Wes looked worried for the first time. "Do you think that's likely? They'd arrest her, instead of hushing it up?"

"No," Cara insisted.

"Maybe I should go with her. I could pose as one of her sons," Wes suggested.

"Ewww!"

"We don't know who went with her before. Just that it was a man. It's too big a risk to impersonate two people. Let me make some calls."

"In the meantime, I'm going shopping!" Cara crowed.

CHAPTER FIFTY-ONE

The theatrical supply house proved easy to locate, and Wes held the shopping basket while Cara gushed over the different products she found.

"Skye is going to die! This stuff is so impossible to get!" she said, dropping several tubes in the basket. She referred to her phone several times, where she was carrying on a text conversation with Skye.

"Skye says the latex cheek pads will work best to soften my jawline… I guess the swelling will do some good after all." She looked up and wrinkled her nose. "Courtney looks phenomenal for her age but still…" Wes suspected Cara was getting a little enjoyment out of dissecting her stepmother's looks. After the misery the woman had put Cara and her family through, a little mental payback was deserved.

"I'm sure she'll get surgery soon," Cara mused. "There's only so much diet can do. Genetics gets you every time, and she's getting a little jowly, and the bags under her eyes…"

Wes looked at her skeptically. "Don't get carried away. The woman may be Medusa on the inside, but she's still extremely attractive."

Cara scowled at him but put back a few of the pads. "You're right."

"What did you tell Skye? She's met Courtney. She must have questions, and the fewer people who know, the less likely you are to get in trouble later."

"I said I was working on a project for my brother. I sent her some close-up photos of the nose and jawline, but I don't need help with the hair or aging around the eyes, thanks to the practice I got from the movie. It would be easier if her nose were narrower, then I could contour. Skye didn't recognize the pictures, and I promised to fill her in when I get back."

After Cara had found everything she thought she needed, they stepped out into the icy drizzle.

"Speaking of when we get back."

Cara's eyes flit to his.

Wes cleared his throat. "You know, I was only staying in the house while I was house hunting. I never intended on staying in that house for a long time."

Cara halted on the sidewalk, her fingers turning white where they clutched the bag.

"I know now isn't the time to talk about it. With so much going on…"

"You're moving out." Cara wouldn't look him in the eye.

"Well, yeah."

"Wow," she breathed, crossing her arms over her chest.

Wes's stomach clenched. This was going wrong. "I want us to find a place together." Cara glanced up at him. She looked adorable, with her nose turning pink in the cold despite the heavy makeup she wore to cover her bruising.

"Together?"

Wes took her hands. "I know you have a lot going on with your family and everything that happened with Colin." Her eyes flickered. "I know this isn't the best time to talk about it, but I don't want to wait. I don't want to go back to that house."

"We have some wonderful memories there." She began walking again.

Wes put his hand on her arm to stop her, turning her to face him on the crowded sidewalk. His hands stroked down her biceps. "And bad ones, too. I know you'll need a place close to the city for work, but I can work from anywhere."

"You've put a lot of thought into this already."

Why does she sound worried?

Cara's eyes were serious when they met his. He thought this was what she wanted to hear, that they would be together.

Isn't that what she wants, too?

"I mean we haven't finished all the Star Treks yet." He joked lamely, but she didn't smile as he'd hoped.

"A few days ago, you were convinced Melody was the love of your life, and now you want us to what… move in together? Not roommates but together, as a couple?"

Wes stared, feeling helpless. He didn't know what to say.

Cara tugged at her scarf. "You're right though. This isn't the time. I need to concentrate on what I have to do tomorrow." She must have read the hurt in his face because she pulled him down to her level by the front of his shirt and placed a firm kiss against his lips.

"I'm not saying no. I'm saying the last few days have been all adrenaline and…" She smirked. "Great sex, but I need to be sure you know what you are doing. You need to be sure this is what you want. I don't want to be someone you've slipped into your fantasy of happily-ever-after."

She stepped back then. "Come on, I'm freezing."

Wes's heart sank. He was silent as they got in the car and rode back to the hotel. The quiet didn't seem to bother Cara as she stared out her window which only worried him more.

CHAPTER FIFTY-TWO

"It's about time! I've been texting you!" An annoyed Luke opened the door to Declan's suite.

"What are you doing here?" Cara asked in a choked voice, before dropping the bag and hurling herself into her brother's arms. Luke clutched her snug against his chest.

"James wanted to come, but he's in the middle of something," Luke said cryptically. "One of us needed to be here to take care of you."

Cara pulled back. "It's great to see you, but Declan is here."

"He's not as good of a hugger as I am," Luke joked.

Wes stood back watching them, feeling more alone than he had in a long time. After what Cara had said on the street, and now seeing her with her family, he felt like she was intentionally putting a distance between them.

Luke looked suspiciously at Wes. "I didn't realize you would be here. I thought you went back to Atlanta."

Cara frowned. "Leave him alone, Luke. I need him here." Wes brightened at her choice of words. He would definitely follow up later on what she had meant by that. *Need is good, right?*

"Have you seen Declan?" Cara worried her lip.

Luke looked wary. "Not in person, but he left me a key. He knew I was coming."

"Well, that's something," Cara said. "He seems better."

"He's always thrived on turmoil, so that sounds about right," Luke drawled.

"I think we're getting closer to knowing what happened, Luke."

They each took a seat on one of Declan's couches while Cara filled her brother in on everything that had happened. Her accusing Courtney, the conversation with Dr. Keller, and their plan for the next day. Luke looked at him with a new respect when Cara mentioned it was Wes who discovered the connection between the music and the pin number.

"But you don't know for sure that's what the pin number is?"

"No." She agreed. "But it's our best bet. Courtney would have tried all the other pin numbers she knew. It can't be a coincidence that he changed the security pin and then insisted that my mom send me the snow globe."

"I hope you're right. There may be nothing other than money in there, and that is rightly Courtney's," Luke cautioned.

"If there isn't something related to Dad's death, then I'll just close it and leave. It's getting late, and Declan will be back soon. I need to go do a practice run on the makeup so we can take a picture and get it to whomever Declan's using to make the fake…"

Luke put his fingers in his ear. "La la la la—I'm not hearing a crime being planned—la la la."

Cara stuck her tongue out at her brother and walked to the door with the shopping bag in her hand. She stopped at the door, and nonchalantly said, "Wes, can you help me? I need to dye my hair first."

Luke's face darkened, and he glared at Wes. "I'll help you."

"Don't be such a child, Luke. I'm doing it in the sink, not the shower. Unless?" She winked at Wes.

"I'd prefer not to have your brother murder me, if you don't mind."

"Fine, I'll do it myself." Cara gave a dramatic sigh.

Avoiding Luke's suspicious gaze, Wes retreated to the dining table in the suite with his computer, using the excuse that he needed to catch up on emails. In reality, he needed a minute away from Cara's brothers' scrutiny. The Blooms were intense.

When Declan returned it was almost as if the two brothers communicated silently. They took seats opposite Wes at the table and began grilling him.

"You've helped my sister. We appreciate that," Luke began. "You've lived with her for months?"

What the fuck?

The brothers exchanged a look.

"Separate bedrooms, right?" Declan interjected.

Wes decided silence was the best option. Luke grinned, recognizing the tactic.

"Nice. He's smart," he said to Declan, but it was Cara who interrupted by opening the suite door.

"What do you think?"

"Holy shit, that's scary." Luke's mouth hung open.

Dressed in her pajamas she posed with one hand behind her head and one on her hip.

"David, you terrible tease!" Her whole voice changed, and while Wes recognized what she was doing, the slack nature on her brothers' faces showed how effective the transformation was.

"Uncanny." Declan let out a disbelieving laugh. He walked close to Cara to inspect her makeup, but Wes noticed him take his sister's hand as if the smooth skin reassured himself it was still the younger woman.

"This might work. Damn! Is this what you've been doing?"

Luke was as dumbstruck as Declan, but pride sounded in his voice.

Wes's chest expanded as Cara's face transformed with happiness. Even though this was to reveal her father's killer, her brothers were finally seeing what she could do.

"We should take the picture," Declan finally said.

Cara obligingly stood in front of the white wall, and Declan snapped several pictures before walking to the door.

"I'll get these to," he looked at Luke, "my friend. It shouldn't take long."

After Declan left, Cara turned to Wes. "Believable?"

"Eerily."

"Excellent! I'm going to go take this off because, believe it or not, it's not the most comfortable thing in the world."

Cara disappeared, leaving Wes alone with Luke.

"I never saw it before," Luke said absently, walking to pour himself a hefty portion of whiskey from the bar.

"Didn't see what?"

"How much Courtney looks like Corinne. I mean Corinne is in a class of her own, but it is a little weird." Luke shook his head. "Love is a funny thing. I wonder if it was because Corinne was the one who didn't want him, that he ended up marrying a woman who looked similar?"

Wes wasn't sure what he should say. Collapsing on the sofa, Luke slugged the drink back. "Cara's told you about us, right?"

Wes nodded, not exactly sure what the man meant.

"You grew up in foster care?" Luke waved the glass. "We checked up on you, obviously. She mentioned you were in love with a girl you'd been in foster care with."

Wes bristled. This was none of their business, but as much as he would like to tell them to fuck off, they were Cara's brothers, and on some level, he understood they were looking out for her.

"I love Melody, my foster sister, but not like that."

"But a few days ago, you thought you did."

The door opened, and Wes knew Cara had returned. She leaned against the wall just inside the door, waiting for his answer.

His eyes were on her when he said, "For a long time, I confused the love I felt for Melody with something else. I didn't have the benefit of siblings. There are very few people in my life who have ever made me feel... I didn't understand how to differentiate." Wes stared into her eyes, across the room, willing her to see. "What I feel for Cara is different. There is nothing I wouldn't do for her, nothing I wouldn't do to make her smile, laugh, make her dreams come true."

Luke leaned back, a smirk on his lips, aware of what was happening, but Wes wasn't embarrassed.

"I don't care how you *think* you feel about my sister," Luke finally said. "Just know that if you break her heart, I will destroy you. Now, that I've done my brotherly duty, I need to find where Declan is hiding the good whiskey cause this," he waved his glass, "is *shiite*."

Luke disappeared into the second bedroom of the suite, but Wes's eyes were all for Cara as she made her way towards him.

"You love me?"

"I told you I did."

She came to stand before him. "And it's different from how you felt about Melody?"

Wes grabbed her hips and pulled her hard against him. "I watched Melody for days with Luca and didn't care, but the sight of that ass Damon touching you made me want to break out every dirty fighting trick I'd ever learned." His hands lifted to frame her face, his thumb carefully brushing the lurid marks on her jaw.

"I love you. I want to take care of you. You aren't fitting into a fantasy of mine." He brushed his lips across hers. "You *are* the fantasy."

She gasped when his hands slid beneath her and hoisted her against him, and she wrapped her legs around him for stability.

"I don't care if your brothers hate me. I love you, and if it takes the rest of my life, I'm going to make you believe it."

"I don't know about the rest of my life, but you are welcome to try for the rest of the night."

Wrapped around each other, they heard Luke yell. "Take it to your own room please, before I throw up!"

CHAPTER FIFTY-THREE

It was a little awkward to face her brothers over coffee, but she'd met plenty of her brothers' *friends* sneaking out of their father's pool house in the early morning hours, so they could deal with the fact she'd spent the night with Wes. Cara still wasn't sure what would happen when they got back to Georgia, but she knew Wes loved her.

But would it be enough?

The old whispers sounded in her brain. Could it last? Was she a substitute? When he got bored, would he want Melody again? She shook herself mentally.

No!

She trusted him.

"You, okay?"

Luke emerged from the bedroom in sweatpants and a UGA T-shirt, his dark hair tousled from sleep.

"Yeah." She forced a smile. "Just nervous about today."

"You don't have to do this. We can find another way."

Cara shook her head, and Luke looked at her with a knowing expression. "Does the brooding have anything to do with you asking me last week if I believed in love?"

Her mouth quirked. "He says he loves me."

"You think he's lying?" Luke's question seemed simple, but she knew him well enough to know that there was a wealth of subtext behind his words.

"I know he *believes* he does."

"Are you unlovable then?" Luke poured a stream of rich coffee into a mug. "I happen to think you are extremely lovable."

"No." She took a sip of coffee. "But it's not that straight forward."

"Ah, so he's a gold digger after your nonexistent fortune."

She glared. "Ha-ha. Hilarious."

"Clout chaser? Looking to cash in on the Bloom name?"

"No, he didn't even know who I was when we met."

"Hmm." Luke sipped his coffee. "What's his angle?"

"He doesn't have an angle," she said, instantly defensive.

"He's not stupid. He knew what he could get by helping the Blooms."

"He knew who Declan was, eventually," she admitted. "But that's not how he is."

"Wasn't he just in love with someone else? And then he just gave up? So, he's a quitter?"

"He's not! I mean, she's engaged to this Italian guy with all the connections she ever wanted, and then..." she gestured to her face. "This happened."

"Ah, he only started showing interest after he got shot down by the model."

"No! Oh my god! You are the worst!" She laughed, throwing her napkin at him.

Luke caught it against his chest. "I'm just saying the man I saw the night of your break in, the one who sat up the rest of the night, despite the fact I live in a doorman protected building, is not someone who suddenly decided a couple days ago he was in love with you."

"I didn't know he'd done that. Do you really think so?" She hated how vulnerable she sounded.

"I know so." Luke kissed the top of her head. "Now go start your creepy transformation. You have a big day ahead."

It took Cara well over an hour to style her hair and apply the stage makeup and clothing required to transform her into an approximation of Courtney Bloom. Wes walked with her to the suite.

"It's impressive," Luke said, taking in the look.

Cara placed her hands under her chin and posed. "Isn't it!"

Declan swallowed thickly. "Wow." He nodded, his lips folding in. "Yeah. Just…"

Wes stood back, not wanting to intrude. It was interesting. Declan's face was a mixture of horror and admiration while Luke's was all delight.

"You look just like her!" Luke said. "Say something Courtney-like."

"Oh, David! You are simply the best!"

Wes thought he might be the only one who caught Declan's flinch while Cara and Luke dissolved into laughter.

"Do you have the IDs?" Cara asked. "I'd like to get this over with."

"Yeah, of course." Declan walked to the manila folder on the bar and pulled out a passport and driver's license.

"These are what you need."

Wes noticed he didn't look Cara full in the face. And this time Wes wasn't the only one. Luke and Cara exchanged glances.

"Ready?" Wes asked. Cara cast one more quick look at her brothers before squaring her shoulders.

"Absolutely!" Cara tucked a leather portfolio under her arm, and then threw a white fur coat Declan had procured over her arm.

They settled in the cab and stayed silent on the ride to Waterloo Place. Wes would have thought she was unaffected, except her hand crept across the seat to lace her fingers with his, even though she kept her gaze steadfastly forward.

There was so much he wanted to say. Last-minute warnings. What if they had guessed wrong about the pin number? Suddenly, the risk Cara was taking felt very real. After spending time with Declan, he didn't doubt that Cara's time with the Garda would be limited, but still… A cold sweat broke out along his spine at the image of handcuffs being put on her.

"It's not too…"

"I won't be but a minute." She looked meaningfully between him and the cab driver as they came to a stop at the curb. Then, she was gone, as if the slightest hesitation would derail the whole thing, and he was left to sit in the cab, wondering what was happening inside.

CHAPTER FIFTY-FOUR

Cara kept her breathing even as she clicked across the marble foyer in four-inch heels. Thankfully, the rain had kept up, so her patting at her rain-dotted scarf, wrapped around her head and neck, seemed believable enough. "Left foot, right foot," she told herself, a fake smile curling around her lips.

Reaching the desk, she asked to speak with a private banker. She didn't know if Courtney already had one, but as she slipped the ID across the wooden surface and the woman skittered back, she felt a momentary satisfaction that the name Bloom still held weight. Less than two minutes later, the woman was back.

"I'm so sorry Mr. Murphy isn't in today. Did you have an appointment?"

Cara controlled her exhalation of relief. "No, I found the piece of information I was missing yesterday to access my poor deceased husband's account. I was hoping to get back to the States tomorrow." Cara affected a simper, which felt saccharine enough to gag her, but the woman seemed to buy it.

"Oh, yes. Mr. Murphy mentioned you had come by. Did you want to access your husband's box?"

Box? That ruled out art or any significant amount of gold or silver.

"If it's not too inconvenient." Cara let the sarcasm drip from her tongue the way she thought Courtney would.

"Of course," the woman hurried to assure her. She shuffled through some papers and typed something on her keyboard. "It seems everything is in order." She looked up nervously. "You have the four-digit pin?"

Cara hoped the woman couldn't see the sweat on her upper lip. The woman turned a small keypad toward her. Cara stared at it for a second, and then taking a breath keyed in 1,1,5,5.

The young woman raised her eyes. "I'm sorry, Mrs. Bloom, that pin is incorrect."

Cara's heart rate picked up. *It had to be right.* Oh god was she going to be arrested? What else could it be? He'd sent her the snow globe—Twinkle Twinkle Little Star. She looked again at the keypad, and her brow cleared. "I'm sorry. I must have hit a key by mistake. May I try again?" She was proud of how cool her voice sounded, but the woman looked unsure and put her hand out to pull the keypad back.

Cara didn't give her a chance to object, swiftly keying in the numbers. Her eyes on the monitor, the woman's whole body sagged with relief.

"Excellent, Mrs. Bloom. If you'll follow me."

Ten minutes later, Cara struggled to keep her expression calm as she walked the short distance to the cab where Wes waited. When she slid in next to him, she couldn't hide the triumphant light in her eyes. "Holy shit," she mouthed at him. Cara's lips stayed shut on the ride to the hotel, and when they were in the elevator, Cara tugged the scarf loose.

"We were right!" Wes punched the air in excitement.

"No." She shook her head. "Not 1155. It was 7827."

His brow furrowed, and Cara knew he was trying to work out the significance.

"On a phone keypad, it's the word *star*. It was just like I thought. My father left the message for me. I was standing in front of the lady, thinking I'm screwed, and an image of the note flashed in front of me. My father wrote STAR in all caps. I knew I only had one more chance, and it was my best guess."

Wes pressed a smacking kiss against her lips. "What's in the envelope?"

"Bullshit," Cara muttered. Her brothers were waiting in the hallway when the elevator doors opened. She shoved the envelope into Declan's chest, but her eyes were on Luke. "It's total bullshit. Don't leave him."

Wes arched a brow but followed her back to their room. Cara had just started applying the oil to loosen the fake pieces when Declan's voice exploded in the hallway, followed by Luke's angry voice.

Cara looked up and met Wes's eyes in the mirror.

"What was it?" he asked.

She swallowed hard. "Pictures, and a USB."

"Pictures of what?"

Cara scrubbed roughly at her face. "A car accident."

Wes's brows drew down.

"I didn't look at them closely. The second I opened the envelope, I knew they were what my father wanted me to find. I just don't know why he had them, or what he wanted me to do with them." She rubbed at her forehead, fighting back tears. "It's bad, Wes. Really bad."

He paled and then stepped forward to wrap his arms around her. He pulled her back against his chest and dropped a kiss to the top of her head.

"We'll figure it out."

CHAPTER FIFTY-FIVE

Wes held off asking any more questions until they had rejoined the two men in the hotel suite. A frown seemed to have taken a permanent spot between her eyes. Whatever Cara saw in the envelope had upset her deeply. She gnawed at her lip.

"Declan can be a controlling jerk, but I know there is an explanation. Don't judge him."

Wes could see how important this was to her, so he simply nodded. After the shouting in the hall, he didn't know what to expect when they reached the suite.

Luke opened the door, his face drawn, before wandering back to stare sightlessly out the window to the city beyond. Declan was slugging back whiskey, the decanter sitting on the table in front of him.

Declan's eyes burned with anger. "They aren't real. I swear."

Cara didn't hesitate. She crossed to him and threw her arms around his stiff body.

"I know."

"The real questions are why did our father have them and where did they come from?" Luke turned back to the room with his hands shoved in his pockets.

Wes stood back, not wanting to intrude, but the curiosity was eating him alive.

"They could be doctored, right? Photoshopped?" Cara sank onto the sofa next to Declan.

Luke nodded. "They're pretty blurry, so it wouldn't have taken an expert. There's a police report which is more of a problem. We need to find out if one actually exists in the system, or if it's a fake."

"Was our father setting me up? We were battling for control of the company. Was he going to use this to blackmail me?" Declan's voice cracked a little, and Wes looked away.

"No!" Cara cried. "He had them hidden. He must have been trying to protect you."

"Protect me from what? Don't be stupid! I knew he hated me, but not this much!" Declan roared in Cara's face. He threw the file folder across the glass coffee table, scattering the papers and USB. Luke took a step forward, his face tight, but Wes beat him to it.

"*Never* speak to her like that again." Wes's voice was low and fierce and took the three Bloom siblings by surprise. Declan's face was stormy, but Luke chuckled.

"Couldn't have said it better myself. Now…" Luke bent to grab a handful of the papers. "We need to find the source of these and why our father was hiding them in a vault in Dublin."

Declan grabbed the decanter and poured another large drink.

Luke nodded at the glass. "I know you are upset, but that's not helping."

"I'm not upset," Declan growled. "I'm fucking furious! I've never even been in a car accident, much less killed a prostitute!"

Wes's eyebrows hit his hairline. *Shit.*

"As your counsel, I think we should have these conversations in private."

"I would never say anything!" Cara sounded outraged, but

from the look Luke sent his way, Wes realized he was the one they were worried about.

Declan straightened, sending Wes a death glare.

Cara, watching the byplay, blurted out, "There are pictures of Declan driving a car, and then the same car after a car accident." She paled a little. "There's a dead woman on the road."

"Cara!" Luke snapped.

"Too late now. He can't unhear it." Cara turned toward her brothers. "I trust him. With my life." Despite the situation, warmth flooded through Wes at her words. "I won't have secrets from him."

"He's not family," Declan insisted, sloshing his whiskey when he jerked it toward Wes.

"Not yet." From the expressions on their faces, Wes wasn't sure which of them was more surprised. He hadn't planned on saying it, but once the words were out, nothing had ever felt more right.

"This is just fecking grand," Declan muttered, turning away in a huff, but Wes met Luke's appraising stare.

Luke gave him a faint smile. "Good luck with that."

Cara's face had a warm flush, but she didn't speak. He wouldn't let himself worry about that now. Wes knew she was still concerned about his feelings for Melody and that he was moving too fast, but suddenly it felt like they weren't moving fast enough. He grinned at her and got a confused look back.

"I'll call James. He should be able to pull up the case number." Luke pulled out his phone.

"Absolutely not!" Declan snapped.

"I don't have access in New York. It would have been a lot easier if you'd managed to get yourself framed for murder in Georgia."

"If it's even a real death," Wes injected.

Declan's eyes narrowed, but Cara nodded. "The photos may

not be real. Show Wes. He knows more about this than any of us do." The brothers exchanged a look. "Do it!"

"Might as well." Declan huffed. "She'll just show him herself."

"Who said you weren't smart?" Cara teased. "I have a feeling this is going to take a while, and I'm not interested in listening to you throw up all night. I'm going to order some food to soak up some of that alcohol."

"That might be the meanest thing you've ever said to me. I'm an Irishman. We don't get sick from whiskey."

"Half-Irish," she pointed out, but winked at Wes. "Everyone good with Thai?"

Wes listened with half an ear as Cara placed the order. He spread the pictures out, side by side on the coffee table. Luke plucked what looked like a police report from the pile.

"I have to call James. Even if he can't find the information, he'll kill us if we don't let him know what's going on."

Declan's mouth flattened. "I don't want him involved." He looked away. "If it goes bad–and someone finds out he's pulled records—his career with the prosecutor's office will be over."

"He's your brother. Besides, I'm not sure he'll be there much longer."

Wes kept his eyes on the pictures, the tension between the brothers palpable.

"He's a boy scout. What are you going to do if he tells you no?"

Luke let out a harsh laugh. "He might be a boy scout, but underneath it all, he's a Bloom, and he's your brother. He won't say no."

Luke stepped out of the room to make the call. Wes lifted the photo, showing Declan behind the wheel of a vintage Porsche going through a toll booth. Systematically, he traced the lines of the photo with his eyes and then repeated the process with the one depicting the dead woman.

"Here." Declan shoved a tumbler at him, and the scent of

whiskey filled his nose. Declan tumbled onto the sofa facing him, propping one foot on the coffee table and resting his glass on a bent knee. "She's not as tough as she looks."

"She's not as fragile as you all seem to think."

Declan's eyes narrowed. "You told her about working for me? About your arrest?"

Wes met his eyes. "Yes."

"Huh." Declan took a swig, and then looked to make sure they were still alone. "It's a cliché, I know, the big brother threats." He leaned forward, his foot hitting the ground with a thud, and braced his elbows on his knees. "But believe me when I say, if you break my sister's heart, I will ruin you and everyone you care about."

Wes didn't flinch. Normally he hated bullies, but in this case, not only did he know Declan was doing it for the love of his sister, but also that he meant it. "And I'll deserve it. Luke beat you to the threat, by the way."

Declan assessed him for another minute and then leaned back with another grunt. Considering the amount of liquor the man had put away, Wes was a little surprised he hadn't slumped over.

Wes held up the photo of the car after the accident. "I think this one is real."

"Bullshit!" Declan spat.

"But this one is a fake. A decent one, not a great one. If you know what to look for, there are a few obvious signs."

"Show me."

Wes handed him the first photograph. "Look at your head."

Declan's eyes went to the photo, his mouth pinched in an angry line. "Okay?"

"The shadow is wrong."

Declan squinted. "What shadow?"

Wes took the photo from him and pointed to the section he meant. "When the car traveled under the lights of the tollbooth, a shadow is cast from the driver onto the woman." Declan still looked blank. "The shadow that should be cast from the driver's head onto the passenger doesn't line up with the head in the photo. See how the other shadows line up with what is casting them. There is a gap where the top shadow begins. If I were to guess, they have replaced the head of the driver with yours, but whoever manipulated it didn't account for the height difference between you and the actual driver in the original picture."

"But that's my head. How did they put it on that body?"

Wes shrugged. "It's actually pretty simple if you've got photo manipulation software. Photoshop, for example. All they needed to do was select the area where the original driver's head was and remove the layer. Then, they replace that section with your head taken from another photo. The other mistake they made was they tried to line it up too precisely. Because you must be taller than the driver, they left out your neck. That's why it looks like your chin is on your chest, but they weren't experienced, and that's why the shadows don't line up."

Declan took the photo back and held it close to examine.

"There are some other discrepancies, too." Wes continued. "The line where your head meets the seat is wavy. I think whoever it was took out too much the first time and tried to re-layer the plaid pattern of the headrest. See how the lines don't match?"

Declan met Wes's eyes with an intense concentration. "If necessary, could we prove it wasn't me in the photo?"

"If the original is on that USB, I could run an Error Level Analysis on it. That will show right away where all the spots of manipulation are and when it was done."

Declan handed him the USB. "Do it. And I want to know who the actual face is."

Wes took the memory stick. He had his computer with him, and it would only take a few minutes to run the diagnostic with his software. "That I can't do. Once the layer is deleted, you can't get it back, not once the new image has been saved."

The muscle in Declan's jaw flexed, but he dipped his chin. "Run that test."

Wes got up to retrieve the computer from his messenger bag and returned to the sofa, sticking the USB into the port.

There were only a handful of files on the drive, and it didn't take long for Wes to find the photo in question.

"What's going on?" Cara asked, coming back in the room.

"I'm running an ELA on the photos. The photo of Declan is definitely fake, but the same car after the accident is most likely real. Do you want me to run the rest of the pictures, too?" Declan nodded.

Her forehead crinkled. "How is that possible? You love that car. I think you would have noticed if it had been in an accident. Where is it now?"

"I sold it."

"Really? I didn't know that."

"It was after…" He stopped, paced to the windows, and shoved his hands in the pockets of his suit pants, his head down.

Cara bent over Wes's shoulder to watch. "See the green and red places?" He pointed at the screen. "That shows where the photo was manipulated." He pulled up the metadata. "Looks like they did it on a MacBook Pro."

"Who's?"

"Maybe if they uploaded it to their cloud, the IP could be traced from the server, but there's no reason for the server company to have done that. It's a picture of someone at a toll-booth. It wouldn't have raised any red flags."

Wes began running the other pictures. "The rest appear to be originals. The ones of the car and… also, there is a photo of you with a broken arm."

Declan turned back. "My broken arm?" His expression shuttered, and Wes looked to Cara with a question in his eyes, but she shrugged.

"The photo of me driving looks real though, doesn't it?"

"To the average person, yes. Unless someone knew what to look for, they look genuine."

"Our father must have thought they were real."

"No." Luke's voice was firm as he rejoined them.

"He had to have!" Declan shook his head bitterly. "Why else hide them? Why not ask me about them?"

"You don't know that—"

"What's the date on the police report?" he asked Luke.

"April, two years ago."

Declan exhaled harshly through his nose. "I was here in Ireland. That was when Seamus... had his trouble."

"What trouble?" Cara asked, but Declan shook his head, refusing to answer the question about his older half-brother.

"What did James say?"

"He is going to check on it and get back to me. He's going to call in a favor so that none of our fingerprints are on this. Just in case."

CHAPTER FIFTY-SIX

The food arrived, but none of them had much of an appetite.

"So, what do we do next? There has to be a reason Dad wanted me to get these from the vault."

"Maybe he had second thoughts about them being real?" Wes suggested.

"Or maybe he knew the end was near, and he didn't want Courtney to get her hands on them." Cara winced at Luke's bluntness, but she couldn't dismiss it as a possibility.

"I thought he left everything to his wife?" Wes set his napkin on the small table they had spread the food on.

Cara made a face. "He did. In the new will."

Luke suddenly sat up straighter. "The new will was signed the day after he returned from Dublin."

"Under the terms of the old will, except for bequests to individuals, all of his assets and holdings were to be sold and split equally among his children."

"This is proof he didn't change the will." Cara shook her head and looked pointedly at Luke. "You can't believe he wanted Courtney to have evidence that Declan committed a crime! And if he didn't want her to have the photos, he wouldn't have left them in the vault and sent me the clue to the pin number. He must have thought, at the time, we would still inherit."

Luke looked over her head in thought. "It's not proof," he intoned. "But I think you're right. Proving the will was forged is going to be extremely difficult."

Declan's phone rang, but he silenced it, placing it on the table. "If he didn't want the information out there, why didn't he destroy it?"

The question was fair. It didn't make sense that her father had kept the information, even if it was hidden.

"Maybe he had his suspicions but didn't know how to go about finding out if they were real."

Cara shot Wes a grateful smile.

Declan's phone rang again, and he frowned at it, saying. "He could have just fucking asked me."

"You two weren't exactly close, at the time," Luke reminded him, and Declan scowled.

His phone signaled a notification, and Declan smiled at whatever the message was.

"What is it?" Cara asked.

"I had someone watching the building at Waterloo Station. Call it morbid curiosity, but I wanted to see what Courtney's reaction would be when she realized we got there first. I wanted to know who the man was who accompanied her."

"Was it Chris?" A knot grew in her stomach, but before he could answer, Cara's phone rang, and she held it up to show the group. "Speak of the she-devil."

"Don't answer it. Let it go to voicemail."

"She must know it was me. Do you think she'll call the Garda?"

"I think it's time for Cara and me to go back to Atlanta," Wes said.

"I agree. Let's put some geography between you and this," Luke took a bite of his food.

Her phone pinged with a voicemail notification. Cara put it on speaker so that everyone could hear.

"I know it was you, you little bitch. And I know what you took. It's not the only copy. If you and your brother keep pushing with your ridiculous accusations, I will make sure that information ends up with the proper authorities."

"It doesn't matter if there are other copies. It's easy to prove they are fake," Wes said.

"We don't know the police report about finding the body is fake. It says the vehicle was no longer at the scene of the accident. In fact, if you don't think they manipulated the accident picture, I'm inclined to believe the police report is real. That woman died, and the police know about it," Luke added.

Declan stood, walked to the windows, and chuckled.

"This isn't funny, Declan!" Cara felt queasy. "She knows we have the pictures and the USB. Even if they are fake, the notoriety of an investigation is bad!"

Declan shook his head. "She won't go to the police, and since our father went to great lengths to hide them in Dublin, I bet they were the originals. She just admitted she knew what was in there, which means she was involved in creating them."

Breaking glass drew all of their eyes to Luke, who had knocked his glass onto the floor but was staring at them with horrified eyes.

"The date on the police report." Cara watched his Adam's apple bob when he swallowed. "That was right before he told us he was getting married."

It took a second for the information to process, but as she realized what Luke meant, it felt like all the blood had left her head, and she was suddenly ice cold.

"Fuck." Declan looked like someone had sucker punched him, and he dragged in a ragged breath. "No. Fuck. *Fuck!*"

Wes's eyes ping-ponged among the three of them. "What does that mean?"

"Do you remember when I told you about when my father married Courtney that it was the ultimate break with Declan? How much it hurt that he was finally marrying, and it was to that witch! How Declan and…"

She stopped when Declan swore. "Jesus, Cara!"

Luke, however, was looking at her with a strange soft expression. "You really told him everything, didn't you?"

Cara's eyes went to Wes. "Yeah," she smiled. "He knows everything about me. The good, the bad and the ugly."

Ignoring her brothers, Wes lifted her hand and kissed her fingers.

"If he married her to protect you—" Luke began.

"You don't know that!" Declan interrupted his brother.

Luke lifted one brow. "You're right. It could totally be a coincidence that, days after you supposedly killed someone in a car accident, our father announces that, after sixty-five years of being a bachelor and having numerous love affairs, he is suddenly marrying his current girlfriend." He held up his hand and began ticking off his points with his fingers. "Look at the evidence. After he announces the engagement, he refuses to discuss it with any of us. Declan and Dad never really spoke again, and then shortly after, we all lost access to him. Courtney's son is suddenly given a position in the company that he is in no way qualified for, and we now know Courtney knew about the photos." He paused, grimacing. "It also explains his sudden irrational anger with you, the argument you said he picked."

Cara frowned. "What argument?"

Her brothers ignored her.

"I can't accept he married her because he thought…" Declan's voice broke, and Cara sprang to her feet and rushed to him. At first, he was stiff under her embrace, but eventually, he put his arms around her holding her tight.

"If he did, it means he loved you so much that he would do anything for you." Cara felt a shudder go through him. "And in the end, he must have known the truth. That's why he wanted me to be the one to find it." She pulled back and gave him a crooked smile. "He must not have thought you would listen, or maybe he was ashamed he'd believed it and couldn't face you. What matters is he wanted to make sure you were still protected!"

Declan put her back a step and patted her shoulder. "Or he still thought they were real and wanted to make sure no one but the family saw them."

Cara watched helplessly, unsure what to say to make him feel better. Declan tugged at his cuffs, straightening his sleeves, and when he spoke, he was dispassionate. "I'll have Cecile get the two of you on a flight back to Atlanta."

Cara frowned. "Declan, we have to plan for what to do next."

Declan held her eyes for a minute. "We can't do anything until we find out if the police report is real, and if someone really killed a woman in my car. Then we can work backward and discover how Courtney knew about it, and how she got her hands on the evidence. I'll convince whoever it is to tell me their connection to Courtney. We could use that as leverage. But we need to know more about what was happening in the house in those last months. How did she make him sick without the doctors figuring out what was wrong? I'll call Mrs. Woodson in the morning. She's our best chance."

"What about Vincent?" Luke asked.

"I can't find him," Declan said. "He took a job doing private security in the Middle East. I can't pin him down."

"Who's Vincent?"

"Head of my dad's security," Cara explained, and almost laughed at the surprise on his face. "You see why I'm not sorry that part of my life is over?"

~

CECILE FOUND them seats on flights out of Ireland early the next morning. Cara and Wes had the earliest flight back to Atlanta, with Luke on a separate flight a few hours later. Declan would return to New York later in the day.

Their last night in Dublin, as they lay in the bed happily snuggled together, Cara broached the question that had been floating around in her mind since she realized that this time the next day she would be back in Atlanta.

"Where are we going tomorrow?"

"Hmm?" Wes asked sleepily, nuzzling the back of her neck. She rolled to face him, tucking her hands under her chin.

"Tomorrow. When we get off the plane, where are we going?"

Wes's eyes flickered open and understanding flashed. He brought his own folded hands under his head. "Where do you want to go?"

"I think Luke expects us to go back to his place."

"As much as I like your brother, I'd like some time alone with you, where I don't have to cover your mouth when you—"

"Hey!" she laughed, swatting at his arm. "You don't have to look so smug."

"I think I do." He laughed.

Wes's expression became serious. "Yesterday you didn't seem sure. Are you saying you want to give us a shot?"

Their faces were only inches apart, and she could see the vulnerability behind the gold flecks of his eyes. "I don't think I'd call it giving it a shot. I think we just..." Cara shrugged one shoulder, "are."

A sweet smile spread across his face. "I like the sound of that."

Wes reached out and tucked her hair behind her ear. His fingers lingered sliding the strands between his fingers. "You are so beautiful."

"Even with bleached hair?"

Wes leaned forward brushing a kiss across her lips. "I bet you'd be gorgeous bald."

Cara released a breathy moan as his lips found the sensitive spot under her jaw. In an abrupt movement, Wes threw back the thick duvet that covered them.

"Off," he ordered, rising to his feet, at the foot of the bed and pointing at his T-shirt that she wore. Cara wasted no time stripping it away, as she watched him kick his boxer briefs to the corner of the room. Her heart pounded, and fire raced along her veins as she met his eyes. The bed dipped as he crawled toward her, his mouth searing a trail up her body until she was writhing.

Cara's hands balled into the cool sheets beside her. His kisses trailed slowly up her inner thighs making her forget to breathe. "Wes. Please!" She begged.

"What is it you want?" His warm breath wafted over her core. "This?" Wes pressed a light kiss against her and Cara moaned in frustration. He looked up at her and arched an eyebrow. "More?" His tongue flicked against her, finding the bundle of nerves. But he was as impatient as she was, and with a growl, Wes's firm lips closed over her sensitive flesh and her back arched. His tongue circled and stroked driving her crazy.

"Oh my god!" A high-pitched cry escaped her, even as her fingers found his hair and held tight. Pleasure escalated almost painfully, and she wasn't sure if she wanted him to stop or continue the exquisite torture. Wes gripped her twisting hips, holding her still beneath him until Cara's eyes rolled back in her head.

Before she could catch her breath, she heard the foil of the condom packet rip. Cara lifted her eyes to meet his.

"You don't have to… I'm on the pill." Wes hesitated. "I trust you," Cara whispered.

Wes's face stilled. A look she couldn't decipher crossed his face and then his weight was pressing her deep into the mattress as he thrust into her. He bent his head murmuring her name over and over into her hair. Cara gripped at sweat-slicked shoulders as one arm wrapped around her back, pulling her up to match his movements as his other hand found her breast. He turned his face to her, claiming her lips. His tongue swept in, matching his body's movement. Urgent. Needy. Cara clasped her legs tightly, her heels locked on his back. Wes lifted her hips higher and she shattered around him.

Their hearts still pounding against each other, Wes pulled back and stroked his thumbs across her cheekbones, looking deep into her eyes. "I love you, Cara Bloom."

Happiness suffused every cell of her body. "And I love you, Wes Evans."

CHAPTER FIFTY-SEVEN

EXHAUSTED FROM THE EVENTS OF THE PAST FEW DAYS, CARA SLEPT most of the flight back to Atlanta. They stayed at a hotel for a few nights rather than returning to the house. Knowing that Colin was locked up in a psych ward in Europe helped, but with the dramatics in her family, she hadn't had time to really process how she felt about being stalked by one of her oldest friends. The thought of going back to the house made her feel slightly ill.

There had been an intense conversation about where they should live. Cara couldn't afford to buy anything, but she also couldn't imagine not waking up with Wes every day.

"What if you pay me rent again?"

"Is that weird?"

"I think so, but I know you won't agree to let me pay for everything."

That was true. Her independence had been hard won. "Smart man."

"Still," Wes framed her face with his hands. "I want it to be *our* place, not mine. The realtor sent me some houses this morning, and there is one that I think we should go see. I think you will love it, but if you don't, we'll find something that suits us both."

"I'm sure it will be great." Cara didn't care where they lived as long as they were together, but the home he took her to in the Brookhaven area, was perfect. It was a new construction and close enough so that she could commute to whichever production she was working on.

Her brothers had been predictable with the 'it's too fast' and 'you just got together' comments, but she almost throat punched Luke when he compared it to her mother's string of love affairs. The only thing that saved him was when he finished with, "I'm worried you just went through an ordeal, and you aren't thinking clearly."

"It's not fast at all," she said through gritted teeth. "I've felt this way for months, and it's not like we weren't already living together."

"I like Wes. I just want you to be sure. Until a couple of weeks ago, you insisted he was in love with someone else."

His words brought a twinge of doubt, but she shrugged it off. Either she was going to trust Wes with her heart, or she wasn't.

The bid for the house was accepted, and they expected to move in a little more than a month. After a week in a hotel, Cara was ready to be around her own stuff again. Wes needed to travel to Jin and Nina's house to work every day because the Wi-Fi wasn't secure at the hotel, and with Atlanta traffic, that was a nightmare. It made sense for them to return to the little house in Chamblee.

It wasn't as painful as she expected. The house had been cleaned since they left, and no sign of the break-in remained. Skye called her soon after she returned from Ireland and asked Cara to work with her on a new TV show at Magnolia Studios. While Cara was flattered at first and enjoyed the new job, it made her realize that being a makeup artist wasn't where her passion lay.

She loved makeup and the camaraderie of the set, but in her off hours, she found joy mixing new concoctions and experimenting with oils for the skin. Cara sourced a natural foods wholesaler where she could order large amounts of ingredients for the beauty products she was making at home. Needing feedback from someone who had been in the industry longer than she had, Cara invited Skye over and tentatively laid out her plan.

"I know everyone thinks they've got the next best thing—"

Skye rubbed a dab of the face cream between her fingers. "I like the texture." She rubbed it into her hand and raised it to her nose for a sniff. "The light honeysuckle is nice, too. Floral but natural." She cocked her head. "So, where are you going to sell it? The Peachtree Farmers Market?"

Cara beamed, her excitement growing. "Do you think people would buy it?"

Skye appeared thoughtful. "I think if you get some cute packaging and play up the all-natural benefits, you've got a shot. Also, we'll get people we know in the entertainment industry to post on social media to drum up some interest. Can't hurt to try, right?"

"This calls for bubbles," Cara said, getting a bottle of champagne from the fridge. The ladies were two glasses in and searching the internet for packaging ideas when Wes came home slinging his messenger bag over the back of the sofa.

"What are we celebrating?" he asked, with a smile.

"I showed Skye the creams." Cara couldn't contain her grin, and Wes smiled at her proudly.

"They are pretty great even I have to admit." He rubbed his cheek. "My skin feels better since she started using me as a test dummy." Wes came around behind her chair and bent to kiss the side of her neck. "But I don't know how I feel about all these other girls running around Atlanta smelling like you."

Skye pretended to gag. "Could you two be any cheesier?"

Over the next couple weeks, as they slowly packed up the house, Cara created enough of her product during her off hours to display at the farmer's market.

The only ugly spot on her new happiness was that the investigation into Courtney's connection to their father's murder had stalled out after Dublin.

James could find no record that matched the police report in the official files, and they concluded it was fake, too. It also explained why Courtney hadn't repeated her threats. Declan was still trying to track down Vincent Menardi, her father's head of security, and Mrs. Woodson had remembered nothing new.

Cara knew Declan wouldn't give up, but she needed to move on with her life.

CHAPTER FIFTY-EIGHT

"I'm sorry I can't come with you today." Wes stacked the last box in the back of her car. "I've got to finish this report."

Cara gave him a kiss as she opened the door. "It's not a problem! Skye is coming with me, and she'll help set up. She's proven to be an exceptional asset. No offense, but somehow I don't think sitting at a table, talking to people about skincare, is a great fit for you."

"Skincare I could do… in measured amounts, but people." He gave a mock shudder, and she laughed as he had intended. Wes watched as Cara buckled herself in and shut the door.

For the next couple of hours, he concentrated on the reports he needed to get out. Their closing on the new house was Tuesday, and the movers were coming on Wednesday. Shutting his computer, he went to the refrigerator to get a drink.

Hearing heels on the tile, he asked, "How did it go?" But the words died in his throat when he saw Melody standing just inside the front door with a suitcase at her feet. "Melody? What are you doing here?"

"Aren't you happy to see me?" She sashayed toward him.

Wes frowned. He didn't like the look of this. Now that the

blinders had fallen from his eyes, he was more wary of his old friend. "It's always great to see you," he hedged. "I'm just surprised. Where's Luca?"

She didn't answer his question, casting a glance at the boxes stacked around the room. "Did you finally find a house?" She lifted her hands in front of her mouth in an expression of excitement, but it didn't ring true. "I can't wait to see it."

"*We* did." He saw the second his deliberate word choice registered with her. A small twitch in her eyes gave her away, but Melody didn't acknowledge it. Instead, she licked her lips, and moved closer to him. He felt a tinge of sadness for her. "Melody, what's going on? Why are you here?"

"I've made a mistake." Her hands clutched at his shirt front, and she looked up at him through her lashes. It was meant to be seductive, but he was completely unaffected. Well, that wasn't completely true. He felt irritated. Wes removed her hands.

"No, you haven't, Mel."

"I have," she insisted. When she moved to touch him again, he stepped away. "I see now that I should be with you. We belong together."

Wes sighed. Her feelings for him were no more real than his had been for her. "I will always care about you, Melody, but I'm in love with Cara. My future is with her.

Melody's face crumpled, but she steeled herself, letting out a dismissive laugh. "You've had a fun fling. It's okay. I forgive you."

"You forgive me?" Wes's voice was disbelieving. "Forgive me for what?"

Her expression faltered. "You're in love with me, Wes. I've always known it. I always knew I'd end up with you."

"I'm not in love with you, Melody."

She shook her head vigorously, her voice growing more desperate. "But that's why you came to Italy, right? To show me I don't belong with Luca, that I should be with you. You used her to make me jealous. Okay, you win. I'm jealous!"

How many times had he wished she would say those words to him? That they could start building a life together. He knew better now. Wes had never felt about her the way he felt about Cara. He had always been Melody's safety net, and once she saw that was gone, she panicked. "Did something happen with Luca?"

"No."

"Then why did you leave him?"

Tears welled in her eyes. "Suddenly, it was just so real. He's pushing to set a wedding date, and I just... I needed to see you." She blinked, looking unsure. "Because I realized I should be with you."

"You're just scared. I understand more than anyone else in the world. We are both so close to having everything we've ever dreamed of, and it's fucking petrifying."

He gentled his voice. "But it's not real. It's just fear. Life dealt us a bad hand growing up. That wasn't our fault, and it doesn't dictate what our future should be. We can be happy. We *deserve* to be happy."

"I thought you wanted to be a family with me. It's what you always said." Melody fitfully played with the front of his shirt. This time, he didn't remove her hands.

"I did," he agreed. "But not because I was in love with you, any more than you have ever been in love with me." He continued when her eyes flew to his face. "We were safe together. Our hearts weren't at risk, not in that way. You will always be my family. No one else knows what we went through, but that's different from how you love Luca."

"I'm scared," Melody whispered. "What if I fuck this up like I have every other thing in my life? I'm a fraud. I don't know how to love someone or how to be loved... What if Luca figures out that I'm a mess?"

"You're not a fraud, and he already knows you're a mess." He laughed when she hit him. "You are infuriating and annoying. That's true. But Luca knows you. The first time I met him, he was making you food because he knew you were going to get hangry. I've seen you like that. It's not pretty. And if he's sticking around, he must really love you," Wes teased.

"He could break my heart."

"He could." Wes nodded. "But isn't it worth the risk? To finally let go of all our crap and feel everything?"

"You're speaking from experience?" Melody sounded dubious.

"I am. I have never felt so much myself as I do when I'm with Cara. She accepts me for all my weirdness. My love of Star Trek, my dread of human interaction—she doesn't judge me or try to change me. I love her." He shrugged.

Melody took a step back, wiping at her cheeks. "I think it was seeing how you looked at her in Italy that scared me so much. I knew she had replaced me."

"You weren't replaced, Melody. It was never like that between us. I see now how I had confused my feelings. I love you, and you will always have a place in my life, but..." He met her eyes, making her see how serious he was. "She is my everything."

"She seems nice," Melody conceded. "And, I guess if she's going to be around for a while, I'll have to like her."

"As soon as I think enough time has gone by that I won't spook her, I'm going to marry her."

At the doorway, Cara echoed Melody's surprised gasp. Melody looked between the two of them and then walked to collect her suitcase.

"That's my cue to leave, I guess." Melody slid into her jacket.

"Don't miss your chance, Mel. Talk to Luca."

Melody bit her lip but nodded, stopping when she drew level with Cara. "Don't break his heart. He's one of a kind."

Cara met the model's stare. "I know."

With one last look over her shoulder, Melody left, closing the door behind her.

"Cara," Wes started. "I didn't know she was coming. I told her—"

"I heard."

Wes was wary. Had she heard Melody saying they belonged together?

"She's having a classic Melody freak out. I told her—"

"Did you mean it?"

He couldn't interpret the look on her face as she walked further into the room. "That I never loved her? That I love you?"

"No, that you want to marry me."

His eyes searched hers. "With every molecule of my body."

"Then you should probably ask me."

Wes's eyes widened. "I didn't think you were ready. You said…"

"Ask me, Wes."

THE END

The Dangerous Blooms **series continues with**
See You There (Dangerous Blooms Book 2)
Luke & Dahlia's story
Order: See You There (Dangerous Blooms Book 2)

SEE YOU THERE (DANGEROUS BLOOMS BOOK 2)

LUKE AND DAHLIA'S STORY COMING AUGUST 2023

~

If you enjoyed this book please consider leaving a review!

~

Don't miss out on Kate's latest book news!

Subscribe to her newsletter? https://katebreitfeller.com/contact/

Or follow her author page on Amazon: https://www.amazon.com/Kate-Breitfeller/e/B07R9XVR55

ABOUT THE AUTHOR

Kate's character driven romantic suspense and romantic mystery series serve as the perfect escape from reality! She frequently refers to her books as "hanging out with her imaginary friends" and enjoys putting them in a variety of precarious situations.

Kate currently lives with her husband, two adult sons, and the rescue dog/writing partner, Charlie, on Florida's Space Coast.